Death
in the Latin
Quarter

Death in the Latin Quarter

RAPHAËL CARDETTI

Translated from French by
Sonia Soto

ABACUS

ABACUS

First published in France in 2009 with the title *Le Paradoxe de Vasalis*
by Éditions Fleuve Noir
First published in Great Britain in 2010 by Abacus

A CIP catalogue record for this book
is available from the British Library.

ISBN 978-0-349-12255-7

Typeset in Horley by M Rules
Printed and bound in Great Britain by
Clays Ltd, St Ives plc

Papers used by Abacus are natural, renewable and
recyclable products sourced from well-managed forests and certified
in accordance with the rules of the Forest Stewardship Council.

Mixed Sources
Product group from well-managed
forests and other controlled sources
www.fsc.org Cert no. SGS-COC-004081
© 1996 Forest Stewardship Council
FSC

Abacus
An imprint of
Little, Brown Book Group
100 Victoria Embankment
London EC4Y 0DY

An Hachette UK Company
www.hachette.co.uk

www.littlebrown.co.uk

When the legend becomes fact, print the legend.
THE MAN WHO SHOT LIBERTY VALANCE

I never travel without books, either in peace or war . . .
'Tis the best viaticum I have yet found out for this
human journey.
MICHEL DE MONTAIGNE, *ESSAYS*

Albert Cadas was a calm, discreet man. Contrary to a well-established university tradition, no outburst of his had ever attracted attention. He harboured no desire for controversy, and had never uttered a single word in anger. One could undoubtedly find in these personality traits the reason he had never attained the heights to which he had seemed destined.

Just after his eighteenth birthday, his keen intelligence and thirst for knowledge opened the doors of the École Normale Supérieure. Three years later, he made his way to Oxford, where he completed a PhD thesis on *The Doctrine of Categories in Duns Scotus* which, on the day of his viva, the renowned Francis Yates declared to be a 'foundation stone of the fragile Scotist edifice'.

Yet despite a solid reputation as a brilliant mind – or perhaps because of it – Albert Cadas had to wait a whole decade before obtaining at last a Chair in Medieval Philosophy at the Sorbonne. By then, the more scheming of his fellow students had long been dispensing knowledge in prestigious institutions, assiduously cultivating publishing houses and frequenting the corridors of power. On the day that Albert Cadas received notification of his appointment, his joy was marred by a certain bitterness, which would never leave him.

In the twilight of his career, the university community regarded Albert Cadas as a living anachronism. He belonged to an ancient breed of scholar that had long ago disappeared from the lecture theatres, able to decipher an eleventh-century Gnostic manuscript sight unseen or recite from memory whole paragraphs of Henry of Ghent's *Summa Theologica*.

Nevertheless, day to day, his incredible erudition was a burden that caused him to be completely out of step with the society in

1

which he lived. The Internet and the digital revolution were as alien to him as were most of the students entrusted to his care. These found him equally remote, and Albert Cadas poured forth his learning in lecture theatres that were three-quarters empty, his audience a scattering of drowsy students, probably too lazy to join their friends in the local art-house cinemas or on the benches of the Jardin du Luxembourg.

His few disciples left his classes exhausted, with the dizzying feeling of having surveyed the whole of Western culture in two hours. Stooping, as if weighed down by the extent of his knowledge, the old lecturer could juxtapose William of Ockham and Gilles Deleuze in the same sentence without its seeming pedantic or contrived. In these moments of grace, his voice came alive, and one almost forgot the hunched body from which it issued.

Albert Cadas's break with the world of the university was subtle, and long imperceptible. As time passed, he gradually stopped attending symposiums and seminars. He reduced his teaching to a minimum, concentrating on the handful of students whose research he still agreed to supervise. His name appeared less and less frequently in specialist publications, before finally disappearing without prompting the slightest reaction from his colleagues. His professional ascent would never take him higher than his office on the third floor, just under the eaves, but Albert Cadas had known for a long time that this was not what mattered.

Of course, he still occasionally felt a painful stab when he thought of the honours that might have been his. But a few glasses of *hors d'âge* Armagnac managed to push these dark thoughts to the back of his mind. His brain clouded by alcohol, he would lie on his bed and recite aloud his favourite passage from St Augustine's *Confessions*: 'Verum tamen tu, medice meus intime, quo fructu ista faciam, eliqua mihi.'

Like his inspiration, Albert Cadas too needed someone to show him the way. Unfortunately, in his case, God would prove to be of no use. He had ventured into places so dark that no one, not even the Almighty, all powerful as he was, could help him escape.

Deep inside, Albert Cadas felt hopelessly trapped. Breaking free would require more than the meagre strength that remained to him. If he could, Cadas would have gone back to a time some thirty years earlier, when he didn't yet know where his quest would lead.

To end up, in the autumn of his life, lacking all certainty, having shared the thoughts and insights of so many great minds, might have seemed laughable, had this recognition not induced in him a terrifying feeling of impotence and emptiness.

For now, however, Albert Cadas was quite indifferent to such metaphysical considerations.

He could think only of running as fast as he was able.

Abruptly, he pushed aside the two attendants in blue uniforms and caps standing at the entrance to the Sorbonne, who were startled to see him abandon his usual slow, formal demeanour. His tie loose, Albert Cadas shrugged vaguely in apology, then ran on across the great paved courtyard, through the teeming crowd of students hurrying towards the amphitheatres for their first lectures of the afternoon.

Outraged at such a lapse in professorial dignity, the Dean shot him a reproachful look as he passed. Oblivious, Cadas rushed past the library entrance, bounded up the few steps flanked by charmless statues of Louis Pasteur and Victor Hugo opening on to the chapel transept, and entered the main university building by a side door.

Already out of breath, he started up the old staircase that led to the upper floors. Despite the absence of a lift, and the triple bypass that made physical exertion difficult, Albert Cadas had always refused to move offices, believing that his location under the eaves was still the best way of discouraging unwelcome visitors. Today, however, feeling his lungs burn with the effort, he painfully regretted his obstinacy. Reaching his office door with

3

difficulty, he pulled a heavy bunch of keys from his coat pocket and inserted one into the lock, but found he could not turn it.

The door was unlocked.

That wasn't how he'd left it the day before, he was sure of it. He remembered perfectly checking twice that it was locked. He pushed it open with unaccustomed violence, and hurried to the metal cabinet he used as a safe.

The doors were wide open. The combination padlock hung down, dangling from the left-hand door. Never, in almost forty years at the Sorbonne, had Albert Cadas left his office without locking the cabinet. It was utterly inconceivable. He was often distracted, but not when it came to the things that were important to him, and locking the cabinet came top of his list of priorities. A simple glance confirmed his worst fears.

Albert Cadas could accept that his career had foundered in mediocrity. He could silently endure his colleagues' contemptuous looks and the students' half-smiles as he wandered, absent-minded and crumpled, through the corridors of the Sorbonne. But that he should be stripped of his most precious possession, the only material object that really mattered to him, was intolerable.

Blinded by his certainties, he'd ignored the signs. He'd thought the Sorbonne would provide greater protection than his tiny two-room flat in the Rue du Cherche-Midi, as if the prestige of the place alone might prove an insuperable psychological barrier. But he was wrong, and the error was his and his alone. If only he'd been less arrogant, this disaster would never have happened.

Still out of breath after the climb, Albert Cadas rushed to the window and opened it wide. For several seconds he gazed at the dome of the chapel where Cardinal Richelieu's remains lay. Suddenly the path ahead appeared glaringly obvious. Albert Cadas, Chair of Medieval Philosophy at the Sorbonne, would show he was worthy of his glorious forebears. Down the centuries, those Brothers who had preceded him within these walls had instituted a moral code from which he could not waver.

He was at once flooded with relief, as if his decision were a natural extension of his entire journey, from the first time he'd felt, at the age of fifteen, through the simple grace of St Augustine's words, an incomparable intellectual communion. He no longer felt any sadness. He simply regretted having failed, so near the end of his quest.

He took off his coat and folded it carefully before laying it over the back of his chair. Then he adjusted his tie, smoothed a crease in his jacket with the back of his hand and removed a tiny, almost invisible, speck of dust that had settled there.

Only then did he close his eyes and fall into the void.

Thus Albert Cadas's life came to an end on the immaculate paving of the courtyard of the Sorbonne, before the eyes of some one hundred witnesses, in a dazzling spray of blood and brain matter.

1

Valentine Savi didn't even look up when the bell rang, announcing the arrival of a customer at her workshop. As if nothing had happened, she continued applying alcohol with a piece of cotton wool to the mould that gave the Madonna – painted at the beginning of the nineteenth century by a hand bereft of any artistic talent – her shrewish aspect.

At least the person responsible for this disaster had had the good taste not to sign it. Of course, the owner of the painting was convinced he had an undiscovered masterpiece on his hands – he'd mentioned the names David and Delacroix to Valentine. The reality promised to be harsh. The awful painting wasn't worth a penny, probably not even the cost of restoring it.

Basically, customers were all alike: they came through the door to the workshop, eyes shining hopefully, hugging a grimy painting that had hung for years over the mantelpiece of some obscure great-aunt in the provinces. They'd endured countless lunches with the old witch, sustained by the hope that one day she'd bequeath them her treasure. Week after week they'd eaten the same *pot-au-feu*, been subjected to the same conversation, eyes pinned to their future inheritance, picturing the marvels hidden beneath the yellowed varnish. Have it properly restored, and they'd be able to get a new people-carrier, maybe even a bigger house.

When the big day had come at last, and they'd buried the old dear and got in ahead of the other heirs, they looked for a restorer who charged what seemed like a fair rate – after all, it just needed a good clean, they could almost have done it themselves with a bit of nerve, solvent and elbow grease – and ended up at the door to Valentine's workshop.

Which was why she no longer even bothered to look up when the bell rang. She hoped the show of disdain would put off potential customers, and spare her the need to rescue from oblivion yet another grubby collectable.

When the Madonna's face finally emerged, Valentine reflected bitterly that it would really have been better to leave the mould alone. She sighed, threw the soiled cotton wool into the bin and pushed the picture away, to the end of the bench that took up almost the entire workshop. She would have loved to give the poor Madonna a happier face, but restoring didn't mean improving. This principle brooked no deviation, even in so desperate a case.

Not the least bit discouraged by her indifference, the visitor waited at the door, motionless in expectation.

Eventually Valentine glanced in his direction. The old man didn't look like her usual customers. His cream three-piece suit appeared to have been made to measure about a century earlier, in Savile Row. He wore a matching panama hat, the kind no one had worn since the fifties. He held a leather briefcase covered in fine cracks that perfectly mirrored the wrinkles on his forehead. A withered rose, forgotten in a cupboard, thought Valentine. Delicate, elegant and deliciously old-fashioned. Like the old bridal bouquets you sometimes found at a flea market.

With a polite smile, the visitor gestured at the chair opposite, on the other side of the bench that was covered in a confusion of paintbrushes and bottles of chemicals. Valentine nodded, but didn't return his smile.

The old man placed his briefcase on the bench and rested the knob of his cane against the back of the chair. He removed his panama with a hand so wrinkled it looked as if it were covered with parchment. Fine, almost invisible blue veins ran beneath the skin, disappearing at the juncture of fingers twisted with arthritis. His face tense with the effort, he seemed to take an eternity to fold his dry body into the chair, before nodding at the small drawing that hung behind Valentine, of a horseman arched back in a position of ecstasy.

His voice echoed in the workshop, much clearer and stronger than his appearance would lead one to expect.

'Remarkable intensity in its simplicity, like your workshop. Marino Marini would have been delighted to see one of his works here.'

The restorer's interest was aroused. Usually, no one noticed the drawing. The few visitors who paid it any attention were unaware who the artist was. Yet she'd paid a fortune for it when she'd bought it from a reputable dealer on the Quai Voltaire almost ten years earlier, the day she'd been hired by the Louvre.

She'd spent her entire first month's wages on the tiny square of Canson paper, yellowed with age, but she'd never regretted her folly. She'd left the drawing unrestored, not even trying to remove the spots of mildew on its lower half. She loved it just as it was, with its imperfections and the signs that it had known another life before ending up in her possession.

The old man's gaze slid from the drawing to Valentine, before coming to rest on the newly emerged face of the Virgin. He smiled tolerantly.

'You can't do anything with it. I've always thought a work of art should suit its container,' he went on, unfazed by the young woman's silence. 'It would make no sense to hang a Picasso or a Chagall in one of those pretentious apartments done up by a fashionable decorator, the kind that puts marble everywhere, floor to ceiling, and covers the walls in bright colours. A splash of crimson here, some yellow there, a few touches of sky blue to finish. You know the sort.'

Valentine nodded. She had no idea where the old man was

9

going with this, but he'd piqued her interest, or at least, idle curiosity.

'On the other hand,' he went on, 'a small picture bought for ten euros can take on a new dimension if it suits its surroundings. You and I both know this Virgin belongs in the dustbin. Yet she's brought joy to her various owners. Basically it's a question of consistency. Your drawing by Marini suits this workshop perfectly. It must mean a lot to you.'

Valentine hated opening up, especially to a stranger. She tried to hide her emotions, but couldn't help twisting her mouth into a grimace. The drawing represented all the promise her life had failed to live up to. Promise she'd clung to for a long time, but had eventually had to relinquish for good because of a few un-cooperative molecules. The horseman perched on his strange mount was a reminder of what she'd lost.

'Could we change the subject, please?'

'Of course. I'm sorry, I didn't mean to . . .'

'It's nothing. What can I do for you?'

'I want to offer you a job.'

'I'm swamped. I've got masterpieces to save,' she added, gesturing with her chin towards the hideous Madonna.

'I see,' was all the old man said.

He seemed to hesitate for a moment, wondering how best to state his case. He decided on the most direct route.

'You're much too good for this, Valentine. I've seen some of your work.' He coughed, a little awkwardly. 'I mean, your work . . . from before. Absolutely remarkable. I need a talented restorer, and I think you're the right person.'

Valentine shook her head. 'That's all over. Look around: do you see an ounce of talent anywhere? I restore worthless old junk. Even if I make a complete mess of it, no one seems to mind. Quite the reverse.'

'You won't always be able to turn away the kind of work you're made for, Valentine. You've been unlucky. Everyone knows how good you are.'

The restorer felt a dull wave of anger wash over her. She tried to suppress it, but didn't quite succeed. She ran her hand through her hair, removing the pins holding it up. Long, light brown locks tumbled over her shoulders, setting off the sparkle of her green eyes.

'You can't imagine what I had to endure. I don't want to go through all that again.'

The old man opened his briefcase and took out a rosewood box about ten centimetres long, which he placed between them in the middle of the bench.

'This is what I'd like you to work on. I'm prepared to pay whatever is necessary. You're the only one I trust for this job. You used to perform miracles.'

'You're right. Remember the miracle of disappearance? That was me.' She tried to sound ironic, but only succeeded in edging her voice with bitterness.

The visitor pushed the box towards her. 'Before giving me your final answer, have a look. If you're still not interested, I'll leave and never mention it again.'

Valentine stared at the box for several long seconds. At last she made up her mind. Her hand hesitating slightly, she undid the red velvet ribbon that was tied around it and opened the lid. Inside she found a rectangular object enclosed in a pouch made of the same red velvet. The whole thing was hardly thicker than a sachet of sugar.

'Go on, take it out.' The old man spoke softly yet firmly. It was the voice of a man used to being obeyed.

Valentine gave in. She put on a clean pair of gloves, slid her hand inside the pouch and pulled out a small and very damaged book.

At first glance, it seemed to be a medieval codex in quarto format, in appalling condition. Devoid of lettering, the binding was in tatters and had a few pieces missing, some the size of a coin. The lower half of the book was blackened, as if it had been held over a flame or, worse still, dropped into the embers of a fire.

Her features drawn in concentration, Valentine inspected the tiny ancient book at length, then turned it over and examined the back with the same attention. She saw nothing to reassure her.

'A work of art should suit its container,' she said as she raised her eyes at last to the visitor. 'If you wanted to be consistent, you should have packed it in an old cereal box.'

The old man smiled indulgently. 'In this case, nothing, not even solid gold, would be luxurious enough. Open it.'

Prompted by his imperious tone, Valentine straightened up and went to the lectern that occupied a corner of her bench. To limit any tension on the binding, she laid the book open on padded blocks. She was breathing slowly, determined to control her emotions this time. Even so, she couldn't help sensing a flutter of excitement, but it immediately turned to disappointment as she saw that the inside of the codex too had suffered irreversible damage.

The opening page had been cut out, and all that remained was a narrow strip about half a centimetre wide, without writing. The next page was adorned with marginal decorations depicting interlaced plants – Valentine could make out violets, daisies, even strawberry plants – on which butterflies alighted, as well as a strange dragon with a lion's head and eagle's wings. Clumsy and without charm, the central illumination resembled the style of those produced during the early Renaissance in Germany or Flanders. In the foreground, two shepherds armed with spears reposed with their flock in a rocky landscape overlooked by a vast fortress. In the margin of the missing page, a few traces of colour showed that it too had been illustrated.

Valentine had restored a number of medieval miniatures, but it wasn't her area of expertise. She could tell at a glance, however, that she was looking at an addition made after the book was produced. In the lighter areas of the main illumination, particularly the sky, the letters of the text over which the illustration had been painted showed through. The difference between the visual brilliance of the opening page and the sobriety of the following pages, which were quite without refinement, seemed to confirm her impression.

It was hard to tell how long after the completion of the codex the addition had been made. Only chemical analysis of the pigments used would give her an idea. The aim of the artificial embellishment was clear, however: to transform an ordinary breviary – a common item of little commercial value – into a book of hours, something much more sought-after. The missing page had probably been cut out and sold separately to an undiscerning buyer.

If the first few pages were disappointing, the rest of the volume was little better. The parchment had lost all suppleness, so that the pages seemed as if they would crack at the slightest touch. Most bore ancient traces of damp, with a proliferation of purple mildew.

Each page was almost entirely covered in a dense network of Greek characters, little darker than the medium on which the copyist had inscribed them. The red of the capital letters had almost completely faded, and it too was almost indistinguishable from the parchment. Deciphering the text with the naked eye was a challenge. Valentine made out a few words, but couldn't reconstruct an entire sentence. To complete the devastation, several pages had come away from the binding and were floating loose inside the volume.

'What do you think?' asked the visitor, his voice quite calm.

Valentine couldn't understand the reason for his confidence. It seemed he was just like all the other customers she got rid of every day. He brought her a mouldy book, insisted she examine it and expected her to go into raptures over pages covered in illegible script that was probably of no interest to anyone.

At first, Valentine tried to evade the question. 'I've rarely worked on parchment. I don't have the expertise to appraise your manuscript. There are specialists far better qualified in this area. There aren't many of them, but I can give you their details, if you like.'

'I know these people. It's your opinion I came for.'

Valentine hated this kind of situation. To spare customers' feelings, she tended to tone down a harsh judgement by overlaying it with a gloss of technical jargon. But she could see in the old man's faded eyes that this tactic wouldn't work.

'It's a *euchologion*, a prayer book. At first glance, I'd say it dates from the thirteenth century, or the start of the fourteenth at the latest. The illumination on the second page was obviously added later, and matches neither the general appearance of the book nor its contents. The origin of the codex is hard to determine with certainty. I can't see a mark of provenance, an ex libris or colophon. But from the size of the capitals and the style of the characters, I'd say it comes from a Middle Eastern monastery. The overall condition is quite simply catastrophic. Restoring a volume in such a pitiful state would take time and lots of money. To be perfectly honest with you, I don't think it's worth it.'

The old man interrupted with an abrupt gesture. 'I'm not in the habit of stinting when it comes to money. As for time, I don't have much, but I can give you a few weeks.'

'I'm not even sure this book is salvageable,' protested Valentine. 'The damage is ancient. You're five centuries too late. It's a miracle it's lasted until now. At best, maybe I could stabilise it to prevent it from completely crumbling to dust. You can find breviaries like this on the market quite easily. If you have money to burn, buy another in better condition. It'd cost you much less than having this one restored.'

Her words slid over her listener as if she'd said the exact opposite. He didn't look in the least put out. A glint of amusement appeared briefly in his eyes.

'For your information, I spent almost two hundred thousand euros to acquire this book. Don't worry, I'm not senile. I wouldn't have paid a hundredth of that for a common psalter. Please, take a look at page ten. It should make you change your mind about the quality of the manuscript.'

In her former life, Valentine had worked on drawings and

paintings worth several million euros, or more. But she'd never seen such a contrast between the nominal value of a work and its outward appearance. She couldn't see what there was in this book to justify such an extravagant price. With extreme care, she turned the pages until she reached the one her visitor had indicated. Nothing appeared to distinguish this page from those preceding it. If anything, it was even less legible, due to numerous dark lines that covered most of it.

Suddenly inspired, Valentine switched on the lamp fixed to the back of the lectern and angled it over the page. The hollow imprint of other characters appeared, in Latin this time, inscribed at right angles to the others and in some cases emphasised by subtle ink shading. Valentine switched off the light and the letters disappeared.

'A palimpsest,' she murmured simply. 'Of course.'

The copy was written on used parchment, as was often done at the time to economise on the rare and expensive material. The scribe had rubbed down the skin with acid, erasing the original words, then sanded the parchment with a pumice stone before reassembling the pages to make his breviary. This dual process, chemical and mechanical, did not, however, destroy all traces of the original text, which remained embedded in the deeper layers of the parchment. Just like childhood memories in the remote strata of one's mind, Valentine liked to think. By accentuating the imprint of the letters, the slanting light had resurrected the original text. It was a little like good psychoanalysis, except that here everything disappeared when you removed the light source.

Medieval manuscripts produced using recycled parchment, most often Greek or Byzantine, were far from scarce. Only rarely, however, was the erased text retrievable, and even more rarely did it turn out to be interesting.

There was, of course, the famous Archimedes Palimpsest, which a few years earlier had fascinated the scientific community, but that was an isolated case. In the end, the owner had spent several million dollars deciphering the three texts by the Greek mathematician that were preserved in the codex. For several years he'd employed a large team of restorers and palaeographers, and even chemists and physicists, at the University of Montreal. Not counting the army of historians of science, mathematicians and specialists in Greek antiquity recruited for the second phase, the actual study of the fragments. Rescuing a palimpsest required investment on an epic scale, without any guarantee of discovering anything important and in the certain knowledge that you would never recover your costs, even in the event of success. From a financial perspective, it was doomed from the start.

'Do you know what this is?' asked Valentine.

The old man shrugged. A shadow crossed his face, which Valentine was at a loss to interpret. The shadow of doubt, perhaps? Unless it was fatalism. The old man's features recovered their serene façade.

'I have some idea, but I'm not sure. I need confirmation.'

At least the owner of the Archimedes Palimpsest knew what he was dealing with before he launched his costly venture.

'Can't you tell me any more?'

'Not yet. First, I need a definite answer. Accept my proposal and I'll tell you everything. I promise you won't regret it.'

Valentine closed the book and returned it to its velvet pouch, then to the box of precious wood. Carefully she tied it shut and pushed it towards her visitor.

'I'm not in the habit of working blind. I like to know what I'm restoring before I start.'

The old man seemed neither surprised nor disappointed. He simply nodded before slipping the box into his leather briefcase. He got to his feet with difficulty, leaning on his cane, then took a business card from the inside pocket of his jacket and handed it to Valentine.

'If you change your mind, please call me,' he said, adjusting his panama. 'Above all, take your time thinking it over.'

With a shuffling gait he headed towards the workshop door. As he was about to leave, he turned back to the restorer.

'You once possessed a rare talent. It's still in you, somewhere. Let me help you retrieve your gift, Valentine.'

2

'Elias Stern? The *real* Elias Stern?'

In disbelief, for the third time Marc Grimberg read the name on the business card the old man had given Valentine. He stroked the letters printed on the little piece of card with the tip of his index finger.

'So it would seem,' said Valentine. 'I don't think he has a name-sake. He was the right age, at any rate. I've seen photos of him when he was younger, and there was a definite resemblance. More lined, and more gaunt, but it was him.'

'I can't believe it. I thought he died years ago.'

'Well, I can assure you it wasn't his ghost. He was definitely here. Not in great shape by the look of him, but it was him in the flesh.'

Grimberg handed back the card reluctantly. He couldn't have been more excited if it had been a Michelangelo sketch or a certified authentic relic of the True Cross.

'So are you going to call him?' he asked.

'I don't know yet.'

'It's the chance of a lifetime, Valentine.'

'I can't make a decision just like that. I need to think it over.'

'You can't let an opportunity like this get away,' insisted Grimberg. 'The man's a legend.'

His face was expressionless, seemingly contradicting the

vehemence of his words. Like many of his colleagues, Grimberg had a complex mix of feelings about Stern: a fascination with the man, and revulsion at the work he did. Calling him a legend hardly approached the truth, for Elias Stern was unquestionably the biggest art dealer of the twentieth century. Like everyone, Valentine knew his story by heart, or at least the little he'd allowed to filter out.

Elias's grandfather, Gabriel, had fled tsarist Russia when the first pogroms against the Jews erupted. He arrived in Paris in 1882 with his wife and children, penniless, his only asset a small portrait attributed to Caravaggio in which he'd invested all his savings a few years earlier.

One day as he was passing Père Tanguy's art supply shop in the Rue Clauzel in Montmartre, he was struck with amazement by some paintings in the window signed by someone called Cézanne. Nothing he'd seen before had provoked such wonder.

The following day, Gabriel sold his Caravaggio and, with the money, bought three of the paintings that had so moved him, together with a dozen sketches and studies, for the sum of fifty old francs. Soon he became friends with a group of artists who had been panned by public and critics alike since 1874, when Louis Leroy had dubbed them, ironically, 'Impressionists' in his newspaper *Le Charivari*. In a few months, Gabriel came to purchase works by Monet, Sisley and Pissarro.

Together with other collectors such as Georges Charpentier and Theodore Duret, Gabriel took it into his head to convince Parisians that his instinct was right. It was at this time that Gauguin's offer of his wonderful *Virgin and Child* was rejected by the Musée du Luxembourg. The seventeen paintings of the Gustave Caillebotte bequest, including works by Renoir, Cézanne and Manet, were also declined, following the indignant reaction of the members of the Institute.

It took a decade for the sneering and sarcasm to subside. Meanwhile, Gabriel had tirelessly accumulated his friends' paintings, selling those he wearied of and acquiring even more beautiful works. When the Impressionists became fashionable, Gabriel Stern suddenly found himself in possession of a considerable fortune. Not only did he own an unrivalled collection of the paintings people were now going wild about in London and New York, but he was also a trusted friend of most of the artists, making him their favoured intermediary. He opened a gallery in the Rue Lafitte, where the most eminent of his fellow-dealers had premises, and bought a large house in the Rue des Saints-Pères, where he settled with his family.

The equal of Durand-Ruel and Ambroise Vollard, Gabriel Stern reigned over the Paris art market for a quarter of a century. His ascendancy was ended by the Spanish flu epidemic of 1918. The day after the Armistice, Gabriel was given by his friend Georges Clemenceau a pass for Vienna, and headed there immediately to meet Egon Schiele, a young painter he'd heard good things about. He didn't know that the artist had died from the disease a fortnight earlier. Gabriel too became infected, and died less than forty-eight hours later in his suite at the Sacher Wien Hotel on Philharmonikerstrasse, far from his beloved paintings.

Promoted to head of the family business in these dramatic circumstances, his son Jacob was thought mad when he dropped the Impressionists, which were too mainstream for his taste. At the end of the war, when nobody wanted them, he started buying eighteenth-century French paintings. At the time, you could get a red chalk drawing by Watteau or a small Fragonard at the Drouot auction rooms for a hundred francs. Ten years later, when prices for these artists went through the roof, they ceased to interest Jacob, who regarded his trade with the eyes of a pioneer.

He then developed a passion for all forms of the avant-garde. A band of young unknowns had only to proclaim their aversion to current artistic conventions for Jacob to turn up the next day, chequebook in hand. He bought everything, often at derisory prices, packed his purchases into the back of his Citroën Traction and drove home. There, he propped them against chairs in the living room and showed them to the young Elias, commenting on and justifying his choices for hours at a time. Occasionally he found himself saddled with a batch of unsaleable rubbish. But mostly the market agreed with him, and he made huge profits when he came to sell.

Thus, in the Sterns' storeroom, next to the Bonnard and Seurat, works by Picasso, Braque and Modigliani started accumulating, soon to be joined by entire crates of Matisse and Chagall.

Gabriel had provided wealth for his family. Jacob now secured status. Film stars, aristocrats and politicians all flocked to his gallery, listening out for his tips as they would at the races. Not a day went by without a mention of Jacob Stern, that paragon of 'French good taste', as they called it across the Atlantic, in the culture pages of *Le Matin* or *Le Figaro*. If he wasn't giving a sumptuous dinner in honour of the President of the Council, Edouard Daladier, he was playing a discreet part in the sale to John D. Rockefeller of the *Portrait of Antoine-Laurent Lavoisier and His Wife*, one of David's masterpieces, for a price hitherto unheard of for a work of art.

This didn't stop Jacob and his family finding themselves utterly alone when the SS came for them in August 1942. After a stay at the Drancy Internment Camp, they were sent to Dachau. Happily, a week earlier, an intuition had caused Jacob to send his eldest son to London, accompanying several containers full of pictures, sculptures and furniture.

Two years later, when Elias returned to Paris, he found the big house in the Rue des Saints-Pères quite empty. Disappointed at missing the most beautiful pieces of the Stern collection, Goebbels had ordered that everything the little upstart Jews had left behind, down to the last coffee spoon, be sent to him.

In addition to an unrivalled stock of masterpieces, Elias inherited his forebears' flair and a taste for risk. He grasped the significance of the main artistic trends of the post-war period before anyone else. When Picasso was at his peak, he bought

Pop Art. When Warhol became a demigod, he developed a passion for narrative painting. Always one step ahead of the competition, his galleries in Paris, London and New York were packed with treasures available nowhere else. Elias could boast of having put together, single-handed, some of the most beautiful collections in the world. Solomon Guggenheim never failed to visit him when he was passing through Paris. As for Calouste Gulbenkian, his many houses, situated on every continent, were full of works chosen by Elias. The flamboyant millionaire followed Elias's advice blindly and bought everything he suggested, without even looking at the price.

Elias Stern was the best in his field because he sold far more than pictures: he offered a privileged few the quintessence of human genius. He possessed a unique eye, refined by decades of observation and analysis. He could recognise an exceptional painting from a poor black and white reproduction. He'd discovered masterpieces hiding beneath daubs or behind impenetrable coats of varnish. Only he could perform such miracles. The wildest rumours circulated about the paintings he was supposed to have in the storeroom of his large house. People spoke of hundreds of pieces, all exceptional, of course, for Stern hated mediocrity. With him, it was the best or nothing.

He passed into legend the day he retired from business, when he was over eighty. Without warning, he sold all his galleries and disappeared from the face of the earth. He never appeared again in public, so that almost everyone thought he was dead.

Hence Grimberg's amazement. 'Do you think it's true?' he asked.

'What?'

'The story about the Van Gogh.'

Among the countless anecdotes that had flourished about Stern over the years, one stood out as improbable. According to the rumour, sometime in the mid-eighties Stern had refused to sell a Van Gogh – an extraordinary version of his *Irises*, far more beautiful than the one in the Rijksmuseum in Amsterdam – to a fantastically wealthy industrialist, with the excuse that he believed him incapable of appreciating its subtleties. The obstinate buyer doubled, then tripled his offer until it reached an obscene figure, the equivalent of the GDP of a developing country. But Stern held firm. The last anyone heard, he still had the painting. As no one had been inside his house for almost a quarter of a century, the story remained unverifiable.

'Do you think the Van Gogh really exists?' asked Grimberg, who would have cut off his right arm for a chance to see it, if only for a minute.

'I have no idea.'

In truth, Valentine didn't care. It had taken her almost two years to get over what she still persisted in calling the 'accident'. Struggling with depression every day, she'd somehow managed to rebuild the semblance of a career. In a dingy workshop, dealing with third-rate work, maybe, but she'd started from such a low point that she was satisfied with little. At least the workshop gave her a reason to get up in the morning – that was something.

In a few moments, Stern had shattered her fragile equilibrium. He'd reawakened painful memories, oblivious of the consequences of his irruption into her new life, plunging Valentine back into uncertainty. He'd trampled his way into her quiet, carefully protected life, knocking it all flying. She was furious. He could offer her work on the Dead Sea Scrolls themselves and she'd still turn him down. He and his mouldy spell book could go to hell.

Valentine stared for a moment at her untouched cup of coffee and lifted it to her lips. The coffee had gone cold. She made a face.

'Shit . . . I can't drink this now.'

She got up and went to pour the contents of the cup down the sink. When she came back, she took two bottles of beer from the fridge and handed one to her former colleague before sitting beside him on the sofa, her legs tucked under her.

'I don't understand,' said Grimberg. 'How can you turn him down? After everything you've been through. After . . .' He searched for the words. 'After the *disaster*.'

It was the first time he'd been so insensitive towards her. Valentine felt tears rise to her eyes. She decided to hold them back until later, when she was alone at home and could give in to her grief without fear of ridicule. There was no way she was going to let Grimberg see her cry.

'You can't say no,' he insisted. 'Not to Elias Stern. You can't spend the rest of your life fixing this awful old stuff. You're far too good for that.'

Grimberg was right. Valentine knew it, but she didn't like hearing it said twice in one day. The urge to cry returned, the tears rising dangerously close to the surface.

'Give me a break. It's hard enough as it is . . . I didn't call you for that.'

Contrite, Grimberg put an arm around Valentine and hugged her. There was affection in the gesture, but also a slightly clumsy sensuality. Valentine shrank back a little. Grimberg didn't push it, and let go. Things should have been clear between them. They were supposed to have settled the question of how they felt about each other long ago.

The second thing Valentine had done after being taken on by the Louvre, just after buying the Marino Marini drawing, was to sleep with Grimberg. An accredited restorer in the Italian Paintings Department, he was about ten years older than her, and owed his great success with the museum's female staff to his good looks and easy charisma. But Valentine hadn't chosen him for his charm, or his thick-rimmed glasses, cashmere polo necks and tousled hair. She actually found these accessories of the melancholy intellectual slightly irritating. For her, sleeping with Grimberg had been like a rite of passage, the celebration of a new phase of her life, and nothing more.

There had never been any question of passion between them, much less love. Grimberg was in the right place at the right time, that was all. Their mutual desire had led them into bed, where they'd had a good time. Neither of them wanted the relationship to go any further. It was obvious: they didn't need to say it.

Grimberg came back into Valentine's life when she was fired, a few weeks after the 'accident'. Of all her former colleagues, he was the only one to show his support. If she'd survived, it was partly thanks to him. He seemed to feel it gave him the right to intervene in her life, even to make his way back into her bed.

Valentine wasted no time in rejecting his advances, in no uncertain terms. It wasn't him; she'd have preferred it if that had been the problem, but she hadn't been intimate with any other man since being fired. In fact, she had so much trouble taking care of herself she had nothing left to give anyone else, not even tenderness. She felt empty, drained of all emotion, and there was nothing she could do about it.

Grimberg took note. He resolved to play the part of best friend.

'Stop feeling sorry for yourself,' he said, getting up from the sofa and taking his leather jacket from the hook by the door. 'You might never get another chance. Think it over.'

Unable to sleep, Valentine spent almost all evening thinking over Stern's offer, staring up at her bedroom ceiling. At ten-thirty, she made up her mind. She dialled the number on the business card.

Elias Stern himself answered at the third ring.

'Stern.'

'It's Valentine Savi. Sorry for calling so late.'

'Don't worry. I'm a poor sleeper anyway.'

'I accept your offer,' said Valentine. 'I'll see what I can do with your codex.'

'Wonderful. I'm so pleased. I'll send my chauffeur round first thing tomorrow. Good night, Valentine.'

'See you tomorrow.'

Stern hung up.

Valentine put the phone down beside her, on the bed. For the past two years, she'd numbed her anxiety with sleeping pills. That night she resisted the urge to reach for the packet in her bedside-table drawer.

3

Every morning, at exactly six-thirty, Joseph Fargue climbed the steps of the Cluny – La Sorbonne metro station. He walked the hundred metres or so to the Bazar, the café on the corner of the Rue de la Sorbonne and the Rue des Écoles, and stood waiting for the owner to unlock the door.

Fargue had been coming to the café since his student days and, for almost half a century, had eaten lunch there every day, invariably ordering the plat du jour, a small bottle of Vittel mineral water – at room temperature because chilled drinks gave him heartburn, and then he couldn't concentrate on his work – and crème brûlée for dessert. He'd had lunch there for so many years he'd become part of the furniture, like the scarlet velvet of the banquettes, the brass handrail on the stairs and the red and white checked tablecloths. He was just a little duller, so no one really noticed the quiet figure in the corner opposite the door.

In the morning, Joseph Fargue's self-effacing nature wasn't an issue, as he was the only customer in the café. After drinking his coffee, he rose, made a vague gesture of greeting to the staff who were just arriving and picked up his briefcase. His mother had given it to him the day he got his *baccalauréat*, and he took obsessive care of it, polishing it every evening with a special cream for delicate leather.

He then headed slowly to the main entrance of the university and waited for it to open, at seven o'clock on the dot. More than five minutes' delay earned the guilty doorman a report, which Fargue delivered in person to the Chief of Security.

Joseph Fargue was always absolutely punctual. And if he could manage it, so could everyone else. In any other way lay anarchy.

He'd experienced anarchy in 1968. He'd seen revolutionaries masquerading as students raise barricades and dig up the cobbles to hurl at the police and representatives of the State. For almost two months, appalled, he'd witnessed a country gripped by paralysis. He'd nearly been lynched when he called for lectures to resume and the troublemakers to be expelled. Fargue knew what anarchy was, and he never wanted to see it again. There was one way to avoid it and one only: you had to establish strict rules, and ensure that they were just as strictly observed.

Unfortunately not everyone agreed. Everywhere permissiveness and sloppiness were gaining ground. People felt free to do whatever they liked whenever they liked. Nobody respected anything any more. As for the basic rules of good manners, they'd disappeared without trace long ago. People now made phone calls on the bus, oblivious of the nuisance they caused. They took perverse pleasure in dropping litter beside the bins. They walked around all day with headphones on.

None of this would have happened if the authorities had eradicated the chaos in time. The world was going to the dogs, but that was no reason to open the front gate to the Sorbonne at 7.05 a.m., instead of the regulation 7 a.m.

It was Joseph Fargue's duty to arrive first at the Research Centre of which he was head. As Chief Administrative Officer, he was responsible for the numerous reference works, rare books and incunabula that made up the collection available to students and academic staff. Among his many tasks, he had to unlock the premises and make sure everything was ready by the time they opened. At that hour in the morning, his colleagues were probably still lolling in bed with their wives, or just starting to prepare their children's breakfast. Fargue had neither wife nor children, but even if he had, he would still have arrived before that bunch of layabouts.

He relished the utter silence that reigned in the stacks, whose system he himself had designed with extreme attention to detail. There, in the rooms where he was absolute master, Joseph Fargue had, over the years, constructed a haven of peace, a refuge based on order and the science of classification refined to the utmost degree. *Everything and everyone in their proper place, and the world is more beautiful*, was the motto that governed his daily life. It wasn't hard to grasp. If only everyone did their bit, anarchy would retreat and civilisation would regain the ground it had lost over the past few decades.

Joseph Fargue's day started going downhill at nine o'clock, when the students and academic staff began filling the rows and desks. You could always rely on the barbarians to talk loudly about subjects of the utmost frivolity, or to put books back in the wrong place. Joseph Fargue would then step in and lecture the culprits, threatening to throw them out or simply withdraw their passes. How much more agreeable life would be without all those ill-mannered interlopers! Books to put away, cards to file and complete silence – it was all a dedicated and conscientious Administrative Officer needed to be perfectly content. When he imagined his ideal world, Joseph Fargue felt shivers of pleasure run down his spine.

As he did every day, he started by taking his pens and inkpad from his leather briefcase. He placed them on the main desk, beside the cards on which users wrote down the reference numbers of books they wanted to consult. Then he slid his case into the top drawer, the one that locked. He made sure not to touch the computer. It had been inflicted on him by an incompetent manager who insisted that you couldn't run a research centre without complete mastery of five or six different software packages. Fargue had drawn up report after report condemning this nonsense, but had been unable to prevent the arrival of the computer. The machine had sat on his desk ever since, a useless, dusty reminder of the vanity of the times.

28

His first task of the morning consisted in categorising all the request forms from the day before, then filing them by name and status of those making the requests, in duly labelled metal boxes. To his colleagues this was a tedious chore. Fargue, on the other hand, didn't see it as a waste of time, and performed the task with real pleasure.

He sat down and glanced around for the previous day's forms. There were usually about thirty to be filed. That morning, however, he couldn't see any. Of course, as exam time approached, students became scarce in the reading room. Staff too willingly deserted the Research Centre in favour of the sunny terraces of nearby cafés. Fargue's disappointment manifested itself as a vexed groan. In his day, end of term or not, teachers taught, students studied and the world went round.

The day before, Fargue had attended a meeting that had lasted all morning. He'd got back to the Centre at lunchtime, around one-thirty, just in time to hear from one of the porters that, following the drama the university had witnessed, the Dean had decided to close the campus for the rest of the day. Fargue had had to ask everyone to leave in a hurry, and had locked up the Research Centre himself.

Puzzled, he picked up the phone and dialled the number of one of his colleagues.

'Hello?' said a sleepy voice.

'Francis? It's Fargue.'

'Joseph, it's ten past seven . . .'

'I know, thanks. Can you tell me if there was a problem with the request forms yesterday morning?'

His colleague thought for a moment. 'No, nothing. It was all as usual. There were about ten requests. You know, same old routine.'

'Thank you, Francis,' said Fargue, hanging up.

There must be a logical explanation for the disappearance of the forms. In the rush to close up, maybe they'd been left in a corner or slipped by mistake into a drawer. In that case, they'd reappear sooner or later, but Fargue wasn't satisfied with such a vague possibility. As a good Chief Administrative Officer, it was his duty to check.

He began searching the Research Centre room by room, starting with the reading room. Half an hour later, he found the forms at last, slipped between the two metal cabinets at the back of the reading room under the windows. Fargue thought immediately that it must have been a prank by a reader annoyed at having to vacate the place unexpectedly.

He pushed the cabinets apart and slid his hand into the gap, scraping his wrist as he did so. He cursed briefly, wiped the few drops of blood away with his handkerchief, then returned to his desk and looked through the forms. He flinched when he saw Albert Cadas's name on one of them. He had made his request at 10.20 a.m. Fargue stared at the old man's slightly shaky handwriting. One of the last things he'd done before his death was to come and work at the Research Centre. Fargue couldn't help feeling proud, and moved.

The title of the book Cadas had requested drew his attention. It was an original edition of the *Theatrum Orbis Terrarum* by the geographer Abraham Ortelius, published in Antwerp in 1570 and considered to be the first atlas in history. As far as Fargue knew, this was outside Albert Cadas's area of interest. To make sure, he opened the metal box where he kept academic staff requests and went to the letter C.

In the previous five years Albert Cadas had consulted forty-three books. None was dated later than the fifteenth century, and all were connected with either philosophy or theology. He had never shown any interest in geography whatsoever. Indeed, Joseph Fargue couldn't remember Cadas ever mentioning anything other than the history of medieval thought. The lecturer was known at the Sorbonne for his consistent interests. So why this sudden fascination for the *Theatrum Orbis Terrarum*, and the cartographic representation of the world?

To get to the bottom of it, Fargue noted the shelf number on the slip and went to the reserve collection, which only Research Centre staff were authorised to enter. It was where the most valuable books were kept. Fargue unlocked the door and went straight to the shelf section written on the form. He inspected the shelf several times, and then checked neighbouring shelves, until he was forced to accept that the *Theatrum Orbis Terrarum* was not in its place. And if it wasn't there, that meant it had been stolen.

Joseph Fargue's carefully ordered world was falling apart. Anarchy had returned, and he felt powerless in the face of it.

4

A huge black Mercedes limousine drew up. Stern's chauffeur got out, nodded at Valentine indifferently and opened the rear door for her without saying a word. His suit jacket stretched over bulging pectorals, and he radiated controlled strength and absolute confidence in his powers of persuasion. In this he was the opposite of Stern. While the latter brought to mind one of Louise Bourgeois's steel spiders, which are far more solid than their spindly limbs suggest, his chauffeur seemed to have been modelled by Rodin's powerful hands. All sharply defined muscle, his bulk only just fitted behind the leather steering wheel.

Valentine had little time to enjoy the Mercedes' reclining seats and array of luxuries for, despite its size, the car slid easily through the traffic. They reached the Champs-Élysées in a matter of moments, drove past the Grand Palais with its newly refurbished glass roof gleaming in the sun, crossed the Alexandre III Bridge over the Seine and headed towards the Latin Quarter. Less than ten minutes later, the car drove through the gates of the Stern family home at 12 Rue des Saints-Pères, on the border of the seventh arrondissement, and pulled up at the foot of imposing steps at the front of the main building.

Built at the beginning of the nineteenth century, the house was surrounded by a wall so high that nobody could look in, even from neighbouring buildings. From the street, when the front gates were closed, one could glimpse only the grey slates of the roof overhang and, at the back, the tops of trees in the garden. It was easy to see why Gabriel Stern had made this his main residence, almost a century earlier: everything about the house – an austere building without particular style or charm – suggested secrecy.

Less easy to determine was whether the purpose of this fortress was to protect the treasures amassed by three generations of art lovers, or to arouse the curiosity of passers-by. It was probably a little of both.

The Sterns were businessmen, after all. Mystery sustained their myth, which in turn drove business. They had become wealthy because they could tell a masterpiece from an ordinary painting, but also because all three had an innate feeling for what would later come to be known as marketing. The large house contributed to their commercial success just as much as Gabriel's instinct, Jacob's boldness and Elias's sharp eye.

The electric gates swung smoothly closed, the only sound a quiet click as they locked. As Valentine climbed out of the back seat of the Mercedes, the chauffeur grabbed her bag. 'On your way out,' he said, his tone admitting no protest.

Valentine was no match for him; she couldn't have made him relinquish the handbag even if she'd lashed out with nails, teeth and carefully aimed kicks. She gave up the bag without a murmur.

Stern was standing at the top of the steps, as impeccably dressed as the previous day. Today, however, his suit was of a grey rather like that of his own skin. The day before, Valentine hadn't noticed quite how closely it resembled the parchment of the manuscript he'd shown her. In natural light, the similarity was striking.

The art dealer was leaning on the arm of a man with a physique similar to the chauffeur's. Well over six feet tall, the bodyguard wore a jacket that was too tight for prominent biceps moulded by countless hours in the gym. Face blank, he looked Valentine up and down, checking for any sign of a weapon hidden beneath her clothing. Once satisfied that she was no threat, he lost interest.

Valentine felt a strange combination of curiosity and claustrophobia. She was about to enter a house that no one, or almost no one, had been inside for years, at the invitation of a man everyone had thought was dead. It could go to one's head. At the same time, Stern had had no qualms about pressuring her into working for him. He had touched several sore points. However much she turned the matter over, she still reached the same, rather unpleasant conclusion: Stern had imposed his will on her. His old-fashioned manners and inoffensive air did nothing to dilute the forcefulness of his tactics. As she mounted the steps, Valentine almost regretted accepting the old man's offer.

Despite her unease, she took the hand he held out to her with some emotion, aware that the crooked fingers had touched the most beautiful paintings in the world. Indeed, to judge the quality of a picture, whether it was by Piero della Francesca, Francis Bacon or an unknown, Stern claimed he needed to establish physical contact. He liked to touch genius, literally.

The old man held Valentine's hand a little longer than necessary as if, sensing her emotion, he wanted to let her make the most of it. Then he let go of his bodyguard's arm and took Valentine's. As they went inside, the bodyguard stationed himself at the door. He smoothed his jacket, then, arms crossed behind his back, began scanning the courtyard.

'Welcome,' said the old man as they entered. 'I'm delighted you agreed to come.'

'Thank you for asking me. I'm honoured, and, I have to admit, a little intrigued by your invitation.'

'Yes, yes, thank you, Valentine. Let's move straight to serious business, if you wouldn't mind. We haven't any time to waste. Come this way.'

Stern led Valentine down a long corridor. The walls were painted an off-white and were hung with framed photographs of

Stern family members and some of their illustrious guests. In one, Valentine recognised Elias's grandfather, Gabriel, standing between Renoir and Degas, before a silly misunderstanding had ended the artists' long friendship. Examples of their work could be seen in the background. Of the dozen or so paintings visible, two were now in the Musée d'Orsay and a third was in the Metropolitan Museum of Modern Art in New York. Eventually worth hundreds of millions of dollars, in the photograph they were propped against the wall among a jumble of sketches and empty frames.

In another photograph a little further on, a smiling Jacob was posing with Marlene Dietrich, while Erich von Stroheim, familiar cigarette holder between his lips, casually looked on. In the next Elias, as a very young man, stood arm in arm with a laughing Picasso before the Cubist portrait the artist had painted of him, which had ended up in the Pushkin Museum in Moscow.

Stern and Valentine passed a room where several women were absorbed in their work at computer screens. They came to an opaque Plexiglas security door. Its modernity contrasted strangely with the period mouldings and wall lamps of the old house. Stern entered a code on an electronic keypad and pressed a thumb to a biometric reader. A light changed from red to green and the door slid silently aside.

'My lair,' said Stern conspiratorially. 'Among themselves, my employees call this room the "holy of holies". They think extraordinary things happen when I shut myself in here. Actually I spend most of the time daydreaming, but please don't tell them that. I'd lose all credibility in their eyes.'

A magnificent inlaid desk sat imposingly in the centre of the room. Valentine recognised the rosewood box that Stern had shown her the day before, placed between a thick monograph on Giacometti and two carefully aligned Mont Blanc pens. She had expected a profusion of priceless works of art, but the walls were empty, except for the one facing the desk on which hung the *Irises* that so fascinated Marc. This version of Van Gogh's famous picture was quite simply astounding. Even behind protective glass, the mauve flowers glowed with an hypnotic radiance. It took Valentine's breath away, and she stood staring for a moment. She could see why Stern hadn't been able to part with it, even for a mountain of gold.

Used to the effect the Van Gogh had on unprepared visitors, Stern waited for Valentine's astonishment to subside before indicating a pair of armchairs in the corner, facing a large bay window that looked on to the garden.

He sank into one of the armchairs with a slightly artificial sounding sigh of relief, and invited Valentine to do likewise.

'I apologise for all the security measures,' he said. 'Excessive, no doubt, but necessary. There are a lot of precious objects here. You have to deter thieves. What can you do? In my grandfather's day, you could walk through the streets with a masterpiece under your arm. Nowadays, you only have to have your picture taken in front of a valuable painting and all the thieves in the land are queuing up outside your house.'

The Plexiglas door slid open again. One of the young women they'd seen earlier in the computer room came in. She was carrying a tray with a teapot and two Sèvres porcelain cups. Placing them on the coffee table between the armchairs, she poured the tea with deft movements. She picked up a sugar lump with silver tongs and offered it to Valentine, who shook her head.

'Thank you, Nora,' said Stern. 'You're a treasure.'

Nora smiled back at him. She must have been about twenty-five or twenty-six. She was wearing a close-fitting trouser suit that accentuated her slim, well-proportioned figure. Her blonde hair was swept into an impeccable chignon, showing off her delicate, refined features. Nora was beautiful – glacially so, admittedly, but undeniably beautiful – and she knew it.

'If you need me,' she said gently, 'just let me know.'

'Don't worry, we will. We'll call if we need anything else.'

Stern eyed his employee's harmonious curves as she left the room.

'Ah, Nora . . . She can twist me round her little finger. What can I do? Surrounding myself with charming creatures is the last true luxury for a man of my age. The paintings should be enough, you might think. But I lack the moral strength to give up Nora and her like.'

Valentine took a sip of tea. The hot liquid helped her get a grip on herself. She tried to ignore her surroundings, to forget her host's fame and the compelling presence of the *Irises*. She wanted an explanation, and was prepared to walk out if Stern refused to provide one.

Coming straight to the point, she asked: 'Why me?'

Stern didn't answer immediately. Lost in thought, he gazed at the garden for a few seconds. Through the window, the branches of ancient oaks bearing the first buds of spring swayed in a gentle breeze.

'Do you know why I retired, Valentine?'

Stern had a disconcerting habit of evading questions. In his profession, it was probably an asset. A dealer had to be able to listen to his clients so as to choose the paintings that best suited their taste and budget. In everyday life, this occupational quirk soon became infuriating.

Irritated by his diversionary tactic, Valentine merely shook her head in response. The elderly art dealer didn't take offence, and continued.

'I was tired of it all, you see. Finding paintings, persuading buyers, negotiating prices – I'd had enough. I was rich, my passion was played out and I had no heir to share it with. I wanted to live out my life in peace, surrounded by my memories and my favourite paintings. Then one day I came upon an El Greco, an absolute marvel. The technique, the style, the composition were all perfect, and magnificent. I couldn't prove it but deep down I knew it was a forgery, the best I've ever seen.'

Stern seemed to search for his words, as if about to confide something a little shameful.

'I went to see the owner of the painting, a collector to whom I'd sold several major pieces, a man of taste, intelligent and cultured. When I told him his El Greco was a fake, he all but called me a fool. He brought out the certificates, the valuations, the provenance . . . The documents seemed irrefutable, and all I had to set against them was my intuition. I had no idea how the forger had done it, but he'd covered his tracks perfectly. He'd managed to place his picture alongside my masterpieces. I know it sounds ridiculous, but I felt he was provoking me, trying to ruin my life's work. And the worst thing was that no one would listen to me. Me, Elias Stern!'

What would have seemed like conceit from anyone else sounded like a simple statement of fact from Stern's lips. Valentine didn't doubt for a moment that he could recognise a fake El Greco at a glance.

'In the collector's defence,' the old man went on, 'I have to admit that the illusion was perfect. Even the varnish looked as if it had been applied four hundred years ago. But that El Greco was a forgery. I could feel it, but I couldn't prove it. Not alone, anyway. I needed help.'

He paused briefly and waved his hand as if to dismiss a crowd of irrelevant details.

'I expressed my doubts to a small group of experts I'd worked with before, mostly art historians and archivists. They acted as my legs and eyes. They spent months searching archives all over the world, until at last one of them found the document I was lacking.'

He waited a few seconds for a question that didn't come. Valentine simply looked at him with curiosity.

'It was just a letter,' Stern continued, 'tucked away in a corner of the *archivio storico* in Florence. In it, Cardinal Colonna recounted how two young painters from the Court of the Grand Duke of Tuscany, whose names have unfortunately been lost to history, challenged each other to paint a picture in the manner of El Greco. Colonna described the winner's painting in detail: it was my collector's picture, beyond any possible doubt. It resembled an original so perfectly that eventually its history was forgotten and it was erroneously attributed to El Greco.'

Valentine supplied the conclusion to the story herself. 'So both you and the owner were right. It wasn't a present-day forgery, but it wasn't an authentic El Greco either.'

Elias Stern nodded. 'Needless to say, he hates me for it.'

He poured himself another cup of tea, after offering one to Valentine. She declined, keeping the teacup resting in her lap.

'I'm boring you with my little stories, aren't I? You're thinking what a rambling old fool I am. No need to look embarrassed, Valentine, I quite understand. When I was young I too hated having such anecdotes inflicted upon me.'

The old art dealer had a tendency to overdo it, but his skill as a storyteller could win anyone over. Valentine started to relax despite herself.

'I'm getting to the point, don't worry,' Stern continued. 'Believe it or not, this success revived me. It made me feel I still had a purpose. I realised that, in fact, the prospect of retirement bored me deeply.' He made a sweeping gesture that took in the entire room.

'I'm not suited to moping on the sofa, even surrounded by the works of great masters. From time to time, private individuals or institutions entrust a painting or objet d'art to me so that I can authenticate it. For legal and practical reasons, I've set up a foundation. It's a very small organisation, but sufficiently well endowed to have the means to continue functioning after my death.'

'I've never heard of it,' said Valentine.

'I've always felt that discretion was the key to business, especially in my field. I've never revealed the names of my clients, or the sums of money involved. Without secrecy, I wouldn't have lasted a week. I've made it one of the basic operating rules of the Stern Foundation. Infrastructure, staff, logistics, have all been kept to a minimum. I set great store by it. Many doors would be closed to us if our activities became public.'

'You still haven't answered my question. Why me?'

'When I got hold of the manuscript, I thought of you immediately. What's there deserves every attention, and you're the
best in your field. My sources have confirmed it. This job is your
rightful due. It goes without saying that you'll be paid appropri-
ately for your work. What do you think?'

'What's in the book? Isn't it time you told me?'

Stern placed his cup on the tray and looked directly at
Valentine. The gleam of complicity that had shone in his eyes
until now suddenly disappeared, giving way to an expression she
couldn't interpret. For a moment, she had the feeling he was
gauging whether she was worthy of becoming an initiate.

At last he made up his mind to reveal the information she had
come for.

'Does the name Vasalis mean anything to you?'

At the sound of the name, Valentine's teacup slipped from her
hands and fell to the floor. The Sèvres porcelain lay in pieces.
Only vaguely aware of the damage, Valentine stared at the old
man's withered face. The name he had just spoken echoed in her
head, and everything around her – the garden, the magnificent
Louis XV desk, even the Van Gogh – suddenly receded, leaving
only Stern.

She shook her head, like a stubborn little girl.

'Vasalis is a myth. He never existed.'

Stern held Valentine's defiant gaze, his blue eyes fixed on hers.
His quiet confidence didn't falter; quite the reverse.

He shook his head. 'You're mistaken, my dear. The man really
lived, and the codex is the only physical trace left of his time on
this earth. You're going to make Vasalis live again, Valentine.
Isn't that an exciting prospect?'

5

Elias Stern must be senile. That was the only possible conclusion, the only rational explanation.

Like countless elderly people, he lived in a world of memories and fantasies. The only difference between him and other old men was that he paid his employees well for looking indulgently on his whims. Besides, what if his bodyguards and secretaries were in fact carers who lifted weights, and nurses recruited for their looks? In that case, perhaps the tall gates of the house in the Rue des Saints-Pères now served a different purpose from the one they were designed for. Perhaps it wasn't a case of deterring intruders, but of preventing news of Stern's failing mental health from leaking out. It was an appealing theory. It explained the silence that had surrounded his sudden disappearance.

Such were Valentine's thoughts as she followed Nora's slim, supple form through the maze of corridors in the large house.

Stern had brought the meeting to an end, saying he was very tired, soon after Nora entered the room, brush in hand, to sweep up the scattered pieces of Sèvres porcelain. In fact, it was Valentine who needed to recover.

The art dealer really must have been senile to offer her fifteen thousand euros for two months' exclusive work for his foundation. Valentine was stunned. Fifteen thousand euros . . . It was half her annual salary when she worked for the Louvre.

In exchange for this princely sum, Stern's only requirement was that she leave her workshop and devote herself full time to the manuscript and related research. He would place a room in the house at her disposal, supply any equipment she needed and pay all the costs she deemed necessary for the restoration and deciphering of the codex, without question.

In short, he was paying her handsomely to work on ideal terms, doing exactly what she normally did for a pittance.

But as with all wonderful opportunities, there were a number of problems. The first had to do with the manuscript itself, or rather its contents. Stern had not been the first to look for proof of Vasalis's existence. But as far as Valentine knew, no previous attempt had succeeded. The conclusion was obvious: the figure of Vasalis was an intellectual construct, the invention of a group of scholars with nothing better to do; the equivalent of the Loch Ness monster for medievalists in search of excitement. For that reason, and because she'd stopped believing in fairy tales about thirty years ago, Valentine couldn't for a second imagine that the codex contained an original text by Vasalis.

Something else troubled her. Despite her attempts to find out more, she still knew nothing about the mysterious organisation she would be working for. According to the art dealer, its official name was 'The Stern Foundation for the Dissemination of the Arts'.

This generic designation meant nothing. Half of all the arts-related organisations in the world had similar names. In ordinary conversation, Stern referred to it as the 'Foundation', the capital F conveyed by a short pause, as if the old man were about to speak a magic word or reveal a wonderful secret. He might just as well have said 'Thingamajig' or 'Whatsit', so vague did everything to do with the organisation seem.

When Valentine asked about the aims of the Foundation, its funding or its board of directors, Stern remained stubbornly silent. He refused to say any more, claiming it had nothing to do with the job he was entrusting her with. As long as she was being paid – and she was being very well paid – what did the nature of her employer's corporate structure matter?

A similar vagueness surrounded the staff employed by the Foundation. From what Valentine could gather, Nora's job description was hazy, something between private secretary and all-round assistant. As she and Valentine passed the computer room, Nora introduced the two women busy at their machines as Virginie and Isabelle. They looked up briefly from their screens, polite smiles barely disguising their indifference. Nora made the remaining introductions: the brawny chauffeur was called Franck, and the mute bodyguard Eric. Ordinary names, interchangeable at will, and no surnames.

Valentine's uneasiness grew. Nothing rang quite true. The large house felt like a theatre set full of silent figures with blank faces.

Nora was a case in point. Her features never showed the slightest emotion, and she kept her voice absolutely neutral, whatever she was saying. In fact, she addressed Valentine in a whisper, as if fearing to shatter the harmony of this artificial world with too sharp a tone. Even the heels of her court shoes made no sound on the parquet.

Above all, Valentine hated not knowing what she was getting into. If her financial position hadn't been so precarious, she would have refused to work on such terms. But the fifteen thousand euros Stern was offering were an unexpected godsend. So she'd suppressed her doubts and signed the contract he'd handed her, including the confidentiality clause which, if she was indiscreet about the job or the contents of the codex, meant she could be sued for considerable damages.

Anyway, even if she did manage to stabilise the condition of the codex, she probably wouldn't find anything interesting in it, and would therefore have nothing to tell. The logic of this convinced her in the end.

The rooms of the large house were arranged around a marble staircase with a wrought-iron banister of elaborate curlicues. A beautiful piece of work, thought Valentine as she climbed the stairs, produced at a time when people still believed objects should outlast them. How things had changed. She suddenly pictured ladies in evening dress and men in tailcoats, champagne glasses in hand, streaming up and down the majestic staircase.

She made a rough calculation: ground floor, two upper floors, about ten doors per floor. The place could easily accommodate a couple of hundred guests, an orchestra and an army of servants. Such a stately setting wasn't suited to emptiness and silence. Valentine realised her mistake: it was wrong to compare the house to a theatre set. Even cardboard scenery seemed more alive than this tomb of marble and wrought iron.

On the first floor, the two women passed a series of closed doors, before stopping in front of a security system like the one outside Stern's office. Nora repeated the art dealer's actions of an hour earlier. The thin panel of tinted Plexiglas slid silently into the wall.

Though it was at the back of the house and looked on to the garden, the room was in darkness. Thick curtains hung over every window, blocking out all sunlight. When Nora pressed the switch, white light, intense but not blinding, streamed from spotlights in the false ceiling.

Valentine couldn't help starting at the sight of the walls, which were covered in shelving from floor to ceiling, filled with books without a single gap. The books were arranged according to size. The folio volumes were on the lower shelves, while the quarto and octavo books occupied the higher ones.

'Mr Stern is placing his personal library at your disposal,' Nora explained. 'This is where you'll be working.'

'Great.'

Curious, Valentine entered the room, while her guide stood back. She ran her index finger along the plain limed oak shelves supporting the books, reading the titles and authors' names on the spines. She stopped at a book bound in ancient ivory vellum, and cast an enquiring glance at Nora, who shrugged.

Valentine took this as assent. She carefully slid the book out and opened it. The frontispiece showed a palm tree surrounded by a banner bearing the motto *Curvata, resurgo*.

Amused, Valentine softly read out the text beneath the engraving. '*Le Cid*. Tragi-comedy. Paris, Augustin Courbé, Bookseller & Printer to His Royal Highness the King's brother, at the small Salle du Palais, M.DC.XXXVII. By Royal permission.'

Nora completed the description: 'An original edition with one hundred and twenty pages, in remarkably good condition. Only one other copy of this edition is known to bibliographers. It's in the Guyot de Villeneuve collection, and has a modern binding. The vellum on this one is of the period. Two other editions, with one hundred and thirty-six pages, were published in the same year, but this is probably the earliest. The text contains several interesting variations compared with the final version.'

Valentine saw a fleeting gleam in Nora's eyes just before she regained her mask of impassivity. So, she was a living human being after all. Perhaps she even had feelings. You just had to talk about antiquarian books for her to show emotion. There was something reassuring, if poignant, about it.

Both women seemed embarrassed by the revelation. There was a heavy silence as Valentine put the book back.

'I didn't know Mr Stern dealt in rare books as well,' she said, to ease the atmosphere.

'Elias has never sold a single book. He collects them for his personal use.'

Valentine noted the move from 'Mr Stern' to 'Elias', but didn't dwell too long on the rather surprising sign of familiarity. She'd never read anything anywhere about Stern being a bibliophile, or that he could even distinguish between a run-of-the-mill volume and a rare edition. There were definitely gaps in the old art dealer's official biography.

Nora saw that she was surprised, and felt obliged to justify her employer's discretion.

'Art is his work; books are his real passion. They're different. He doesn't need to talk about it.'

'I see . . .'

In fact, Valentine couldn't see at all how someone who owned so many works of art could prefer mechanically reproduced objects. Most of the books in the library had been printed. Incunabula and first editions, certainly, and no doubt priceless, but they didn't have the same effect on Valentine as unique pieces.

She headed towards the door.

'Elias's behaviour often makes his guests uncomfortable, you know. He's done it to you, hasn't he?'

Caught off guard by Nora's question, Valentine stopped in the doorway. She hesitated a few seconds before answering. 'I just can't quite figure him out, that's all.'

'That's how most people feel. Some even think he's insane or senile, or both. I can assure you they're greatly mistaken.'

Valentine felt herself blushing. She looked down to hide her embarrassment and let out a little conspiratorial laugh, which sounded too forced to be convincing. Nora wasn't taken in, but she smiled back, or rather made the barely visible beginnings of a smile. According to her personal code of communication, it probably signified the start of a lasting friendship.

She waited for Valentine to step out of the room before switching off the light. Then she keyed in the code to lock the door, and gestured towards the landing.

'I suppose he told you his El Greco story?' she said almost warmly, as she preceded Valentine down the stairs.

'Yes, and the one about boring a charming young lady with his anecdotes.'

'That's one of his classics,' admitted Nora. 'But don't reduce him to such trifles. He was testing you. It's his way of amusing himself. He's done it to all of us.'

Valentine decided to take the plunge. She wanted to confide in Nora her doubts about the Foundation, but the moment Nora's foot struck the tiles on the ground floor, she became the dedicated professional once again, the efficient employee of the Stern Foundation for the Dissemination of the Arts.

'Mr Stern will expect you here at nine tomorrow. Please let me know if you'll be needing any specific equipment.'

'I will.'

'Franck will collect you at eight-thirty, like this morning. I'll have the manuscript ready in the library, so you can start work immediately. Make sure you get plenty of rest this afternoon and tonight. Believe me, you'll need it. You've got a lot of work ahead of you. Does all that suit you?'

'Perfectly,' was all Valentine said.

'See you tomorrow then,' said Nora as she opened the door of the Mercedes.

'Yes, see you tomorrow. Thanks for everything, Nora.'

As she passed through the gates of the large house, ensconced in the back of the limousine, Valentine set aside her doubts. At worst, she thought, she'd spend two months in a sumptuous setting surrounded by valuable works of art, light years away from her workshop and the dreadful paintings that were her bread and butter. Even if she didn't succeed in bringing poor Vasalis back to life, she'd have a pleasant time.

Grimberg was right. A little luxury was always welcome, especially when you had been at the edge of the abyss, as she had. Valentine needed to get her breath back before she re-entered reality. She sank a little deeper into the comfortable leather seat as she gazed at the illuminated façades along the banks of the Seine. For the first time in a long while, she almost felt relaxed.

6

Almost twenty-four hours after the suicide, the dark stain was still visible, despite the efforts of the Sorbonne cleaners to remove all traces of the event.

Two of them were busy on their knees, brush in hand, following the Dean's orders. All too aware of how damaging the continued presence of Albert Cadas's blood on the courtyard paving stones was to the image of his institution, the Dean was issuing instructions in an irritable voice.

He considered the Sorbonne to be his private domain, so the suicide of one of his academic staff was like an insult, first to him personally, then to the venerable institution over which he had the honour of presiding, and lastly to the university system as a whole. Had Albert Cadas not already been dead, he would have forced him into early retirement.

'He's going to be a nuisance to the very end,' he grumbled, deploring both the impertinence of the dead man and the porous nature of Parisian stone.

As he passed the small group of spectators gathered round the Dean, David Scotto hunched into his jacket collar, hoping not to be noticed. A friend had phoned him in the late morning to tell him of Albert Cadas's death. Masochistically, David had come to see for himself that his PhD supervisor was indeed dead.

Beyond the human tragedy, the blood on the paving stones

symbolised the end of all his own prospects. David could say goodbye to any hope of completing his research, or getting the job he wanted. Five years' worth of work had just been brutally consigned to the graveyard of unfinished PhD theses. His career now rested beside Albert Cadas in a drawer at the morgue.

David felt quite ill. He was stunned, almost out of his mind. Yet he'd never been particularly fond of the old professor. To be honest, he found certain aspects of the man's personality exasperating. In the space of a few minutes, this charming man could turn cold and distant, and it was impossible to fathom why his mood had changed.

An inopportune word, an incorrect quotation were enough to prompt the abrupt reversal. He would then refuse to see David for weeks, claiming that his mere presence would disturb his thinking. Even when behaving relatively benevolently towards his protégé, Albert Cadas could be so curt that some days David considered bringing his research to a premature end.

But Cadas had proposed a subject for David's thesis when all his colleagues had refused, so this deserved at least a certain kind of gratitude. Later, when the university scientific committee questioned the viability of David's work and turned down his grant application, Albert Cadas had been vocal in his defence, so that David could give up his odd jobs and devote himself fully to his thesis. He had begun by expressing his low opinion of each of the committee members, then had initiated the appeal procedure. For weeks, Albert Cadas's ranting resounded through every administrative department of the Sorbonne.

In the end, the Dean summoned them both. Sitting behind his huge desk, surrounded by portraits of illustrious predecessors, he must have thought his status alone would impress them sufficiently to make them realise how foolhardy it was to clash with the committee. He hadn't, however, expected the extent to which the two men couldn't care less about what he had to say.

Elated at having found a PhD supervisor at last, David was still picturing his future as a triumphant march towards academic heights. He could always smooth over any problems once he'd taken the viva, he thought. In his view, the rest didn't matter. The Dean could get as worked up as he liked. He could have a heart attack right there and then, for all he cared.

As for Albert Cadas, he knew his career was too far advanced for his superior's threats to have any consequences. He listened to the Dean's lecture with indifference.

When the Dean at last fell silent, Albert Cadas gave him a reply which, in the smooth, civilised world of the university, was like a nuclear bomb.

'Listening to you, I couldn't help thinking of the lines from Sophocles: "Whoever approached a tyrant, even as a free man, became his slave." What could you possibly offer me in return for my allegiance? A bigger office? A committee to chair? An extra bookshelf? Come now, let's be serious. We shouldn't even be having this discussion. You don't object if we leave now, do you?'

The Dean blanched. As always when he felt ill at ease, his hand went to the rosette of the Légion d'Honneur on his lapel. He recovered some of his composure as he reflected that those same words of Sophocles' were on Pompey's lips when he was assassinated then decapitated on the seashore in Egypt, where he had fled to escape Caesar.

Just as Pompey had perished because he believed he was protected from assassins by his merciless enemy, Albert Cadas's certitudes were working against him. If he wasn't careful, he'd make a fatal mistake. Come that day, the Dean himself would gather his head at the foot of his still warm corpse and delight in displaying it on the wall facing his desk. He might even have Sophocles' absurd saying engraved beneath the trophy. You had to be pretty stupid to believe that a pure soul was any match for the sword of the mighty.

'Well, if that's your attitude . . .' he said, pretending to become engrossed in a ministerial circular of the utmost importance. 'Gentlemen, there's the door. Please close it behind you.'

As the two men were on their way out, the Dean raised his

head slightly and, his voice shaking with anger, issued a final warning.

'I'm not surprised by your reaction, my dear colleague. But, as you know, in this world everything has a price. I'll be waiting for you to make your next false move. And when you do – as I know you will – don't expect any leniency from me. As for you, young man, you will find your choice leads to doors closed to you far more firmly than mine. I fear you'll only realise the grave consequences of your decision once it's too late.'

Albert Cadas shut the door without waiting for the Dean to finish. The last few words were muffled by the heavy wood.

As they walked down the gloomy corridor, the old philosophy professor placed a hand on his student's shoulder. It was the only sign of affection he ever showed David in all the years they worked together.

Despite his satisfaction at having stood up to the Dean, Albert Cadas's face betrayed deep fatigue, etched by forty years of mutual incomprehension between him and the institution for which he worked.

'Let's leave that imbecile struggling with his own stupidity,' he said with a weary smile, 'and return to our fascinating dialogue with the past. At least that won't stab us in the back. Well, I hope not.'

From that day on, David's gratitude towards Albert Cadas just about counterbalanced his terror of the Dean whom, superstitiously, he avoided like the plague. He took care to stay well away from the corridor reserved for the managerial staff of the university.

This precaution was even more pertinent now that his protector was dead: he no longer had anyone on his side to prevent the Dean from crushing him if he suddenly felt like it. And David had no doubt that his supervisor's sworn enemy would derive enormous pleasure from doing just that.

The hope of passing unnoticed proved futile. The Dean caught sight of him in the distance, and elbowed his way towards him through the crowd of onlookers. He called out as David was about to enter the library.

'You there! Yes, you, Scotto. Wait, I want a word with you . . .'

David stood still, unsure of what to do. The library had seemed like a good refuge, but it had only one entrance. Once up the stately steps and through the great door, he would have been trapped like a rat in a cage.

The Dean knew that David had no escape, so he approached him unhurriedly, with the regal bearing of the victor in his hour of triumph. News of the affront he had suffered years earlier because of David had circulated around the university. Such an insult called for exemplary punishment.

'You must be devastated,' he said, loud enough for everyone to hear. 'Such a loss to the university. He was one of the pillars of the Sorbonne. We all mourn your late lamented supervisor.'

He didn't mean a word of it, of course. His face showed obvious relief. Not only had he got rid of a troublesome lecturer sooner than he'd hoped, but now he had a free chair to grant to one of his many protégés. His victory was complete.

Give and you shall receive. The Dean had made the age-old saying his own. The kingdom of which he was absolute ruler was riddled to its very core with the canker of ambition. The more the Dean scattered the crumbs of his power to the beggars around him, the more he felt the wonderfully gratifying miasma of obligation rise as he passed. Albert Cadas was the exception in a world in which every gesture originated in an unquenchable thirst for recognition. He had no place in such a world. His death was part of the natural order of things.

The Dean grabbed David's arm and brought his face up close to the young man's. The skin around his eyes was deeply lined. This sign of the passing of time emphasised a disturbingly piercing gaze, like that of a raptor spying prey, and preparing to swoop and tear it apart.

This time, the Dean spoke quietly so that no one else could hear.

'I warned you that you were making a grave error letting that old fool lead you by the nose. I could crush you in the blink of an eye, and no one would bother to defend you.'

He left a brief moment of silence, during which he peered into the young man's face to make sure his words had sunk in. He seemed pleased by what he saw.

'You're in luck, however,' he went on. 'Your determination to provoke me has finally aroused my interest. I'm curious to know how Cadas convinced you to follow him so blindly. I'll expect you in my office tomorrow to discuss it. You'd be well advised to attend. Is that understood?'

David nodded, unable to speak. Satisfied, the Dean let go of his arm and left him surrounded by amused observers.

David had never felt so alone, not even when his first love had slapped his face in front of the whole class on receiving his declaration of ardour. He stood rooted to the spot for some time.

'What a bastard!'

David turned with a start. Raymond Agostini stood behind him, dressed as usual in a faded velvet suit. Though smoking was forbidden on campus, he lit a cigarette and took a long drag.

'I suppose he threatened to throw you out?' he said, exhaling smoke. 'I was too far away to hear what he said, but I'd be surprised if the weasel didn't take the opportunity to settle a few old scores.'

'I haven't been banned from the Sorbonne just yet, but exile looms.'

'I'm not surprised. He wants to do things by the book to cover himself. Don't worry, Scotto, I'll try to sort things out. The good thing about idiots is that they're too stupid to persevere when the tide turns. I'll stand up for you if he picks a fight.'

Raymond Agostini knew what he was talking about. He'd been appointed lecturer in Ancient Greek literature only a year after Albert Cadas. In the course of his long career, he'd sat on most of the university committees. If anyone knew the workings of the Sorbonne, he did. This hadn't prevented him, as he neared retirement, from being gradually sidelined by some of the young

Turks of the Classics department. On the face of it, he seemed to take it calmly. His wife had been pushing for some time for them to move to their house on the Côte d'Azur. It was understandable: why spend so much on a villa overlooking the bay of Saint-Tropez – on which they were still paying off the mortgage, incidentally – and only stay there three weeks a year?

Agostini had so far heroically withstood the dual onslaught of his wife and his colleagues, but he was about to reach the fateful age of sixty-eight and automatic retirement. The prospect of spending his days, winter and summer, going for walks on the beach, hand in hand with his wife, wasn't particularly appealing. Not to mention the endless games of Scrabble and suppers in front of the television. Even the Chinese hadn't invented such a form of torture. Raymond Agostini was counting on his diabetes and delicate heart to get him out of that ordeal.

As well as sharing Albert Cadas's taste for *hors d'âge* Armagnac, he had a similar liking for peace and quiet. Indeed, he'd chosen the office next to Albert Cadas's, on the top floor of the main building. The two lecturers spent hours between classes arguing over literature with the energy and passion of undergraduates.

Raymond Agostini was suddenly overcome at the memory of those times. His eyes clouded with tears. Even his irritation with the Dean was eclipsed by this wave of grief.

'How sad,' he said, shaking his head. 'What could have possessed poor Albert?'

'Maybe he was depressed,' ventured David. 'Or ill. With his personality, he'd never have endured a long terminal illness.'

'Don't be ridiculous. If Albert had been ill, he'd have told me. I saw him yesterday and he seemed fine. Fuming about his colleagues, and most of the students at the university, as usual, but not at all depressed.'

Instinctively, David glanced up at the window from which his supervisor had thrown himself. Agostini did likewise, and immediately looked away.

'Horrible . . .' he murmured. He stared at David. 'What are we going to do with you now, Scotto?'

David shrugged and smiled. 'Can you recommend a good place of exile? A desert island, or an active volcano, perhaps?'

Raymond Agostini didn't answer. He drew on his cigarette in silence. His thoughts were already elsewhere. On a beach on the Côte d'Azur, with his wife, to be precise.

His expression became grim.

7

Sometimes a person's destiny hinges on very little – poorly judging a bend in the road, missing the start of a meeting, changing a number at the last minute to turn a losing lottery ticket into a winning one. Or chemicals reacting unpredictably, as Valentine had discovered to her cost. A silent, imperceptible loss of control that alters the course of your life for ever.

Valentine had lost control of her destiny for just a fraction of a second, the time it takes to blink an eye or take a breath. She'd paid a heavy price for it. Not financially, of course. That had been up to the insurance company, which paid out a hefty sum in compensation for her mistake.

More spectacularly, Valentine's punishment had taken the form of a modern-day version of the pillory. She hadn't been physically harmed, of course. But she had been condemned to public vilification, which was just as painful and humiliating.

For weeks Valentine had been lambasted mercilessly in the press, with no opportunity to defend herself. Having abuse hurled at you in the papers is never pleasant. Seeing your name amid a torrent of epithets such as 'incompetent', 'irresponsible' or even 'criminal' is even less so.

Valentine's thoughts turned to her new assignment, and to the palimpsest's putative author, Vasalis. He too had let go of his destiny and hadn't been able to rectify the course of his life. In an interesting contrast, his punishment had been quite the opposite of Valentine's. Indeed, rather than have him publicly reviled, Pope Clement IV had decided, around the year 1265, to erase him from the memory of man. He had condemned Vasalis to the dungeon of history, along with the numberless multitude of the defeated and the damned. But before this, as was the quaint habit of the time, Vasalis had been put to the stake and reduced to a pile of ashes, which his executioners scattered to the four winds.

Once the unfortunate's mortal remains had gone up in smoke, it was easy for the papal censors to consign his memory to eternal limbo. On pain of the identical punishment Vasalis had undergone, they forbade all mention of his name or commentary on his writings. Whatever Vasalis had done, he had provoked a reaction of unprecedented violence, even for such troubled times.

Clement IV's plan worked perfectly. Half a century later, no one could remember why Vasalis had incurred his wrath. By the middle of the fifteenth century, no one would have dared affirm that he had ever really existed.

So was the macabre story told by its adherents. There weren't many of them, but Hugo Vermeer was one. Actually, Vermeer was inclined to give credence to any tale, as long as it was suffused with mystery, conspiracy and scandal. If, in addition, it involved art or philosophy, with a hint of anticlericalism, he rushed in with the fervour of a Spartan on the day of battle.

Hugo Vermeer was a fighter, a doughty warrior, quite unlike his illustrious ancestor from Delft – at least, he claimed to be a direct descendant, though he never provided any proof – whose stoutness and heavy features, though, he did possess. Apart from that, Hugo Vermeer was short, unshaven and usually reeked of alcohol, even on the rare and short-lived occasions when he was sober. His addiction did nothing to improve an unfortunate temperament, not unlike that of an enraged Rottweiler. He spent his days railing at politicians, the cost of living and dissolute youth, and had a tendency to string together shameless lies with considerable virtuosity.

When he wasn't skulking at home in a foul mood, Vermeer was an entertaining companion, with a sharp – or, more accurately, lacerating – wit. He was also unfailingly loyal, and would happily sacrifice an entire case of Château Pétrus to help a friend in need. So on those evenings when he was determined to cheer her up, Valentine knew she was in for a massive hangover.

Vermeer poured himself another glass of Gevrey-Chambertin, the wonderfully velvety 1992 vintage. He signalled to the waiter for a second bottle and enthusiastically attacked the gargantuan rib of beef occupying his entire plate. He swallowed an impressive mouthful of the meat, which was cooked to perfection, and completed the gastronomic assault with a handful of frites, washed down with more wine.

'Ah, 1992,' he said at last, catching his breath. 'A great year for Burgundies. But only for Burgundies. That year's Bordeaux are unspeakably mediocre. And as for the Beaujolais, what can I say? They make you want to weep!'

Hugo Vermeer spoke perfect French, exclamations and curses included. Only a slight tendency to mistreat his vowels betrayed his Dutch origins. He glanced contemptuously at the Diet Coke beside Valentine's plate.

'How can you drink that stuff? It's not worthy of you, my lovely. You know it eats away at your insides. It starts with an ulcer and then degenerates into cancer. They do it on purpose, the bastards. Why do you think they've never revealed the recipe? So that they can peddle their filthy drugs to us, take our money and . . .'

'And steal our souls,' finished Valentine, who knew her friend's rants by heart.

'I'm not kidding, Valentine. If I'm going to damage my arteries, I'd rather do it with good things. Cheers!' he concluded, emptying his glass.

'You were born in the wrong century, Hugo. You should have lived in Dumas's and Flaubert's time.'

'Don't!' grumbled Vermeer, eyes full of longing. 'Ah, Madame

Bovary's dinner! Sirloin, fricassée of chicken, braised veal, leg of lamb, roast suckling pig, andouille sausage with sorrel . . . Not to mention the tiered cake for dessert and wine by the caseload. Eight hours at the table . . . Those people really knew how to live!'

He refilled his glass and proposed a toast. 'To the great Curnonsky!'

'To the prince of gastronomes!' added Valentine, raising her glass of Diet Coke. 'And to all the writers who died young and obese and in terrible agony!'

Hugo Vermeer stroked his stomach dubiously. 'Pah! We're all going to die one day, so why deprive yourself before the fateful moment?'

He put his philosophy into practice immediately by cutting himself another chunk of meat, smearing it with Béarnaise sauce and wolfing it down. His face radiated lascivious pleasure, in a rather convincing imitation of Goya's Saturn devouring his son.

'What's bothering you, Valentine?'

'How can you tell I'm worried?'

'Please, don't try that with me.'

Valentine looked down and applied herself to crushing the lemon slice in her glass with the stirrer.

'I can't talk about it, Hugo. I've signed a confidentiality clause. I don't want to get into trouble.'

'Your worried little face wouldn't by any chance have something to do with a certain manuscript, purchased last week by a certain elderly art dealer who's gone to great lengths lately to stay out of the spotlight? If the answer's yes, blink once. If it's no, stick your tongue out. Even if Stern's lawyers are watching, they won't be able to use it against you in court.'

'How did you hear about the codex, Hugo?'

'It's my job to know everything. And I'm pretty good at it, may I remind you. I say so in all modesty, of course. Now, let's see, premise number one: I've heard that old rogue Elias has paid a fortune for a book so mouldy no library would touch it. So he needs a good restorer. Premise number two: you're the best in your field and – a factor not to be discounted – you're available and penniless. Conclusion of this brilliantly constructed syllogism: Elias contacted you, offered you the job and, judging by your face, you've accepted but have doubts.'

Valentine clapped limply. 'Not bad for a bloke who didn't get his *baccalauréat.*'

'The only reason I didn't get it is that my dear parents wouldn't let me mix with the offspring of the lower orders.'

To say that Vermeer belonged to the elite was something of an understatement. Indeed, from birth his parents had prepared him to assume his position as a gentleman of private means with absolute self-assurance. No member of his family had done any paid work for the past hundred and fifty years, and it was out of the question that this should change. The only clubs the Vermeers deigned to join required an entry fee of at least ten thousand euros, not including annual membership.

Hugo's education had at first been entrusted to a succession of tutors, none of whom could endure the little monster for more than a year. Eventually, out of weariness, his parents had sent him for his teenage years to a boys' boarding school in Switzerland. It was isolated, expensive and deadly dull. As well as a definite, though not exclusive, attraction to members of his own sex, Vermeer had left with an enduring hatred of teachers, together with a contempt for those who submitted to their authority – in other words most people.

Hugo Vermeer belonged to the elite, and loved it.

What he considered his job was therefore more of a hobby, from which he got nothing but huge enjoyment, and also endless problems. Almost three years ago he'd set up an Internet site called Artistic-Truth.com, on which he published a constant stream of irreverent news about the art world. Tales of wheeler-dealing and embezzlement were listed, categorised, commented on and condemned.

Though often unverifiable, his scoops were remarkably

reliable. No one escaped the virulence of his pen, or rather his keyboard. If Vermeer had something interesting to expose, he didn't hesitate, regardless of the trouble it would cause.

His work had earned him quite a few enemies. The year before he had had to shut down the site for a time, when he had been sent a photograph of himself with a red target superimposed on it. A classic tactic, and highly effective.

The message was clear. But its authors had overlooked one thing: having always been kept apart from society, Hugo Vermeer couldn't give a damn for the moral considerations that constrained ordinary mortals. He ignored all obstacles, and took advantage of his social status to claim certain privileges, beginning with freedom from accountability to any government department. Nothing scared him and nothing stopped him, especially not the law.

This natural tendency to walk on the wild side had influenced his career choices. Vermeer cashed in on the collapse of the Eastern bloc in the early nineties by embarking on the large-scale importation of ancient icons, mostly stolen.

When the competition became too fierce, he realised he needed a change of career. The disappearance of one of his intermediaries, of whom only the torso was found five months later in a Moscow rubbish dump, prompted him to make this wise move. He bought an antique shop specialising in art nouveau, and created a life that matched his ideal in every way. He lived in a grand apartment on the Avenue Hoche, halfway between the Champs-Élysées and the Parc Monceau, ate in Michelin-starred restaurants and drove a turquoise 1961 Maserati 3500 GT.

But his paltry turnover couldn't support such a lifestyle. There was a rumour at the time that much of the art stolen in France ended up in his hands. As is often the case, the rumour was well short of the truth: Vermeer could get hold of anything, from a solid-silver salt cellar to a fresco by Tiepolo, as long as you were discreet, paid top dollar and didn't expect an invoice.

This profitable business came to an end when the police, after months of investigation, caught him in possession of compromising items. But despite the evidence, Vermeer was released from police custody and all legal proceedings were dropped. The reasons for his release remained mysterious. He was rumoured to have given the police information on some of his colleagues who also dealt in stolen works of art. As no one could prove it, and the police made no major raids in art-crime circles, theories about his good fortune went no further than conjecture.

Nevertheless, Vermeer fell in line. In the space of a few months, he constructed a façade of impeccable respectability. He sold his apartment and bought a modest house in the suburbs, put the Maserati in store and, at least officially, stopped his illegal activities. But he kept in touch with every shady character on the continent, from the Urals to the Atlantic.

So some of these persuasive friends gave the creators of the threatening photograph to understand that they'd better put an immediate end to their attempt at intimidation. They didn't even have to insist too forcefully. Vermeer was able to reopen the website within a week, and no one had tried to threaten him since.

'What have you heard about the manuscript?' asked Valentine.

'Not much, really. Stern acquired it after a hard fight, in a private deal. There were two of them after the codex, at any cost. I don't know who the other bidder was but he was also a man of considerable means.'

'Do you know who the seller is?'

'No, but I bet he can't believe his luck. When you manage to sell a piece of crap like that at that price, you tend to shout it from the rooftops. I could probably find out who he is quite easily, if you'd like.'

'That would be great.'

Vermeer wiped his mouth with his napkin. 'What interests me,' he went on, 'is why Stern was so keen to get the codex. He's not stupid. He must know what he's doing, spending that much money on a manuscript. I'd be curious to know what it contains.'

He gave Valentine a meaningful look. She pretended not to notice, but it took more than that to put Vermeer off.

'It'll stay between us,' he promised. 'I won't mention it on the website. Not a line, nothing. Not a hint.'

'Liar. You can't keep quiet.'

'Valentine, please!' Vermeer tried to look his most angelic. The result was only moderately successful.

'You look like Jack Nicholson in *The Witches of Eastwick*,' said Valentine. 'You dreadful ham.'

'Nicholson is a faggot. Even when he's playing the Devil, he remains profoundly human compared to me.'

Vermeer loved to play the bad guy. The question was, was he a good guy disguised as a two-bit baddie, or a real bastard who didn't even try to hide his true nature? Ever since she'd met him, Valentine had swung between these two views. But as the years passed, the more she tended to believe the second.

'Tell me about the Foundation,' she said.

'Valentine, it really isn't nice to keep me waiting.'

'How about you scratch my back and I'll scratch yours?'

'You're cruel. If you weren't a vulgar plebeian, I'd find it charming. But actually you're getting on my nerves.'

'Don't be mean, Hugo.'

'OK, you win,' conceded Vermeer. 'Only because you're cute and I haven't given up hope of you succumbing to my charms one day. This is the little I know: Stern appeared last year with his new toy, this "Art Foundation", or whatever he calls it . . .'

'Foundation for the Dissemination of the Arts,' said Valentine.

'If you want my opinion, it's all bullshit. The guy disappears from the face of the earth for three years, everyone thinks he's dead and suddenly here he is again at the head of a foundation whose activities are non-existent.'

'How do you mean?'

'Your Stern Foundation hasn't done a thing so far. No exhibitions, no sponsorship, nothing. It's an empty shell. For an organisation with twenty million euros at its disposal, that's a bit surprising, isn't it?'

'What about the staff, then? I saw five employees. They looked like they were working. At any rate, there's a room full of computers.'

Vermeer shrugged. 'I have no idea what they do, exactly. There's total secrecy. Nothing ever filters out of the Stern house. But I'd imagine the heavies are there for more than just moving paintings. I've tried my hardest but I still haven't found out anything, and I don't like it. I don't like it at all. The whole business smells bad. Your turn now: what's the deal with this damn codex?'

You could never be sure of anything with Vermeer. Even as his friend, it was best to stay on his good side.

'Vasalis,' said Valentine reluctantly.

Vermeer's face lit up. 'So what's the deal? Invisible ink? A palimpsest?'

Valentine nodded.

'A palimpsest,' repeated Vermeer thoughtfully. 'So the rumours were right.'

'What do you mean?'

'You've heard of the *De forma mundi*, haven't you?'

'I've never had your taste for fables. I've always thought Vasalis was a sort of parable. Something to edify the faithful.'

'You don't even know why he died?'

'No.'

Vermeer took on a long-suffering expression. 'Vasalis was executed because he wrote a treatise, the *De forma mundi*, which displeased the Pope. When Clement IV got rid of Vasalis, he also burned all copies of the book. But one of them is said to have survived. Stern must have got hold of it. I've got a file on Vasalis on my computer. I'll send it to you this afternoon. We can talk again when you've read it.'

Valentine indicated the laptop on the banquette beside her friend's ample posterior. She gave him a seductive glance.

'Why don't you give me a taster now?'

Vermeer took a gulp of wine, savouring it at length. A crimson droplet formed in the stubble at the corner of his mouth.

'The suspense will do you good. How did you put it just now? Ah yes, "You scratch my back and I'll scratch yours." And also it'll teach you for drinking that crap instead of my Gevrey-Chambertin.'

Pleased with this, Hugo Vermeer gave himself up wholly to the gentle thrill produced by the wine on his taste buds, heightened by the sight of Valentine's aggrieved face.

8

Joseph Fargue sat on the parquet floor of the room where the rare books were kept, feeling utterly humiliated. He would never have thought such a catastrophe possible. He had never even considered it. This was the most disastrous day of his life. Worse than the day his mother had died.

As soon as he had discovered that the *Theatrum Orbis Terrarum* had disappeared, he had rushed to the Dean's office. He'd explained what he'd found out, in particular that Albert Cadas was involved. The Dean had been surprisingly understanding, given the gravity of the situation. He hadn't raised his voice, hadn't said anything about an administrative investigation or disciplinary action against Research Centre staff. First, he'd asked Joseph Fargue to exercise the utmost discretion, and then he'd accompanied him to Cadas's office. A quick search had convinced the two men that the stolen book was not there. Vexed, Fargue had returned to the Research Centre, thrown out the few remaining students and sent his colleagues home before shutting himself in there, alone. He needed peace and quiet in order to check some things. He didn't want to be disturbed.

Inventorying the valuable books took almost three hours. The laborious task did not improve his mood – quite the reverse. Unfortunately, the *Theatrum Orbis Terrarum* was not the only book to have disappeared from the shelves. Three other books were missing. They were all irreplaceable, either because of their rarity or because they possessed some exceptional feature.

Several pages from the missing treatise *De la Sagesse* by Pierre Charron had been annotated by Montaigne, to whom the author had given the work as a token of admiration. The *Institutiones in Linguam Graecam* by Nicolas Clénard, published in Leuven in 1530 and subsequently reprinted one hundred and twenty-four times in under a century, one of the bestsellers of the Renaissance, had also disappeared. And as for the first edition of Libri V of the *Epigrammatum* by Bernard Bauhuis – a Jesuit famous for his one-line tribute to the Virgin Mary, whose words could be arranged in a thousand and twenty-two different ways, which was the number of stars known at the time – there were only three other known complete copies in the world. And none had belonged, as this one had, to Cardinal Richelieu, who had written his name in ink on the title page.

The disappearances were an absolute catastrophe, a disaster. Fargue made a quick calculation and estimated the financial loss at half a million euros, at least (the *Theatrum* alone was worth a good two hundred thousand, and the Charron probably more because of Montaigne's annotations). But there was worse still. The books had been part of the Sorbonne's collection for hundreds of years. They would be unobtainable today and, even if comparable copies did appear for sale one day, the university wouldn't be able to afford them. The theft was an incalculable loss to both academics and students.

To see the Sorbonne's heritage thus affected was deeply upsetting to Joseph Fargue, who had been its faithful, conscientious guardian. In his role, he'd always fought to maintain the Research Centre collection intact. He had never agreed to the loss of a single book, even when times were difficult and funding uncertain.

But, despite his pains, he hadn't been able to prevent the theft of four important books. His career, which had been beyond reproach until then, would be indelibly tainted by it. Nothing else would make sense until he had found out how the books had been removed from the Centre and, more importantly, until he had recovered them.

He decided to set to work immediately. The first thing he did was to take another look at Albert Cadas's request forms. As he expected, none was for the missing books. The professor must have removed the relevant slips, just as he had tried to do with the one for the *Theatrum*, in order to erase all trace of the theft.

Fargue could picture the scene clearly. Cadas had probably done the same with the other missing books as he had with the *Theatrum*. He'd asked to look at them and had somehow managed to slip them discreetly into his briefcase, and had made the only physical traces of his crime – the request forms bearing his name – disappear. He'd then simply waited for the member of staff whom he'd dealt with to go off duty or on a break before calmly leaving the Centre.

The human factor was the weak link in the system implemented by Joseph Fargue. He was aware of the flaw. Despite his best efforts, he'd never managed to convince his colleagues of the importance of efficient communication. The incompetents forgot everything as soon as they were off out of the door in the evening. Cadas had been careful to avoid Fargue when making his requests, knowing that Fargue would never have left without checking that the books were back on their shelves. The extreme conscientiousness of the head of the Research Centre was a legend in the university. He was often mocked for it, as if doing one's job well was a failing. Until now, his application had never been faulted. Fargue hadn't imagined it ever could be. Events had proved him painfully wrong.

The only thing Fargue couldn't understand was why Cadas had hidden the bundle of request slips when he'd stolen the *Theatrum*. He must have been interrupted before he'd had the chance to remove the one bearing his name from the pile. Having run out of time, he must have got rid of them quickly, probably planning to return later that morning to put the slips back in their usual place. If he hadn't thrown himself from the window, overcome with remorse – this at least was how Fargue interpreted the suicide – no one would have realised that the *Theatrum* and the other books were missing.

As Chief Administrative Officer, Fargue was partly responsible for the tragedy. Waves of guilt and shame washed over him. He would willingly have given in to despair had the dignity of his office allowed it.

But that was inconceivable, especially on university premises, so he did the only thing that might bring him solace: he got back to work.

9

When she got home, Valentine went straight to the computer. In her inbox she found the file Vermeer had promised to send. He'd sent it just as she left the restaurant. The Dutchman's mischievousness knew no bounds. Valentine swore she'd make him pay. She clicked the print button. Humming gently, the laser printer began spewing out pages. It took about ten minutes to print the mass of documents Vermeer had sent.

Containing several subsections, the file was almost three hundred pages long. The bulk of it consisted of excerpts from books and articles that had appeared in journals with such catchy titles as *Studia Phaenomenologica, Archives d'histoire doctrinale et littéraire du Moyen Âge*, or *Internationales Jahrbuch für Hermeneutik*.

The earliest texts dated from the start of the twentieth century. Three-quarters, however, were written after the Second World War, as if the end of the conflict had given a boost to Vasalis studies. Some of the articles were in French, but many were in English or German, languages that Valentine read only with difficulty, especially in their technical form.

The authors were academics, mostly specialists in medieval philosophy or theology. They seemed to take perverse pleasure in a convoluted style, dense with references that were quite incomprehensible to a layperson. Valentine had envisaged a gentler awakening for her brain, made sluggish by two years of inactivity. Before attacking the mountain of documents, she went to make coffee.

It took her the rest of the afternoon to get through the file. She was finished by suppertime, with a splitting headache and a feeling of despondency that was almost as intense.

Actually, the file Vermeer had put together contained very little factual information. Relying on third- or fourth-hand accounts, the authors of the texts all agreed that Vasalis's existence was not in doubt, and that he had probably lived around the middle of the thirteenth century.

In detail, though, their versions diverged markedly. Half of the scholars claimed that Vasalis had spent his whole life in the tranquillity of Cluny Abbey. According to the rest, he had dispensed his knowledge at the Sorbonne, where he had played an active part in the intense philosophical debates taking place in the university at the time.

Similarly, while the title of his treatise was unanimously agreed upon, its contents remained a mystery. To some, the *De forma mundi* was simply a reformulation of Arab cosmology, influenced by Siger of Brabant and Boethius of Dacia, the leading members of the Averroist movement. For opponents of this theory, Vasalis had on the contrary devised an audacious prefiguration of the floating bodies theory that earned Galileo a papal interdict three and a half centuries later. These conflicting views gave rise to endless arguments among the experts. In fact, nobody really knew what the *De forma mundi* contained.

At around eight o'clock, when Valentine was about to throw in the towel, a bleep indicated that she'd received an email. Entitled *Highway to Hell*, the style was pure Vermeer.

Hi, baby. You've suffered penance enough for today. Still saying 'you scratch my back and I'll scratch yours'?

The message had a document attached. Valentine opened it without much hope, sure it would be the kind of bad joke her friend loved.

For once, it wasn't. Vermeer had sent her a reproduction of a rather accomplished sketch, probably black stone or lead point on a medium that was difficult to determine. The image was of very poor quality, almost blurred, as if it were a scan of an old photograph rather than of the original piece. Valentine hadn't seen the study before, though the composition reminded her of a drawing she'd had in front of her a few years earlier when she was doing her end-of-course work placement at the Vatican Library.

She printed the page, then went to the untidy heap of boxes that contained her museum catalogues and artists' monographs – a treasure trove accumulated from innumerable museum visits over the years. She searched through the boxes until she found what she was looking for. It took her only a moment to find the right page.

She placed Vermeer's scan and the illustration in the book side by side. The two drawings were remarkably similar, both in line and composition. The stylistic similarities suggested that both came from the same hand and that, if so, the study could be a preparatory piece for the final version.

The latter belonged to a series of drawings on parchment that Botticelli had made to illustrate *The Divine Comedy* at the request of Lorenzo de Medici, cousin and namesake of Lorenzo the Magnificent. In this instance, it was the illustration accompanying Canto 10, in which Dante recounts his visit to the sixth circle of Hell, reserved for the Heretics. Drawn with a metal point, then traced with pen and partially coloured, it dated from the early 1490s. It showed the Florentine poet, easily recognisable in his usual bonnet and long red cloak, walking through a cemetery with his guide Virgil, depicted as a bearded old man. The faces of the damned, contorted with pain, were visible among the terrible flames rising from open tombs. The two men appeared several times in the drawing, as they advanced. Starting at the top right-hand corner of the page, their journey ended at the bottom left, before a tomb larger than all the others, whose lid bore the inscription: *'Anastasio papa guardo'*.

Botticelli had followed the verses of *The Divine Comedy* to the letter. Dante himself had simply followed the medieval tradition, reproaching the Pope for his tolerance of the Monophysite schism led by Acacius of Constantinople at the end of the fifth century. For malevolent medieval theologians, such open-mindedness was ample justification for a one-way ticket to the fires of Hell.

The study found by Vermeer was less detailed, but anticipated the final version of the illustration fairly closely. The main difference was the inscription on the tomb: there was no mention here of Anastasius, but instead of a certain 'Vasalius Sorbonae', thus appointed by Botticelli the champion of all classes of heresy. This alteration was important, for several reasons, the main one being that there existed no other ancient mentions of Vasalis in the documents assembled by Vermeer. If the sketch was authentic, it was undeniable proof that the figure of Vasalis was not the invention of a bunch of lunatic academics. And the fact that Botticelli dared name him meant that at the end of the fifteenth century, in cultivated circles, or at least the Neoplatonic circle in which the painter moved, the legend of Vasalis was taken to be true.

The second interesting aspect of the study was purely artistic. No preparatory sketch by Botticelli for his important work on *The Divine Comedy* had ever been found. And, drawn on the back of the parchment on to which a certain Niccolò Mangona had copied Dante's text, the illustrations themselves had disappeared not long after they were created.

Nine of them, including the one Valentine had before her, had been found by chance in the seventeenth century in the Vatican Library, inserted in a book of miscellany that had belonged to Queen Christina of Sweden. A second group, consisting of eighty-three leaves, was identified two centuries later in a Parisian bookshop. It passed through the hands of the Duke of Hamilton, before being bought in 1882 by the King of Prussia's librarian for the royal drawings and prints room.

While almost all of Botticelli's drawings had reappeared, no trace of any preparatory work had survived. To experts, this sketch would provide valuable information on the creative process of a painter whose works were all thought to be known.

From the perspective of art history, Vermeer had made an extraordinary find. Valentine didn't dare consider the kind of price it would fetch if it were put up for sale. The mention of Vasalis only increased its value, for it added an element of drama – something the art market always sought – to Botticelli's prestigious signature.

Valentine picked up the phone and dialled her friend's number.

'Well, if it isn't my favourite little pleb,' said Vermeer as he answered. 'Did I make you happy, at least for a moment?'

Valentine wasn't in the mood for banter, and she came straight to the point.

'Where did you find the drawing?' she asked curtly.

'The Lord works in mysterious ways, as you know.'

'Don't be a pain in the arse, Hugo. I've wasted all afternoon on your crap. If you'd sent the sketch straight away, I could have saved myself a bad headache. I ploughed through about fifteen articles in German because of you.'

'You had to drown in that sea of irrelevant documents to truly appreciate the importance of the drawing. Simple psychology.'

'Where is the drawing, Hugo?' asked Valentine.

'If I said I had no idea, would you believe me?'

'No.'

'Well, it's the truth. All I have is a photographic repro-duction. And the photo's pretty old and poor quality, as you've seen. I don't know what's become of the original. I've never seen it.'

Vermeer paused before continuing. Valentine wasn't going to like what he had to say. He knew it, and was prepared for another fit of temper.

'To be absolutely frank, I'm not even sure that it really is a Botticelli.'

'You're kidding! So why the hell did you send it to me?'

'Calm down. It's actually the way I got hold of the photo that's interesting. Do you want to hear about it or not?'

Valentine seemed to relent a little. 'OK, tell me.'

'It was about six or seven years ago, just before my little run-in with the law. Well, you know all about that . . .'

Vermeer was always uncharacteristically coy when the subject of his legal difficulties came up. At the time, he and Valentine had already met. She'd called upon his services a few times for tricky valuations, quite unaware that he was at the centre of an art-smuggling network. She was stunned when Interpol agents summoned her to make a statement. After this, she'd refused to have anything to do with Vermeer. It had taken him almost a year to convince her that his criminal activities had been exaggerated by the police, and that, anyway, he'd drawn a line under that period of his life. His support when Valentine was fired from the Louvre had removed any lingering doubts she might have had.

Vermeer had dubious morals, but he was loyal to his friends and immensely knowledgeable about art.

'The photo was sent to me,' he went on. 'I got orders like that every month. I'd be sent a reproduction of a piece, the address where it could be found and a cash advance. When I got hold of the item, I arranged delivery, was paid the rest of my fee, and I erased the memory instantly. I had an incredible gift for forgetting in those days. Except in this case, I never had time to use it. The police turned up at my place the day an intermediary was supposed to be giving me the address where I was to collect the drawing. I've always felt it wasn't entirely a coincidence.'

'What makes you say that?'

'The police spent hours questioning me. I didn't know who ordered the theft, but I negotiated a full amnesty in return for the name of the intermediary who contacted me.'

'And the police caught him?'

'They found his body a week later in his car boot, with a couple of bullets in the head. I realised it wasn't in my interest to pursue the matter. But I kept the photo, just in case.'

'So you don't know where the drawing is?'

'At the time, it was in Paris. According to my information, stealing it was going to be a piece of cake. It had no particular protection – no guard, no alarm, no safe. I could have got it out in less than five minutes, with no risk. Pity . . . I'd never have been paid so well for a job that easy. I expect someone else did it. Lucky man.'

'Who would have been interested in it? I bet you have some idea.'

'It's a long list: almost all the museums in the world, most private collectors, anyone with the slightest bit of sense. And the bastards at the Vatican, of course. It's not in their interest for Vasalis's name to resurface.'

'Aren't you exaggerating a little?'

'Their churches are empty. They'll lose the last few believers if yet another name is added to the list of guys reduced to ashes for no reason.'

'What crap, Hugo. I'm really not up to listening to this kind of thing tonight. Please stop, right now.'

Her plea had no effect. Vermeer had no intention of letting an opportunity pass to expound his personal conspiracy theory.

'I forgot to mention the CIA, Nike and all the bloody multinationals. If there's money to be made, you can be sure those bastards aren't far away.'

Even after all these years, Valentine wasn't sure if Vermeer was serious when he came out with this rubbish, or whether he just pretended to believe it to amuse himself. If he was joking, he didn't show it.

She tried to bring her friend's diatribe to an end: 'I know, I know, money's taking over the world and the masses are being brainwashed.'

'Bloody hell, Valentine, they're going to eat us alive, and you just sit there doing nothing!'

When he was off on one of his rants, Vermeer was impossible to stop. He could go on for hours about the Kennedy assassination, or the takeover of European financial markets by drugs cartels. Besides, he was up most of the night visiting Internet sites where all the world's conspiracy theorists met to exchange supposedly confidential information.

'Listen, Hugo,' said Valentine, 'I've heard enough for tonight. If you don't have anything more specific to tell me about Vasalis, I'm going to bed. I'm exhausted.'

'Don't be grumpy. I've sent you all the documents I have. I haven't got anything else. Now, if you want the address of Elvis's retirement home, I can give you the details. Interested?'

'Of course. I've always wanted to know.'

'Really?'

Valentine didn't have the energy to get angry. She put down the phone.

Vermeer could go to hell with his rich-boy whims. It wasn't even worth trying to correct his failings. He was just like that, and always would be. You had to put up with it, or stop seeing him.

Valentine put her fit of temper down to her wasted evening, and turned her thoughts to bed. She had a hard day's work ahead of her tomorrow at Elias Stern's house. She needed to get some rest.

The pile of Vasalis articles was still on the floor, by the computer. Valentine gave it a good kick. As the pages of German scattered over the parquet, she immediately felt a lot better.

10

David knew exactly what Anna was like, but still he fell for her little ways. They hadn't seen each other for almost two months. From long experience he knew he could count on a major attempt at seduction, but he hadn't expected her to be quite so full-on. She sat on the sofa facing him, crossing and uncrossing her fishnet-clad legs until she found the perfect position to give him the best view of them. She pretended to smooth her miniskirt, and sighed helplessly at its blatantly inadequate length. Her big green eyes looked straight into David's.

Despite his best efforts to convince himself to the contrary, he was attracted to Anna. He felt his hormones surge whenever he laid eyes on her slender, supple body. She knew it, and never missed an opportunity to exploit his weakness.

David tried to free himself from Anna's gaze, but her eyes held his. Her smile went from innocent to frankly lewd as Paul, her current partner, entered the apartment. He shook David's hand, mumbling a mechanical 'Hi, how are you?', took off his velvet jacket and sat on the sofa beside Anna.

Meanwhile, Anna's eyes had not left David's. Her skirt rode up imperceptibly, exposing another few centimetres of her gorgeous legs. Determined not to give her the satisfaction of a single glance, David tried to maintain an air of detachment.

He managed at last to tear his gaze away from Anna's and

looked at Paul, a little sheepishly. He didn't know how much Anna had told him about their relationship. With her, there were only two possible tactics: total surrender or escape. David had spent a good part of the last ten years wavering between the two, finally reaching a status quo that was, all in all, pretty frustrating. He had his life, and Anna had hers, which was far richer and fuller, but neither was entirely happy with the situation, especially David.

Having said that, it wasn't all bad. At least his mental health no longer depended on Anna's moods. Anna was an absolute fury. Which was no bad thing when it came to sex, but it made life hell generally speaking. Life with her was an endless series of crises, rows and furious arguments, interspersed with equally furious bouts of passion. The slightest spark set off a nuclear explosion. Moderation, a happy medium, were alien concepts to Anna.

For Anna, life as a couple amounted to a permanent challenge to her loved one. There was never any respite. When day-to-day problems weren't enough to inflame her senses, she invented frivolous excuses to trigger hostilities. It always ended in a wild session in bed, but the fleeting pleasure didn't make up for all the problems.

David had lived with her for ten months in his second year at university. It had taken him three years to get over it. Since then, they slept together when the occasion arose – in other words, often when Anna was single, and only slightly less when she wasn't. The rest of the time they tried to avoid each other.

For his part, Paul seemed to be dealing well with his girlfriend's stormy temperament. He didn't have the drawn features, mad, staring eyes or touchiness typical of Anna's other victims. At least, not yet. It would come. With her, the fairy tale always ended badly. There was no way out. David had paid dearly to discover this.

Paul and Anna had met the year before at a seminar at the Collège de France. She was putting the finishing touches to her PhD in art history. He had just got a prestigious appointment at the École Normale Supérieure. The two of them were the quintessence of the achievements of the French education system, the mixed-doubles version of the nation's elite. Years of relentless study, thousands of euros in grants and bursaries, dozens of teachers ordered to deliver the best of their knowledge to those fizzing brains – all of it just so the two lovebirds could spend all their time in bed, instead of pondering the future of the nation. What a waste.

The reason Anna had asked David to come round soon became apparent.

'Good news,' she began. 'Paul and I have decided to get married.'

They were no doubt hoping for David's approval, or at least a reaction of some kind. Their faces moved closer together, with the conspiratorial look of lovers made smug by feelings of perfect harmony. Their fingers intertwined.

David couldn't help feeling slightly sick. His only response was to smile foolishly, and wait resignedly for the follow-up. Anna wasn't the type to announce an engagement and leave it at that. She loved exaggeration, putting off reflection till later, especially where her love life was concerned. She had an unfortunate tendency to follow her hormones rather than her head, and often came to regret her urges.

But she wasn't one to admit her mistakes.

'I really want Paul to be the father of my children,' she went on, gazing at Paul with a look dripping with tenderness.

As predictable as they were, her words increased David's feeling of nausea. Paul was at least the fourth 'love of my life, father of my children' that Anna had introduced him to, but he still couldn't stand the idea that she was happy while he floundered in emotional despair.

'That's great,' he felt obliged to say. 'Have you set a date?'

'Anna's really keen for us to get married before the first anniversary of when we met,' said Paul. 'You know what she's like – fiery and passionate . . .'

Fiery and passionate, my arse. She'll dump you just before the wedding, when the guests have arrived and you've given her a diamond as big as a golf ball, David finished in his head. *Then she'll come knocking at my door in floods of tears. You'll be a laughing stock for the rest of your life, and it'll serve you right.*

He summed up these thoughts in a few words: 'I'm sure you'll be very happy together.'

The comment was in keeping with the tone of the occasion – apparently warm and sincere, but with an undertone of contempt.

The last few years had made David disinclined to believe in even the possibility of earthly happiness. That a nightmare like Anna should get anywhere near it was inconceivable, and quite unfair.

'Do you really think so?' asked Anna, who had caught the subtle nuance.

'I'm absolutely sure. You're made for each other – it's obvious.'

David was lying disgracefully, and Anna knew it. She loved these situations. Nothing gave her more pleasure than watching him thrash about in a tangle of emotion.

A long silence followed. Anna and Paul took the opportunity to kiss passionately. David's nausea turned into deep revulsion.

Paul then felt obliged to show an interest in David, no doubt to further underline his happiness compared with his guest's personal and professional misery.

'So what are you up to at the moment, David?'

'Not a lot, to be honest.'

Paul hesitated for a moment. To a brilliant mind like his, idleness had meaning when praised by Cicero or some idiot dead for two millennia. In those blessed times, *otium* was a sign of distinction. But nowadays, the idea of indulging in shameless idleness was abhorrent to him.

He gave David an appalled look, straight out of an eighties TV series. 'How do you mean?'

'I'm trying to set a record for the length of time it takes to

81

complete a thesis. I'm aiming to finish when I'm forty. Though now my supervisor's taken the big leap, I think it'll be more like sixty. Then I'll retire. Not a bad career plan, is it?'

Paul's sympathetic smile prompted David to play up the role of depressive dropout. Unfortunately it was one that fitted him like a glove.

'And as no woman has granted me her favours since the dawn of time,' he went on, 'my life is truly miserable. Any more questions? Can I go home now and end it all?'

David had achieved his aim. Paul looked as if he were sitting on a bed of nails. He shifted from one buttock to the other.

'I didn't mean to offend you,' he mumbled.

'Don't worry,' Anna said. 'David's only kidding. He loves making people feel uncomfortable.'

Actually, he just wanted to be left in peace, but that wasn't Anna's style.

'You were kidding, weren't you?' she insisted. 'Go on, tell him . . . You can be a real pain when you get started, David!'

'That's right, I'm joking,' he said, still trying to appear indifferent. 'I'm having a ball, really. I have to fight off the army of models chasing me. No way am I going to top myself before I chat up the whole of the Elite Agency, including the secretaries and cleaning ladies.'

David had forgotten that one of Anna's skills was an ability to plunge you into the depths of despair with just a few words. He was reminded of this as she went on.

'Oh, stop the overgrown teenager routine. People'll start getting divorced soon, so you're bound to find someone then.'

David imagined Anna's angelic face surrounded by a halo of blood. To complete the picture, he added a flash of distress to her eyes and a touch of suffering to her lips. Mantegna couldn't have done better.

As if she could read his mind, Anna pretended to be embarrassed. 'Oh, sorry! I didn't mean to upset you . . .'

It wasn't true, of course. Not only did Anna *mean* to make

David feel depressed, but the sight of his stricken face positively delighted her.

The last time David had seen that smile of satisfaction, eight years earlier, Anna had just dumped him, out of the blue. Like an idiot, he hadn't seen it coming. He'd had the same murderous urge then as now. He wondered again how he had managed to resist.

The worst thing was that Anna was right. David had spent five years slaving over his philosophy PhD without much to show for it. His supervisor had committed suicide. The Dean – the most powerful man at the Sorbonne – detested him, and had threatened to crush him like an insect. He had little cause for optimism. In the short term, his career prospects hovered between middling and nil. If, by a miracle, he managed to finish his thesis, a brilliant future as an unemployed scholar lay before him.

In the meantime, David survived thanks to a part-time job. It consisted mainly of wandering down endless corridors, retrieving books from dusty shelves and being lectured on his return by grumpy slave drivers, who took revenge on him for their thirty years in a dull job. And his salary – if you could call it that – was so low that his bank manager rang once a week to demand that he repay his overdraft.

In turn, David resorted to his parents. It was a recurring game between them: David rang his mother to beg her for help, she pretended to hesitate and said she'd have to speak to his father, then hung up, cursing her offspring. In the morning, David got a cheque in the post and rushed to cash it, as ashamed as if he'd got it dealing drugs. He then made a point of forgetting to thank his saviours until the last day of the next month, when another demand from his bank manager prompted him to dial his parents' number once more.

He was pondering the question of how overqualified thirtysomethings could fit into the cut-throat consumer society, when Paul suggested they have a drink.

They moved to the table where glasses, a half-empty bottle

of Martini and a plate of shop-bought tapas were waiting for them.

Anna took the opportunity to resume hostilities. 'You can't go on like this, David. You've got to do something.'

'Thanks for the advice. I'll be sure to follow it when the opportunity arises.'

As well as being annoying, Anna was tenacious. Maybe because she'd reached a stage in her life where material comforts were more important to her than anything else, she couldn't understand David's fascination with Albert Cadas. In her view, David was wasting his time with the weary old recluse in his dusty, anachronistic world. That David might, on top of that, be passionate about illegible old manuscripts made her doubt his sanity. Not to mention the paltry career opportunities a supervisor whose influence extended no further than his office might offer. What's more, now a dead supervisor.

Five years earlier, Albert Cadas had persuaded David that he must devote his days and nights, weekends included, to searching for an obscure treatise written in the late thirteenth century by a mysterious scholar whose existence had long been forgotten. The man who was to become his mentor assured him conspiratorially that Vasalis's only known work, the *De forma mundi*, had exerted a rare fascination over the few privileged enough to have a copy, or to have read a few passages in isolation. In reality, the quest turned out to be far less appealing. Despite Albert Cadas's optimism, David found no clues anywhere to help him unlock the mystery of the *De forma mundi*.

Anna returned to the attack: 'Finish your thesis. Get a move on. Find a real job. Anything rather than what you're doing at the moment.'

This was too much. David felt a wave of anger rising.

'So what are you saying? That I should become a secretary, like you?' he retorted. 'Please! I do have some pride left.'

Since finishing her PhD, Anna had taken an underpaid job in an art gallery on the Right Bank, near the Place de la Bastille.

She did a bit of everything, from managing the staff to organising exhibitions. But she earned a secretary's salary, which diminished the job in David's eyes. And even if he refused to admit it to himself, it annoyed him that she'd sorted herself out while he wallowed in self-pity.

To his despair, his low blow didn't have the effect he'd hoped for.

'You don't understand,' she replied calmly. 'I'm not a secretary, I'm assistant to the gallery director. It's quite different.'

'You wear miniskirts and make your boss's coffee, don't you? You're just a skivvy, that's all. You can call it what you like if it makes you feel better.'

'Arsehole.'

'Tart.'

Paul wished he could melt, disappear into a gap between the tiles. His face took on a greenish tinge. He got up and went to the bathroom without a word. He didn't realise that this frank, brutal display of aggression had actually calmed things down.

'Are you coming to the private view at the gallery tomorrow?' asked Anna.

'I'm not sure yet.'

'I'm not going to beg you, David. I'd just like you to come, that's all. I've worked like a mad thing to set the exhibition up.'

David glanced in the direction of the bathroom door, making sure Paul was still out of earshot.

'Are you really going to marry that idiot?'

Anna wasn't put out by his bluntness.

'Yes. Why? Don't tell me you're concerned about my love life now.'

'Admit it: you're bored stiff by him. OK, he's a nice guy and he's got a real job, I give you that. But God, he's boring!'

'You're just jealous because Paul is capable of living with a woman without driving her crazy.'

'You've got it back to front. You're the hysterical one. I was simply responding to your histrionics. In real life, with normal people, I'm a quiet man. Come on, be honest for once: you miss me, don't you?'

Anna was expert at giving clear answers. Under the table, she placed her bare foot on David's knee and moved it up his leg.

David wasn't expecting this. Instinctively he clenched his thighs. Anna had the rare ability to induce vague anxiety in any man who knew her even a little.

'It's OK,' she whispered huskily. 'I don't want to hurt you. Quite the reverse.'

The rubbing of her toes sent an electric shock through him. Maybe this was an unknown characteristic of fishnet tights, or maybe it was David's body telling him he was ready to sleep with Anna again. He preferred the first possibility, as the second seemed rife with problems.

'You're right,' Anna went on. 'Paul has qualities you lack completely, but you're more fun. And I don't just mean your sense of humour . . . You complement each other, in a way. If you like, we could resume our little conversation where we left off last year. Married life for him, the extras for you. Paul need never know. He's far too busy to be jealous.'

David didn't have time to say how much the thought of sharing intimate moments with her, even occasionally, terrified him.

Paul returned, mumbling excuses for his hasty exit. Anna smiled at him affectionately, while her foot moved inexorably towards her ex-boyfriend's crotch.

11

Despite the poor quality of the reproduction, the Botticelli drawing held a strange attraction for Hugo Vermeer, which was
nothing new. He'd been obsessed with the drawing for six years
now, from the moment he'd taken it out of the envelope handed
to him by an intermediary.

Vermeer had pondered the matter at length, but had failed to
reach any firm conclusion. He couldn't explain his weakness for
a sketch that he'd never actually seen with his own eyes. It was a
mystery to him.

In his previous life, hundreds of works of art had passed
through his hands. Most of them were hardly worth the risks
he'd taken to steal them. Others were of such quality that he'd
been reluctant to hand them over to the client. But none had ever
aroused such strong emotions in him as this one. Those few pen
strokes had fascinated him, carrying within them a force he could
neither grasp nor identify. The possibility that the drawing might
be an original Botticelli wasn't sufficient explanation of the way
he felt. Vermeer wasn't a fetishist. A famous signature was mean-
ingless to him if the piece didn't live up to the supposed talent of
the author.

The more he tried to understand his obsession, the more he
had to acknowledge the truth: the arrival of the sketch had coin-
cided with a major turning point in his life.

The sequence of events was too clear to be accidental. Even if it seemed insane, his fate now seemed bound, one way or another, to the drawing. Had he believed in a divine being, Vermeer might have seen it as the instrument of some sort of redemption.

When the police turned up at his place that morning, Vermeer realised that a new chapter was beginning. Knowing he was under surveillance, he was usually obsessively cautious. Until then, he'd never brought home anything that might give away his criminal activities. But the day he received the Botticelli reproduction, he had made an exception. He hadn't been able to resist taking it home to examine it more closely.

The following day, at dawn, the police had burst into his apartment and dragged him out of bed. In less than two minutes they had found the envelope containing the photograph, together with a considerable amount of cash intended to cover his initial expenses. In a decade of art smuggling, Hugo Vermeer had just made his first mistake. It was one too many.

He resigned himself to a long stretch in prison, regarding it as the lesser of two evils – better to spend a few years behind bars than all eternity under a marble slab. It was an unpleasant prospect, of course, and regrettable, but when he got out, he'd still have a good few years ahead of him.

In a surprising development, the police officer heading the investigation decided to concentrate his efforts on the client who'd ordered the theft. He was even prepared to make significant concessions in order to catch him. He offered Vermeer a deal. In return for the name of the intermediary coordinating the operation, he would release Vermeer and drop all charges.

The superintendent thought he'd get other opportunities to catch Vermeer. Sooner or later one of his accomplices would agree to collaborate with the police and give them Vermeer's head on a plate. All the superintendent had to do was wait. And in the unlikely event that Vermeer evaded him, he was bound eventually to run into someone who coveted his market, gun in hand. Vermeer wanted to play in the big leagues. Too bad for him.

The officer realised his mistake when his men found the intermediary's corpse a couple of days later. The body was discovered in a car about fifty kilometres outside Paris. As usual, the local residents hadn't seen a thing, and the killer had left no clues, neither cartridge cases nor fingerprints. The client's trail simply vanished and, with it, any hope of solving the case. The superintendent could hope for nothing more. He could always, he thought bleakly, make origami figures out of the file if he didn't want to feel completely useless.

Hugo Vermeer was his last chance of salvaging the case, so the superintendent combed through his bank accounts and those of his gallery, but failed to find anything compromising. In desperation, he interviewed all of Vermeer's acquaintances, in the hope that one of them might provide interesting information.

His efforts proved futile. To everyone he questioned, Vermeer was certainly a bit of an oddball, even downright eccentric, but an honest, knowledgeable gallery owner. The last straw came during the interrogation of the restorer from the Louvre. Valentine was astounded when she heard what Vermeer was suspected of. Completely trusting her friend, she had on several occasions given him valuable objects and paintings for appraisal. Vermeer had returned them all to the museum, including a series of Poussin studies which he declared authentic and valued at a million and a half euros.

Behind the one-way glass, the superintendent had watched the disaster unfold, powerless. This last statement was the nail in the coffin of the investigation. Vermeer was now whiter than white. The law couldn't touch him.

This miraculous outcome had nevertheless changed Vermeer profoundly, more than he could have imagined. As he left the headquarters of the Brigade Criminelle, he felt suddenly weary. He was tired of having to keep covering his tracks to elude the forces of law and order. He'd had enough of checking under his car every morning to make sure no one had fixed a bomb to it during the night.

For a long time he'd found the risks exciting. It was what got him out of bed in the morning. He'd had enough money since birth to live at least a dozen lives of ease. Only his taste for adrenalin justified his criminal activities. He could have chosen motor racing, or bungee jumping, or even alcohol or drugs. He'd opted for dealing in stolen art purely out of snobbery because the tradition of his family made him consider all the other choices too vulgar for a man of his station. A therapist would have understood this in a second, but the superintendent failed to see it. It was his principal error of judgement.

But the blade had only just missed Vermeer's neck, and he took it as a warning. It could have made a great story, worthy of a gossip magazine: the dealer in stolen art, rotten to the core, renouncing his wicked ways because of a vision of Hell sent to him from who knows where. Saints had been beatified for less. St Vermeer, on the road to Damascus. It sounded pretty good.

The Dutchman believed in many things, including the imminent arrival of extraterrestrials, but all forms of religion were completely alien to him. Not to mention that, by definition, the concept of redemption only applied to those in possession of some sense of morality, which he wasn't. Vermeer had chosen the path of legality, not honesty. The difference was subtle but significant, and he made it a point of principle. He was quite happy to appear angelic in the eyes of society, but he had no intention of dying of boredom.

Lost in thought, he mechanically slid his thumb into his mouth and chewed off a tiny sliver of nail.

He read through the short text on his screen once more. These few lines had occupied him for a good part of the night. He'd weighed every word, every comma. The result seemed to satisfy all the criteria he'd had in mind when he started.

He was about to take an irrevocable step. Once he'd sent the text, there was no going back.

His only concern was Valentine's reaction. She'd be furious, and quite rightly. But their friendship had not only survived revelation of his nefarious past, it had even become stronger. Valentine would understand. She was a bright girl. He'd just have to explain things to her.

Vermeer couldn't go back now, anyway. He had to do something. He'd already waited too long. He had no idea what the consequences would be, but he felt ready to face them.

A slight shiver ran through him as he clicked Send.

12

As Nora had said, everything was in place by the time the limousine dropped Valentine outside Elias Stern's house. The elderly art dealer was nowhere to be seen, however, leaving his employee to greet her.

After their conversation the day before, Valentine had expected Nora to be friendly, or at least warmer. Instead, the Stern Foundation assistant's manner was restrained and professional, as if nothing special had passed between them. Her fifteen minutes of humanity must have been over for the month.

Wasting no time, she told Valentine to follow her to the library. The doors on the ground floor were all closed today, so Valentine didn't see any other Foundation employees. The house appeared to be deserted, the only sound the young women's footsteps on the marble tiles as they walked down the long corridor.

'Is no one else here yet?' Valentine asked Nora as they started up the grand staircase.

'Virginie and Isabelle are having a few days off. Mr Stern wanted you to work undisturbed. There's only me and the security staff here.'

'I'm sorry if he made you come in just to look after me.'

'That's OK. I like my work. Holidays don't really suit me.'

Valentine interpreted the confession to mean that Elias Stern's assistant had no private life, and was bored to tears as soon as she stepped outside the large house. It must be difficult for obsessive twentysomething bibliophiles to find like-minded people in the outside world, though Nora didn't seem unduly bothered.

When they reached the library, she keyed in the code to unlock the door and gestured for Valentine to enter.

The codex was waiting on the table, resting on a padded lectern like the one in Valentine's workshop.

'Have you brought everything you need?' asked Nora.

Valentine raised the impressive doctor's case she was holding. 'Everything's here. If I need anything else, I'll go and get it from the workshop.'

'Perfect. I'm going to lock you in, Valentine. For security reasons. You understand, don't you?'

Somewhat taken aback, Valentine looked doubtful. Nora quickly sought to reassure her.

'Don't worry. Soon you'll be able to come and go as you please. We just need to configure the biometric system for your prints. We have to call out a technician for that. In the meantime, I'll let you in and out.'

'How do I get hold of you if I need to?'

Nora showed her the intercom on the wall beneath the control box for the door.

'The intercom is connected to my office. Just press the button and speak. It'll be your only link with the outside world. The walls are soundproofed, and a jammer blocks mobile-phone signals throughout the building.'

'You're serious about security, aren't you?' said Valentine. 'It's like being inside a museum.'

'Our security measures are much better than most museums, believe me.'

'OK. Well, I'll try not to panic. If I get an attack of claustrophobia I'll simply press the button and you'll be here straight away?'

'My office is on the ground floor, next to Mr Stern's. I just need to come up one flight of stairs. You won't have to put up with this for long. As soon as your biometric data are entered, you'll be independent.'

'Great.'

'You're sure you've got everything you need?'

'Positive. Don't let me keep you.'

'I'll see you later then.'

Nora stepped out, placed her thumb on the biometric reader and keyed in the locking code. The indicator light changed from green to red, and the heavy Plexiglas panel slid back into place.

There was now absolute silence in the room, as if the outside world had suddenly ceased to exist. Valentine pressed her face to the Plexiglas. She stood there for several seconds, unable to tell whether the fleeting shapes she could distinguish through the opaque panel were human figures or tricks of the light.

Resisting the urge to check that the intercom was working, she lifted her bag on to the table and began unpacking her basic kit – several pairs of gloves, paintbrushes of different sizes, tweezers, cotton wool, blotting paper, small bottles of distilled water, alcohol and chemical reactants – which she laid out around the lectern.

When she was at the Louvre, she had always begun by reading all she could find about the piece she was restoring. Once she'd got into the artist's mind, and felt she'd decoded the subtle mechanism of his technique, she set the documents aside and got down to work.

Valentine had chosen her profession because it combined both manual and intellectual work. For her, physical contact with the medium always went hand in hand with stimulation of the mind. Spending her days on the rubbish people brought to the workshop was completely different: her brain cells weren't involved. They could take a complete rest without its affecting the quality of her work.

Elias Stern had understood this. He'd offered her an intellectual rebirth.

13

Stonily, Stern eyed the man, whom he knew as Julien Sorel, facing him across the desk.

'Tired already, Mr Sorel?' he asked severely.

The visitor stopped yawning immediately. He could have pointed out to his host that it was not yet ten in the morning, that his plane had landed only three-quarters of an hour ago and that he hadn't had time to shower or change or even eat breakfast. This was what he'd have liked to say, but he couldn't, so he held his tongue.

The two men had been due to meet the following day. This was what their respective secretaries had agreed some time ago. When he landed, therefore, Sorel had followed the Stern Foundation chauffeur without a second thought, and climbed into the luxurious limousine thinking he had a whole day ahead of him in which to relax at his hotel. Instead he'd found himself at the elderly art dealer's house for this surprise meeting.

Sorel hated being caught off guard. He liked to be prepared for anything, and was often meticulous to the point of obsession. There was nothing wrong with that. In fact, in his job it was essential, at least if you wanted a long life. And Sorel had every intention of making old bones.

The unexpected summons had made him nervous. Stern had rushed him so as to gain a psychological advantage. The strategy wasn't very original, but it was certainly effective. Sorel's head didn't feel too clear, and he hated the fuzziness.

But this was no time to pick an argument. He hadn't come all this way to tell Stern what he thought of him as a host. He could have done that from his office several thousand kilometres away, and at a convenient hour, thus avoiding an eight-hour flight and three days' jet lag. Not to mention the fact that Stern was quite capable of reporting him to his superiors as soon as his back was turned. The art dealer had the direct numbers of certain people to whom Sorel did not have access, even after seventeen years with the firm.

He had no desire to ruin his career over a pointless outburst, so he opted for prudence.

Despite the tie constricting his neck, he tried to breathe slowly. His expression remaining absolutely unchanged, he focused on his breathing, and soon felt the calming effects of the exercise. When he spoke, his tone was perfectly neutral.

'I do apologise. My plane landed less than an hour ago at Le Bourget. I haven't slept in almost thirty-six hours. I'm exhausted.'

'Well, you know what they say: "The future belongs to those who rise early",' the old man said sanctimoniously.

'We're not interested in the future, Mr Stern. You know that. We focus on the present. And that's a hard enough job as it is.'

'Ah, yes, that's true . . . The future falls within the remit of your competitors.'

'Our colleagues,' corrected Sorel. 'We work in perfect coordination with them.'

Stern smiled as if he'd heard an amusing joke. He was enjoying the conversation, especially as the dice were loaded in his favour: he could launch attacks freely, while his adversary was boxing with one hand tied behind his back. Elias Stern knew that an agent of Sorel's rank couldn't touch him. He thought he'd make the most of his advantage and have some fun. His smile broadened from wry amusement to outright mockery.

Keep messing me around and I'll slit your throat like a pig.

Sorel could not, unfortunately, permit himself to kill his host. He loosened his tie and took a deep breath, eyes half closed. This time, he didn't try to hide his attempt to control his emotions. His anger did not disappear completely, but it subsided sufficiently to restrain his murderous feelings. In his defence, Stern's way of treating him like a moron really was irritating.

The fact that you knew twelve different methods of killing with your bare hands didn't mean you couldn't also be cultured. It was actually the reason he'd been chosen to be Stern's principal interlocutor: like Sorel, several of his colleagues had PhDs in literature, but he was the only one to have studied art history as well. He also spoke perfect French, the legacy of a Basque grandmother and summers spent at the family home in Saint-Jean-de-Luz. But still Stern insisted on treating him like a brainless gorilla.

'Let's focus on the reason for my visit, shall we?' Sorel said, to cut short a confrontation he knew he'd already lost.

Stern assented half-heartedly. 'I suppose your superiors have sent you to pass on instructions. None too pleasant ones, I imagine.'

'Instructions? Certainly not. At most, advice on how to conduct this affair. An annual subsidy of ten million dollars justifies some intervention on our part, I feel. We want to ensure our money is wisely invested.'

It was Stern's turn to look annoyed, his smile replaced by a scowl. With the tip of his index finger, he spun one of the two pens on the desk before him, then realigned it with the other.

'You have no reason to doubt it,' he said. 'I send you a detailed report on the Foundation's activities every six months. Our accounts are impeccable.'

'That's not the problem,' retorted Sorel. 'Your accounts are clear. They can't be faulted. Actually it's the choice of your latest recruit that my superiors, and I myself, question. Let's just say we're a little puzzled.'

'Recruiting Valentine Savi is absolutely necessary. She's an outstanding restorer. I have high hopes for her. She'll be very

97

useful to the Foundation in the future. Besides, she's already at work on the codex.'

'I don't doubt her skill. The only question that interests me is this: is she reliable?'

Stern opened his arms in a gesture of powerlessness, palms turned upwards.

'As reliable as anyone can be who's emerging from depression. As far as I'm concerned, I'm sure she'll get over it now that she's back at work. My judgement should be enough. I'm rarely wrong about the people I choose to work with.'

'There's been too much media fuss about that girl,' said Sorel brusquely. 'Before taking her on permanently, the question of her past will have to be settled once and for all. If she really did make the mistake she's accused of, she'll have to be ruled out. You have no choice. Foundation employees must be above reproach. We can't expose ourselves to attack.'

'I've asked Nora to shed some light on what happened. She's outside, if you'd like to speak to her. Shall I ask her to come in?'

Sorel shook his head. 'No. It's your problem. I don't want to intervene just yet. But I'll need a clear picture of the situation fairly soon.'

Sorel fell silent and looked around the room. As always, his eyes came to rest on the Van Gogh. For a moment, he lost his train of thought. He heard the art dealer's voice, and had to make an effort to return to reality.

'When are you leaving?' repeated Stern.

'I have orders to remain in Paris until this matter is sorted out. My superiors were quite clear. There's a lot at stake, for us and for you. As supervisor of this project, I must see that it succeeds, and lend you a hand if required.'

'You're staying at the usual place?'

'Yes, the same suite as always. Keep me informed of progress.' He paused a moment, then added reluctantly: 'I'm not here to wage war. We're only at the start of our collaboration. I'd very much like things to improve between us.'

Stern obviously didn't believe a word of this. He said nothing, and simply triggered the Plexiglas panel from where he sat by pressing a button under his desk.

Sorel stood, nodded to his host and left the room without looking back.

He was now smiling broadly. He felt much better. The meeting had gone well, and he had kept his cool despite Stern's childish provocation. This victory over himself was intensely satisfying, made even more so by the prospect of soon being able to get into his hotel bed.

The ability to suppress his emotional urges had not been part of his training. He'd been taught to melt into a hostile background, to contain possible threats or, failing that, to eliminate them, not to relax by controlling his breathing. Sorel had learned this himself, on the job. He had soon realised that in his profession losing control led to humiliation, even death. And while he disliked the thought of dying, he hated even more the thought of appearing to his colleagues like a fool with no self-control. So he'd perfected a system for calming his impulses, at first using medication, then techniques based on yoga together with moderate, regular use of soft drugs.

Thanks to all this work, he'd managed to put up a good front before the judge during his divorce, when his wife had claimed the house, the car, custody of their two children and even the dog. Despite the urge to kill her, Sorel contained himself for the entire hearing. He had not insulted his wife, as his instincts prompted. He had on the contrary responded to her demands with arguments crafted in a spirit of moderation and forgiveness.

OK, so he'd been unfaithful. Several times, he couldn't deny it. He'd even hit her. Not frequently, but it had happened. He was quite willing to admit it. He had a stressful job. Such slips were understandable, if not excusable. Anyway, he couldn't change the past. So why not start from scratch, as civilised adults? He had concluded his appeal with a contrite air. Eyes shining with bottled-up emotion, he'd ended his speech with a tremor in his voice. He was the picture of humility.

He'd spent a long time practising the expression in the bathroom mirror, in his hotel room the week before. The effect would have been even better with a whip and a crown of thorns, but these were banned in court, so he'd made do with self-restraint.

Still, Sorel had been pleased with his performance. Awarding marks, he'd have given himself a good eight out of ten. But his efforts had come to nothing, and the judge had ruled against him. The idiot had given his wife everything she wanted, including custody of the dog.

Losing the children didn't bother Sorel much – his paternal instincts had never been strong, especially as he spent three or four days away from home every week – but the prospect of giving up his dog was heart-wrenching. But he'd said nothing on hearing the decision. He'd focused all his thoughts on his breathing, and it had worked wonderfully.

He'd felt the anger ebbing away to distant corners of his mind, so that he had even been able to give his wife a conspiratorial little nod as she got into the car, a bright red Honda S2000 convertible, as if to say: 'You see, I'm a good sport, even after everything you've put me through.'

That evening, before going to bed, he'd gone home – *her* home, from now on – and methodically smashed up the car with a baseball bat decorated in the colours of the Chicago White Sox, his favourite team.

Destroying his ex-wife's car had been soothing, relaxing even. Back in his hotel room, he'd collapsed in a heap and, despite his awful day, slept for almost twelve hours straight. He hadn't done that for years. There was nothing like a good surge of endorphins for relieving stress.

Despite this mild crisis of loss of control, from that day on Sorel knew that he could take anything. His meeting with Stern had just confirmed it once again.

Nora was in the corridor, leaning against the wall. She straightened up as Sorel came out of the office, and stared at him as if she'd never met him before.

'What are you looking at?' snapped Sorel.

'It's nothing, really,' she said. 'There's just something I'd like to know. Just a simple thing.'

'Go ahead and ask.'

'I was just wondering if Julien Sorel is your real name. I mean, like the character in the novel.'

Sorel ran his hand through his hair to repair the damage from the journey, and adjusted his tie. He chased away all thoughts of Stern in order to give the young woman his full attention.

Nora had ignored him on previous occasions. This sudden interest seemed promising. Sorel felt the little vein on his left temple throb. He knew the feeling well. He was attracted to the girl. This was what the muted beat was telling him. He found Nora very sexy, with her formal manner and perfect chignon. This was exactly how he pictured the heroines of all the nineteenth-century novels in his grandparents' library, which he had read voraciously as a teenager when he spent the summer holidays with them. Madame Bovary and Anna Karenina must have looked like her. Maybe a little plumper, with bigger breasts, according to the fashion of the time. Sorel had always had a taste for the classics, in both novels and women.

He intended to get Nora into bed by the end of the mission. It would be his bonus, in a way. He hadn't crossed the Atlantic to sleep alone in his suite at the George V for the entire stay. He didn't for a minute doubt that he'd succeed. Women rarely resisted him, at least, not those he picked up in the bars near his home when he needed company. Nora must have forgotten what a real man was like, spending all her time with Stern. A little reminder would be good for her.

His tiredness suddenly evaporated. Sorel felt fine again. He forgot the hours spent on a plane, the time difference and his empty stomach. He stared back at the young woman, letting his gaze roam freely over her neck to the top of her breasts, even a little lower. Pure desire, which he didn't try to hide, shone in his eyes.

101

'And what's your conclusion?' he asked eventually.

Nora resumed her position leaning against the wall, her chest slightly forward.

Her reply was cool. She smiled knowingly. 'No matter. Clearly my thoughts about your name are of less interest to you than other, more basic impressions.'

Sorel's breaths came deeper and faster as the implications of her remarks sank in. His chest grew tight, but one thought kept his focus. Elias wasn't immortal. He wouldn't always be around to protect Nora inside his little fortress.

He could take his time.

14

Valentine's unease at being locked in disappeared as soon as she started work. She put on her glasses and protective gloves and began examining the manuscript in detail, from the binding to the pages inside.

Unfortunately this thorough inspection only confirmed her first impression. The slightest touch caused irreversible damage, and the lectern was soon dotted with tiny fragments of parchment too small to be gathered up and stuck back on.

The collagen in the deeper layers of the hide had lost its original elasticity and resilience. The molecular structure had been damaged by prolonged exposure to damp. The fire that had blackened the binding and a good number of the pages had made them as brittle as dry leaves. The manuscript had probably been in this condition for several centuries, maybe even since the end of the Middle Ages.

At this stage, Valentine still didn't know the full extent of the damage – it might be spectacular but superficial. Indeed, chemical and bacteriological analysis sometimes contradicted initial visual impressions. This possibility gave Valentine hope.

Bent over the manuscript, she didn't hear the Plexiglas panel slide open. She jumped as Elias Stern entered the library.

'Everything all right?' he asked.

Recovering, Valentine set her glasses down on the desk and nodded. 'Apart from the depressing state of the codex, yes.'

'Do you think you can do anything with it?'

'It's still too early to say. I need to carry out more thorough tests.'

'How would you like to join me for lunch? You've been working for four hours. You must be starving.'

Valentine glanced at her watch: it was one o'clock. She'd lost all sense of time since Nora had left the room. This was a good sign.

'Why not?' she said. 'I'm used to regular hours. My stomach's going to send me a sharp reminder if I don't fill it soon.'

'Perfect. Nora is already in the car. She's got your jacket.'

Stern and Valentine went down to the courtyard where the limousine was waiting. Nora was sitting in the front seat. The chauffeur helped Stern into the car.

Wearing an impeccable, tight dark suit as always, Franck closed Stern's door but left Valentine to close her own. She managed rather well, considering she was sunk deep in the exquisitely soft leather seat. The Mercedes was wonderfully comfortable, but getting in and out required the skills of a contortionist.

Once they were settled, Franck sat at the wheel and started the engine. He took the Rue de l'Université, then turned off almost immediately towards the Seine.

The journey took only a few minutes. Franck parked the limousine outside the Musée d'Orsay and Nora helped Stern extricate his weary body from the back seat.

As he had the day before, Stern took Valentine's arm, leaning his other hand on his cane as they walked the few metres to the small esplanade in front of the museum. While Stern and Valentine were making their way to the entrance, Nora went ahead and whispered a few words to one of the attendants. He gestured for them to enter without queuing.

There are places you tend to idealise, to make more beautiful in memory than in real life, but the Musée d'Orsay is not one of them. Valentine was always awed by the elegant majesty of the building.

The conversion of the old railway station into a museum had been a great success. The vast central hall, almost a hundred and forty metres long and edged by six levels of terraces rising up to over thirty metres, didn't dwarf the works of art on show as one might have feared. On the contrary, it gave an impression of freedom from all constraint, quite unlike a traditional museum layout.

Nora, Valentine and Stern didn't linger at the entrance, but took the lift up to the restaurant on Level Two. The head waiter led them to a small room off the main dining area and gave them a table slightly apart from the others, next to a large window looking on to the Musée de la Légion d'Honneur.

A regular at the restaurant, Stern ordered the lamb shank without even looking at the menu. Valentine and Nora both chose the risotto with white truffle shavings. Quite unconcerned about seeming pushy, Stern insisted they also have the dessert of the day, a delicious gratin of red fruits with *sabayon* sauce.

After coffee, Stern suggested they take a stroll around the museum to aid digestion. Although she knew most of the paintings by heart, Valentine accepted graciously, curious to find out what kind of guide the elderly art dealer would make.

Stern avoided the rooms devoted to the Impressionists, which were always packed with tourists, instead leading her up the escalator to Level Five, off the main visitors' circuit, where they wandered among the paintings of the Post-Impressionists and the artists of the Pont-Aven School. From time to time, Stern stopped in front of a picture and proffered a comment about a detail of the composition, or a delightful anecdote about the artist.

In the wing devoted to Les Nabis, Stern stopped before a strange painting in subtle shades of yellow and ochre. For a long time he followed with his eyes the blurred outline of the figure that occupied most of the canvas.

The painting showed a man of around sixty, seen from the front, in an awkward on-guard position, bare-chested, fists clenched, one arm held up in front of his torso. The plaque said that it was a self-portrait by the artist Pierre Bonnard, titled *Le Boxeur*.

Bonnard's depiction of the ravaging effects of age on his body was uncompromising. His skin was sallow and his chest sunken. Drooping shoulders supported puny arms. Roughly painted, his features expressed intense fatigue, as if just raising his arms were an effort.

'This painting . . .' began Stern in a voice full of contained emotion. 'I think I was one of the first people ever to see it. It had just come from Bonnard's studio. The paint wasn't quite dry. I was a child at the time, but I can remember it perfectly.'

'You knew Bonnard?' asked Valentine.

'I went to his studio several times, yes. But I saw this in Ambroise Vollard's shop. He opened it around the same time as my grandfather opened his, in the early eighteen-eighties. Their shops were next to each other and they became good friends, despite being in competition. They understood each other. They had the same tastes and admired the same artists. In those days they were the only ones, or almost, to recognise the Impressionists' huge potential. Everyone called them mad. That must have brought them closer together. Vollard had lunch at my grandparents' house every Sunday.'

'Didn't Vollard die quite a long time after Gabriel? Did he continue to visit?'

Stern nodded. 'Vollard got on well with my father, too. After lunch he'd invite him home to show off his latest acquisitions. They could spend hours discussing the paintings. It went on until Vollard's death, just before the Second World War.'

Stern was silent for a long time. He became lost once more in contemplating the painting.

Valentine sensed that she should leave him in peace. She waited patiently for him to resume his story.

'My father started taking me with him as soon as I could tell the difference between a rattle and a sculpture,' Stern went on. 'It was his idea of education: he thought being able to tell a Cassatt from a Valtat was far more important than learning to read. And I'm hardly exaggerating when I say that. It has to be said that I was fertile ground. I loved going to Vollard's. There were paintings all over the flat, stacked on shelves or on the floor, unframed. There were Renoirs, Cézannes, Rouaults . . . And Bonnards, of course, all magnificent. I must have been four or five when I first saw this one. It was the early thirties, if I remember rightly. Vollard had just been to Bonnard's studio and brought back a whole set of pictures, including this self-portrait. He wanted to know what my father thought of it.'

'And how did Jacob react?'

'He immediately pointed out that there was no signature. It was true! Bonnard hadn't signed the picture. He hadn't signed anything Vollard bought that day. In fact, Vollard had got the paintings for such a modest price that he didn't dare ask Bonnard to come and sign them, for fear he might change his mind if he saw them again and raise his price. Vollard was like that – unbelievably stingy. He was a genius, but what a skinflint! I'd give anything to go back to that flat, even for a second, with dear old Vollard in his skullcap, always moaning. Pah! It's all so long ago. No one but me is interested in this old stuff now.'

'That's not true,' protested Valentine. 'Otherwise the museum would be empty.'

Stern turned from the painting to look at Valentine.

'You have the power to prevent my memories disappearing with me, Valentine. When I spoke of your gift the other day at the workshop, that's what I meant. It's a talent not given to everyone. The Foundation needs someone like you. And not just to restore the Vasalis codex. There's so much to do . . .'

A shadow of nostalgia passed across the old man's face, giving way almost immediately to weariness. He leaned more heavily on Valentine's arm.

'The walk has tired me out. Would you be so kind as to see me to the car?'

Valentine helped Stern back to the Mercedes, and he dozed on the journey home.

Nora woke him when they arrived. Looking exhausted, Stern had Franck accompany him to his apartments.

Valentine returned to the library. Deep in concentration, she spent the rest of the afternoon meticulously photographing each page of the codex so as to have a permanent record of its original state, before she began the restoration work.

Every two hours or so, Nora came to see if she wanted something to drink, and check that everything was going well.

In the late afternoon, Valentine's attention was attracted by a faint scratching sound. Her first thought was that a bird must have landed on the window ledge, and was tapping on the window with its beak.

She thought she'd make the most of the distraction to stretch her legs. Putting down her digital camera, she went to the nearest window. She pulled aside the heavy curtain blocking out the light. She did likewise at the other two windows but didn't see a bird. Beyond the glass, the grounds of the property were in deep gloom, accentuated by seasonal drizzle. Valentine peered into the darkness, but could see nothing out of the ordinary. There was no movement in the garden. Even the trees were motionless, as if the oppressive atmosphere of the house extended outside.

She heard the sound again. This time it seemed to come from inside the house. Valentine left the window and went to the Plexiglas door. She was right. The sound was coming from that direction.

She could see a blurred figure through the glass. Nora must have come to open up for her so that she could go home. But there was something odd about Nora's demeanour. From the little Valentine could see through the glass, Stern's assistant seemed to be struggling with the control panel and failing to get the door open. After a minute, she appeared to give up. Her outline became increasingly indistinct as she walked away down the corridor.

Valentine felt the stirrings of anxiety. The fear of being trapped inside the room erased all other thoughts.

She tried to calm herself by seeking an explanation for Nora's behaviour. If there was a fault in the door mechanism, she must have gone for help. A technician would soon be there. She'd be free within the hour. And it wasn't all bad. She could get the technician to enter her fingerprints into the memory of the biometric reader. From tomorrow, she wouldn't have to put up with being locked in.

Valentine had no choice but to be patient. She sat down on the floor facing the door and, hugging her knees, prepared herself for a long wait.

Suddenly the figure reappeared. Shoulder first, it struck the Plexiglas panel.

With a cry of surprise, Valentine fell backwards. Her glasses fell off, and she hit her head on the parquet with a dull thud. Half stunned, she saw the figure hurl itself against the door again. She no longer had any doubt – it wasn't Nora.

Valentine started to scream as loudly as she could, but the sound of her terrified voice simply bounced off the soundproofed walls.

15

'Tell me about Vasalis.'

David had been expecting anything but this. He had arrived at the meeting in a despondent mood, certain that the Dean had summoned him simply to confirm that his academic career was over. He wouldn't have been surprised to be told to follow his mentor's example and jump out of the window. After all, the cleaners were now adept at getting blood off the courtyard paving stones, and at least it would put an end to the curse that seemed to have afflicted David since he'd begun his thesis.

'Tell me what you've learned about Vasalis,' the Dean repeated, as if David hadn't heard.

That the unfortunate monk, eight hundred years after his death, should now arouse the interest of the highest authority at the Sorbonne left David perplexed. If his working hypothesis proved correct, Vasalis was dead, his name forgotten and his treatise reduced to ashes. So why did the Dean want to know more about him? He was well aware that David had made little progress with his research. He didn't need to have David confirm it aloud in order to kick him out of the Sorbonne.

While David was pondering this, the Dean glanced exasperatedly at his watch.

'I have another meeting at seven, in other words in ten minutes' time. That's exactly how long you have to save your skin.

Tell me what you've found out about Vasalis, and I'll see what I can do for your thesis. I'm listening.'

Within the space of two days, the Dean had moved from threats to questions. Now David had to find out whether this was a good sign or not.

'What would you like to know?'

'What documents are you working on?'

David had spent the morning at home preparing his defence. He'd phoned in sick at work, claiming he had the beginnings of bronchitis. His boss probably hadn't believed him, and would no doubt take his absence as yet another example of his poor attitude.

Caught off guard by the Dean's dramatic volte-face, David suddenly felt lost. The thousands of pages he'd trawled through in the past five years now merged into a confused muddle in his mind. It took him several moments to gather his thoughts. He launched at last into a faltering explanation.

'With regard to direct sources, I've collected about twenty references to the *De forma mundi* in texts or letters dating from the fifteenth to the eighteenth centuries. Simple allusions, mostly veiled, at least for the most ancient ones. Vasalis is never actually named in them, because of the Pope's ban, but—'

The Dean interrupted, more stiffly even than usual.

'Let's not beat about the bush. I'll rephrase my question, and I expect a straight answer: have you found conclusive proof that the treatise exists?'

'Several contemporary witnesses state that Clement IV's envoys spent almost six months scouring the courts of Europe. They also searched the libraries of the main abbeys. The Pope sent his men anywhere that copies of the *De forma mundi* might have gone.'

'Or maybe their mission had an entirely different purpose, and your suppositions are baseless.'

Reluctantly, David conceded the possibility. 'Yes, that is something to consider. Except that I haven't found any other explanation for the Pope's relentlessness. You must admit, it's rather strange that the Pope should send his henchmen to the four corners of the continent without anyone knowing why.'

The Dean made some notes on a card. He glanced at the clock facing him, behind David, then added: 'In short, all your rambling is based on an unverified hypothesis? It doesn't seem very . . .' He hesitated for a few seconds, searching for a concluding phrase. 'It doesn't seem very scientific. We don't even have proof that the Pope really did anathematise Vasalis.'

David shrugged. 'The only way of obtaining irrefutable confirmation of my "rambling", as you call it, would be to find a passage from the treatise or, better still, to get hold of a complete copy. For the time being, you're right, I don't have proof.'

'In five years' research, you haven't come close. So why, apart from the fact that he was as stubborn as a mule, was Cadas so sure that a copy existed somewhere?'

'I don't know,' admitted David. 'It was something he'd been interested in for a long time. He'd searched most of the big European collections, from the Bibliothèque Nationale de France and the Vatican archives, to the Cambridge University Library and the Biblioteca Nacional de Madrid. He really did look everywhere but he never found anything conclusive, though he never seemed disheartened. He was always convinced that a copy was waiting for him somewhere, and that they were destined to meet some day.'

'So, to sum up: Cadas spent a quarter of a century following an intuition. Is that it? And all at the taxpayer's expense. Some would call it a waste.'

David resisted the urge to jump across the hideous mahogany desk between him and the Dean and make him take back his harsh words.

The man's tactic was obvious. He was trying to force David up against the wall, to provoke a disastrous reaction so that he wouldn't even need an academic justification to have the security guards eject him from the Sorbonne. He'd be able to settle David's fate at last without getting his hands dirty. Deep down, David had accepted that his academic career was dead and buried.

112

Punching the Dean's smug face was an appealing thought, but he wasn't about to fall into such a crude trap.

'Your summary is a little simplistic, but yes, you could call it intuition.'

David couldn't believe what he'd just said. Albert Cadas might have been a stubborn old mule, but he was no fool. He wouldn't have devoted so much time to chasing after the *De forma mundi* if it had been just an illusion. The Dean's view was partial and restrictive, far from the open-mindedness that an academic should display. But nothing David could say would change this.

A different angle would reveal how wrong the Dean was about his colleague. The intuitions of the old professor of philosophy should properly be interpreted as a stream of logical deduction. They were the fruit of a perfect knowledge of the intellectual context in which Vasalis had developed.

Albert Cadas hadn't needed to unearth physical proof of Vasalis's existence to know that his thought was still real, buried somewhere in Western collective memory. He'd read so widely that he'd reached a point where certainty became irrelevant. Limited people like the Dean could hardly conceive of such a lofty perspective, let alone approach it.

'To your knowledge,' the Dean went on, 'did Cadas have money problems?'

'Money wasn't important to him. He couldn't give a damn about it.'

'Personal problems, then?'

'Why are you asking me this?'

'One of my academic staff has committed suicide. I'm just trying to understand what happened.'

Unsettled by the Dean's insistence, David raised his voice. 'I've had enough of your questions. I'd like to know where you're going with all this.'

The Dean looked irritated. 'Think carefully before going down that path. I'm the only person who can rescue you from the impasse you've got yourself into.'

'You can also finish me off. If you're going to throw me out, just get it over with.'

'If I'd been determined to get rid of you, you wouldn't be here this evening. Do you really think I've got time to waste?'

This admission slightly calmed David. He decided not to storm out after all.

'Did you notice anything unusual about Cadas in the last few months?' the Dean continued.

David reflected on the days leading up to his mentor's death. Something surfaced from the depths of his memory.

A week before his suicide, Albert Cadas had called to say that he had made definite progress with his research. He'd just got back from Naples, he'd said, sounding very cheerful. He'd found a remarkable document in a private archive, and had purchased it.

He'd said more, but at the time David hadn't paid much attention. His supervisor had announced several times before that he was about to make a major discovery, but his hopes had always been dashed. David had assumed it would happen again. It was probably a trivial incident. David decided not to mention it to the Dean.

'I don't know why he killed himself. I'm sorry, I can't help.'

'Well,' said the Dean, 'if you have nothing else to say, that will be all.'

'About my future . . .' ventured David.

'I don't know yet. I need to give it some thought, and discuss it with the members of the University Scientific Committee. You'll have our answer within the next few weeks. Until then, watch your step.'

David needed no translation. He understood immediately.

After Albert Cadas's spectacular suicide, the Dean wanted a less showy conclusion to this matter. David would not have to endure a public execution. He would be put to death quietly and discreetly, without publicity, in a dark, anonymous room.

It made no difference. David's last remaining hopes had vanished.

16

Despite the violence of the blow, the Plexiglas panel barely trembled.

Valentine stopped screaming. She was in no immediate danger. The intruder would never get through the door by ramming at it with his shoulder. He'd have to do far worse than that to break it down. She wasn't sure if he'd seen her from the corridor or not, but she thought it best to get out of sight, just in case.

Still lying on her back on the floor, she used her heels to shift herself towards the nearest wall. She hid in the blind spot between the door and the end of the shelves. Hardly daring to breathe, she stood up slowly, her back to the wall, until she could reach the intercom with the tips of her fingers. She turned and pressed the button, praying that Nora was right about it working.

'Nora,' she whispered. 'Answer please, Nora.'

Nora's voice rang out in the room, reassuring. 'What's the matter, Valentine? Do you want to go home?'

'There's someone outside in the corridor. I don't know who it is. He's trying to break down the door.'

Valentine realised that she didn't need to whisper. The intruder couldn't hear her from outside the room. She tried to stop shaking, and continued in a normal voice.

'You have to come upstairs, Nora. Right now.'

'I'll call security and be there straight away.'

Valentine released the button. She waited a moment, then took a deep breath and peered through the Plexiglas. The intruder had disappeared. The corridor seemed empty again.

Thirty seconds later, two figures appeared. One of them quickly tapped a code into the control panel and placed her finger on the scanner.

The door opened and Nora entered with Eric, the bodyguard Valentine had seen the day before with Stern. Both were holding guns.

'Nora!' cried Valentine. 'I'm so pleased to see you!'

'What happened?'

'There was someone behind the door. He tried to unlock it using the control panel, then he started slamming into the Plexiglas.'

Nora signalled to Eric to search the other rooms on the first floor. Then she grabbed a walkie-talkie from her belt, raised it to her lips and spoke, pressing the call button.

'Franck, Valentine has confirmed that there was an intruder. Lock Mr Stern into his office and check the grounds.'

The chauffeur's voice emerged from the device with surprising clarity. 'Roger. I'm on my way.'

Nora clipped the walkie-talkie to her belt and thumbed the safety catch on her gun. Then she slid the weapon into a holster under her jacket, in the small of her back. Valentine would never have dreamed that Nora knew how to use a gun, even less that she carried one all the time. It jarred with her delicate, almost fragile appearance and her love of ancient books. The Stern household certainly held surprises.

Overcome by a flood of conflicting emotions, Valentine leaned against Nora, who held her up by her waist.

'It's all over.'

'I was so scared, Nora!'

'Don't worry. If our visitor is still here, Eric and Franck will find him.'

The walkie-talkie on Nora's belt crackled and she raised it to her lips.

'Nora,' said a male voice.

'I'm listening, Eric.'

'There are footprints along the outer wall. One man on his own, it looks like. The motion detectors in the grounds didn't work. The intruder must have disabled them somehow.'

'Come back inside. Meet us downstairs.'

'Understood.'

Now Franck swiftly entered the library, still holding his gun pressed to his thigh.

'Did you find anything?' asked Nora.

'The garage door was forced open. The alarm was deactivated with an electronic jammer. Nice work.'

'I can't believe it,' exclaimed Nora. 'In broad daylight. It's incredible.'

'I thought the security here was better than a museum's,' said Valentine.

'I thought so too.' Nora seemed very disappointed. She turned towards Franck.

'You didn't see anything else? Has the intruder gone?'

Franck nodded. 'I've been all round the building. There's no sign.'

Nora took Valentine's hand and led her out of the room.

'Come on. Let's go and see Elias. You can leave your things here.'

'What about the codex?'

'It stays here. It's the safest place in the house. The door withstood one assault. It'll hold up if the visitor comes back. But we'll make sure it doesn't happen again.'

Valentine left the room. As soon as she was in the corridor, Nora engaged the lock.

Franck went downstairs ahead of them. Eric was already standing outside Elias Stern's study. Nora unlocked the reinforced panel.

'Go on in,' she said to Valentine. 'I've got a few calls to deal with in my office. I'll join you later.'

Stern went over to Valentine as she came in, looking genuinely worried. He placed his hands over hers, and she felt his rough skin against her own. The simple touch dispelled much of her nervousness.

'Valentine, are you all right? You're not too badly shaken?'

'I've had a hell of a fright, but I'm OK now.'

'I never thought the manuscript would arouse such interest so quickly. We operated very discreetly. No one was supposed to know about the deal, or that the manuscript was here.'

'Well, obviously someone does know, and really wants to take it from you.'

The old man looked anxious. 'This is highly regrettable. I didn't want to involve you in anything like this, Valentine.'

'It's not your fault. It wasn't serious. I've had a bit of a scare, that's all.'

'You could have been hurt. This should never have happened.'

They heard car tyres crunch on the gravel of the courtyard.

'That must be the police,' said Valentine.

'We haven't called the police.'

'But someone's just tried to steal the Vasalis manuscript!'

'The Foundation has its own security. We don't need to call in outside help. We handle our problems ourselves.'

There were footsteps in the corridor and a knock at the door. The reinforced panel slid into the wall and a man entered the room. He could have been anywhere between forty and fifty. He wore a dark suit, like all the male staff at the Foundation. His thin hair was cut short. He was unshaven, and he looked as if he hadn't slept in days – dark shadows ringed his pale eyes. He seemed furious at having been disturbed.

Anger. Intense, constant anger. The man exuded nervous tension, thought Valentine. She tried to see if there was the bulge of a revolver under his arm or in the small of his back, but couldn't tell for sure if he was armed.

The aggressive light in the newcomer's eyes made her think he must be.

'What's happened?' he asked curtly.

'Someone broke in,' said Stern, not seeming to take offence at the man's abruptness.

'The codex?' The man didn't show his host any particular respect, as if Stern were not his superior.

'The manuscript's still here, thank goodness. The library door withstood the attack. Valentine was in the room at the time. It was she who alerted us. If she hadn't been there, it would probably have taken us a few days to realise what had happened. The break-in might even have gone undetected.'

The man suddenly seemed to become aware of Valentine's presence. He held out his hand, looking her up and down. Valentine realised that it was an instinctive thing in him. She could also tell that he liked what he saw.

'Julien Sorel,' he said.

Valentine took his hand, giving a start at the name.

Since choosing the pseudonym – with the agreement of his superiors who had not, of course, caught the reference – for his operations in Europe, Sorel had realised that most people lacked any knowledge of classic French literature. At best, the name rang a bell, but few could remember where they'd heard it before.

Sorel could see in Valentine's eyes, however, that she had made the connection.

Valentine withdrew her hand quickly, almost embarrassed at this physical contact with the incarnation of a character from a novel. This response, too, was common. Usually, Sorel found it amusing. This time, however, he would rather have avoided it.

Not knowing how to dispel the uncomfortable atmosphere, he glanced at Stern.

The old man took over.

'Mr Sorel is our Head of Security. This is Valentine Savi. I've told you about her. She's the Foundation's latest recruit.'

Sorel nodded at Valentine.

'You'll have to review your security measures,' she said to him.

119

'We'll see. That's my concern, not yours. Your job is to prise Vasalis's text from that goddamn book.'

He had a slight accent that Valentine couldn't quite pinpoint. She placed it somewhere between the United States and the depths of the Massif Central.

'Did you see the intruder?' he asked.

'The glass is not transparent. I saw a figure, that's all. I don't know what he looked like. I'm not even sure it was a man. It could just as well have been a woman. Actually, I thought it was Nora at first.'

Sorel turned to Stern. 'Eric said the sensors in the grounds malfunctioned. The security cameras might still have caught something, though it's unlikely as they're linked to the sensors and normally they're triggered at the same time. I'll take a look later.'

'Do as you think necessary,' said Stern quietly.

Sorel seemed unhappy with this answer. As if overtaken by nervous spasms, his body began to shake. He stepped towards Stern and hissed angrily: 'I've been saying for months that you need more staff. You should have listened to me.'

'Eric and Franck are quite enough. Even if we'd had ten more guards, the intruder would have got in the same way. It's the electronic security devices that failed, the outside sensors and the alarm. It wasn't human error.'

'With the funds at your disposal, a few extra guards wouldn't come amiss, whatever you say. You're playing with fire.'

'I said no. That's my final answer. I'll take responsibility for the consequences if necessary. As I have always done.'

Sorel looked sceptical. Installing Stern at the head of the Foundation had been a huge mistake. Sorel still couldn't understand why his superiors had agreed to work with Stern, or why they'd given him all the executive power. Sorel had been firmly opposed to the Foundation project from the beginning. He couldn't see the point of setting up such an organisation, and feared it would eventually become unmanageable – as it had proved. But his bosses loved the idea of being able to intervene where, in theory, they had neither the possibility nor the right. They had jumped at Stern's proposal without gauging the practical problems involved.

It was all very well wanting to play at being big shots on another continent. But you had to have the capability to step in quickly, and they didn't. In practice, Stern had a free hand to make the important strategic decisions. Field agents like Sorel had to pick up the pieces.

Nora entered Stern's office. 'Already here, Mr Sorel? You look tired. Actually you look like death warmed up.'

'I was asleep when you called.'

'Congratulations on your efficient security system,' she mocked.

'Oh, that's right . . . Screw you. Give me a break, OK? If your boss listened to me occasionally, this wouldn't be happening.'

The atmosphere in the room was suddenly electric. After a long silence, Sorel pointed at Valentine.

'Anyway, if that little fool hadn't let on that the manuscript was here, none of this would have happened.'

Valentine was stunned. 'What are you talking about? I haven't told anyone!'

Sorel took a folded sheet of paper from his jacket pocket. He unfolded it and handed it to her. 'Read this. It might jog your memory.'

Valentine quickly read the page, then crumpled it into a ball. Her mouth twisted into a grimace of barely contained fury.

'Hugo, the bastard . . .'

17

The man didn't look good.

His head was lolling to one side and his tongue, covered in thick foam, protruded from his emaciated face. His frighteningly thin, disjointed body seemed to be floating in the air. The butcher's hook between his shoulders, by which he hung from the ceiling, must have had something to do with it.

Two other bodies swung beside him, hanging by the neck. They too were ravaged by deprivation and ill treatment. Given their state, it looked as if it had been a favour to finish them off. Execution had simply precipitated the inevitable end a few days early.

The nightmarish sight provoked the same reaction in everyone: at first, they walked past without really paying attention or understanding what they were seeing. Then they began to distinguish the outlines of the three figures against the background, which was a subtle palette of grey and beige. After a few seconds the information sank in and their expressions changed completely. The fake smiles became grimaces of disgust and terror.

Zoran Music hadn't pulled his punches. His depiction of the concentration camps was horrifically realistic. At a society event like this cocktail party, with canapés and women in evening dress, the contrast was striking.

Alex Cantor, the director of the gallery where Anna worked,

had based the small exhibition on the theme of 'The Representation of the Body Transfigured by Suffering'. This, at least, was the title of the lavish catalogue given free to every guest.

Beside Music's painting hung a huge *Figure* by Yan Pei-Ming, dating from the early nineties. A little further on there was a print of Pierre et Gilles' *Saint Sebastian*. His body pierced with plastic arrows, the handsome young man looked into the photographer's lens with an unequivocally languorous expression. In the middle of the room *The Dying Slave*, a sculpture by Yves Klein, writhed in pain, the subject matter strangely at odds with its colour, Klein's signature intense blue.

The exhibition was put together very cleverly. There was nothing particularly original in it, but it was a skilful mix of well-established artists and promising young talent. For different reasons, and in varying degrees, they all embodied the spirit of provocation that so many collectors now favoured.

In charge of the gallery's PR, among countless other things, Anna had done a fine job. She'd invited the potential buyers and personalities who mattered, those whose opinion was listened to at dinner parties. It was a safe bet that the exhibition opening would make the front pages of the specialist press the next day, particularly as the gallery was in an ideal location between the Boulevard Saint-Michel and the Seine, a stone's throw from the church of Saint-Germain-des-Prés.

After fifteen minutes, David grew tired of watching middle-class ladies with immaculate hair give exaggerated little cries before Zoran Music's emaciated corpses. He found a waitress with a tray of drinks.

He needed to relax after his meeting with the Dean. He downed two vodka and oranges one after the other, smiling sheepishly at the waitress as he put the empty glasses back on the tray and grabbed a third. The sudden flood of alcohol in his bloodstream made him feel good. He started wandering among the guests, glass in hand.

Strangely, David had felt almost relieved since leaving the Sorbonne. An external force over which he had no control – in this case, the Dean – had made him abandon his PhD. Deep down, David knew he should have made the decision himself a long time ago. He had nothing to gain by persisting in his vain quest. Academic life, with its rigidity, low blows and compromised principles, wasn't for him.

At last it was over. The Dean hadn't made it official yet, but he might as well have done. It was just a matter of time.

David's future was a blank page, and exciting new possibilities now opened up before him. Oddly euphoric, he decided to abandon himself entirely to this feeling of newfound freedom. Tomorrow he'd see all the problems involved in the conquest of this unknown territory. When he awoke and glimpsed the gaping void of his new life, he'd fall back to earth and probably go through hell for a few months.

But tonight, he refused to think about it. He wanted to enjoy this state of grace, even if it was only temporary. *Especially* because it was only temporary, in fact.

David Scotto was back, in an exquisitely simple anthracite Hedi Slimane suit he'd bought six months earlier in a fit of madness. By the time he'd realised his mistake, it was too late to return it. Contrite, he'd left it, unworn, at the back of his wardrobe. It was no coincidence that he'd worn it for the first time tonight. The suit symbolised a new start.

Lost in thought, David stumbled into the blue slave's pedestal. The statue swayed perilously, while at least half the vodka went down the Hedi Slimane jacket.

'Oh shit . . .'

A woman's hand held out a paper napkin. 'Don't you think he looks as if he's suffered enough?'

The voice came from behind him, deep and sexy like Marlene Dietrich's. The voice of a dark angel.

David turned slowly, savouring the wonderful sound. There were nine chances out of ten that his disappointment would be as great as his hopes. That was the game. He had little to lose, other than time and some of his illusions about feminine perfection.

He turned round. He knew immediately that he'd been right to spend all his savings – his parents' savings, actually – on the designer suit. The girl who'd spoken was breathtakingly beautiful. A slim brunette, her low-rise jeans were only slightly too tight. Her t-shirt, proclaiming a love of Dior, perfectly complemented her artfully tousled hair.

David's mouth suddenly felt dry. At last, when he managed to speak, he said the first thing that came into his head.

'You're not married, I hope?'

He gave himself a virtual slap on the back of the head. He was pretty rusty after all this time.

His opening line had been so unexpected that the young woman smiled forgivingly.

'You get straight to the point, don't you?'

'I'm sorry. That's not what I meant to say.'

'Don't worry. You're not one of those horrible men who just wants to get a girl into bed, are you?'

'OK,' said David, 'it's a draw. Let's start again. David Scotto.'

'Pleased to meet you, David. Are you always as forward with women and as careless with works of art?'

'Only when I'm bored. I feel like a fish out of water. This isn't your element either, is it?'

Bull's eye. A look of collusion shone in her eyes.

'How do you know?'

'You don't look like the other people here. You don't seem like the kind of person who goes to fashionable private viewings. You lack the blasé air, and that indefinable hair colour which is somewhere between the very elaborate and the frankly ridiculous. Actually, you look too real.'

As a chat-up line, it couldn't have been worse, and he knew it. Of all the thousands of guys who must have flirted with this girl, probably none had gone about it so badly.

'That's a pretty in-depth analysis!'

125

'Am I right? Tell me the truth.'

The young woman ran her hand through her hair, tousling it, and laughed.

'It's true. I avoid fashionable gatherings as much as possible.'

'What do you do for a living?' Another sparklingly original line.

'Let's see if you really are perceptive, or if you've just been lucky so far. You have to guess.'

'Hm . . . Are you a student?'

She looked horrified.

'Try again.'

'Model?'

'Now you're just trying to flatter me. You're disqualified.'

She made as if to turn and leave. David had no choice. He decided to go for broke.

'Let me buy you dinner to make up for it. We can slip out discreetly and leave all these morons pretending to swoon in admiration. I know a great little Italian place just round the corner.'

She shook her head. 'I don't think your girlfriend would be too happy.'

'What girlfriend?'

'The one who's been staring at us for the past few minutes. Over there, by the stairs.'

David turned in the direction she'd indicated. Anna was watching from the opposite corner of the room. She gave them a friendly little wave and blew David a kiss. A languorous kiss, of course.

Anna had ruined the atmosphere. It was her speciality. She had an undeniable talent for it.

David made a desperate attempt to rescue the situation.

'Listen,' he said to the girl, 'it's not what you think.'

'Don't worry. I won't tell her what a terrible flirt you are. Congratulations, by the way, you've got good taste.'

'But we're not together.'

The girl placed a finger on David's lips.

'In that case, unless you're a complete idiot, you should rush into her arms.' She winked at him and disappeared into the crowd.

David watched her walk away without even trying to stop her. He downed the rest of his vodka and orange.

Beaming, Anna came to join him, holding a glass of champagne. 'What did she want?'

'Just to chat, and more if we hit it off. Unfortunately, thanks to you, I think that's as far as we're going to get. Happy now?'

'She was so full of herself, it stood out a mile. Did you see that hideous t-shirt? And the hair . . . She could have gone to the hairdresser before coming. She looked like something out of a circus.'

'Listen, Anna, just in case you haven't got it yet, you and me, we're not together any more. The fact that you've seen me naked doesn't give you the right to pull this crap. You can't stop me having a love life.'

'Oh calm down, darling. Admire the wonderful art around you and have a drink. That's what you're here for, isn't it? And stop flirting with any tart within reach.'

David raised his eyes to heaven. 'Thank God you were here to stop me making such a terrible mistake. My virtue is safe. Go on, go and lick your boss's arse. Earn that shitty salary.'

Anna gave him a long, hard stare. 'You can be a real jerk sometimes.'

She sighed and threw the contents of her glass in his face.

18

Displayed in a million pixels on screen, the extent of the disaster was even more apparent than on Sorel's printout.

Vermeer had gone ahead, the bastard.

The whole world now had access to the information that Valentine had disclosed after swearing him to secrecy. She'd believed him when he'd promised to tell no one. She should have known – the scoop had proved far too tempting.

Hugo Vermeer was an absolute bastard, and she was a fool. Sorel was right. In disbelief, Valentine reread the post at Artistic-Truth.com yet again. She'd read it so many times she knew it by heart.

Vermeer had called the piece *The Vasalis Paradox*.

Such is the Vasalis paradox: when everyone thought him dead and buried, cut down by the obtuse scepticism of certain scholars of little faith, he appears again, livelier than ever, ready for battle.

Indeed, it is rumoured that one of our most knowledgeable art lovers – let's call him Mr S, and just say that he senses masterpieces the way others scent killings on the stock market – has just spent a small fortune on a worm-eaten manuscript. What is this aesthete going to do with such a mouldy old book? Use it as fuel in one of the fireplaces of his legendary mansion? We doubt it, and so do you, dear readers. Unless . . .

Unless another text is hidden in its pages.

Not just any text, but *the* text. The one we all dream of reading one day. The *De forma mundi*, a treatise we thought lost for ever.

Vasalis was burned at the stake for writing it. For our part, we'd sell our soul to the highest bidder to read a single page.

Mr S is so sure of his good fortune that he hasn't hesitated to recruit the best there is in the world of art restoration in order to penetrate the manuscript's secrets.

The question is, what will he do with the *De forma mundi* once he's rescued it? Will he let the world benefit, or will he make millions of dollars from it as only he knows how?

The answer is uncertain. No doubt grouchy philistines couldn't care less. Everyone else – and we're sure that includes you, dear readers – is quivering.

With delight or disappointment? We don't yet know.

Valentine could quite understand Sorel's fury. Vermeer couldn't have made it more explicit. Behind the pompously flamboyant language, it was all there, crystal clear to anyone in the least familiar with the art world.

By suggesting Stern was the owner of the *De forma mundi* even before Valentine had finished examining the palimpsest, Vermeer had made the old man a target. And had probably got Valentine the sack at the same time.

A few hours earlier, when she'd admitted her mistake, Stern had said nothing. Valentine would have preferred it by far if he'd hauled her over the coals and torn up her contract there and then. She could have understood, even accepted, such a response. Instead, he'd got Franck to drive her home. He'd promised to call her in the morning, advising her to get some rest and try to forget the break-in. It seemed like she was being fired, but gently.

This was nothing like her abrupt departure from the Louvre, but the end result was the same.

'Dammit,' muttered Valentine, eyes glued to the screen.

She couldn't bear to look at the web page any more. She switched off the computer, then leaned back in her chair and had a long stretch. The words of the article were still dancing behind her half-closed eyelids.

Other words, just as cruel, then took the place of Vermeer's. Except in this case, millions of people had read them. They told of a huge loss to humanity caused by one person's error. Hers. Valentine Savi's.

Her name on the front page of the papers, vilified as if she were a murderer, or worse.

Valentine felt her stomach clench. She'd made a complete mess of things. Yet again.

Whatever she did, she never got anywhere. No matter how hard she tried to extricate herself from the net she'd been trapped in for the past two years, her efforts came to nothing. She was wasting her energy. Things would never get better. She'd never get her old life back.

Valentine hid her face in her hands. Even tears had deserted her. But the feeling of failure was there, gripping her inside. She had reached the limits of her moral strength. A huge wall rose before her, and she felt too isolated to attempt to climb. She reached for her mobile and dialled Marc Grimberg's number.

'Hello?' he said.

'Marc . . . I need you. Can you come over?'

'I'm on my way.'

He didn't ask questions, but hung up without another word as if he already knew that, tonight, Valentine would not refuse him.

19

The toilets lived up to the gallery's status. They were worth a visit on their own. There was marble everywhere, the taps were by Philippe Starck and the interior designer had favoured patrons with aluminium urinals in which they could see themselves peeing. Here was everything for the modern man. Classy.

Having availed himself of all that was offered by the urinal, David rinsed his face and took off his jacket in order to dry it. His shirt and tie had more or less escaped the vodka and champagne spills, so at least he was spared the indignity of having to stand half naked in the men's toilets. That was something.

A prolonged spell under the hand-dryer left his jacket crumpled and still reeking of alcohol. If anyone came near him, David would have little chance of avoiding a reputation as a drunk.

The two giants in dark suits who entered also seemed concerned with their appearance. Their funereal garb perfectly suited their brutish faces. The more presentable of the two looked like Mickey Rourke after the boxing and botched facelifts. The other made Winston Churchill look like a male model. The gun holsters bulging beneath their jackets only enhanced the effect.

The second man locked the door to the toilets and stationed himself in front of it, legs slightly apart and arms crossed.

By now, David was feeling a little anxious. It didn't look like the pair were there to answer the call of nature. An internal alarm started flashing rapidly. If these two were what they seemed, booze stains on his jacket were the least of his worries.

Without much hope, David prayed that a batch of spoiled canapés might cause a rush for the toilets. No one came to his rescue, of course.

The bigger of the two men – the post-op Mickey Rourke – advanced towards him, with all the nonchalance that his great bulk would permit. David opened his mouth to ask for an explanation, but the man didn't give him a chance to speak. His punch struck David's left temple, landing him on his backside, head full of thousands of brightly coloured stars shooting in all directions. The devastating pain came a fraction of a second later, while blood poured from his brow.

David moaned in agony. He tried to make it sound manly but, in all fairness, it was simply pitiful.

'What the fuck do you think . . .'

By way of answer, the brute kicked him in the stomach, just under the ribs. A horrible burning sensation spread rapidly through his middle, where he was supposed to have abs. For a moment, the pain in his belly blotted out the pain in his skull, but then the two began working together.

David would never have thought it possible to be in so much pain. He felt as if he had a particularly unfriendly alien in his stomach, and its only slightly less vicious little brother in his brain.

He didn't even have the strength to groan. He curled up on the floor in a survival position, knees to his chest and forearms in front of his face. He could take the idea of being beaten up. He'd got a pretty thorough pounding a few years earlier, coming out of a club, and had recovered without lasting damage. But his face was his main business asset. David needed it for his new start. He had enough problems already. He couldn't let them disfigure him without even knowing why.

'Shit,' he moaned, 'that really hurts.'

The man grabbed him by the tie and lifted him up about

twenty centimetres. He wound his fingers around the knot and twisted it by a quarter of a turn, which instantly cut off the oxygen supply to his victim's lungs. He let David choke for a good minute, long enough to extinguish any hint of resistance. This little flourish was quite unnecessary, as David had no intention of challenging his attacker.

Just as David was about to lose consciousness, the man let go and allowed him to take a deep gulp of air. Then he helped him up by yanking on his tie.

Though he was bent double by the pain, David made a point of trying to stand unaided. Even half dead, he still had some pride.

'David Scotto?' asked the man.

'Nice time to check . . . What would you have done if it wasn't me?'

The thug mimed the barrel of a revolver with two fingers of his free hand and placed them against David's temple. His lips then formed a silent 'bang'. He was someone who knew how to be persuasive even with a limited vocabulary.

Don't try to be clever. And whatever you do, don't provoke him. David turned this basic rule over in his mind. The brute was capable of drawing his gun and killing him there and then, without a second thought. And the place lent itself to violent death – there was more marble in here than in the whole of Père-Lachaise. A simple wipe-down, and all traces of blood would be gone in no time. The interior designer had done a really good job.

'What do you want from me?' asked David between gasps.

'Where's the illumination? Where've you hidden it?'

David was speechless for a few seconds. He racked his brains, but couldn't for the life of him think what the brute meant.

'If I say I don't know what you're talking about, you're going to hurt me again, aren't you?'

The man smiled, emphasising a jaw worthy of a Neanderthal. 'What do you think?'

'Well, let's be practical then. Could you be a little more precise?'

'The page with the illumination.'

'Again, I don't have any illumination.'

'So your teacher had it, then.'

'My teacher? You mean Albert Cadas?'

The Neanderthal nodded. David looked down and began closely examining the tip of his shoe.

'Well?' said the man.

'You're not going to like this . . .' David muttered, not daring to look up.

'Try me, you little bastard.'

'Cadas never showed me any illumination. And he's dead now.'

The Neanderthal sighed and raised his fist.

'Wait!' cried David. 'Tell me exactly what you want and I'll do it.'

'We want that page, so you'd better find it, and fast. It's easy: you find and you bring.'

'Have you got a photo or a reproduction?'

The Neanderthal shook his head.

David felt a deep despair. As the moments passed, he sank lower and lower. It seemed as if he'd never hit bottom.

'How can I find the damned thing if I don't even know what it looks like? Describe it to me, at least.'

'It's a page torn from some old book. With a kind of painting on it.'

'Thanks for the information, but I already had some idea of what an illuminated vignette was before I met you.'

David bit his lip. *Don't try to be clever. And whatever you do, don't provoke him.*

To his great surprise, the remark didn't earn him another punch.

'Can you give me something more to go on?' he continued quickly, before the man had time to regret his magnanimity. 'Do you know where it might be?'

The Neanderthal simply shook his head from side to side, as if dealing with a half-wit.

'D'you think we'd be here if we knew? You'll have to manage somehow. You've got a week to get hold of it and bring it to us.'

David was about to ask what would happen if he didn't but refrained, aware that the answer to his question was predictable.

The man scribbled a telephone number on a piece of paper and forced it into David's hand.

'You can reach us on this number, day or night. And you'd better get in touch, or else . . .'

He left the sentence hanging, and gave David a shove with one hand. He fell backwards, hitting his head on the edge of the washbasin and awakening the alien nestled in his skull. He fell to his knees and threw up over his trousers.

The two brutes swore in disgust and left, sniggering.

David didn't take his eyes off them until they had disappeared out of the door. He intended to recognise them if he ever ran into them again.

He struggled to his feet, promising himself he'd go back to working his abs as soon as he was better. He'd really let himself go lately. A few self-defence classes wouldn't go amiss, either.

A quick look in the mirror confirmed his fears. He was a sorry sight, with a bloody face and soiled clothes, but he couldn't stay in the toilets all night. One of the other guests would eventually need to evacuate the excess alcohol and canapés. He tried to tidy his hair. But there was nothing he could do about the bruises on his face or the stains on his suit.

As raising his arms caused him pain, he gave up putting on his jacket and slipped the piece of paper with the telephone number into his trouser pocket.

He staggered to the door, hoping to make as discreet an exit as possible. With a bit of luck, if he hugged the walls and kept his head down, people back in the outside world wouldn't notice his grotesque appearance.

As he re-entered the gallery there was a burst of applause.

David stood open-mouthed for a moment, before remembering the title of the exhibition: 'The Representation of the Body Transfigured by Suffering'. Suddenly David understood, and a wave of contempt for the whole of humanity rose from his painful stomach. The guests thought it was a piece of performance art, part of the exhibition. As if you could feign such pain . . . Human stupidity really knew no bounds.

Out of the corner of his eye, David just had time to glimpse Anna and the girl in the Dior t-shirt rushing towards him.

He vomited again before fainting.

20

Valentine sighed sleepily. She stretched her neck slowly, and gazed at her lover's body. Grimberg had made the most of her departure from the bed, at just after four in the morning, to appropriate the bedding and wrap it around himself like a child.

For a moment, Valentine wondered if she'd been wrong to break the rules of the game like this. She'd opened the door halfway, but she had no intention of opening it any further, and definitely not of giving her former colleague the keys to her life. She didn't want him to latch on to her moment of weakness and use it to establish habits which would quickly become stifling.

Grimberg, however, had played his part perfectly. He'd understood that Valentine needed physical release, and given her what she wanted, but hadn't felt obliged to provide any artificial tenderness, which she didn't want.

Out of the window, the first light of dawn was timidly attempting to pierce the darkness. Valentine glanced at the clock above the breakfast bar. She still had a good hour to waste before she could decently throw Grimberg out.

She switched on the computer and slipped the memory card into the front slot. She created a new folder on the hard disk, and imported into it all the pictures she'd taken the day before in the library at Stern's house. Then she began retouching the photos using image-processing software. It was a tedious job but, at that time of night, she needed something intellectually undemanding, and this fitted the bill perfectly.

She opened each file in turn, adjusting the brightness and contrast of the photographs so that the text copied by the scribe who'd made the codex stood out.

The results were mixed. Most of the Greek characters now showed up clearly, but Vasalis's palimpsest remained locked in the depths of the parchment. Having said that, almost all the pages were legible.

Valentine chose a few fragments of text at random and amused herself deciphering them. Despite her meagre knowledge of Ancient Greek, she was soon convinced that it really was a book of prayers. She printed all the pages, then copied the first line of each prayer on to a separate sheet. She hoped that by focusing on the choice and order of the texts she'd be able to work out the date the manuscript was made, as well as establish with greater precision the geographical area it came from.

Out of curiosity, she ran Internet searches using the opening sentence of each prayer. Most were not indexed by any search engine. But Valentine did manage to identify two texts. One was an exorcism of impure spirits by St Gregory, the other a Communion prayer by John Chrysostom. According to the information she found, by the High Middle Ages the texts were widespread almost throughout the Christian Middle East. Nothing useful there, then.

The research had taken her less than forty-five minutes. It was still too early to drag Marc out of bed. A little envious, Valentine watched him sleep. She felt exhausted, but knew she wouldn't fall asleep, even if she lay down again beside her lover's peaceful body.

She spent the next twenty minutes testing the different functions of the image-processing software. She opened the file containing the photograph of the first cover board – the only one without any text – and amused herself by stretching the image in every direction, inverting and altering the colours.

Two small dark stains in the upper left-hand corner of the photograph suddenly attracted her attention. She reframed the image and adjusted the parameters until the stains became clearer. Valentine allowed herself the first smile of the day.

She rushed to the bed, placed a hand on Grimberg's shoulder and shook him gently.

'Hm . . .' he murmured, still half asleep.

Valentine shook him harder. 'Marc, I need to know something. Please wake up.'

'What?' he grumbled, barely opening his eyes.

'Do you know anyone who specialises in bookplates or stamps?'

'Bloody hell, Valentine . . . Have you seen the time? It's still dark outside.'

'I know. I'm really sorry, but this is important. Well?'

'Well what?'

'Someone who can decipher provenance marks – any ideas?'

'If I give you a name, will you leave me alone?'

'I'll even let you use the bathroom when you get up.'

Grimberg closed his eyes and turned towards the wall. He pulled the bedclothes over his head, so that only a few tufts of hair remained visible.

'Hélène Vailland,' he mumbled, his voice muffled by the duvet.

Valentine kissed him quickly where his head protruded from the covers.

'Thanks. Don't forget to close the door behind you.'

21

Thierry Moreau made a face as he recognised Joseph Fargue in the distance, approaching the security office.

'Damn,' he said.

He turned to the three security guards in the office with him: 'Which one of you got here late this morning?'

One after the other, they all shook their heads.

'Come on, guys, you know I couldn't care less. Spill the beans.'

The men remained silent.

The head of security sighed.

'Look, guys. Because of your nonsense, I'm going to have to listen to the old fool moaning. Thanks a lot. I'll remember it when you need a day off.'

Moreau would have liked to slip out, but Fargue pushed open the glass door before he had time. The Chief Administrative Officer stood in the doorway and looked round at the four men in the room. He came towards the counter where the Chief of Security was sitting.

Moreau didn't stand up to greet him but remained at his control console, from where he could see all ten screens in front of him at once.

'Mr Fargue, you haven't been to see us for three days. To what do we owe the honour of your visit this time?'

In fact, Moreau knew exactly what his visitor was going to

say: he hadn't been able to get into the Sorbonne at seven on the dot that morning. It was unacceptable and, as Chief of Security, it was his duty to make sure that the gates were opened at the time stipulated in the internal regulations of the institution.

Fargue ignored his question. Without asking permission, he came behind the counter and indicated the row of screens.

'Your screens here, do they just display, or do they record as well?'

Pulled up short by the question, Moreau forgot to order him back to the public area.

'We record everything the surveillance cameras see.'

'And do you keep the tapes?'

'There aren't any. Everything's recorded digitally. The data is automatically overwritten every Sunday at midnight.'

'Overwritten?'

'We record over it,' explained Moreau.

'Today's Friday. So the recordings from last Tuesday haven't yet been . . .' Fargue searched for the word Moreau had used a few moments earlier.

'. . . overwritten,' Moreau filled in.

Fargue paused before declaring, as if it were obvious: 'I'd like to see the recording.'

'Impossible.'

'Why?'

'The data's confidential. There's a very strict legal framework regulating access. Only certain people can see it.'

Fargue stiffened. 'Do I have to remind you of my rank?'

Moreau was about to point out that Fargue held a very lowly position in the university hierarchy and that, in a less tolerant environment, a person as insignificant as him would have been told to get out. Charitably, he kept these thoughts to himself.

'Only the police can view the recordings, with the Dean's consent.'

Fargue hesitated. Nervously, he smoothed down over his skull the long strands of hair with which he tried to hide his baldness.

He'd hoped it wouldn't come to this, but he'd run out of options. It was a desperate step, probably doomed to failure, but he didn't want to abandon his investigation without eliminating all possibilities.

He was visibly pained as he made his proposal: 'What if I promise never to come and bother you again about opening times?'

Moreau saw at once an unexpected opportunity to be left in peace for the decade remaining before Fargue's retirement.

He grinned. 'Never again? Really?'

'Never.'

'Well then, that's another matter.'

With an authoritative jerk of the chin, Moreau signalled for the security guards to leave the room.

Once they'd left, Moreau drew up a chair for Fargue at the control console.

'Tuesday . . . that was the day Cadas died, wasn't it?'

'Indeed.'

'May I ask why you're interested in his suicide?'

'Several books have disappeared from the Research Centre. I think Cadas stole them. I'd like to get them back.'

Moreau looked sceptical. 'Which camera would you like to see?'

Fargue pointed through the window to the building from which Cadas had thrown himself.

'I went in there earlier. I saw a camera at the top of the stairs, on the fourth-floor landing.'

Moreau reached for a folder on the counter and began leafing through it. He stopped at a map that showed all the cameras on campus, then slid a finger to the one Fargue had mentioned.

'That's camera twenty-seven. What are you hoping to see?'

'I don't know. Something you may have missed.'

Moreau raised his eyes to heaven, but refrained from comment.

'What time shall I start the recording from?'

'Cadas died at around one o'clock. Start then.'

Moreau tapped away on his keyboard. When he'd finished, he placed a finger beneath the middle screen.

'Ready?'

'Go ahead.'

Moreau pressed the Enter key. An image with faded colours appeared. There was a digital timer in the bottom left-hand corner of the screen. Placed as it was, the camera provided a perfect view of the landing and the corridor leading from it. After a few metres, however, the corridor turned a corner beyond which nothing was visible.

'You can't see Cadas's office,' Fargue pointed out.

'It's the only camera on that floor,' replied Moreau. 'Not many people go up there. I didn't even know academic staff still had offices up there.'

'Is that staircase the only way up?'

Moreau nodded. 'The camera records anyone going up or coming down. No one can avoid it.'

A few moments later, a blurred figure appeared on screen. Even with its back to the camera, Fargue recognised it immediately.

'Cadas . . .'

As the lecturer disappeared around the corner towards his office, the timer showed 13:03.

'Shall we continue?'

'Yes, go on.'

For some time the two men watched the empty landing in silence. As the timer showed 13:07, several figures ran past the camera.

Moreau paused the recording again. He tapped his finger on one of the frozen figures.

'That's me, there.'

He was with two uniformed security guards.

'We arrived straight away,' he explained. 'A number of witnesses saw Cadas jump. So we didn't waste any time looking for the place he fell from. We didn't pass anyone either, on the stairs or in the corridor, and his office was empty. If there'd been

143

someone with him at the time he died, we'd have seen them. It was definitely suicide.'

Fargue groaned in disappointment. 'Can you go back? Before Cadas arrived.'

Moreau flashed him an annoyed look. He couldn't understand why Fargue was persisting. Cadas had committed suicide, and that was that. In his view, the matter was closed. But Fargue didn't seem prepared to leave the security office without viewing the recording in its entirety. He crossed his arms, eyes on the screen.

Moreau gave in. 'If you insist. I suppose we may as well.'

He pressed the fast-rewind key. He and his men waddled backwards comically until they vanished from the screen. A few seconds later, Albert Cadas too reversed and disappeared down the stairs.

Once again, the picture of the empty landing filled the screen. Only the numbers rushing past on the timer in the bottom left-hand corner broke the hypnotic monotony of the recording.

'Stop!' cried Fargue suddenly.

Moreau obeyed. He set the recording to run at normal speed again.

A man came round the corner of the corridor and advanced towards the camera. When he reached the landing he realised he was being recorded – a look of surprise crossed his face, and he immediately lowered his head.

Moreau rewound the recording and paused it at the exact moment the man was caught staring into the camera. Aged around forty, he was wearing a navy suit and light-coloured tie. His blond hair was cut short with a perfect side parting.

'Do you know him?' asked Moreau.

'I've never seen him before.'

Increasingly puzzled, Moreau captured a screen shot, saved it and printed it out. He pointed to the timer on the image.

'Look at the time he was there: eleven fifty-five. He left the floor an hour before Cadas's suicide. Why is he of interest to you?'

'He's holding something under his arm,' was Fargue's only reply. 'I'd like to see what it is. Can you enlarge that part of the picture?'

In a hurry to finish, Moreau pressed the zoom button.

Fargue couldn't help crying out in indignation as he recognised what the man was carrying. He counted four books. The largest was the size of the *Theatrum Orbis Terrarum*. The image wasn't clear enough to make out the lettering on the spines, but Fargue was in no doubt: these were the books that had disappeared from the Research Centre.

He pointed out a fifth object, slimmer than the others. It was rectangular and about twenty centimetres long. It stood out from the books, as it was much lighter in colour.

'What's that?'

'No idea. I'll try to zoom in closer.'

With the mouse, Moreau selected an area of a few centimetres around the mysterious object and clicked on it a few times until it filled the entire screen.

'It looks like some kind of box.'

'It's an archive box,' said Fargue. 'It's what we use for fragile books when they're being stored. But this one's too slender to contain a book. Look: it's only a couple of centimetres thick.'

'What the hell's he doing with this stuff?'

'We have to find out what time he arrived,' Fargue said, ignoring the question.

Moreau rewound the recording until the man appeared on screen, his back to the camera. This time he was empty-handed.

The timer showed 11:15. The man had spent almost three-quarters of an hour on that floor, before Cadas arrived, and he had left with the books the lecturer had stolen from the Research Centre. Fargue was baffled.

'When you got to Cadas's office,' he asked Moreau, 'did you see any signs of forced entry?'

The Chief of Security gathered his memories. 'The door was

unlocked, but it didn't seem to have been forced. I didn't notice anything unusual, at any rate.'

He took the screen printout from the printer tray and placed it before Fargue on the control console.

'Are you sure you don't know who he is?'

'Yes. I don't think he's a member of staff. Between the two of us, we must know almost everyone here. And he looks too old and too well-dressed to be a student.'

Suddenly Fargue had an idea: 'You keep a record of all external visitors to the university, don't you?'

Moreau indicated a spiral notebook on the counter. 'We check their ID and note them down here. If your man isn't a member of the university, he must have had his name recorded here to get into the building.'

He reached for the notebook and flicked through it until he came to the page for the previous Tuesday. He pointed immediately to the first name on the list.

'Here he is. Simon Miller. Arrived at eleven-thirteen. It takes about two minutes to get up there if you know the way. It fits. He arrived and went straight up.'

'Do you record departure times as well?'

Moreau shook his head. 'No, only arrivals. The only way of finding out what time he left would be to view the recordings from the courtyard cameras. But spotting one individual in the crowd is almost impossible, especially at that time of day. The courtyard's always packed with students at lunchtime.'

Fargue seemed disappointed with Moreau's reply. He stared for a long time at the photograph of the man who had taken his precious books.

'Tell me his name again, please.'

'Miller,' Moreau reread. 'Simon Miller.'

Fargue thought the name sounded familiar. He said it to himself quietly several times.

'Dear God!' he murmured suddenly. He leaped from his chair, grabbed the photograph and rushed out.

Moreau watched him leave the security station without making the slightest move to stop him.

'What the . . .' His exclamation hung in mid-air.

Too busy elbowing his way through the crowd in the court-yard, Fargue didn't even hear.

22

For a moment, as he opened his eyes, David Scotto was disorientated. He was lying in a bed, stark naked. His last memory was the moment just before he fainted at the gallery. The room, however, seemed vaguely familiar. He wasn't dead, or else hell looked a lot like his bedroom. The discovery delighted him.

Energised by the good news, he tried to sit up, despite the painful vice gripping the left side of his head where the first blow had struck. He managed to raise his upper body from the bed, but then he felt as if his stomach muscles were tearing and he fell back against the mattress, grimacing. His euphoria evaporated. Being alive was agony.

His attacker was certainly good at his job. Every move reminded David of their encounter the night before. The simple act of breathing made him groan in pain, and his mouth was filled with a very unpleasant metallic taste.

Awoken by his contortions, Anna emerged from beneath the sheets, in a little nightie she'd pretended to forget at his flat a few months before. One of her breasts swung freely outside the white lace bodice.

David was suddenly seized with doubt. 'You and me, we didn't . . .'

Given his condition, the thought that he and Anna might have had sex last night was absurd. But with her, nothing was impossible. She could have brought a zombie back to life if she'd wanted to.

Anna was still half asleep. Eyes closed, she shook her head, one hand adjusting the strap of her nightdress. The breast disappeared. She mumbled a few unintelligible words and snuggled against him, just like in the good old days.

She slid her hand over David's bruised abdomen, drawing a groan of pain from him.

'How are you feeling?' she asked.

'How do you think? Like I've been trampled by a herd of mammoths. By what miracle did I get home?'

'Paul brought you, with a stop at A and E on the way. You were completely out of it. I couldn't leave you on your own.'

'That's nice. You're sure Paul isn't going to come round and finish me off? I seem to remember he's the jealous type. I know he's not Mr Universe, but in my present condition a disabled dwarf could thrash me.'

Anna sat up in bed. She seemed wide awake now, furious even. Life as part of a settled couple hadn't completely extinguished her fiery nature.

'Is that all you have to say? You gave me a fright, you moron!'

'D'you think I got myself beaten to a pulp deliberately?'

'If you stopped messing around, this kind of thing wouldn't happen to you. Bloody hell, David, grow up. You go looking for trouble.'

Even though, objectively, David was in no way responsible for what had happened the night before, he felt like a little boy caught peeping through the keyhole of the girls' changing rooms. Anna had a knack for making him feel like a kid. She'd always treated him like this. After pondering the matter, David could only come up with one explanation: for her it was a subtle way of manipulating the male brain.

Such a strategy could only work, of course, with David's consent, whether conscious or not. Sorting out his Oedipus complex should have put an end to it, but this permanent abdication of responsibility basically suited him, too. It meant he didn't have to make difficult decisions, such as quitting smoking or breaking up with Anna for good.

She slid her fingers up David's chest to his face, leaving pale streaks on his swollen flesh. David gritted his teeth but managed not to groan. Anna knew what she was doing, without a doubt. He resisted the urge to push her to the other side of the bed, as far away as possible.

'Who did this to you?' Anna went on.

'Two men.'

'Why? Did you tell them one of your stupid jokes?'

'For your information, they smashed my face in before I had time to say a word.'

'Just like that? Without warning?'

'Yeah.'

'Maybe you earned it in a previous life, when you were a rabid dog or a corrupt politician.'

'Very funny . . .'

'All right, sorry. What did they want?'

'They asked me weird questions about Albert Cadas. About an illumination he was supposed to have.'

'Did you know about it?'

'He never mentioned it. On the other hand, he didn't inform me he was going to commit suicide before he jumped out of his office window either. We weren't *that* close.'

'Did you tell them that?'

'Of course I did, but they didn't believe me. I've got a week to find the illumination and hand it over.'

'Then what?'

'You'll have to find a window in your schedule to visit my grave. No plastic flowers, please, or inscriptions on my tombstone about "Eternal Love". I can't stand that sort of thing.'

Anna didn't seem to take this possibility seriously. She moved her head close to David's and pressed her lips to his ear.

'Oh, by the way,' she said playfully. 'I almost forgot: the

little tart from yesterday left you her number. In your shirt pocket.'

'I'm surprised you didn't throw it away. It's not like you.'

'I thought about it, but I felt sorry for you, with your little face all puffy. You haven't had much luck lately. I decided not to take away the only source of happiness in your day.'

David didn't reply.

Resting on her elbow, Anna raised herself about thirty centimetres and leaned right over David. She gave him the same languorous smile as the evening before, when she'd interrupted his conversation with the girl in the Dior t-shirt, then she made the vulgar pout that usually had an immediate effect on him.

But usually he had full use of all his muscles.

'What shall we do now?' whispered Anna, pressing her chest against him.

Forgetting his pain, David grabbed her by the shoulders and pushed her down on the bed beside him.

'You're getting dressed and going home. And I'm going to inspect the damage. I'd like to feel depressed on my own, if you don't mind.'

He got up extremely slowly, and took shelter in the bathroom from Anna's stream of abuse.

His clothes from the previous day were strewn all over the tiled floor. A quick inspection confirmed his fears: the suit was ruined. What with the blood, alcohol and vomit stains, it was only fit for the dustbin. This enraged David far more than the stitches in his brow. Other than that, he'd got off pretty lightly. Apart from slight bruising around the eye, he was almost presentable. Nothing to write home about, but not the end of the world either.

Then he remembered that it was the first day of his new life.

As Anna had said, in his shirt pocket he found a metro ticket on which the girl in the Dior t-shirt had written her mobile-phone number. He placed it on the shelf beneath the mirror, together with the piece of paper the Neanderthal had given him

151

just before smashing his skull. Two telephone numbers in one evening. David was rarely so successful.

But his heart wasn't in it. He crumpled the metro ticket and threw it in the bathroom bin. He considered doing likewise with the Neanderthal's number, but didn't. Guys like that didn't mess about. He'd better keep the option of contacting them if he needed to. He opened the mirrored cabinet and slid the paper in beside his razor.

He took a long shower; then, in case the two heavies from the night before wanted another chat, he put on a faded t-shirt and threadbare jeans. He wasn't about to sacrifice any more expensive clothes.

By the time he emerged from the bathroom, Anna had disappeared. She'd laid the nightdress on his pillow, as if to make him endlessly regret her absence.

He went through the flat to the kitchen and collapsed on the only chair. The room was the size of a Portaloo, and just as depressing.

It was almost nine o'clock. He felt incapable of swallowing anything solid, but he was terribly thirsty. Two cups of pure caffeine and Damon Albarn's voice blasting from the hi-fi helped him regain some clarity.

Even after recovering full use of his brain, he still couldn't understand why he'd been beaten up. He was of no importance to anyone. He was just a mature student aged thirty-one, jobless and up to his ears in problems – another potential benefits claimant. But that was no reason to wipe him off the face of the earth.

He suddenly remembered that he wasn't unemployed quite yet. He picked up the telephone and dialled his boss's number.

'Hello,' said the man David hated most in the world after the Dean of the Sorbonne, his voice wrecked by nicotine.

'It's David Scotto.'

There was a brief silence at the other end. David could clearly hear the man exhaling, even though smoking was banned in public.

'What the hell are you still doing at home, Scotto?' said the gravelly voice at last. 'You should have been here ages ago.'

'How do you know I'm at home?'

'It's called caller display. Welcome to the modern age, young man.'

David didn't respond to his boss's sarcasm. He decided to launch straight into his sob story. He hadn't rehearsed it, but he'd used it so often in the past he had it off pat.

'Actually, I can't make it into work again today. I'm terribly sorry.'

The tone was perfect. Hesitant, but not tearful. David had been using it with his mother since the age of twelve. She fell for it every time, so that David had come to a firm conclusion: his mother was astoundingly naive, and it would be a dreadful waste not to exploit her weakness. He might as well try it out on someone else.

'Still bronchitis?' asked his boss. 'That's nasty . . . Once you've got it, it's hard to get rid of. I had it last year and it dragged on for weeks. Do you remember?'

'In fact,' David felt obliged to admit, 'the bronchitis is much better.'

'So quickly? Count yourself lucky, Scotto. By the way, I'll need a doctor's note for your absence yesterday. No need to post it. You can hand it to me in person.'

'No problem,' David lied.

'What's up with you now?'

'I had a slight accident yesterday evening. I slipped in the bathroom and—'

'In other words,' his boss interrupted, 'you came across a gang of mean boys and they gave you a good thrashing. I imagine your ego took a bash, too.'

'My ego's fine, thanks. I can't say the same for my body. I'm bruised all over.'

'You'll get over it.'

'Easy for you to say. You didn't get your ribcage kicked in. And I won't even mention my face. I'm quite a sight.'

David was well aware that he was exaggerating his injuries. It must have been apparent from his voice, as his boss remained unmoved.

'Listen, Scotto, I couldn't give a damn what state you're in. Fit or not, you'll always be a skiver and find a way to skulk in a corner. So if you don't turn up to work in the next twenty minutes, I'm firing you. Is that clear?'

He hung up without waiting for a reply, so he didn't hear David swear.

David was furious, but he had no choice. He needed his job at the library, at least while he was retraining. Whether he liked it or not, he'd have to tolerate his boss's high-handedness. He sighed and hoisted himself painfully from the chair. From the hi-fi speakers, Damon Albarn began to sing his hymn to Clint Eastwood.

David wasn't in the mood for upbeat music. He switched it off angrily. His new life was beginning as badly as the previous one had ended. Come to think of it, there was something consistent about the sequence.

23

As always happens when an ancient institution undergoes profound changes, the Bibliothèque Nationale de France's move to the banks of the Seine had caused violent controversy. Accustomed to the old site in the Rue de Richelieu, which was inconvenient but imbued with the charm of tradition, many researchers had been critical of the new location as well as of the architectural style. Erected on an embankment marooned at the edge of the thirteenth arrondissement, the four massive glass towers, shaped like open books, dominated the riverside.

Ten years on, the main causes for complaint had lost some of their substance. The area had been injected with a semblance of life, at least during working hours, and the steps leading to the central esplanade, responsible for a wave of fractures during the first downpour, had even been resurfaced. New habits had gradually replaced old ones. Many of those most nostalgic for the former building had retired, and library users had become more tolerant of the persistent faults, such as the waiting time for books, or the leaks that meant that rooms sometimes had to be closed.

Valentine had had quite a battle to obtain a precious pass to the lower level of the building, reserved for authorised researchers. It took a quarter of an hour for the librarian at the reception desk that day – a sour-looking woman who clearly did not believe that young ladies of pleasing appearance were capable of carrying out intellectually demanding research – to agree at last to issue her with a day pass.

Five minutes later Valentine set off, down a series of gloomy corridors and escalators, on the long descent to the reading rooms. Dismal and unwelcoming, these appeared to be populated by wax figures in a state of deep concentration. The background noise so typical of university libraries was missing. Entry to this pantheon of French culture was not granted to just anyone. Indeed, ordinary mortals had to make do with the garden level. Only a privileged few were allowed inside the belly of the beast. They wouldn't waste a second of their precious time there in idle chatter.

Valentine had no idea what the woman she had come to see looked like. But for once she'd been lucky. When she'd phoned the École des Hautes Études en Sciences Sociales where Hélène Vailland worked, her secretary had said that the scholar always spent Fridays at the Bibliothèque Nationale. And she'd been happy to tell Valentine which room she usually sat in.

At that hour of the morning, many seats were still empty. Valentine looked round the room. By a process of elimination, she selected a woman of about fifty bent over a large in-folio volume. Plainly dressed in a simple jumper and unfashionable jeans, she had long grey hair gathered untidily into a bun. Clearly elegance wasn't her primary concern when working at the library.

Intent on her book, the scholar was unaware of Valentine's arrival. Valentine coughed discreetly as she approached. The woman looked up. She put her magnifying glass down and turned a severe, lined faced towards Valentine.

'Yes?'

'Mrs Vailland?'

The woman gave a slight nod. Valentine took it as assent, and gestured to the free seat beside the scholar.

'Could I speak to you briefly?'

'Of course. I was going to take a break anyway.'

Valentine sat down.

'Thank you. My name is Valentine Savi.'

Hélène Vailland peered at her closely for a fraction of a second. Valentine couldn't tell whether she had made the connection with the Louvre scandal. The scholar's face betrayed no particular emotion.

'Your secretary said I'd find you here,' explained Valentine.

'Academics are creatures of habit. If we were intrepid, we'd be in a different job.'

Hélène Vailland's dry laugh echoed in the silent room. She turned and glanced anxiously at the library assistant at the central desk. To her relief, he didn't look up from his newspaper.

'What can I do for you?' she asked.

'I wonder if you could help me decipher the provenance marks on a manuscript,' said Valentine.

'Why didn't you make an appointment with my secretary? I don't like doing appraisals in a hurry. As a rule, I need several days if I want to do a good job.'

'I understand. I would have made an appointment if I'd had time, but this is urgent. The manuscript I'd like you to look at is rather special.'

The scholar sighed. 'All right, let's have a look . . . You're lucky I'm not a stickler for protocol. Have you got it with you?'

Valentine regarded her gratefully. She opened her bag and took out the photograph of the cover board of the codex, folded in half.

'If there were ever any bookplates, they've been removed, and all the marks of ownership or provenance have been scraped off or chemically erased. But I've managed to make two visible by adjusting the image parameters. Even so, the marks aren't very clear and the result is poor. Do you think you might be able to identify them?'

'It's always difficult to give an opinion based on a reproduction. I much prefer to work with the original. But let me have a look anyway. I might see something.'

157

Valentine unfolded the photograph and passed it over. Hélène Vailland pushed aside the incunabulum she'd been working on. She laid the picture in front of her and examined it in silence for several minutes, an eye to her magnifying glass.

When she looked up, her expression had hardened. 'May I ask where you found this?'

'I'm sorry, but it's quite confidential. The owner of the manuscript has had some problems recently. He'd rather not be identified.'

The scholar handed back the photograph. 'In that case there's nothing I can do for you, Miss Savi.'

'You've identified the marks, haven't you?'

'That's exactly why I can't help you.'

'At least tell me why you refuse,' pleaded Valentine.

The scholar hesitated. She took several seconds to make up her mind, while Valentine watched her eyes.

'Someone has already shown me these marks,' Hélène Vailland said at last. 'About six months ago. I remember it very well. The marks hadn't yet been erased. I identified them without any problem and retraced the book's journey, at least in part. I must say I didn't like what I found at all.'

'Why do you say that?'

'You know, what I do might seem rather dry, but actually it's detective work. My job consists in following a book's journey from its birth to the day when it's entrusted to me. I identify its previous owners, trace its pedigree and search the archives to fill in the gaps. Medieval codices like yours have often taken meandering paths to reach us, and that may often be why they've survived.'

She pointed to the photograph. 'Your manuscript is an exceptional case,' she went on. 'It's had too many lives for one book. In my line of work, that's never a good sign.'

'What do you mean?'

'Have you heard of the *Codex Sinaiticus*?' asked Hélène Vailland.

Valentine shook her head.

'The *Codex Sinaiticus* was made around AD 330. It's one of fifty original copies of the Scriptures that the Emperor Constantine had made after his conversion to Christianity. Most of the manuscript is now in the British Library. The rest is divided between the St Catherine Monastery in the Sinai Desert, where it was found, the Leipzig University Library and the National Library of Russia. I mention this because the man who discovered it, Constantin Tischendorf, was closely linked with your manuscript.'

Valentine's mobile phone started vibrating in her pocket. Hélène Vailland paused, visibly irritated by the interruption.

Valentine took out her phone. Vermeer's number was displayed on the screen. She diverted the call before switching it off and putting it back in her jacket pocket.

'I'm so sorry,' she said. 'Please go on.'

The scholar pushed back a strand of hair that had come loose from her bun.

'When he discovered the *Codex Sinaiticus* at the St Catherine Monastery on Mount Sinai, Tischendorf borrowed it from the monks in order to study it, promising to return it. In fact, he sent it to Tsar Alexander II in exchange for a title and nine thousand roubles – a fortune at the time. There was also a loose leaf in the parcel with it. It came from another manuscript, and bore a rather poorly executed illumination. According to Tischendorf, this sheet of parchment was as valuable, if not more so, as the *Sinaiticus* itself.'

'It was the opening page of my manuscript, wasn't it?'

'I'm sure of it,' said Hélène Vailland. 'Here, take a look at this.'

She picked up the photograph by a corner and indicated a faded patch about a centimetre square in the top half of the cover board. If you looked closely, you could make out a capital M set inside an ovoid cartouche.

'It's the mark of the library of the Metochion, the Monastery of the St Sepulchre in Constantinople,' explained the researcher. 'In 1846, two years after finding the *Sinaiticus*, Tischendorf brought out a book called *Travels in the East*. It contains a short passage about his visit to the Metochion. Tischendorf doesn't go into detail, but I'm certain he saw the manuscript and realised it was a palimpsest. He didn't manage to get it out of the library as he did with the *Sinaiticus*, but he tore out the first page as proof. He probably intended to go back later for the rest of the codex. But his negotiations with the Tsar failed, and he died without returning to Constantinople.'

'And what has happened to the manuscript since then?'

'It remained at the Metochion until the end of the nineteenth century. In 1899 someone called Kerameus updated the library catalogue. The note on your codex states that the opening page is missing, and that the manuscript is in very poor condition.'

'So the damage is long-standing,' said Valentine. 'That's what I thought.'

'But that's not all,' Hélène Vailland went on. 'A few months after writing his description of the codex, Kerameus noticed that it had disappeared. No more was heard of it for several years. It was found again by chance at an antique dealer's in Jerusalem in 1906, and returned to the Metochion. A Danish scholar, Johan Ludvig Heiberg, then became interested in it. He published an article in the journal *Hermes* in which he confirmed Tischendorf's theory about the palimpsest. Heiberg also recounted the ancient legend that had circulated in the Metochion for several centuries. It was his research that gave rise to all the rumours.'

'What do you mean?'

'All the nonsense about Vasalis. Don't tell me you don't know. I imagine that if the manuscript's owner has called on a restorer, it's because he thinks Vasalis is—'

She broke off suddenly and turned round. A library assistant, hands resting on the handle of a metal trolley full of books, was standing behind her. He took a book from the top of the pile and handed it to her.

'The book you asked for. Apologies for the delay.'

'Ah, yes, thank you. I'd completely forgotten about it.'

'Is there anything else you need?'

The assistant turned towards Valentine and gave her a charming smile, to which she did not respond. She noticed a nasty purplish bruise on his cheek.

The young man's gaze slid towards the photograph she was still holding and lingered there.

'Can I keep the book all afternoon?' Hélène Vailland asked him.

'Until closing time, at eight. I can put it aside for you for tomorrow if you haven't finished with it by this evening.'

'Thank you.'

'You're welcome.'

'See you later then.'

The assistant nodded and walked away slowly, pushing his trolley.

'How was the book removed from the Metochion?' continued Valentine, once she was sure he was out of earshot.

'At the end of the First World War, when the Turks took over the region, the Greek authorities discreetly transferred the monastery library to Athens. But a number of crates never arrived. That's why books bearing the Metochion mark can be found all over the place. The Cleveland Museum of Art, the Bibliothèque Nationale and Duke University, for instance, have acquired some. The Greeks kept quiet about it at the time because they needed the political support of France and the United States to counter the Turkish threat. Your manuscript was part of the lost lot of books, but it's taken much longer to reappear.'

She placed the tip of her index finger on a second mark made in blue ink, which was even less legible than the Metochion mark.

'It's the signature of Charles Gervex. He was a French soldier who served in Greece during the First World War and was then sent to Turkey in the early twenties, just after the Treaty of Versailles. He acted as an intermediary in the sale of books stolen from the Metochion. He kept this one for himself, probably because he'd heard about the palimpsest. In the early fifties, he tried to sell it to settle his debts. But he had no luck: none of the individuals or institutions to whom he offered it would buy it, as they feared the Greek government would demand its return. So the codex remained in the Gervex family. It was Charles Gervex's granddaughter who asked me to trace the book's history. She'd heard her grandfather talk about the Vasalis palimpsest since she was small, and she wanted to know if it was a fantasy.'

'And what did you tell her?'

'That I wasn't able to find out how the codex got to Constantinople, so there was nothing to link it to Vasalis. And I explained that the Metochion mark made selling it difficult, if not impossible.'

'Without the marks of provenance, it became much easier,' concluded Valentine.

'Quite. I didn't for a second imagine she'd do such a thing. Erasing the marks – it's outrageous.'

'What became of the page Tischendorf cut out of the codex?'

'I have no idea. It disappeared from the imperial collections during the Russian Revolution. It hasn't reappeared since.'

Valentine thought for a few seconds. She had one last question.

'Are you still in touch with Gervex's granddaughter?'

The researcher picked up her bag and reached inside. She took out a small red leather diary.

'We haven't been in contact since I gave her my report, but I must still have her details.'

She flicked through the first few pages. 'Here we are. I'll jot them down for you.'

She tore a page from the diary and wrote down the name and address of Charles Gervex's granddaughter. She handed the piece of paper to Valentine, who slipped it into the back pocket of her jeans.

'Thank you for all this information,' said Valentine. 'I'm very grateful.'

'You're welcome. Do you really think the manuscript is worth all the trouble you're taking?'

Valentine stared for a moment at the photograph of the cover board before folding it and putting it away in her bag. She shrugged.

'Well, the new owner of the codex thinks so. He's paying me to think so, too. It's not much, but for the time being I'm hanging on to that. And if I needed certainty in life, I'd be in a different job, wouldn't I?'

Valentine waited until she was outside the library to take her mobile phone from her pocket. She checked her voicemail to see what Vermeer had to say, but the Dutchman had hung up without leaving a message when she hadn't taken his call.

She decided not to ring him back straight away. She had better things to do for now than argue with him. Instead of Vermeer, she dialled Charles Gervex's granddaughter. After three rings, a pre-recorded voice informed her that the person she was calling couldn't answer the phone and suggested she try again later. Valentine hung up without leaving a message. She looked at the address Hélène Vailland had written down. Marie Gervex lived in the next arrondissement, the twelfth. Valentine knew the area. It was only about twenty minutes away.

Aware that her persistence was verging on the irrational, she decided to go straight there. It was unlikely that the codex's previous owner would be at home, but Valentine didn't want to have any regrets. After all, Stern hadn't yet phoned to tell her she was fired. Until she had proof to the contrary, she was still working for the Foundation. Even if she had only a few hours left to devote to the manuscript, she should do all she could to get closer to the truth. She should do it first for herself, but also for all those who had crossed the manuscript's path and believed that it was exceptionally important. Their faith in the human intellect deserved respect.

On a childish impulse, Valentine switched off her phone again, as if she could postpone being fired simply by refusing to hear the bad news. She walked a few metres across the square in front of the library, then stopped and closed her eyes. Her face turned towards the sky, she let the sun's rays caress her cheeks and forehead. She was overcome by a strange feeling. The walk to Marie Gervex's house was probably the last thing she'd do for the Stern Foundation. After that, her path and the manuscript's would diverge for ever, and she'd go back to her workshop, growing frustration her only prospect, day after day. Better not to think about it.

She opened her eyes and contemplated the majestic scene laid out beyond the esplanade of the library. Marie Gervex lived near the Gare de Lyon, next to the railway line. Her apartment block was just below it, probably behind the first or second row of buildings, a few hundred metres away as the crow flies. To get there, she simply had to cross the Seine and head in a straight line.

Valentine had no idea what to expect. She didn't even know what she was hoping to find. Yet a conviction was taking firm root within her: for once, she wouldn't just let herself be swept along by events. She didn't want to miss this chance, even if it came to nothing. It was still better than waiting and submitting.

Newly inspired, she set off with a resolute step.

24

'There you are, you crook,' muttered Fargue.

He glanced first at the small photograph on his computer screen, and then at the picture caught by the surveillance camera. There could be no possible doubt – it was the same man.

Just because Joseph Fargue refused, for ethical reasons, to use a computer, didn't mean he didn't know how. When the machine had been installed in his office, he had been obliged to go on a training course. On principle, Fargue had expressed his reluctance but, as he wasn't in the habit of disobeying orders, he had given in. He hadn't had any occasion to congratulate himself for his compliance. Until now. The search engine had come up with twelve pages of Internet links for the name Simon Miller. By refining the search, Fargue had easily identified the man he was looking for.

An English bookseller based in London, he specialised in high-end deals. There was a photograph of him on his website home page. Fair-haired, blue-eyed, around forty, a blasé aristocratic air – he was identical to the man caught on camera.

Though interesting, this was not enough for a perfectionist like Joseph Fargue. He opened the metal box marked with a capital M in black felt pen and went through the cards. His memory had not deceived him. There were five in the name of Miller.

The bookseller had been to the Research Centre three times in the space of only four months. On his first visit, he'd requested to look at the *Theatrum* and the *Institutiones in Linguam Graecam*. Then he'd returned for the Charron and, on his final visit, two weeks ago, the Epigrams of Bauhuis, and a first edition of *Letters On the Blind* by Diderot. By a happy coincidence, Fargue had lent the latter out for an exhibition only a few days before Albert Cadas had committed suicide. Otherwise it was safe to assume that it too would have disappeared from the strong-room shelves.

Simon Miller was a conscientious book dealer. He'd come in person to inspect the books he was interested in. God only knows how he had persuaded Albert Cadas to get them out of the Centre. With money, no doubt. It always came down to that.

Before going to tell the Dean what he'd discovered, Fargue decided to check one last thing. He wanted to be absolutely sure he hadn't missed anything important. He had half an hour before his colleagues got there, and another fifteen minutes after that before students started arriving. He'd have to hurry if he didn't want to be interrupted every thirty seconds.

He took another look at the bundle of cards filled in by Albert Cadas. At the top of the pile was the one for the *Theatrum*. He placed it on the desk in front of him and selected another ten at random, which he spread out before him.

It took him a good minute to see something rather obvious.

When he'd noticed the theft, he'd only paid attention to the name on the card. He hadn't thought of comparing the handwriting with that on the other cards. But there was absolutely no resemblance. The professor wrote in a regular, upright, if nervous hand. The person who had taken the *Theatrum* had less confident, almost shaky writing, and formed some letters back to front. Perhaps he or she was left-handed? Albert Cadas's handwriting was typical of somebody who was right-handed. So he had never requested the *Theatrum*. The thief had passed himself off as Cadas. He wasn't running much of a risk putting someone else's name on the form. The only thing staff checked was the occupation of the person making the request, to make sure that he or she was entitled to consult Research Centre books. They couldn't care less which name was on the card since, in theory, books couldn't be removed from the premises.

The person who had assumed Cadas's identity must have wanted to take an additional precaution, in case he didn't manage to remove the card. Thus, if the theft was noticed, it would be Cadas who was suspected, not him. For the plan to work, however, one essential condition had to be met: the thief must have been of the same status as Albert Cadas. He must have been a lecturer, or at least a member of university staff.

Fargue now knew enough to inform the appropriate authorities. He grabbed the card for the *Theatrum*, and the ones Miller had filled in, locked the door of the Centre behind him and headed for the stairs.

Before his foot had even landed on the first step, he was pushed violently from behind. His ankle twisted under him and he lost his balance. He tried to hold on to the handrail, but it was too late. His hand slipped on the wooden rail, unable to get a grip. He fell head first down the stairs.

His left femur gave way three steps down. Fargue clearly felt the bone shatter, piercing flesh, then skin. He didn't have time to cry out, or even feel pain. He tumbled to the bottom without managing to slow his fall. As he struck the floor with a dull thud, he felt an intense pain at the back of his neck.

Fargue didn't lose consciousness. Lying on his back at the bottom of the stairs, his first instinct was to check if he'd broken his back. It hurt too much to turn his head, but he could move his fingers and his unbroken leg. He must have dislocated or even cracked a vertebra, but hadn't damaged his spinal cord. He'd been lucky.

His colleagues would start arriving soon, and would rescue him. He must stay calm, try not to move so as not to intensify the pain in his broken leg, and wait. Shouting for help would be futile, since the Research Centre was in an isolated wing of the Sorbonne.

He heard a stair creak somewhere above him.

'You should always take care on the stairs, Mr Fargue. Didn't your dear mother tell you that?'

With a huge effort, Joseph Fargue managed to lift his head slightly. He could see only the shoes of the man who had spoken. It didn't matter – he recognised the voice.

'You . . . pushed me,' he said.

'Of course I didn't,' replied the voice. 'You were rushing down the stairs and you had a bad fall. At least, that's how the police will explain your accident.'

'My . . . neck hurts . . . Help me . . . Please.'

'Of course.'

The man came down the stairs and kneeled beside him. He slid a hand under Fargue's neck and felt it.

'Is this where it hurts?'

Fargue screwed up his eyes, indicating that it was.

The man removed his hand and gathered up the cards scattered around Fargue.

'Lucky Moreau called me,' he continued, standing up. 'You really worried him; he told me what you asked him. When you ran out of the security office, he took you for a madman. It has to be said that with your reputation . . .'

'But . . .' stammered Fargue.

'I knew I had to act immediately. Once you'd identified Miller, it was only a matter of time before you realised that Cadas wasn't the thief. And, as I didn't take the trouble to disguise my handwriting on the card, you'd have identified me eventually. When you're overconfident, you make mistakes. I never dreamed the old fool would jump out of the window. He messed everything up with his suicide. And you, with your stupid persistence.'

'You . . .' Fargue took a deep breath. Every word made him grimace with pain. '. . . stole . . . the books,' he finished.

'Of course I stole your wretched books. Your security measures are so ridiculous I couldn't resist. In a few days they'll be in the hands of a Russian collector, near Moscow, and I'll be about twenty thousand euros richer.'

'And the . . . box? What was in it?'

'If I told you, I'd have to kill you.'

He placed the sole of his shoe against Fargue's cheek, and then gave a sharp push against his face. The already damaged vertebra gave way with a sinister crack.

'Oh, I was forgetting . . . You died in the fall. What point would there be in telling you my little secret now?'

25

The block of flats where Marie Gervex lived faced the railway line. Once reserved for the working classes, the district was, like the rest of the capital, gradually being taken over by the more well-to-do. The transition was more or less advanced depending on the area, but it was under way everywhere, with the inevitable consequences, such as rising rents and the more vulnerable groups being pushed to the outskirts of the city. Supporters of the trend spoke of an unavoidable process of social homogenisation. Others protested that it was a scandal, and demanded emergency measures to halt price increases and restore the diversity that was part of Paris's charm until a decade ago.

The main entrance to the building was of an indeterminate colour that was probably once blue. The paint was flaking badly, leaving patches of bare wood exposed. You simply had to push a small door set into the large arched gate to gain access to the inner courtyard. A feeling of neglect reigned in the small yard with its old, uneven paving stones. There was an abandoned car at the far end, and dustbins overflowing with refuse sacks stood in a corner. Gentrification hadn't reached here yet, but it would probably only be a matter of months before developers took an interest and made house prices skyrocket.

Valentine stood before the board listing the residents. The labels were all different. Some were simply hand-lettered pieces of paper taped to the board. Marie Gervex lived on the fifth floor, at the front of the block.

Valentine circled the courtyard vainly searching for a lift. Eventually she started up the worn staircase.

There were three flats on the landing. Fixed to one of the door-frames, above the bell, was an old brass plate bearing the name Gervex. Valentine rang and waited.

She heard floorboards creak inside, and a ray of light showed briefly at the spy hole.

'What do you want?' asked a woman's voice through the door.

'Mrs Gervex? My name is Valentine Savi. I'd like to talk to you about the manuscript you sold to Elias Stern.'

'You must be mistaken. I haven't sold anything.'

The spy hole cover fell back. Valentine heard creaking again, growing fainter as Marie Gervex walked away from the door.

Valentine rang again and kept her finger on the bell, causing a din inside the flat. A few seconds of torture convinced the owner to return.

This time, she opened the door a crack and looked out.

'What do you think you're doing? Stop it right now!'

Valentine took her finger off the button. It wasn't like her to do something like this. She felt bad about it, but didn't have time to be more diplomatic.

She felt even worse when she saw that Marie Gervex was a tiny bird-like woman. In her late fifties, or possibly early sixties, she wasn't more than five feet tall, despite her high-heeled shoes. Skinny as a rake, she floated inside a flowery dress, which looked as if it had been made for a teenage girl. A life too hard for such a frail body had left its mark on her face. She had drawn features and dark rings under her eyes, emphasising sharp cheekbones. This wasn't the manipulator Valentine had pictured, capable of erasing the provenance marks of a codex.

'I just want to talk to you,' the restorer insisted. 'I work for the Stern Foundation. I won't take much of your time.'

Unsure, Marie Gervex stared hard at her for a moment.

Behind her, Valentine glimpsed a narrow corridor, with a room cluttered with boxes at the end. A sofa covered in transparent plastic sat in one corner.

Marie confirmed Valentine's suspicions. 'I'm in the process of moving. It's chaos in here.'

'Why don't we go out then?' suggested Valentine. 'I saw a bar on the corner.'

Marie hesitated, then nodded and took a woollen cardigan from the hook behind the door.

'Why not? It would do me good to get out. I've been packing up for a week now.'

She locked the door and preceded Valentine down the stairs. They made their way to the ground floor without a word. She still seemed a little uneasy, turning to glance nervously at Valentine every few steps.

'Do you really work for Stern?' she asked as they reached the courtyard.

Valentine said yes. She didn't think it necessary to expand. The less Marie Gervex knew, the more willingly she'd answer her questions.

'I tried to phone just now to tell you I was on my way,' Valentine went on. 'But there was no answer.'

'Mr Stern called last night. He said word had got out about the book. He warned me that I might be contacted, and advised me not to answer the phone or open the door.'

'But you did open the door!' said Valentine with a smile.

Marie seemed to relax a little. A flash of amusement crossed her emaciated features, but they quickly regained their humourless cast.

'Mr Stern said he was going to get in touch with you,' lied Valentine. 'He's solicitous about the people he does business with.'

'Yes, he's very thoughtful.'

Marie stepped out into the street first. The two women walked side by side on the pavement towards the bar.

'So you're moving?' asked Valentine.

Marie nodded her little birdlike head.

'At last I can get out of this awful area. I'm not sorry to be leaving.'

'Where are you moving to?'

Marie dodged the question with a shrug. 'I've been waiting for this moment for twenty years,' she said. 'And all this thanks to an old book! Can you believe it?'

'Your grandfather had good instincts.'

'He knew the manuscript was valuable. He always said so.'

'Did he ever tell you why he was so sure?'

'He mentioned an old legend about a monk, or something. I always thought he was talking nonsense. He was quite confused towards the end, when we put him in a nursing home. Still, eventually I had the manuscript valued. It cost a lot, but it was worth it!'

'You went to Hélène Vailland, I know. I spoke to her this morning, just before coming to see you.'

On hearing the academic's name, Marie stopped dead. Her eyes appeared to withdraw even further into their sockets.

'So you know about the marks?'

'I know that you had them erased, yes.'

Overcome with alarm, Marie started trembling and tugging nervously at the sleeve of her cardigan.

'You want to cancel the sale, don't you?'

Valentine immediately sought to reassure her. 'No, that's not why I'm here. Mr Stern wants to keep the manuscript, even though you lied.'

'So why are you here?'

'I know that another buyer made you an offer. I'd like to know who it was.'

'Hasn't Mr Stern told you?'

Valentine was about to make up another lie, but changed her mind. She couldn't help feeling sympathy for the woman. Marie Gervex seemed as if she might shatter at any moment, exploding into shards like a glass dropped on the floor.

'Listen,' said Valentine. 'Let's go and sit down. I'll explain everything. There are things you need to know about the manuscript, and about Mr Stern.'

The bar was just opposite, on the other side of the street. The two women started across the pedestrian crossing.

Suddenly, with a deafening roar, a van came hurtling round the corner towards them. Valentine barely had time to step back out of its way. Her companion's reflexes weren't as good. The vehicle hit her head-on. Marie was lifted off the ground by the impact. She bounced against the windscreen and rolled over the top of the van before falling heavily on the tarmac.

Valentine watched the scene, unable to react, aware only of the metallic black of the van and the red puddle spreading around Marie Gervex's broken body. She lay a few metres away, in the middle of the road. Valentine was struck by her strange position. Sticklike in her bloodied, flowery dress, she looked like a doll whose limbs had been twisted in all directions by a perverse little girl.

A loud shrieking of tyres jolted Valentine from her stupor. The van had turned round in the middle of the road. From behind the crazed windscreen, the driver stared at her for a moment, then put the van into first gear and accelerated brutally. The rear tyres spun for an instant before propelling the van forward in a cloud of smoke.

Valentine realised immediately what he was about to do. She tried to run, but couldn't – her muscles simply would not obey her. She stood frozen with fear. Her feet were stuck to the ground as if glued.

She heard a screech of brakes behind her, very near. She turned round to see a scooter come to a halt fifty centimetres from her feet, then the driver's voice, muffled by his helmet.

'Jump on!'

In shock, Valentine didn't move. The driver repeated the order: 'For fuck's sake, jump on!'

Suddenly Valentine regained the power of movement. As if

in a dream, she leaped on to the back of the scooter behind the driver.

The scooter shot off, straight for the van. Valentine shut her eyes and gripped the driver's waist, holding on with all her might.

26

Hugo Vermeer had been expecting a visit, but not quite so soon.

The woman rang at the shop door less than a minute after he'd opened. Vermeer had just raised the metal shutter and was about to have his third espresso of the morning, the one that enabled him to face the day with relative optimism, when the bell started massacring the opening notes of Purcell's 'Cold Song' – the terrifying Klaus Nomi version. The Dutchman was in his stockroom at the back of the shop, where he stored recent acquisitions while he examined them and decided whether they needed to be restored. More prosaically, it was also where he kept his coffee-maker, and a few treats to assuage mid-morning hunger pangs.

Vermeer was loath to leave his steaming cup of coffee and packet of almond *cantuccini* which he ordered from an excellent patisserie in Siena. He'd slept badly the previous night. A dose of caffeine was essential at this time of day.

Eventually his professional instincts won out, and he put his cup down beside the coffee-maker and went unhurriedly to the door.

Catching sight of the visitor from a distance, he slowed his pace even more. He winced when he saw the leather jacket and Louis Vuitton handbag with its showy Takashi Murakami logo. Someone capable of paying a shocking sum for a bag designed by an outrageously overrated artist was unlikely to appreciate the subtle elegance of a Charles Plumet dressing table, or the power of an Eugene Gaillard mahogany armchair. And from what Vermeer could see of her face behind the huge dark glasses, she looked young – no more than thirty, maybe younger. Another bad sign. Purchasing power traditionally increased with age.

Vermeer was ready to take bets: she'd spend about a quarter of an hour in the shop, insisting he open every drawer in the place for her, sliding a hand over the shagreen screen and trying to sit on Carlo Bugatti's Snail Room chair, then leave without buying a thing.

A woman, on her own, at ten in the morning, never bought anything. Ever. At best she was scouting for locations; at worst, she was passing the time until her manicure appointment. Vermeer undoubtedly had misogynistic tendencies, but this was something he'd seen confirmed many times.

Proper customers, those prepared to pay forty thousand euros for a Bernhard Pankok cherry wardrobe, came as a couple and at an hour more suited to such business – lunchtime, or maybe late afternoon, after the stockmarket had closed. Each played their part: the wife pointed languidly at something, the husband paid without complaint so as to be left in peace for a few weeks, wondering where the hell they'd put the thing. The wife coveted and the husband settled the bill. It was the basic rule, unchanging since the dawn of time, of the antique dealer's trade: women were to be seduced, and men divested of their money.

To Hugo Vermeer, therefore, a woman in the shop on her own at ten in the morning signified above all a waste of time, preventing him from quietly enjoying a *cantuccino* dunked in his espresso. Nevertheless, his look of contempt gave way to a perfect professional smile. He greeted the customer with a dignified nod.

Her response was to slip a hand inside the Louis Vuitton bag and pull out a gun, which she held to the antique dealer's forehead. The icy touch of the steel on his skin was far from pleasant,

177

but the Dutchman didn't flinch or even show surprise. A gun seemed far more menacing when held by a Chechen assassin in the pay of a Russian competitor.

Though the woman seemed to know what she was doing. She was holding the gun with a firm hand, without shaking, and maintaining the pressure of the barrel against his forehead so as not to allow him the slightest opportunity to push the gun away. She locked the shop door behind her.

'Into the back room!' she ordered.

Vermeer obeyed. The woman pushed him into the stockroom and pointed to a polished beechwood chair.

'Sit!' she barked, her tone brooking no rejoinder.

Vermeer sat. With her free hand, the woman pulled two pairs of handcuffs from her bag and attached his wrists to the armrests. The chair had unfortunately been designed for someone of a more slender build than Vermeer, so he had difficulty finding a comfortable position. Made of four bent wooden slats, the backrest pressed into him, digging into his lower back at the slightest movement. Vermeer lifted his buttocks and shifted forwards. He arched his back as much as he could, but still every breath was agony.

The chair was from a furniture collection that had been popular with the Austrian middle classes in the years leading up to the First World War. The one Vermeer had got hold of was, however, one of the very first prototypes produced by the workshops of the famous Jacob and Joseph Kohn furniture company. It had been manufactured from a design by Joseph Hoffman for a Viennese cabaret, the Fledermaus, which gave its name to the furniture collection.

Vermeer had no idea what awaited him but, if he had to die, the thought of doing so in a historically significant chair was some consolation. Meagre consolation, admittedly, but he was in no position to be choosy.

He wasn't confident, however, that it would be a quick death. The woman wouldn't pull the trigger, at least not immediately. For the time being she needed him alive. She had questions to ask him. Otherwise she'd have killed him already. Vermeer held his breath. He focused on the stranger's face, trying to guess her intentions behind the sunglasses. But the barrier of tinted glass proved impenetrable. He couldn't even make out the colour of her eyes.

He'd had no such problem with the Chechens: they didn't need to hide their faces because their victims were in no condition to identify them after they'd gone. And if they failed in their mission, it was they who ended up at the bottom of a hole with a bullet in the head. Vermeer had escaped one of them by a miracle when he was dealing in icons. Few could say the same. He hadn't wanted to tempt fate a second time, so he'd decided to put an end to his business dealings in Russia. He did not expect to be in such a position again a few years later.

After spreading the rumour on the Internet that Stern had found the *De forma mundi*, he'd been prepared to explain himself. His aim had been precisely to get the people interested in Vasalis to come out into the open. So he had been prepared to suffer some inconvenience. Actually, he'd thought he'd mainly have to endure Valentine's wrath. He'd never dreamed he'd be held at gunpoint by a stranger in his shop only two days after posting the information on his website.

He said irritably to the young woman: 'D'you mind telling me what you want? And stop pointing that bloody gun at my head! I'm cuffed to the chair. What d'you think I'm going to do? It's a genuine Fledermaus! I'm not going to pull off the armrests to get away!'

The woman seemed to take notice of this last point. She lowered the gun and placed it on the table, beside the coffee-maker and *cantuccini*.

'What do you know about Vasalis?' she asked.

'What I've read on the Internet. It's remarkable, you can find truly fascinating stuff on it. And I don't just mean porn—'

The woman stepped towards him and gave the chair a violent shove with the tip of her foot.

Vermeer fell backwards. His head hit the floor with a thud, and he felt the skin break. One of the chair slats snapped and pierced his fleshy hip. He moaned.

'I'm going to repeat the question,' said the woman. 'For the second and last time, what do you know about Vasalis? I'm warning you: failure at this next stage will probably remove your sense of humour permanently.'

Vermeer was starting to miss the Chechens. At least with them executions were tidy. They spared the furniture.

'A genuine Fledermaus!' he groaned. 'It's buggered now!'

'If I have to take all the pieces in this shop and smash them one by one, I'll do it, believe me.'

She took off her jacket and dropped it on the floor, then crouched over Vermeer. Her tight t-shirt showed off well-defined biceps.

She placed a hand on the antique dealer's jaw, then shoved his head to the side, crushing his face into the floor.

'This is my final warning,' she said, pressing on Vermeer's skull. Her voice was neutral, devoid of emotion. A chilling voice, even for someone who, like Vermeer, had known true fear, the kind that paralyses you and makes you want to retch.

Mouth pressed against the floor, Vermeer was struggling for breath because of the wooden slat stuck into his back. He still found the strength to growl: 'Go to hell, bitch. I won't tell you any more.'

'Well, that's good, I don't want to hear any more.'

Vermeer had no time to respond. A needle pierced the skin of his neck just below his ear. As if he'd been injected with a massive dose of cannabis, he instantly relaxed. His spirit seemed to float out of his body. Vermeer didn't even try to stop it, but let it roam freely. Fragments of old memories began to surface, like bubbles in a lake. Vermeer was filled with a strange sense of well-being. An ecstatic smile spread over his face.

The secondary effects soon followed. They started with a slight tingling in his feet, which moved up to his pelvis and then to the tips of his fingers. Then, without warning, the tingling became a violent electric shock. His entire body tensed, stretched to its limit in an arc. The spasm snapped one of the armrests.

Vermeer didn't even have time to mourn the Fledermaus. A blinding flash tore through his brain and he lost consciousness.

27

The scooter drove straight for the van. A fraction of a second before hitting it head-on, it swerved and slipped between two cars parked along the pavement.

The van veered, trying to knock the scooter over. It missed the back by a few centimetres and ran over Marie Gervex's lifeless body. Surprised by the scooter's manoeuvre, the driver tried to change course. He slammed on the brakes, but couldn't avoid the parked cars. With a deafening crash of crumpling metal, the van hit the wing of one car before ploughing into another.

The scooter continued on its way along the pavement. At the crossroads, it turned into a one-way street. The rider had to swerve hard to avoid hitting an oncoming car. He managed to prevent a collision, but the back wheel skidded beneath the weight of the two passengers. The scooter lurched perilously. The rider righted it with a heave and they sped away.

The scooter drove on for ten minutes, weaving through the traffic at breakneck speed even though it was now raining. It crossed the Seine, passed the Jardin des Plantes and headed towards the Place Denfert-Rochereau. At the Parc Montsouris, the rider pulled up at last and parked alongside some railings, beside another dozen or so scooters. He helped Valentine down, then pulled her by the hand into a café looking on to the park.

Dripping wet, they collapsed on to a banquette. The rider removed his helmet.

'That was a pleasant little spin,' he said.

Valentine gave a gasp of surprise as she recognised the library assistant who had brought Hélène Vailland her book at the Bibliothèque Nationale earlier that morning. It took her a few moments before she could say anything.

Eventually she murmured reluctantly: 'What were you doing back there?'

'I followed you,' said the man, as if it were obvious.

He didn't seem too troubled by the accident and the chase with the van. Valentine found his calmness and self-assurance so infuriating that it overcame her inertia. She slapped him as hard as she could. The library assistant cried out in surprise.

As one, the customers and staff of the café turned to stare. The library assistant signalled that everything was fine. He gripped Valentine's wrist. He wasn't about to let her slap him again, should the urge possess her.

'What's got into you? Those bastards tried to run you down! I just saved your life!'

Valentine looked down. She wasn't sorry she'd done it – the slap had proved to be an excellent release of tension and she felt much better. She just hated losing control like that. Dutifully, she looked vaguely ashamed and mumbled an apology, though not with any great conviction.

'I'm so sorry. The tension got to me, I needed a release.'

The library assistant seemed to accept this. He let go of her wrist and felt his slapped cheek. Now a red mark was added to the bruise already on his cheekbone. He made a face.

'Congratulations, that's quite a right hand. I hope you're feeling relaxed now.'

Valentine gave a small nod.

'Who are you?' she asked.

'My name's David Scotto.'

'Am I supposed to know you?'

'Not really, no. We've never seen each other before this morning.'

'So why did you follow me when I left the library? Are you a stalker, or something?'

David stopped rubbing his aching cheek and looked amused.

'I wish! But no, that's not it. I heard you and your friend talking about Vasalis. I'm interested in him as well. It was too much of a coincidence to let it pass without doing something. I had to speak to you. By the time I managed to get off work, you'd already left. I jumped on the scooter, but I wasn't sure how to approach you. When you went into that block of flats, I waited downstairs. I just wanted to talk to you when you came out again. I thought you'd be on your own. And then that van came hurtling at you.'

'I got a glimpse of the man at the wheel when he did a U-turn at the crossroads.'

'So did I. I wasn't expecting them back so soon.'

Valentine gave a cry of surprise. 'You know that man?'

'We bumped into each other last night. He was with another guy, a pretty aggressive type. The van driver watched while his mate dealt with me.'

David indicated the injured flesh around his eye. He went on, between clenched teeth.

'I wondered how serious their threats were. Now I know. The bastards are capable of anything.'

Valentine had a sudden flashback. She saw Marie Gervex's body vaulting over the van and crashing on to the tarmac. The most terrifying thing was the silence that accompanied her fall, as if the life had drained from her even before she hit the ground.

'Marie, she needs help,' she said with difficulty. 'We have to go back.'

'Out of the question. Did you see the accident, the way she fell to the ground? She's dead. No one could survive that. There's nothing you can do for her.'

'What about the van driver? There might still be time to stop him.'

David shrugged helplessly. 'Dream on. He must be long gone. Or else he's lurking somewhere, calmly waiting for you to rush back like an idiot, straight into his trap.'

Stunned by his reaction, Valentine stared at him wide-eyed. A look of deep disapproval appeared on her face.

'Fine. So we forget the whole thing and go home, is that it? We can't just pretend nothing's happened! We've got to go back and tell the police.'

'That's impossible. If you want to, go ahead, but count me out. Those men are dangerous. I know what I'm talking about. I had a run-in with them yesterday, and I'm not repeating it. I don't want to get myself killed. Why don't you bloody well think for a minute—'

He was interrupted by the waiter shambling up to them. 'What can I get you?' he asked absently.

'A half of beer,' said David.

'And for you, miss?'

'Nothing, thanks.'

The waiter muttered something under his breath and headed back to the bar. He returned almost immediately with a glass of beer and set it down in front of David.

'Warm and flat,' said David, once the waiter was out of earshot. 'Just the way I like it. If he's spat in it as well it'll be nigh-on perfect.' He smiled at Valentine, but she ignored his attempt at humour.

She stared at him, as if at last noticing his delicate features, dark, artfully tousled hair and winning smile. He projected an odd combination of self-assurance and fragility. Valentine reflected that a lot of women probably found it appealing. Overconfidence in a man generally left her cold. Having said that, in purely physical terms, there was no denying that David Scotto was attractive, despite the bruises. They added manly charm to his smooth face. In other circumstances, she'd probably have regarded him with less hostility.

'I don't even know who you are,' said David.

'My name's Valentine Savi. I'm an art restorer.'

'Great. D'you work in a museum?'

Valentine didn't feel like recounting her life story to a complete stranger, so she opted for a simplified version of reality.

'I'm working for a private foundation at the moment.'

David looked at her enquiringly.

'That's all I can tell you,' she said, thinking of the confidentiality clause she'd signed.

But there was nothing in the contract about risking her life. Marie Gervex's murder had just changed the rules of the game. Valentine bit her lip.

'Oh, what the hell . . .' she said. 'Have you heard of Elias Stern?'

'The art dealer? He's dead, isn't he?'

'No.'

David seemed disappointed by the news.

'Why are you interested in Vasalis?' asked Valentine.

'I'm doing my PhD on him. Well I was, until the beginning of the week.'

'Why have you stopped?'

'My supervisor had the brilliant idea of jumping out of his office window. And as the Dean doesn't hold me in very high esteem, to put it mildly, I'm going to be chucked out of the Sorbonne any day. So the past tense seemed appropriate.'

He indicated Valentine's handbag. 'Can I see the picture you were showing your friend at the library?'

'Yes, of course.' She unfolded the photograph of the cover board and handed it to him.

'Do you think this might have anything to do with the *De forma mundi*?'

'I'm more and more convinced that it does.'

'Can you tell me where you got this?'

'Stern hired me to restore this codex. He believes it's a manuscript of the *De forma mundi*. These marks of provenance would seem to prove it.'

David Scotto peered at the picture. He smiled wryly. 'I've spent the past five years searching for this book. And now that I've packed in my thesis, I've found it. Can you believe it?'

Pensively, he handed back the photograph.

'The van driver . . .' said Valentine after a moment's silence. 'You said you saw him for the first time last night. What happened?'

David recounted the events of the previous evening. He passed quickly over the fact of being beaten up in the toilets, and said nothing at all about throwing up.

Valentine listened in silence, gazing into the distance. When David came to the reason for the attack, she suddenly emerged from her trance.

She interrupted brusquely: 'Wait a minute . . . What kind of illumination did they tell you to find?'

'That's the problem. They had no idea themselves. They just said it belonged to Albert Cadas, my supervisor. If I don't get hold of it, I'm going to be in big trouble. Now I know they won't think twice about killing me. That doesn't seem to bother you too much.'

Valentine was staring at him intently. There was elation in her eyes.

'I think I know the illumination they meant,' she said. 'If I'm right, it would be an amazing coincidence.'

'After everything I've been through in the past two days, I don't think I believe in coincidences any more. I just know one thing: you and I are in one hell of a mess. So from now on anything's worth considering, however crazy. What do you have in mind?'

'The codex I've been working on is incomplete. The first page is missing. There are the remains of an illumination at the edge, where it's been cut out.'

'You mean Cadas got hold of a fragment of the *De forma mundi*?'

'It's a bit more complicated than that.'

'What do you mean?'

'The manuscript is a palimpsest. Assuming Vasalis's treatise really is there, it's illegible in its present state. If your professor got hold of the first page of the codex, as I think he did, he probably couldn't get anything from it. The illumination was done after the manuscript was reused. The *De forma mundi* had already been erased and overwritten by then. To find it again, first you'd have to remove the two successive layers of paint, then ink. It would be terribly difficult.'

David gulped the last of his beer and scratched his chin with a look of puzzlement.

'Leave that aside for the moment. Assuming Cadas really did find the missing page, where did he get it?'

'I have no idea,' said Valentine. 'As far as I know, the page disappeared in the nineteenth century. It was sent to Russia by someone called Tischendorf, and became part of the imperial collections. It hasn't been seen since the October Revolution.'

'Be that as it may, Cadas seemed very excited by the discovery. With good reason: after a lifetime of research, he'd found proof of the existence of the *De forma mundi* at last. But if so, he had no reason to commit suicide.'

'You're sure it really was suicide?'

'No one's in any doubt. The police aren't even investigating.'

Valentine's euphoria evaporated. 'It's incomprehensible,' she concluded glumly.

David grabbed his helmet and stood up.

'What are you doing?'

'This place is depressing. Let's get out of here. Time to pay Albert Cadas's office a little visit.'

28

Hidden in a doorway, Sorel watched the scooter speed away. If he'd wanted, he could have stopped the van driver before he acted. But instinct had prompted him not to intervene. Marie Gervex had played her part to perfection. She'd done everything he'd hoped. She'd been an important chess piece but, unfortunately for her, the game had moved on. Sorel had had no qualms about sacrificing her. She wouldn't be enjoying the two hundred thousand euros the Foundation had officially paid her for the codex. Now that she was dead, Sorel was already working out how to transfer the money to an offshore account in his name. It would be a shame if no one made the most of all that cash.

The one remaining annoyance was the restorer. It would have been simpler if she too had ended up beneath the wheels of the van. Sorel still couldn't understand why Stern was so besotted with the girl. No one was asking him to prove that the manuscript really held Vasalis's text. Pretending to restore it would have been sufficient. Recruiting Valentine Savi had been a mistake. Yet another mistake. If only she hadn't stepped back when the van came hurtling out of nowhere, the problem would have been solved.

Sorel had observed the entire scene with the keen eye of an expert, analysing the situation and noting errors and shortcomings in the execution of the plan. His conclusion was unequivocal: it had been an unmitigated disaster. Seeing a

189

professional fail so lamentably made Sorel furious. He had remained calm and focused throughout, of course, but deep down he was seething with rage.

From start to finish, the van driver had proved abysmally incompetent. First of all, his choice of vehicle had been idiotic. To increase the violence of the impact, he'd opted for an old model, with none of the recent pedestrian-safety features, such as flexible bumpers, a deformable bonnet and recessed headlights. But the lack of power steering meant he hadn't been able to turn the wheel quickly enough either to hit the scooter or to avoid the parked cars.

A newer model would certainly have produced less spectacular results. There wouldn't have been such an abundance of blood and broken limbs, but the internal injuries would still have been serious enough to ensure the victim's death. At worst, she'd have ended up in hospital and died after a few days without regaining consciousness. The police would have gone through the motions of an investigation. Then they'd have put it down to reckless driving and buried the file after a week or two, which would have suited everyone.

That was the trouble with amateurs: they confused efficiency with display. They wanted at all costs to show the boss they'd done a good job.

The real problem wasn't eliminating the target. Anyone could kill. In physical terms, it wasn't particularly difficult. The human body was an unstable structure vulnerable to collapse. Prisons were full of people who'd discovered by accident how easy murder was. The real problem was killing with certainty, regardless of external factors. One didn't call in people like Sorel just because of their mastery of the techniques of assassination. They were hired because they could handle the unexpected. They were never overwhelmed by events. They analysed the facts, assessed the situation and invariably made the right decision.

The van driver hadn't known what to do when the scooter appeared. The arrogant bastard had got what he deserved.

Sorel waited for the scooter to disappear round the corner before stepping from his hiding place. Forty seconds at most had elapsed since Marie Gervex's death. The street was still echoing to the sound of the scooter's engine. Sorel could almost smell the blood on the tarmac.

He walked towards the van with a measured, almost nonchalant step. From a distance, he might have been taken for a curious bystander drawn by the noise of the accident. In fact, he was carefully scanning the entire area. No one could enter his zone of security without him seeing.

He walked on, past the corpse lying in the middle of the street. At least the van driver had permanently eliminated the primary target. He'd even managed to crush the face when he ran over the body a second time. With luck, the police would take a few days to identify the bloody pulp. A point in the driver's favour, though Sorel strongly suspected that it had not been deliberate. In a rush of magnanimity, he decided to give him the benefit of the doubt.

The moron had made a mess of everything else, though. He'd even managed to knock himself out on the windscreen when the van crashed into the parked cars. Sorel would bet he wasn't wearing a seat belt. Too sure of himself, the stupid bastard. Hadn't even bothered to weigh up the risks. You really had to be trying to be that clumsy.

The van's engine was still running. Sorel opened the passenger door and slid into the cabin. The driver was slumped over the wheel.

Sorel took a gun from the holster under his jacket. He pressed the short barrel of his IMI Jericho 941 – an Israeli weapon nicknamed the Baby Eagle because of its compact size – to the nape of the wounded man's neck. Brutally, he dug it some way into the flesh, to make sure the unconsciousness was genuine.

The driver moaned, but didn't move. His forehead was resting on the steering-wheel hub. A small pool of blood had already gathered on the carpet in front of the pedals.

'Fucking amateur,' muttered Sorel as he pulled the trigger of his Baby Eagle.

The sound of the shot was contained within the small cabin. The driver made a gurgling noise as he died, twitched briefly, then was still, eyes fixed on the gear lever. The Baby Eagle was a good gun, efficient and discreet. The Israelis really knew how to make weapons.

Sorel grabbed the body by the thighs and heaved it into the back of the van. Then he took its place and, quickly wiping the blood and brain matter from the wheel, put the van into reverse.

Before leaving, he checked that there were still no witnesses around. He could see none. This was as he hoped, for his urge to kill had passed.

A raindrop fell on the windscreen, then another. Soon there was a violent downpour, which would wash away all traces and deter the neighbours from coming out of their houses.

Sorel could feel satisfied. Even the weather was favouring him. Luck always smiled on the meticulous. Sorel didn't depend on it on a mission, but it never hurt.

Everything was working out for the best. This assessment made Sorel euphoric. For once, he allowed himself to bend the rules of prudence, which he usually followed to the letter. A broad smile on his lips, he turned the wheel slightly so as to direct the van at Marie Gervex's body, and pressed the accelerator pedal.

A revolting sucking sound came from beneath the van as the front wheels cleared the obstacle, but the suspension absorbed most of the impact. The vehicle rose only slightly, as if it had just driven over an uneven patch in the road.

The human body was such a fragile thing. It was pathetic. Anyone would think man had been designed to be killed.

29

David parked the scooter in a no-parking zone, between the chapel of the Sorbonne and the entrance to the École des Chartes.

'Isn't it risky leaving it here?' asked Valentine.

David bent down to fit a lock to the back wheel.

'Sometimes you just have to live dangerously. Come on.' He set off quickly towards the university entrance. 'Have you got a business card with you?'

'I think I've still got my old pass from the Louvre. But it's expired.'

'Who cares? They don't check that kind of thing. Take it out.'

Valentine rummaged through her purse as she walked. She pulled out a laminated card with a photograph of her looking a few years younger. She showed it to David.

'Will this do?'

He nodded. 'If the security guards make a fuss, just give them a sexy smile. They love pretty girls. That's why they do the job. Shame you're not wearing a miniskirt.'

'Can you please stop it?'

'Stop what?'

'Your stupid comments. I'm not in the mood. In the past two days I've lost my job and someone's tried to run me over. And let's draw a veil over your driving. Your bloody scooter's ruined my back. Give it a rest, will you?'

David would have liked to make a suitable riposte but there was no time. They were at the entrance. He presented his student card and Valentine showed her Louvre pass, with a finger over the expiry date. Too busy to check thoroughly, the guards waved them through without even looking at the cards.

There was an ambulance outside the library. It pulled away, sirens blaring, just as David and Valentine entered the courtyard. They stepped aside to let it pass, then headed towards a building on one side of the courtyard. They took the stairs up to the top floor.

David led Valentine to a door without a name plaque.

'Where are we?' she asked.

'This is Albert Cadas's office.'

She expressed no surprise, simply stating the obvious: 'It seems to be locked.'

'Are you sure? I don't think so.'

Confidently, David turned the handle while giving the door a shove with his shoulder, close to the frame. With a sharp click, the bolt snapped out of the plate and slid back into the casing.

'That's how Cadas opened the door when he forgot his keys,' David explained. 'You just have to get the knack. Up here, every-thing's a period piece. Nothing's changed since the nineteenth century. Funds always run out well before they get to these upper floors.'

He pushed the door open and went inside.

Valentine didn't move. 'This is really stupid. What if someone catches us?'

'Have you got a better idea? I don't intend to let those thugs kill me without doing something. I want to find the illumination before they come back for it. Hurry up, come in! You can't stay out there.'

Valentine obeyed. David closed the door quietly.

Nothing had been touched since the death of the old professor. His coat was where he'd left it, folded over the back of a chair. Someone had simply closed the window he'd jumped from.

There was a strange feel to the room. It was as if Albert Cadas had only just left, as if he'd popped out to give a class or check a book in the library. It was like being in one of those writer's studies where everything is preserved just as it was at the time of the occupant's death, and fetishistic visitors come to absorb the atmosphere. Time seemed to have stood still in there.

Valentine had the unpleasant feeling of being in a mausoleum. She shivered, uneasy.

'This is creepy. It feels like he's about to come back any minute.'

'I wish he would. It would really help me out. Do you want to see the blood in the courtyard so you can be sure he really is dead?'

Valentine shook her head. 'No, really, thanks.'

'So let's not waste any more time,' said David. 'Let's get to work. If Cadas found the missing page from your codex, he'd probably have kept it here. I'll take this side of the room, you take the other, by the window.'

He didn't wait for Valentine to reply but went straight to the metal cabinet where his supervisor kept the books to which he was most deeply attached. Not only was it unlocked, which was quite uncharacteristic, but the doors were ajar.

This puzzled David: there was nothing of great value in the cabinet, but Albert Cadas was a cautious man. He didn't even trust the reinforced door to his apartment, preferring to store his rare books within the precincts of the Sorbonne. Each evening, before leaving, he checked that the padlock was secured and locked. He wouldn't deviate from this ritual for anything. Like most habits, this one seemed laughable, since the office door was so easy to force open. David had pointed this out many times, but his supervisor was beyond the age of changing his ways. And he would never have dreamed that someone might dare to defile his sanctuary. The Sorbonne was not like other places.

But his supervisor's absolute faith did not explain the open cabinet. It was most unlike Albert Cadas to leave it unlocked.

The urge to die must have been really pressing for him to drop everything like that. And now that David had thought about it, it was most unlike him to commit suicide.

David pulled open the doors of the metal cabinet. Immediately he noticed a gap in the centre of the middle shelf, right in front of him. Over time, Cadas had got used to allowing David free access to his books whenever he needed, so David was quite familiar with the contents of the cabinet. It was the first time he'd seen a space between the two crowning glories of the collection, a copy of Euclid's *Elements* dating from 1482, and the six volumes of the *Letters* of St Augustine, published in Paris at the beginning of the eighteenth century and bound in rather dubious taste, in lemon-yellow morocco leather.

David made a quick visual inventory of the books. From what he could remember, none was missing.

So Albert Cadas must have put something there that David was not familiar with. The space wasn't large enough for a book. A box a couple of centimetres thick, on the other hand, designed to protect a page of parchment, for instance, would fit easily.

'There was something here,' he said, as much to himself as to Valentine. 'It might have been the illuminated leaf. Anyway, if it was here, it's disappeared. What about you? Found anything interesting over there?'

'Nothing special. A lot of dust and stacks of old papers everywhere. Seems like tidying up was an alien concept to your supervisor.'

'You should have seen his flat. It's lucky he never got married. No one could have put up with it. I've never met anyone as shambolic.'

'What's this?'

Valentine pointed to a small cardboard folder on the desk. Though surrounded by an improbable mass of books, photocopies and students' essays, it lay in the middle of an empty space some fifty centimetres wide. It was the only thing that seemed to have a set place in the midst of all the chaos. The words

BROTHERHOOD OF THE SORBONNE were written in red felt pen on the spine.

'Nothing important,' said David. 'Don't waste your time on it.'

Valentine ignored him and picked up the folder. She sat down on the nearest chair, making sure not to lean against the coat the old professor had hung over it before he had jumped. Removing the elastic bands from the folder, she took out a sheaf of papers covered in Albert Cadas's nervous hand and began leafing through them.

'What are you doing?' intervened David. 'We haven't got time for reading. Someone's going to find us.'

'You forced open the door and now you're worried? You've changed your tune!'

Nevertheless, Valentine put the papers back in the folder. She closed it and, holding it sideways, read aloud the title on the spine: 'The Brotherhood of the Sorbonne – what's that?'

David shrugged, annoyed. 'Cadas had a number of obsessions. That was one of them. A load of crap, if you want my opinion. Drop it, believe me. There's more urgent stuff for us to attend to.'

'Don't you think I'm old enough to judge for myself? Well? What is it?'

'Don't you ever listen to anyone?'

'I listen to good advice and, above all, those who dispense it. And?'

David relented. He closed the cabinet and replaced the padlock, without locking it, and went over to Valentine.

He cleared a corner of the table with his arm. A precariously balanced pile of papers fell to the floor.

'Shit!' he grumbled.

He crouched to retrieve them but gave up, daunted by the extent of the mess. He stood up again, nudged the nearest papers out of the way with his foot and perched on the desk. He picked up a pen and started playing with it, spinning it back and forth in his fingers.

Valentine shot him a furious glance. 'Have you quite finished?'

David put the pen down. By way of protest, he raised his eyes to heaven and groaned before launching into the explanation Valentine had requested.

'Good old Cadas had very fixed ideas. He started obsessing about this Brotherhood of the Sorbonne years ago – thirty, at least. I don't know who put it into his head. He was completely fixated on it. When he started rambling on about it, there was no stopping him.'

'Does this Brotherhood have a connection with Vasalis?'

'Yes, of course, otherwise Cadas would never have taken an interest in it. Vasalis was the only thing in life he could get fired up about. He really couldn't give a damn about anything else. He named it "Brotherhood" on a romantic whim, I think. As far as I could tell, it was more like a kind of club of men who wanted to rescue Vasalis from oblivion.'

'I thought the Pope had done all he could to make him disappear.'

'Precisely. To Cadas, this was the most convincing argument: in the face of such a strong will to eradicate it, all memory of Vasalis should have been wiped out, almost automatically. His reasoning was that any other outcome would have been absurd. The only explanation as to why he hadn't been forgotten was that, since the Middle Ages, a resistance movement had sprung up to perpetuate his memory.'

'Cadas must have had some evidence for this.'

David sniggered contemptuously. 'Well, that's the problem. There's no mention of Vasalis in any ancient text. His name only reappeared when Heiberg published his article about the Metochion manuscript. Heiberg didn't discover it all on his own. He simply wrote down an old legend that had been passed down by word of mouth by the monks for centuries. They handed him a fantastic story on a plate: a hero murdered by an unjust power, a nasty pope, a brilliant book vanished without trace. Heiberg had all the ingredients to pull off quite a coup, and it succeeded beyond his wildest dreams. The myth was born because of him.'

His face suddenly froze, as if he'd just realised something important. 'Wait a minute . . . Your codex – it's the one from the Metochion, isn't it?'

Valentine nodded.

'Unbelievable . . . How did you find it? Everyone thought it had been destroyed!'

'Obviously everyone was wrong.'

She paused briefly before continuing. 'There's something I don't understand. What did Cadas base his theory on? I've read a load of articles about Vasalis, but I've never heard about this Brotherhood business. What were his sources?'

'He compiled a corpus of texts in which certain expressions recur in identical form, like a sort of code. To be honest, the passages are so obscure you can make them mean almost anything if you extrapolate a bit. Cadas also noticed that the authors of the texts had all been at the Sorbonne at some stage in their lives, either as students or teachers. Hence the name he gave their little association.'

Valentine looked puzzled. 'It's almost too neat.'

'Wait, I've kept the best till last. Pass me the folder.'

He took the cardboard folder Valentine handed to him. He removed the ties, flicked through the first few pages and pulled out a sheet with a list of names typed on it.

'Here's the list of the merry members of the club, as identified by Cadas. Hold on tight, it'll blow your mind.'

Valentine looked stunned as she read through the list. After a moment, she looked up and stared at David incredulously.

'Not bad, eh?' he said. 'Villon, Montaigne, Erasmus, Guizot, Cousin, Ozanam . . . the crème de la crème. No lack of taste. You can see why Cadas never published anything about the Brotherhood. No one would have believed him. It's too huge.'

David's explanation was like a revelation to Valentine. It all fitted.

Cadas's theory was plausible, but David Scotto couldn't know this, as he hadn't seen the drawing of Vasalis with Dante.

Botticelli's sketch proved that, from the fifteenth century on, artists and intellectuals were perpetuating Vasalis's memory. But it could also be read as a metaphor for the risks involved. Challenging papal authority came at a price. You had to be prepared, like Dante, to plunge into the depths of the Inferno.

Valentine was about to tell David all of this when a voice behind her got in first.

'You're forgetting Dante, young man. Quite unforgivable in a student of your calibre. And would you mind telling me what the hell you're doing in here?'

David leaped to his feet and stared at the door. His face turned pale. He couldn't have appeared more shocked if he'd seen a ghost.

The man standing in the doorway, however, was very much alive, and he looked furious.

30

Despite his best efforts, Hugo Vermeer couldn't open his eyelids. And a rolling motion turning his insides upside-down made him feel as if he were on a ship in the middle of a storm.

Memories surfaced one after another. Intermittently at first, in searing flashes, then they came rushing at him.

It had started with a few notes of music. Purcell murdered by Klaus Nomi. Pretentiousness defused by irony. Vermeer himself summed up in a simple tune. The notes floated in his head for a while, before fading gradually as if, little by little, someone were turning down the volume.

The girl only appeared once there was absolute silence. She approached from afar, just a blurred outline. Young, pretty. Really pretty, with her Louis Vuitton handbag and impenetrable dark glasses. The gun. The cold rim of the barrel against his forehead. Fear.

No, not fear. Not immediately. Later, yes, but not yet. Surprise, questions, fear, in that order.

The back of his head striking the floor. Pain. The needle in his neck. The injection. The flash. The armchair cracking as it broke. More pain. Intense, raging even. Relief at last as darkness engulfed everything.

Gradually, the glue on his eyelids began to dissolve. The pitching and rolling, on the other hand, did not stop. It grew even worse, probably as some sort of compensatory effect. Now, at least, Vermeer was beginning to perceive the outside world. For the time being only a faint light penetrated his closed eyelids.

His body was eliminating the chemical cocktail the girl had given him. He felt neural connections begin to fire again. This wasn't necessarily a good thing. He could now feel pain in his back, where the splinter of wood from the defunct Fledermaus had pierced it. The pain grew worse and worse. Bearable, but highly unpleasant. The girl had really messed with him.

She should have killed him when she had the chance. Vermeer didn't give a damn about pain and humiliation. He'd been through it before. He could live with it. But the Fledermaus, that was another matter. He'd make her pay. That was a promise, and Hugo Vermeer always kept his word.

He groaned with pain and rage.

'How are you feeling, Mr Vermeer?' The voice reverberated in his head, as if played on Jimi Hendrix's guitar at the peak of his musical powers, and his drug use, which amounted to the same thing.

He heard the voice again, still badly distorted in his head.

'Please excuse our rather brutal ways. We thought you'd refuse to attend this meeting if we weren't persuasive.'

'Bastards . . .'

Vermeer's tongue was furred. He was having trouble moving it inside his numb mouth. He couldn't keep his Dutch accent in check as well as usual.

'What have you injected me with?'

'Nothing too nasty. A chemical commonly used by government agencies. It's already starting to break down. It'll be out of your bloodstream in a few hours. The unpleasant side-effects won't last much longer.'

The voice became clearer. It belonged to an elderly man.

'Why?' Vermeer asked simply.

'I've told you. I want to ask you a few questions.'

'Who are you?'

'Why don't you try to see for yourself, Mr Vermeer? Open your eyes. You can do that now, can't you?'

Without much conviction, Vermeer ordered his eyelids to open. They obeyed lazily. A blinding light surged between them, burning his retinas.

'Shit . . .' Vermeer moaned, and closed his eyes again.

He repeated the attempt. The pain eased, ceasing altogether after a moment. Blurred at first, the outside world grew more distinct.

First he saw a headrest in front of him, then the outline of a car seat. He slid his hands down his legs until they rested on leather. A car. That explained the rolling and the sensation of movement.

'Can you see me?'

Vermeer turned towards the man and nodded.

'Do you know who I am?'

'Of course I do, Mr Stern. I've seen old photos of you. You haven't changed much in five years.'

'The privilege of age. Past a certain age, one's inexorable decline is largely complete. The process of decay plateaus, one might say. It's unfortunate, but it happens to all of us.'

The old man was to his left. They were sitting in the back of a limousine – a German car, Vermeer thought. A BMW or a Mercedes; probably the latter.

'Your killer isn't here?'

'Nora? No, she's gone back. I no longer needed her.'

'Pity. With her talents, we could have got up to something kinky.'

'I can understand your anger. I had no choice but to send Nora. Her methods are spectacular rather than truly dangerous. And don't worry, you'll be compensated for the Fledermaus. Though, for your information, it was a fake. I sold the original series myself to an American collector a few years after the war. It's now in a house near Washington. Your piece was a copy. But we'll pay you the price of a genuine one.'

'So life is beautiful, is that it? All is forgiven, and we start from scratch as if nothing had happened?'

'Your reputation is well deserved, Mr Vermeer. You're as sour-tempered as they say.'

A ferocious glint appeared in Vermeer's eyes. 'Just wait till I see that girl again. You'll find that I'm far worse than my reputation.'

Elias Stern adopted the air of an indulgent grandfather dealing with a naughty child.

'Come now . . . What's done is done. Let's not dwell on it needlessly.'

'Why were you so keen to see me?'

'Your Internet article was rather inopportune. I want to ask you some questions about it.'

'The codex, eh? You want to know how I knew you had it.'

Stern shook his head. 'Unnecessary. I know that already. My question is rather, why? Why react so hastily? Vasalis is far removed from your usual concerns. He only interests a few specialists. The public at large couldn't give a damn.'

'They'll give a damn if Valentine can prove that you've got hold of the manuscript of the *De forma mundi*.'

'Valentine has only made a few preliminary observations. She hasn't found anything definite yet. But I can't understand your hurry, Mr Vermeer. It's not like you. Beneath that casual manner you take your job very seriously. You check your information before putting it online. You never post mere suppositions.'

'You seem well informed.'

'I have to admit I find your website highly entertaining. You have a rare talent for dredging up the murkiest things. I know several people whom you've driven quite berserk. We've taken an interest in you for some time. We have a very fat file on you.'

'Who is this "we"? Your bloody Foundation? Let's talk about that. I have a few questions of my own. It's all a bit unclear. At the moment it's just a hunch, but I'm sure that if I dug around I'd find some interesting stuff. About the source of your funding, for instance.'

Stern greeted Vermeer's threat calmly. He continued with his line of questioning without bothering to defend himself.

'Your interest in Vasalis is nothing new, is it? I want to know why you're so fascinated by him.'

'It's a personal matter,' said Vermeer.

'Which you've made a public matter with your tactics. You've put the Foundation at risk. Valentine is in danger because of you.'

'You're out of your mind.'

'Someone paid us a visit yesterday afternoon. They tried to steal the codex.'

'That's rubbish! I put the article online less than two days ago. Your visitor must already have known you had the manuscript. He didn't need to go to my site.'

'We considered that possibility. But be that as it may, things have speeded up since you posted your article. The person who sold us the manuscript was murdered just under an hour ago. Valentine was with her when it happened. She could have been hurt. She was lucky to escape unharmed.'

The news hit Vermeer full in the face. He went as white as a sheet.

'Is she all right?' he asked, a lump in his throat.

'To tell you the truth, I have no idea. She survived the attack, but disappeared afterwards. I've only just heard myself. Several Foundation employees are looking for her.'

'Have you tried her mobile?'

'It's switched off, and she hasn't gone home. I sent Nora to her flat. There was no one there.'

Stern fell silent. He seemed genuinely upset. He turned away and stared out of the window.

'I'm worried about her,' he said, apparently hypnotised by the buildings as they rushed past. 'I couldn't give a damn about you, Vermeer. You're an insignificant little crook, whatever you think. You can do all the wheeling and dealing you like, I couldn't care less. But I feel responsible for what's happened to Valentine. I've involved her in a game that's getting away from me. I didn't expect things to go this far.'

'So what happens now?'

'I need information from you so I can get her out of this,' Stern said. 'This isn't the kind of conversation I imagined us having when I sent Nora to your shop. But the situation has changed. We now have a common interest. So let's put all our cards on the table.'

Vermeer didn't have to think. 'All right, let's go to your house. I'll tell you everything I know about Vasalis.'

Stern leaned forward. He tapped on the chauffeur's shoulder. 'Take us back to the house, please, Franck.'

The chauffeur turned off on to the Boulevard Périphérique and accelerated, quickly reaching the speed limit. Behind the tinted windows of the Mercedes, the cityscape flashed past.

Vermeer's head was now quite clear. The drug had completely worn off. Perfect timing. He was going to need his wits about him to handle this situation. He decided to set aside his grudge against Stern and his killer.

Only temporarily, of course. Just for the time it took to get Valentine out of this mess. Hugo Vermeer wasn't the type to forget his resentment for very long. It must have been the way he was brought up.

31

Raymond Agostini didn't seem prepared to move. He stood in the doorway to the office where his old friend had spent most of his career, staring at the two intruders. As they kept silent, he repeated his question, less aggressively this time.

'What are you two doing here?'

Valentine got up. She took a step towards David and stood beside him, as if to present a united front.

But David drew no strength from this. He stood next to the desk as if paralysed, holding his breath, waiting to see how the situation would unfold.

'How did you get in?' continued the professor of Ancient Greek.

Raymond Agostini was short, balding and sported a dark goatee flecked with white. His dozen or so excess kilos, concentrated around his middle, testified to the fact that he had long ago given up on staying in shape.

Standing at the door, he folded his arms, clearly showing that he had no intention of moving until he'd received a satisfactory answer.

'The door was open,' David blurted out at last, his voice unsteady.

'I like you, Scotto, but don't push your luck. I was here when the Dean locked it yesterday. He took Albert's keys with him, the ones that were in his coat pocket. Given the state of your relationship with the Dean, I doubt he entrusted them to you. I therefore conclude that you forced open the door. Do you realise how serious that is?'

David didn't reply. Beads of sweat formed on his forehead, around his hairline.

'You've picked a poor time to take up burglary,' Agostini went on. 'After the latest tragedy to strike the university, the police are on the alert.'

David and Valentine stared at him, bemused.

'Another member of staff died this morning,' the professor explained.

'Who?' asked David.

'Joseph Fargue. He fell down the stairs outside the Research Centre. He fractured his skull. It was a stupid accident.'

David couldn't believe it. 'Fargue? But the guy practically lived here!'

Agostini shrugged. 'What can you do? It's the law of series. When fate catches you, it won't let go easily. Having said that, I'm still waiting for you to tell me what you're doing here, and I hope for your sakes that you have a convincing explanation. What on earth possessed you?'

'It's true, we broke in,' admitted Valentine. 'But we have a good reason. We need to check something. It may be connected with Albert Cadas's death. We had no choice.'

Agostini stared at her, puzzled, but didn't ask who she was.

'As you'll appreciate, I'm not satisfied with your explanation. Could you be more specific? What exactly are you looking for?'

'It's a long, complicated story,' said Valentine.

'Young lady, I've spent the last forty years of my life studying the *Iliad*. I love long, complicated stories. I'm ready to listen to yours. Then I'll decide whether the Dean should hear of this idiocy.'

Valentine looked at David, but he simply shrugged. In return she raised her eyes to heaven with a look of exasperation. The little pantomime lasted some time, neither of them deciding to speak.

Agostini eventually lost patience. 'Right, well, while you decide, I'm going to my office to do some filing. Come and meet me there. And please put everything back as it was.'

He turned round and walked away down the corridor.

David waited for Agostini's round figure to disappear before relaxing. The colour returned to his cheeks. He wiped the sweat from his forehead with his sleeve, then bent down to gather the papers that were scattered over the floor.

'Who was that?' asked Valentine, helping him.

'His name's Raymond Agostini. He teaches Ancient Greek. He's a dinosaur. I think he arrived around the same time as Cadas.'

'Can we trust him?'

'He and Cadas were old friends. Agostini was the only person in the whole place who seemed upset about his suicide.'

'D'you think he knows about the illumination?'

'If Cadas mentioned it to anyone, it would be him. We could give it a try.'

David stacked the papers neatly, placed them on the desk and headed towards the door.

'Coming?'

'Do I have a choice?'

'I doubt it. Until we understand why Cadas killed himself, we won't know why that guy in the van was after you. You could go home and try to forget about the whole business, but I don't think they'll leave you alone.'

He gave Valentine a smile that was meant to be winning.

'And another thing . . . I'm fed up with all these violent deaths. I wouldn't want a pretty girl like you to disappear from circulation.'

The compliment was worthy of a bad TV soap. In different circumstances, Valentine would have told him where to go, but the morning's events had exhausted her.

She waved him away wearily. 'You go ahead. I need to pull

myself together after all that's happened. I'll come and join you in a few minutes.'

'I'll wait here,' protested David.

'I'd like to be on my own for a bit. I need to do some girl stuff. You know, make-up, that kind of thing.'

But David didn't want to leave without pressing on down the path started by his first compliment.

'OK, I'm going. But you don't always have to be so formal with me, you know.'

Valentine couldn't really see the connection between his leaving and this sudden desire for familiarity, but to get rid of him, she agreed, and even gave him the pretence of a smile.

'Fine. Now off you go.'

David looked delighted. 'So you'll come and join me when you're ready?'

'Out!' commanded Valentine wearily but firmly.

David left at last.

Valentine heard him knock on a door at the other end of the corridor. He said a few words she couldn't make out, then the door closed and there was silence.

She opened her bag, took out a small mirror and touched up her make-up. As she was putting everything away, without thinking she slid the folder containing the documents about the Brotherhood of the Sorbonne into her bag. She would never have thought herself capable of such a thing, any more than breaking into a dead man's office or hurtling across Paris in the pouring rain on the back of a scooter driven by a perfect stranger. It seemed that the past two days spent chasing after Vasalis had changed her.

She shut her bag and went to join David in Raymond Agostini's office.

32

Valentine gave Raymond Agostini a cautious account of recent events. She didn't mention Elias Stern, passed over the attempted theft and left out Marie Gervex's murder, simply describing how the van had attempted to run her down and how David had rescued her. As David listened to this version of the story, his face took on a variety of hues, from scarlet to white, settling finally at a rather unnatural pinkish tone. He was careful not to intervene, and let her finish without correcting or interrupting. Valentine was aware that she was lying by omission, or even out-and-out lying, but her new conscience could put up with it. The changes in her weren't all bad.

Her account was riddled with gaps and inconsistencies, but Raymond Agostini didn't seem to notice anything unusual. He listened patiently to the end, hands folded beneath his chin.

'Albert never mentioned an illuminated leaf to me,' he said when she'd finished. 'I'm sorry, I can't help. I know nothing about it.'

His two visitors were visibly disappointed.

'Are you sure?' insisted David.

'Absolutely. Albert and I no longer discussed Vasalis much. Like everyone else, I'd ended up tiring of his quest. You must have been the only person who was always willing to listen to him, Scotto. I'm not criticising you. You were his PhD student. You were too close to him to be objective about his work.'

'But what about the manuscript Valentine is examining?' objected David.

'Despite what you've told me, I still don't believe a copy of the *De forma mundi* could have survived. Miracles like that don't happen.'

David gave up. He sat hunched sullenly in his chair.

'Are you going to tell the Dean about our visit?' Valentine asked Agostini.

The professor shook his head. 'I doubt he'd be interested. The Dean is a very busy man. I wouldn't want to take up his time with such a trifle. What do you think?'

Valentine looked at him gratefully. 'Thank you.'

'No problem. But don't go near that office again, all right? Albert is dead. Let's let him rest in peace for now. We'll deal with his affairs later on.'

He turned to David. 'I can understand you clutching at straws. Your thesis is well advanced, and you'd like to finish it. It's perfectly understandable. You have my esteem, and even my friendship, so I'm going to speak plainly: Albert was the only one who believed you'd succeed. No one else will agree to take over from him. You could spend the rest of your life chasing after Vasalis, and you'd never find anything. Albert wasted his life on that nonsense. His suicide is proof of his failure.'

He uncrossed his hands and placed them before him on the desk, to emphasise his point.

'There's nothing to hope for, Scotto. Don't lose yourself like Albert did in this pointless search. I don't want you to end up like him. There's been enough waste already.'

Despite the bluntness of these words, David tried to put on a brave front.

'I understand,' he murmured.

'If you like, we could try to find a new subject for your thesis. Some of your research might be salvageable. You wouldn't have to start from scratch. In a year, two at most, you could get it finished. Think about it.'

David didn't reply. He stared at the blank wall in front of him, looking as if he'd just been slapped.

'What are you going to do now?' Agostini asked Valentine.

'I'm not sure. David doesn't think I should go home straight away.'

David perked up. 'You could stay at my flat for a few days, until everything blows over.'

Valentine shook her head. 'That's very sweet of you, but I'd rather not. I'd like to talk all this over with a close friend of mine. He'll know what to do.'

David looked disappointed. 'OK, fine.'

He jotted his phone number on a piece of paper and handed it to her.

'If you want to get hold of me . . . You never know. One day we'll look back and laugh, and reminisce about this.'

'I'm sure we will,' said Valentine, slipping the paper into her pocket. 'In the meantime, learn how to ride a scooter properly.'

David tried to smile, but his heart wasn't in it. Looking into her eyes, he said: 'Take care of yourself. The big bad wolf might still be lurking. Don't let him gobble you up.'

'Don't worry. I'm too tough to chew. And thanks again for everything, you know, earlier.'

'You're welcome. Next time, look both ways before crossing.'

Valentine said goodbye to Raymond Agostini before leaving the room. The lecturer nodded in reply.

'Let me know if by any chance your manuscript does turn out to be the *De forma mundi*.'

'So you believe in miracles now, do you?' asked Valentine with a sardonic smile.

'As Homer said, "Miracles are honey to pure spirits." Who am I to contradict him?'

33

'Where the hell are you?'

Almost a roar, Hugo Vermeer's voice burst from the handset. A hint of concern, however, was audible in his imperious tone.

Valentine objected weakly: 'Listen, Hugo, you don't have to deafen me. I've had a hard day and—'

'I know. Where are you?' he interrupted.

'In the Place de la Sorbonne, by the fountain.'

'Stay there. Don't move. We'll be there right away.'

'We?'

'Never you mind. Mingle with the crowd but don't move far. We'll be there in less than fifteen minutes. Be careful.' He hung up.

The limousine arrived exactly twelve minutes later. It double-parked on the Boulevard Saint-Michel, just in front of the Place de la Sorbonne.

Surprised to see Stern's Mercedes, Valentine rushed to the rear door, which opened to reveal Vermeer's unshaven face. She flung herself into the seat next to him and the car drove off.

'What are you doing here, Hugo?

'Riding to the rescue of a damsel in distress. I've dreamed of doing this ever since I was twelve years old, when I saw *Robin and Marian* for the first time. Such a shame! I've left my skintight jerkin in the wardrobe. I'll have to remember to bring it with me next time you get into trouble.'

'I mean, what are you doing in this limousine, idiot!'

'I'm into luxury, as you know, and this car pretty much meets my comfort criteria. It could do with a minibar, of course, but I'll suffer in silence until we arrive.'

He sprawled on the leather seat and patted Valentine's thigh.

'You have a devoted admirer, my dear. I don't know what you've done to old Stern, but he adores you. He was worried sick about you after the accident.'

Valentine stared at him wide-eyed. 'How did he know about it? I left before the police arrived, and I didn't see any witnesses.'

'A man who works for the Foundation got there just after it happened. A guy with a strange accent and a name out of a novel.'

'Sorel.'

'That's right – Sorel. He saw your knight in shining armour carry you off on his two-cylinder steed. Who was he, by the way, this saviour?'

'A disciple of Vasalis.'

Vermeer sighed. 'That's all we need . . . Another freak in your menagerie. I include myself, naturally. Why can't you mix with normal men, Valentine? You know, the kind who marry you, have children with you, take you to the cinema. It would be so much more relaxing for your nearest and dearest. I mean, tearing around Paris on a scooter like that . . . For a well brought-up young lady, you go too far.'

Valentine gave up on the idea of changing the tone. At times of stress, Vermeer was incapable of being serious. Joking was his way of dealing with tension.

'Do men like that exist?' she asked.

'If you look hard, you should be able to track one down. At your age, he'd be a second-hand model, but that would do, wouldn't it?'

'Elegance and refinement . . . You really know how to talk to a woman, Mr Vermeer.'

A self-satisfied smile appeared on Vermeer's fleshy lips. He pretended not to catch Valentine's sarcasm.

215

'Class – you're just born with it. I come from the right side of the tracks, that's all. There's no great merit in it.'

The limousine drove into the courtyard of Stern's house and pulled up at the magnificent front steps.

'Speaking of class,' mused Vermeer, 'not a bad place.'

'Don't tell me you're impressed. Surely your family has something like it in its portfolio.'

Vermeer thought for a moment, scratching his chin as he always did when trying to concentrate.

'My family has bought many pieces from the Sterns. Too many, probably, and for too high a price, judging by this house. Having said that, yes, we do own a few places like it. I'll show you a couple some time, if you're good.'

Before getting out of the car, he straightened his velvet jacket by giving each sleeve a sharp tug. The English fabric, cut to fit his outsize figure, must have been designed for such adjustments, as it didn't tear and did appear more presentable. Pleased, Vermeer put the finishing touches to it by smoothing away the remaining creases with the back of his hand. His attempt to restore order to his hair, however, was an abject failure. He gave up and started to get out of the car. As he swung his legs out, he groaned loudly. He had to lean on the doorframe to help himself out of the vehicle.

Once out, he lifted the back of his jacket and made a face when he saw the bloodstain on his shirt, a little to the left of his spine.

'What's happened to you?' asked Valentine, worried. 'Are you hurt?'

'I met your friend Nora. Quite a character, that girl.'

Valentine didn't have time to enquire further. Elias Stern appeared at the top of the steps, in a charcoal grey suit with a blue silk square in his breast pocket to match his tie. Leaning on his cane, he waited for his guests to come level with him and held out a hand to Valentine. She took it in both of hers, in a gesture that from then on became almost a ritual between them.

'Valentine! I'm so relieved you're all right!'

216

'Thank you.'

'Come in. Let's go and sit down in my study. You need to recover from all the emotion. You can go back to work on the manuscript tomorrow.'

Valentine was pulled up short. She let go of the old man's hand.

'I thought you'd fired me.'

'Did I really give you that impression? Forgive me if I did, but that's not the case. The Foundation doesn't let employees go so easily, especially when they're as talented as you. I didn't go all the way to your workshop to find you only to throw you out at the first hurdle. I had enough trouble convincing you to join us!'

'Your head of security seemed to think differently yesterday evening. He sounded as if he never wanted to hear of me again.'

'Sorel will get over it. He loves to get worked up over nothing and strike an exasperated pose. It's his job. And his temperament too, I should imagine. But I don't hold it against you in the least, Valentine.'

'I don't understand . . . Because of me, someone broke into your house.'

'The Foundation is equally responsible. Our security system wasn't as good as we thought, but we've made the necessary modifications. The site has been secured, as Sorel would say. I hope we're no longer at risk.'

Stern took a few steps towards the door.

'As for your lack of discretion,' he added, 'don't let it trouble you. I took your relationship with Vermeer into account when I hired you. In fact, I expected you to tell him about the codex, and that he would yield to the temptation to post the information on his website. Though I have to admit that the speed with which he did so rather took me by surprise.'

Valentine was stunned. Vermeer, on the other hand, didn't react. He looked down, focusing on a weed that the gardener had missed, sprouting between two paving stones.

Valentine noticed his embarrassment. 'Did you know this?'

217

The Dutchman nodded. 'Elias told me about it earlier, when we were looking for you.'

'Elias,' echoed Valentine thoughtfully. 'So you're on first-name terms now, are you?'

'Our concern for you brought us together,' said Vermeer in self-justification. 'While we were waiting to hear from you, there wasn't much for us to do. Elias and his father have sold my family a number of pictures, you see . . .'

'Only masterpieces,' said Stern. 'First-rate ones. Hugo comes from a long line of men of taste. He is one himself. Thanks to your misadventures, we've met at last. I'm delighted, despite the circumstances. I hope you no longer bear me a grudge for the rather unsubtle methods I used to summon you, Hugo.'

'I have to say, the bottle of 1975 Cheval Blanc you so kindly opened in my honour was a help. And your cheque for the Fledermaus has erased any remaining unpleasant memories.'

Vermeer had been brought up to put on a good front in all cir-cumstances when in company. He excelled in the art of concealing resentment, so that he could have sounded sincere to someone who didn't know him well. Deep down, though, he was still seething at having been ill treated, even if he had to admit that Stern had subsequently been very generous. For now, Vermeer agreed to a truce, no more. His peace would cost Stern far more than a bottle of vintage wine and a few thousand euros.

Stern led them to his study. He and Valentine sat in the same armchairs they had a few days earlier, while Vermeer occupied the sofa against the wall, on the other side of the coffee table. A silver tray with three stemmed crystal glasses, a decanter three-quarters full of dark red liquid and three antique-looking napkins embroi-dered with the initials ES had been placed on the table.

Vermeer helped himself without waiting for his host's per-mission. He inhaled the wine at length before savouring a mouthful. He gave a sort of yelp.

'Hmm . . . Perfectly chambré. You were right, Elias, it had to be left to breathe a little.'

218

'I'm so pleased you like it. I'll have a case delivered to you after you leave.'

Stern had just taken an important step towards a ceasefire. Vermeer raised his glass to the elderly man in thanks.

For a whole minute, nobody spoke. Vermeer savoured his wine while Valentine, gaze unfocused, tried to take in Stern's revelations. She didn't know who she was most annoyed at – Stern, who'd manipulated her from the moment he stepped inside her workshop, or herself, for being so naive.

Stern broke the silence, with a statement of fact rather than an attempt to revive the conversation.

'I didn't think they'd dare.'

Valentine took a few seconds to react.

'I'd like to know what you've got me mixed up in, Mr Stern.'

'Elias, please.'

'Fine. What's going on, Elias?'

She stressed each syllable of her host's name, as if to show that she wasn't taken in by any of it. She'd had enough of all the pretence. She needed definite answers, and intended to force Stern to provide them.

'This is about more than Vasalis, isn't it?'

Stern didn't try to dodge the question. 'You're right. I owe you an explanation. But not immediately. We have to settle something. Would you mind getting up and coming over to the *Irises*, please?'

Valentine did so. Once she was standing in front of the picture, she turned round. She looked puzzled, but also a little curious.

Stern was certainly an expert at creating drama. The old art dealer had lost none of his skill. He still knew how to arouse his audience's interest, getting them to focus their attention on the piece he wanted to show them.

'Raise your hand to the lower left-hand corner,' he ordered. 'You'll find a button set into the frame, on the side of the moulding.'

Valentine placed her fingers on the frame with care, as if afraid she might do irreparable damage to the painting. Starting at the lower corner, she slid them slowly upwards. Almost immediately she felt a little knob beneath her index finger. She took a deep breath and pressed it.

A sharp click echoed in the room. The side of the painting where the button was placed moved away from the wall, pivoting on an invisible axis. Valentine then noticed the hinge on the other side fixing the picture to the wall.

'Go ahead. Pull it towards you. Fully.'

Valentine did as Stern said. She pulled the Van Gogh until it was at a right angle to the wall. She saw a small safe set into the wall behind it. It was surmounted by a keypad, at the centre of which shone a green light.

'There's no better place for a safe,' explained Stern. 'People are blinded by my *Irises*. They could never imagine that such a treasure could hide others. It's an old conjuror's trick: distract the audience by showing them something extraordinary and they forget everything else, even the obvious. They see nothing but what you want them to see. That's why I've always refused to sell this painting. None other would serve as well.'

He pointed at the safe with his cane. 'Go on, open it. It's unlocked. Just press the green button.'

Valentine obeyed. The door of the safe opened. The interior, some thirty centimetres deep, was divided into four sections of equal height, separated by steel shelves. On the lower one, Valentine recognised the rosewood box containing the Vasalis manuscript. On the others, in untidy piles, there were files and notebooks, as well as several jewellery cases and wads of banknotes.

'Top shelf,' specified Stern. 'The brown envelope. Would you bring it to me, please?'

Valentine came and sat down again with the envelope. She handed it to Stern.

'Thank you. You see, I'm not hiding any of my little secrets from you. You no longer mistrust my motives towards you, I hope?'

Valentine didn't answer. She crossed her arms and tried to look casual. In fact, she was intrigued, but on no account was she going to let Stern know.

He pulled an unmarked archive box from the envelope. He placed it before the restorer, then sat back.

'I'd like to have your expert opinion on this. Hugo, would you mind removing the lid so that Valentine can see what's inside, please?'

Despite his love of the Bordeaux and the fact that his glass was still half full, it didn't occur to Vermeer to disobey Stern's request. Curious as well, he placed his glass on the tray, slid forward nearer to the coffee table and lifted off the lid of the box with a theatrical gesture. Inside lay an oblong piece of paper covered in transparent plastic film.

Vermeer was the first to react. 'What's this?' he exclaimed irritably. Exasperated, he turned towards Valentine and, pointing at the contents of the box, asked, 'Do you understand any of this?'

His friend didn't even hear the question. She was staring, horrified, at the inside of the box.

Except for the Louvre stamp in a corner of the sheet, there was nothing. No lettering. Not the slightest mark. Nothing.

Vermeer spent several seconds straining his eyes, trying to make out anything on the uniformly blank surface. The conclusion he came to was unsettling, even for someone so whimsical and open-minded: the folder contained nothing but a blank piece of paper, slightly yellowed with age. A piece of paper of no value.

Elias Stern was the king of conjurors. Or a first-rate con artist. Vermeer would have wagered a case of 1975 Cheval Blanc on the latter.

34

It took Valentine a good ten seconds to be able to speak.

'H-how did you get hold of this?' she stammered, her eyes fixed on the page.

'I still have a few good friends at the Ministry of Culture,' Stern explained. 'Prompted by certain people close to the Minister, the Louvre has lent it to me free of charge for a few days. The head conservator raised little objection. True, it's unspectacular, to say the least.'

Finding his turn of phrase distasteful, Valentine glowered. 'I had a ringside seat for the disaster. Thanks.'

'Don't be angry, Valentine. I'm not showing you this to provoke you.'

'Why, then?'

'I want to understand.'

Quiet until then, Vermeer now joined in. 'Would you mind letting me in on the secret? Or give me another bottle of this wonderful Cheval Blanc, and I'll go and shut myself in the toilet with it.'

'Such a sacrifice would be pointless, my dear Hugo,' said Stern. 'Though it may not look like it, what you have before you is a preparatory sketch for the face of St John the Baptist made by Leonardo da Vinci soon after his arrival at Amboise. I don't think it's an exaggeration to say that it's a perfect example of a failed restoration.'

Vermeer gave an admiring whistle. 'Congratulations!' he said to Valentine. 'When you balls it up, you don't do things by halves. The press never showed the result of your great work. Impressive . . . You should set up an industrial cleaning business. You'd make a fortune.'

Valentine opened her mouth to respond, but instead poured herself a glass of wine and took a big gulp. The excellent wine had an immediate calming effect.

The reviving effect of the alcohol allowed her to control her response. Six months ago she would have burst into tears or, more likely, wanted to smash the decanter over her friend's head. Seeing the sketch again was painful, of course, but her self-destructive urges had gone. Only slight stirrings of rebellion remained, and they were growing.

Valentine knew that her wounds wouldn't miraculously heal. For now, she simply wanted to regain her self-control. She was on the right track.

She prepared her riposte as she finished the rest of the wine.

'I've already been called every name under the sun in the newspapers, Hugo. Your sarcasm is nothing compared to all the horrible things that have been said and printed about me. You've lost your touch. Surely you can do better than that.'

'I had enough trouble convincing you not to jump in the Seine. I don't want to have to start all over again, entertaining as it was watching you lie in bed moaning all day.'

'Not another word, please.'

Valentine's tone was neutral, as if she was asking him to lower the volume on the television or make her a coffee. But Vermeer understood that she was drawing a line beyond which he should not step, for both their sakes. As a sign of goodwill, he replaced the lid and handed the box back to Stern.

'Now that we've seen what Miss Savi here is capable of when she doesn't like a drawing, why don't you explain the point of your little demonstration?'

Stern slid the archive box back inside the brown envelope and placed it in a drawer in the coffee table.

'I can't believe you were responsible for this disaster, Valentine. I want to understand what happened.'

Valentine looked exasperated. 'Why? It's all in the past. I fucked up and they sacked me, full stop. We're not going to go over it all again. There's no point endlessly rehashing the same old stuff. Let's move on. It's what I'm trying to do, and I can tell you, it's not easy.'

'It's unlike you to make such a stupid mistake. They entrusted you with cleaning the sketch because you were the person best qualified for the job.'

'Well, apparently *they* were wrong. I wasn't as competent as *they* thought.'

'It was a straightforward job for someone like you. If the sketch hadn't been by Leonardo, they'd have got a trainee to do it. Something isn't right here.'

'There's no big mystery. I worked on the drawing on my own. No other restorer touched it. I made a mistake, that's all. I'm not sure what the mistake was, but there's no other explanation.'

'Please forgive me for asking such an obvious question, but I assume you followed all the usual procedures?'

'Of course. I used a standard aqueous solution, and performed a stability test on a peripheral area beforehand. Everything was normal. But when I went ahead with the rest, the drawing disappeared within a few hours, as if . . .' She paused. 'As if the ink composition had changed overnight. It must sound silly, but I can't think how else to put it.'

'No preliminary chemical analysis was carried out?'

Valentine shook her head. 'There was nothing to suggest that such a reaction might take place: the inking was uniform, carried out on a well-prepared medium and in a perfect state of preservation. Leonardo worked with good-quality inks, and the procedure I followed had been used successfully on pages from the same notebook. There was no reason to think it might go wrong.'

Stern took in the information and reflected a moment.

'Did anyone have access to the drawing between the time you tested your cleaning solution and the time you applied it to the entire surface?'

'Do you think there was malicious intent involved?' asked Vermeer.

'We must consider every possibility. We can eliminate them one by one until we find the explanation.'

'But this is the Louvre we're talking about, not some provincial museum! This is crazy!'

Valentine silenced him abruptly. 'Calm down, Hugo. Maybe Elias is right to want to examine this methodically. Even if I'd rather never hear about the sketch again, it's the only way of getting at the truth. He's right that I need to know what my mistake was so that I can come to terms with it.'

Offended, Vermeer picked up his glass of wine, sank back into the sofa and withdrew into a sullen silence.

'Hugo, don't get in one of your moods . . . Please.'

Despite Valentine's plea, Vermeer was well into a sulk.

Valentine knew that insisting would only make things worse. When Vermeer was in that frame of mind, the outside world ceased to exist. A bomb could have gone off in the next room, and he wouldn't have budged from the sofa. She shrugged, before continuing to explain things to her host.

'I considered the possibility of malicious intent, but I can't think who would have wanted to damage the drawing. It doesn't make sense.'

She seemed so sure that Stern didn't push the argument. He tried a different approach.

'What other pieces were you working on at the time?'

'I'd just finished an eighteenth-century red chalk drawing. An academic study from the workshop of François Boucher. Nothing important.'

'Did you do anything different before starting to clean the drawing? Alter the proportions of your solutions, for instance, or use a different supplier for your products?'

'No, nothing like that. Restoring the red chalk drawing turned out to be easier than I expected. I finished it several days ahead of schedule, and moved straight on to the Leonardo drawing. I didn't change anything, not my products or my methods.'

'What became of the materials you used?'

'I have no idea. I expect my colleagues threw everything out after I left, to ward off bad luck.'

'Maybe not everything was destroyed,' said Stern. 'They must have kept certain items, at least long enough to carry out valuations. Did you get any information about that?'

'I asked to see the file, but they refused. The drawing didn't belong to the Louvre. It was on loan from a private collector for a temporary exhibition. In return, the Louvre was to restore it, which is fairly common practice. When the drawing was destroyed, the insurers reached an out-of-court settlement with the owner. As there were no legal consequences, the valuation file remained confidential.'

'I expect it suited everyone to avoid going to court,' said Stern. 'The owner of the drawing wouldn't have wanted the sum he received in compensation to be disclosed, and the insurance company wouldn't have wanted to lose a client as important as the Louvre. As for the museum managers, their priority was to bring the affair to an end, and quickly. A court case would only have damaged their reputation further. That's why they sacrificed you so easily. Everyone had something to gain from it. The financial stakes were high.'

'I never found out how much the drawing was insured for. Probably something outrageous.'

Stern nodded. 'The insurers were rumoured to have paid the owner around ten million euros, which seems excessive for a sketch, even one by Leonardo da Vinci. All the parties involved, however, were remarkably discreet on the subject. I'd be very curious to know the exact amount of compensation paid. I haven't managed to get hold of the insurers' file yet, but I've chased up some contacts in the last few days and I'm pretty hopeful.'

He was pensive for a few moments, then abruptly changed the subject. 'If you like,' he said, 'you can stay here tonight, Valentine. We've got more guest rooms than we know what to do with. Nora can lend you some clothes.'

'That's kind, but I'd rather go home.'

Valentine's answer roused Vermeer from his torpor. His voice full of indignation, he spat out the words.

'You can't go back to your place when someone's just tried to kill you! That's the first place the killer will look.'

'I don't think Valentine is running any risk at her apartment,' Stern interjected.

'Easy for you to say, in your ultra-secure mansion. You saw what the guy was capable of! He reduced that poor woman to a pulp!'

'Sorel believes he was only targeting Marie Gervex. In his view, Valentine isn't in any danger.'

'In that case,' Valentine said, 'I expect the police will get in touch with me for a statement. I didn't get a good look at the killer, but I can describe what happened.'

'The Foundation takes care of its own problems, whatever they may be, as I've said. It's been our rule of conduct from the start, and we stick to it. That's what Sorel is here for. He's going to deal with this business.'

'But . . .'

Valentine left the word hanging. Opposite her, Stern's face hardened. No longer the benevolent elderly art dealer, he was coldly determined.

'I have every confidence in Sorel,' said the old man. 'If he assures me that you're in no immediate danger, you can go home with your mind at peace.'

Something in Stern's tone stopped Valentine pursuing it further. She'd suddenly lost all desire to know more. Even Vermeer seemed affected by the hard look on Stern's face. His inquisitiveness vanished, as did his urge to argue. A heavy silence settled on the room.

Valentine remembered the glint she'd seen in Sorel's eyes when they'd met the evening before. At the time, she'd thought it was fury. But she'd been mistaken. It wasn't that at all.

Sorel wasn't angry. He was insane. He was a dangerous madman, and Stern had hired him for that very reason. But Valentine wondered to what extent the art dealer could control his employee.

Sorel was protecting her from those who were trying to kill her. Fine, she was willing to believe Stern on that score. But was anyone protecting her from Sorel?

35

David looked at his watch. The afternoon was wearing on. There was nothing more for him to do at the Sorbonne. Though reluctant to go back to his flat, he'd soon have to think about going home. But before he left, he had a delicate question for Raymond Agostini.

He cleared his throat before launching in. 'Did Homer really say that?'

'I'm sorry?'

'The quotation about miracles. The thing about the honey . . . Did Homer really say it?'

The lecturer made a face, like a child caught lying. His expression changed from mock indignation to amusement.

'I made it up,' he admitted. 'I thought it sounded good at the time.'

David smiled back at him. 'Since when have lecturers at the Sorbonne invented quotations?'

'Since their best friends threw themselves out of windows for no reason. Or since complete morons have been running universities: your choice. Consider this infringement of my professional code of ethics as a sign of distress that's entirely forgivable in the circumstances.'

Agostini gazed at the impressive book collection that filled a wall of his office – hundreds of books, whose worn covers were perfectly lined up on the shelves.

'The important thing is not that Homer uttered those words,' he went on, 'but that he *might* have done. After all, doesn't our job consist of twisting the texts of our favourite authors so that they say what they never dreamed of saying? There's a fine line between analysis and falsification. The best among us find a satisfactory equilibrium. The others overstep the limit and lose their way.'

David thought he caught the allusion, but he wasn't sure.

'Do you mean Albert Cadas?'

'You don't always realise straight away that you're heading in the wrong direction. There's no alarm bell that goes off in your head and tells you, "Careful, you're on the wrong track." It takes months, sometimes years, to see it. In fact, Albert went astray the day he first started chasing that chimera. When he realised, it was too late to turn back, so he killed himself.'

'You don't believe in the existence of Vasalis?'

'Albert lost his way, Scotto. That's what I believe. As for the rest, I have no idea. Whether Vasalis really existed, whether he wrote the *De forma mundi* and a copy survived, it hardly matters. Albert persisted in trying to break down doors that were too firmly closed. He died of exhaustion, or weariness if you prefer. You don't pursue chimeras relentlessly for thirty years without some damage. When the moment of disappointment comes – and, believe me, it always comes – it's hard to recover.'

He looked enquiringly at David, but David didn't respond. The lecturer's words had left him nonplussed. He couldn't understand this outburst against his supervisor, especially from someone who'd always claimed to be his friend.

Agostini sensed his puzzlement. He waved his hand, as if to dismiss everything he'd just said.

'Forget my silliness, Scotto. You're listening to an academic at the end of his career. I'm afraid my last few illusions have been lost, this week, with these two deaths. Go home and get some rest.'

'What about you? What are you going to do?'

'I'm going to see if I can sort through Albert's things. I expect the Dean will want to clear out his office as soon as possible. All trace of Albert will disappear even before he's been buried. It's a sad metaphor for the life of the academic: die, and nothing remains of you but some ink on dusty paper.'

'*Vanitas vanitatum . . .*' concluded David solemnly.

The appalling triteness of the quotation drew a tense smile from the lecturer in Ancient Greek.

36

From a great height, the colossus lowered his head. First he stared at the carpet in front of him, then at the tips of his shoes.

'What do you mean, he failed?' said the man standing in front of the huge window on the fifty-fifth floor of the Tour Montparnasse, his voice shaking with anger.

From behind, Maxime Zerka looked ten years younger than he really was. You would never have thought, seeing the lightly grey-ing hair and the slim figure with narrow hips, that he was over sixty. His narrow-striped suit, cut to disguise the slight excess fat that surgery had not been able to remove, enhanced the effect.

The colossus hunched and made himself as small as possible which, given his size, was an impressive manoeuvre.

'The restorer is still alive,' he admitted sheepishly. 'I saw her arrive at the old man's house in the Mercedes. I couldn't get any-where near her. They've tightened up their security. This time they're on the alert. From a distance, she looked unhurt.'

'What about the other woman?'

'She wasn't in the Mercedes. Maybe José took her out, I've got no idea.'

'Where is he, the idiot? Why isn't he here, giving me his report in person?'

The colossus looked as if he wanted the ground to swallow him. He thought it preferable not to answer.

Zerka stopped gazing at the view from the window and turned round. Power and wealth hadn't altered his deepest nature, or his speech. Zerka spoke exactly as he thought and acted: in other words, without pointless deviation.

'Where is José, the bastard? You must know, you're always together. You're like a couple of pansies.'

Although he was a good fifteen centimetres taller and thirty kilos heavier than Zerka, the colossus began to tremble.

It wasn't that he was afraid of dying. That possibility had shadowed him for the past twenty years, ever since he'd joined the army, but especially since he'd chosen to apply his skills in the service of the worst predators on the planet. He accepted the possibility of death. But not the kind this man would dispense if he decided to kill him.

Zerka continued to stare at him. All trace of anger had disappeared from his eyes. What remained was far more disturbing. The visible signs of his success – the diamond watch, the bespoke suit, the walls hung with old masters, the entire floor rented for his holding company – would never disguise his bestiality. In the midst of all this sophistication, it stood out all the more.

The colossus looked away, unable to endure the strain any longer.

Zerka repeated his question with venom in his voice: 'Where *is* that bastard José? I don't need to tell you, but you'd better have a convincing explanation.'

He didn't need to be specific. The colossus was well aware of Zerka's capabilities.

'He's . . . he's disappeared,' he stammered.

'What do you mean, disappeared?' Zerka clicked his fingers to emphasise his words. 'The bastard's vanished into thin air? Like a fucking magician?'

'Sort of,' admitted the giant. 'He didn't come back from the job. The van's disappeared too.'

'Didn't I tell you to do it yourself? Rack your brains, loser. Think! Anything coming back to you?'

233

The colossus tried to justify himself. 'I didn't think we could fuck up . . . on paper, it was a cinch.'

'Proof. Did you go back and check, at least?'

The colossus nodded. He hadn't had much of a chance to shine so far, so he seized the opportunity to show off his work.

'There was blood on the road and bits of broken headlights all over the place. Several parked cars had been smashed up. The paint marks on them were the same colour as the van.'

The colossus was recovering some of his loquacity. He went on, 'The way I see it, José crashed into the parked cars after hitting the woman. I called all the hospitals. She isn't in any of them.'

'Your conclusion?'

'She's been eliminated. Like you wanted.'

This information seemed to mollify his employer slightly.

Marie Gervex's death hadn't been necessary. It was simply a selfish little pleasure Zerka had treated himself to. The bitch had had the nerve to reject his offer, which had been generous. And he couldn't stand being turned down. When he wanted something, he always got it. Otherwise, to escape his vindictiveness, you'd be well advised to know a travel agent who specialised in remote destinations.

In his head, Zerka drew up the schedule for the next few days. One: bring this business to a quick conclusion. Two: get rid of this bunch of losers who claimed to be experienced mercenaries. Incompetent imbeciles, that's what they were. Only good for throwing away once used. Which is what he planned to do.

He grabbed the remote control lying on a glass table, and pressed a button. The window grew dim, while a panel in the wall opened to reveal a gigantic television screen showing the Bloomberg channel. Then, opening a cabinet beneath the TV, he poured himself a whisky and sank into the leather armchair that faced the screen.

'Right,' he said, peering anxiously at the latest financial

information. 'One out of two – that's something. Where have you got to with the illumination?'

'We've put the fear of God into that guy Scotto. I've given him till next week to find it. He didn't seem to have much of a clue, but he knew the old teacher well.'

'Push that side of things. I want the illumination as soon as possible. The more time passes, the more we risk losing it. If need be, press the guy again.'

'How hard?'

'You can damage him a bit if you like, but don't kill him. We still need him. You can have your fun later, when all this is over.'

'Fine.'

'This time, I want you to do the job yourself. No delegating, understood? Can you cope or do you need a battalion of mercenaries to help you?'

The colossus took the humiliation on the chin. 'I'll manage,' he mumbled.

'Wonderful. And find José. I've got a few things to say to that son of a bitch.'

Eyes glued to the curves of the stockmarket graphs, Zerka raised the glass of whisky to his lips and dismissed his henchman with a wave of the hand.

'Now get out. And don't think I won't find you if you decide to disappear as well.'

A shiver ran down the colossus's muscular back. He backed out of the room, relieved and surprised to be still alive.

37

On impulse, Vermeer turned the wheel sharply. The Maserati 3500 GT crossed the middle lane of the Périphérique and ended up in the left lane, thirty kilometres an hour above the speed limit. He did it all without hitting anything, which was something of a miracle at this time of night.

With lofty disdain, Vermeer ignored the driver of the four-by-four who flashed his lights for cutting in front of him spectacularly. When you drive a 1961 turquoise Maserati, you have every right to despise the rest of humanity. It may not have been part of the Highway Code, but Vermeer followed this rule to the letter.

Without slowing down, the Dutchman let go of the wheel, lit a joint and handed it to his friend. Valentine grabbed it, but didn't smoke it.

'I thought you'd sold this,' she said.

'You must be joking! A beauty like this? I just put it in a safe place for a while.'

'What about your good resolutions?'

'Which ones?'

'Discretion, honesty, abstinence, following the Highway Code . . .'

'I never said anything about abstinence.'

'I know. I was just checking to see if you were paying attention. But what about the rest?'

'I'm fed up with all that. I've been bored to death since I've been keeping my nose clean. I need action.'

'You've had plenty of that the past couple of days, haven't you?'

'Yeah . . . Would have been better if your friend Nora hadn't fucked up my back.'

'I still can't believe she beat you up.'

Vermeer took the joint from her and inhaled deeply.

'Your naivety is absolutely staggering,' he said, blowing the smoke out of the window. 'That girl's explosive. You can tell just by looking at her.'

He suddenly slowed down. With an ear-splitting screech of tyres, the four-by-four slammed on its brakes to avoid crashing into the back of the Maserati.

Vermeer ignored the furious hooting from behind. He was now driving at a sedate speed in the fast lane. About fifty metres further on, he threw the joint out of the window, made an obscene gesture at the speed camera on the central reservation and put his foot down on the accelerator. The sports car roared off, leaving the four-by-four far behind.

With the indicator on the speedometer fixed at a hundred and forty, the Maserati wove between cars for a few kilometres. Vermeer switched lanes at whim, as if the road were empty. Eventually he turned off on to an exit ramp and headed into the centre of Paris.

Twenty minutes later, Vermeer parked the vintage Maserati outside the Hotel Lutetia. With the ease of one who'd been doing it since he owned his first pedal car, he threw the keys to the doorman, who caught them and rushed to sit behind the wheel.

Valentine got out of the car, her legs like jelly. Her stomach was even worse. She felt as if she'd been inside a cocktail shaker. Unsteadily, she followed Vermeer through the lobby.

They entered the bar. The small room with mirror-clad walls and red velvet seats was packed. At the bar, a writer, a regular on television, was drinking with a young actress famed for having the body of a goddess and a bird's brain. A few days earlier, Valentine had read an article in which the writer deplored the intellectual poverty of the starlets on our screens. Obviously, he was less fussy when it came to his own personal tastes. But then he probably hadn't asked the actress out to discuss literature.

'Wait here,' said Vermeer. 'I'll be back soon.'

He went over to the couple, kissed the writer and whispered a few words into the ear of his arm candy, peering appreciatively at her décolleté. The girl blushed and thought for a few moments before bursting out laughing.

Vermeer had a brief, more serious exchange with the writer, then took his leave, casting a final glance at the starlet's chest. On his way back, as he manoeuvred his bulk carefully between tables, several people called out friendly greetings, to which he responded exuberantly.

At last, he got back to Valentine.

'Do you know everyone here?' she asked.

'Some of my forebears more or less lived here. Their ghosts must still be lurking. Seriously, it's a good place to do business.'

'What kind of business?'

'I'd rather not say. You'd blush. I know you.'

'You're a pain in the arse, Hugo.'

'Really?'

Vermeer gazed at his friend with a look of pure innocence. It was his speciality. He'd produced his frightened-little-mouse face for Valentine at least a thousand times before, with a one hundred per cent success rate.

She gave up arguing and changed the subject.

'Why have you brought me here? I'm not doing business.'

'I want to introduce you to someone.'

'I suppose you're not going to tell me anything, are you, to keep the suspense going?'

'You suppose right.'

Valentine was sorry she'd followed her friend without asking more questions. She felt uncomfortable in these luxurious surroundings. Vermeer, by contrast, was in his element. He had changed clothes since leaving Stern's house. In his Hugo Boss suit and Berluti loafers, he looked exactly what he was: the son of a good family, stinking rich, arrogant and potentially detestable.

Had Valentine known he was dragging her here, she'd at least have made an effort with her clothes. In her jeans and worn leather jacket, she looked quite out of place in this elegant environment.

Besides, the maître d'hôtel was staring at her with a look whose meaning was quite clear: you could dress as you liked here, as long as you had a minimum degree of fame. Scruffy nonentities were not welcome.

Valentine gave him a beaming smile reminiscent of Kelly McGillis in *Top Gun* when, in Ray-Bans with hair flying in the wind, she simpered on the back of Tom Cruise's motorbike.

Clearly, the maître d'hôtel wasn't a fan of the film, or maybe he'd seen a recent photo of Kelly McGillis. He raised his eyebrows expressively: all scruffy nonentities were to leave immediately.

Valentine put away her smile and deliberately shifted closer to Vermeer. The maître d'hôtel got the message. He turned away contemptuously.

Vermeer headed towards a man at a table right at the back, in a dark corner. Well over fifty, he was flicking casually through an auction catalogue, mobile phone to his ear. In front of him, on the coffee table, stood a cocktail of a strange pink colour with chunks of fruit floating in it.

'That's him,' said Vermeer.

'Who is he?'

'An old friend.'

'Is that it?'

'He's the policeman who tried to arrest me.'

Valentine was stunned. Unsure whether Vermeer was joking or not, she watched as he went over and stood in front of the policeman, arms crossed.

The man continued his phone call, unruffled. The Dutchman's stout body completely filled his field of vision, but it didn't seem to bother him. He nodded a couple of times, mumbled, and concluded his conversation with a 'Listen, I'll call you later', before hanging up.

He casually acknowledged Vermeer's presence.

'Hugo Vermeer . . . I can't say I'm particularly pleased to see you.'

'Hello, Superintendent. It's been a long time.'

'Not long enough. I'd have preferred to hear that you were in the Seine wearing concrete boots. Your longevity never ceases to amaze me. How does a bastard like you last more than a week in this world?'

'Come, come, Superintendent, why the animosity?'

'Because you ruined the end of my career, perhaps? Or because you're a dirty bastard art smuggler? Or maybe it's just because I can't stand your face, you pretentious ponce. So many reasons. I don't know which to pick.'

'I've changed, you know that. I've gone straight.'

'Men like you never change. At best, they pretend to, until the day they get fed up with taking people for fools.'

'What I like about you is your subtle, nuanced view of human nature.'

'Fuck off, Vermeer. Why did you call me? Need a certificate of good conduct?'

Without being asked, Vermeer lowered himself heavily into the seat facing the policeman. He signalled to Valentine to come and sit in the neighbouring chair.

'Valentine, this is Superintendent Lopez, who ran the Brigade Criminelle for many years, before he was the subject of a departmental reorganisation. That's how they refer to demotion in the police, isn't it?'

Lopez remained stony-faced.

Vermeer went on: 'You remember Valentine Savi, don't you, Superintendent? Your men grilled her thoroughly about me.'

'Don't waste my time, Vermeer. Get to the point or bugger off.'

'Valentine has just been hired by the Stern Foundation. She has a few questions, and I thought you might be able to supply her with some information.'

'And what makes you think I can do that?'

'You wouldn't have shifted your big lazy arse down here if you weren't bored stiff in your broom closet. I just had to mention Stern's name on the phone to hear you perk up at the other end of the line. I'm offering you a bit of excitement, Superintendent, and you'd do anything for some of that again, wouldn't you, even talk to a bastard like me.'

Lopez looked at him wearily. 'Have you finished?'

'Be a sport, Superintendent, tell me I'm right. You made my life a misery. Do me this little favour now.'

The policeman took a gulp of his cocktail and grimaced in disgust.

He turned to Valentine. 'This crap cost me nearly fifteen euros, would you believe. It's outrageous. There's no other word for it.'

For a few moments he tried to fish out a piece of pineapple from his drink with the cocktail stirrer before eventually using his fingers and putting it in his mouth.

'I followed with interest your troubles with your previous employer,' he said, eating the pineapple. 'To be honest, if you mix with idiots, you always end up suffering collateral damage.'

'My sacking had nothing to do with being a friend of Hugo's,' objected Valentine.

'Everything always has something to do with everything else, Miss Savi. Your relationship with Vermeer probably didn't cause your expulsion from the Louvre directly, but it may have meant that certain people failed to give you their full support when you were in the shit. Or maybe even pretended not to know you. You were a bit of a golden girl in your job, weren't you? So how come no one – absolutely no one – wanted to keep you on when it happened? Just because you can't see a link between two things doesn't mean there isn't one.'

241

Valentine didn't reply. She'd turned pale.

Lopez seemed to regret being so harsh. He added, more gently, 'What would you like to know about Stern?'

Valentine glanced enquiringly at Vermeer. He gestured for her to answer.

'The Foundation . . . I don't understand how it functions, or what it does exactly.'

The policeman ran a hand over his slicked-back hair. It must have been a good thirty years since anyone had worn their hair like that, but it matched his crumpled three-piece suit and thick, horn-rimmed glasses. Lopez didn't exactly blend in at the bar of the Lutetia. But he didn't fit the image of the ruthless police-man, either. Really he looked like a fifties crooner transported into the future. Valentine suspected he'd had to show his police badge to get past the maître d'hôtel.

'The mysterious Stern Foundation,' he said reluctantly. 'An astoundingly big budget, henchmen out of Robocop, premises more secure than a fortress and, to top it off, an elusive patri-arch . . . You seem to like trouble, Miss Savi.'

'Aren't you exaggerating a little?'

'I assume they're paying you well?'

'More than well.'

Lopez nodded.

'Your Foundation has pots of money, yet officially it has never made a penny in profit. But that's not surprising, since it's never done anything to earn any money. Actually it's done nothing at all since it was set up. It operates at a loss. And then there's Sorel, who makes your friend Vermeer look like a choirboy. He spends most of his time in the US, with only a few weeks a year in Paris. Rather strange for Head of Security, don't you think?'

Lopez seemed inexhaustible on the subject. He continued, without giving Valentine the chance to interrupt.

'His methods are interesting. A number of journalists have tried to investigate the Foundation in the past few months. The lucky ones received threats. The rest are recovering from their fractures in hospital. In each case it was bad luck: a motorbike accident, a fall in the bath . . . Just about every kind of domestic accident was blamed. I've opened an inquiry into Sorel. I've even sent a request for information to the US State Department, but I've had no response.'

'Who's paying for it all?' asked Vermeer.

Lopez shrugged. 'Who knows? I've never encountered anything so opaque. Anyway, I was inundated with calls from high-ranking bastards telling me politely not to take too close an interest in Elias Stern. I've followed their advice. I've already been put in a fucking cupboard. I don't want to end up in the cemetery. The man's like a god. He's untouchable.'

He started fishing for an orange segment in his cocktail.

'Someone's got a grudge against Stern,' said Vermeer. 'Any idea who?'

Lopez looked sardonic. 'You'd have to be insane to try to attack him. Search the lunatic asylums.'

Valentine stood up and pushed her chair back under the table.

'Thank you so much for the information,' she said, irritated by the policeman's tone.

'You're welcome. If you want my advice, take the cash, do what they tell you without asking questions and forget the Foundation. One last thing: stop hanging around with Vermeer. Your karma's bad enough as it is.'

The policeman seemed to find this last remark very funny. His self-satisfied expression turned to contempt, however, when he looked at Hugo Vermeer. When he didn't get a reaction from the Dutchman, he went back to scrutinising the contents of his cocktail.

Vermeer stood up and tugged his friend by the sleeve.

'Come on, let's go. I've had enough. This was a bad idea.'

He strode off towards the door. Valentine was about to follow.

'There is one man . . .'

Valentine turned back to the policeman. He was still peering intently into his glass.

243

'His name's Zerka, Maxime Zerka. A few years ago he tried to buy a painting from Stern. A Van Gogh, according to rumour.'

'The *Irises?*' blurted Valentine.

Lopez looked up. 'So it does exist. Have you seen it? Is it as beautiful as they say?'

Valentine mouthed a silent 'Yes'.

Lopez went on. 'Not only did Stern reject all his offers, one after another, but he put it about that he would never sell the picture to such an ignoramus. Zerka was made to look like a fool all over Paris. He hated old Elias's guts. But that was quite a while ago. Maybe they've patched things up by now. You never know with that sort.'

'This Zerka – where is he?'

'In the sky, Miss Savi. Look up into the sky.'

Valentine was about to lose her temper.

'What's that? Some kind of riddle?'

'Ask your friend Vermeer. He knows everything, doesn't he? It's his job.'

Exasperated, Valentine shrugged and walked away.

Superintendent Lopez watched her disappear behind the maître d'hôtel.

Everything always had something to do with everything else. When Vermeer realised this, the little prick would get a nasty shock.

38

The telephone rang a little after eleven p.m. At first, David thought it was part of his dream. When he realised it wasn't, he reluctantly left Anna, Valentine Savi and the girl in the Dior t-shirt, who were all lying around him, scantily clad and posing lasciviously, and woke up abruptly. He was alone in his bed, sweaty and disappointed at not finding out how the dream would end, even if it wasn't too hard to guess.

The ringing continued to drill into his ears. He groped around the bed and eventually found the phone under a pile of dirty clothes.

'Hm,' he grumbled into the receiver.

'David?' said Anna's voice.

'Fucking . . . hell.'

At this time of night, David wasn't very articulate.

'I'm really sorry to wake you up, but I need to speak to you.'

'I'm on my own, if that's it . . .' said David, pronouncing the words with a clarity that was heroic, given his state.

'Can you come over?'

'What, now?'

David had progressed beyond monosyllables. It meant he was now wide awake. That was his chance of a good night's sleep buggered.

'I've had a really crap day, Anna. I'm dead. I was out like a light at nine.'

He waited a moment before dealing the final blow.

'May I remind you that you're almost married? Wake Paul up. Comforting you after a nightmare is one of his conjugal duties.'

'He isn't here.'

David recalled that Paul was at a conference for eggheads in a distant, exotic place. He couldn't remember where. Belgium perhaps, or more likely Germany. Anna was bored stiff alone in her double bed. That was why she was calling at this time of night. She couldn't stand being on her own for more than half a day. She was like a cat in her need for affection. In everything else, she was more like a wildcat.

'Please, David,' she begged.

Anna didn't usually ask nicely. David relented.

'Oh, what the hell,' he said. 'I'm on my way.'

He hung up and tried to gather his clothes from the previous day, which lay scattered around the bed. He started putting on his boxer shorts, but changed his mind, threw them across the room and made his way to the bathroom. After all, now that he was awake, he might as well make his dream's conclusion a reality, even if there was only one woman. Anna could wait another five minutes and, anyway, a shower would increase his chances of success.

He parked his scooter on the pavement, just outside the building where Paul and Anna had lived since they'd fallen madly in love. He knew the place well; he'd been there often when Paul was away. He keyed in the entry code and trotted up the stairs.

The door to the flat was ajar. David pushed it open and went in. The light in the kitchen was on, at the end of the corridor.

'Anna?' he whispered.

There was no answer.

In the gloom, David advanced slowly towards the light. Halfway down the corridor, he bumped into something he couldn't identify and swore quietly. He considered turning on the light to avoid any more mishaps, but decided to carry on in the dark.

'Anna?' he said again, a little louder. 'Where the fuck are you?'

Not a sound disturbed the absolute silence that reigned in the flat.

Worried now, David continued down the corridor. All sorts of possibilities went through his mind, from burglary to a simple prank.

The latter wasn't unlikely. Anna was quite capable of waiting for him in bed, surrounded by a sea of candles, champagne glass in hand. Paul had better not stay away too long, or even turn his head.

As David neared the kitchen, there was more light in the corridor. He looked around for something to use as a weapon in case there was a burglar in the flat. He chose a marble paperweight, a hideous thing shaped like a pyramid that Anna had inherited from her grandparents. He held it by the base, with the top facing out.

He advanced the last few metres to the kitchen. At the door, he glanced in cautiously.

Anna was sitting at the table. She was in a dressing gown and had her back to him. She was staring at the window in front of her.

David stood in the kitchen doorway.

'Right, here I am,' he said. 'What's up?'

She didn't turn round. She didn't move, either. She seemed to be enthralled by the darkness beyond the window.

'You could act a bit more pleased to see me,' David pointed out.

Still Anna did not respond.

David realised why when he saw the gag in her mouth. There were handcuffs on her wrists, attached to one of the table legs by a steel cable. She was wide-eyed with terror.

David rushed to her. He put his improvised weapon down on the table and started to untie the gag. Anna shook her head and jerked her chin towards the door.

He turned round and immediately realised his mistake.

In the doorway, his back against the fridge, stood an old acquaintance.

David felt his legs give way.

The Neanderthal looked calm and absolutely in control of the situation. He was holding a gun, pointed down. His physical bulk was just as impressive, and his battered face as ugly.

If this had been a film, David would have distracted the colossus for a fraction of a second, grabbed the paperweight, hit him on the head and made the most of the element of surprise to seize the gun. Then he'd have knocked him out, freed Anna and celebrated the next fifty years as a hero. Unfortunately, in real life his chances of success were almost nil. Such an attempt would almost certainly end in ridicule.

On the other hand, he knew what his opponent was capable of, and had no intention of letting himself be killed without at least putting up a fight. Humiliation or death? David didn't have long to choose, quite apart from the fact that neither option was very satisfactory.

'How do you like my little show?' asked the Neanderthal. It was a rhetorical question.

He went on: 'Your girlfriend's very pretty. We've been getting along great, haven't we?'

For a moment, he looked away from David and slid his gaze over Anna's leg, which was exposed to mid-thigh.

David knew this would be his only chance. He placed both hands behind him on the table, as if to lean on it, and felt for the paperweight. It didn't take long to find. He closed his fingers around the marble pyramid.

The manoeuvre was laughable as well as poorly executed. The Neanderthal realised what David was up to. He raised his gun and pointed it at David's head.

'Keep still. I don't think your girlfriend wants to see the inside of your skull.'

He said to Anna: 'Do you want to see his brains splattered everywhere?'

Anna moaned and shook her head.

The brute turned towards David. 'You see, she doesn't. Now be a good boy and put down the little stone.'

David put the paperweight back on the table and crossed his arms.

'What do you want from us?' he asked.

'I'm disappointed,' said the Neanderthal. 'I waited all day for you to call, but there was nothing: no call, no message, nothing. It's not very polite.'

'You gave me a week to find the illumination. That leaves five and a half days, unless one of us has trouble with mental arithmetic.'

The Neanderthal shook his head. 'There's been a change to the schedule. I need it sooner than planned.'

'It's not very fair, changing the rules in mid-game.'

'When you're grown-up enough to hold a gun, you can make your own rules. Until then, you do as I tell you and say "Yes, sir" to everything I say.'

'Yes, sir,' David couldn't help saying.

Again, the urge to provoke was irresistible.

The Neanderthal looked irritated. 'I really should shoot you.'

David felt this was an interesting opening.

'So why don't you?' he asked.

The brute said nothing.

David pretended to have a sudden inspiration.

'Wait, that's it! It's your colleague who usually does the dirty work, isn't it? He's the real killer. You're just there to amuse the audience, looking like a giant cartoon ape. You're there to scare the kids and give them nightmares.'

Still no reaction from the moron, just a hint of unease.

'By the way, where is he, your colleague?' David went on disingenuously.

A brief tremor crossed the Neanderthal's face. This confirmed David's suspicions: he'd put his finger on a problem. He didn't know what was going on, but references to his associate seemed to make the colossus uncomfortable.

'Not here,' said the Neanderthal after a moment.

David didn't have time to make the most of his fleeting advantage. The Neanderthal stepped towards him, his distress apparently evaporating en route.

With his free hand he gripped David's neck. He pressed the gun against David's lower abdomen with the other.

'You've got till tomorrow to find the illumination and call me. Understood?'

'And if not, what? You've already beaten me up, and you can't kill me straight away or you'll never get hold of it. You don't have many options left. What do you suggest to motivate me?'

The Neanderthal's snarl made David realise that his optimism had been premature.

'Your girlfriend seems to like being tied up. If I don't hear from you by tomorrow night, I'll come back for her, now I know where she lives, and I'll take her back to my place. I've got some equipment there.'

He licked his lips. 'You'll love it, sweetheart, you'll see. I'm in a creative mood at the moment. We can have a party together, you and me. I'll video it and send it to your boyfriend. You're getting married soon, aren't you? Do you think he'd like it as a wedding present?'

Anna moaned. She started writhing desperately on the chair.

The Neanderthal stared at David coldly. 'Is that enough motivation for you?'

39

Sorel had made the decision on impulse when he got back to his hotel room, a little after ten p.m. He'd had enough of waiting for Stern to decide to give him the green light. Deep down, something – what was commonly called experience, but which in Sorel had more to do with instinct – told him that he had to try to get the upper hand over his opponent now.

The problem with Stern was that he always moved his pawns at the wrong time. He would rather let a good opportunity pass than run the slightest risk. If such a strategy sometimes avoided defeat, it rarely ensured victory. But in Sorel's field, only absolute triumph guaranteed the players' survival. Any other result still left them vulnerable.

Sorel entered the lift, in the grey overalls worn by the maintenance staff at the tower. The employee who cleaned the building's top floor but one every night was lying in his underwear, unconscious, in the back of his van.

He unclipped the magnetic pass attached to the pocket of the overalls and swiped it through the reader by the lift door. As the lift rose, he switched on his PDA and looked at the office plan, though he already knew it by heart. During his previous stay in Paris, he'd paid a visit one night to the architects' firm that had designed the interior layout. He'd left with a copy of the plans, which he'd then scanned. At the time Sorel didn't know whether he'd ever use them, but foresight was the cornerstone of his job.

A muffled tune played as the lift reached the fifty-fifth floor. The door opened on to a vast space, divided into workstations by chest-height glass partitions. Having hacked into the database of the premises' security firm, Sorel knew that he had thirty seconds to disconnect the alarm. He went straight to the cabinet that concealed the control box, opened it and entered a six-digit code on the keypad. The warning light on the control panel went out. So far, so good.

According to his information, the place was deserted until the receptionist arrived at seven-thirty in the morning. He had eight hours to search the floor. For a highly trained agent, that was luxury. He took his time examining the communal areas, even though he didn't expect to find anything.

In fact, there was only one room that interested him. To get in, however, he had to get past a reinforced door. Thanks to his digital entry, Sorel knew what kind of lock he'd be dealing with. It took him only a few seconds to open the door.

Maxime Zerka's office occupied half the floor. An impressive window looked out on to the sleeping capital. There were a few paintings on the walls, but Sorel knew that Zerka kept the best pieces of his collection at his home, safe from prying eyes.

He scanned the room. One object attracted his attention because it contrasted sharply with its surroundings. On the glass coffee table, beside the remote control, there was a small black and white photograph in a slender gilt frame. It showed the teenage Zerka standing beside his father, beneath the sign of the small timber merchants his father had founded.

Sorel knew Zerka's file by heart. Childhood in Algeria. Arrival in France in 1962 at the time of independence. Taking the reins of the family firm on his father's death. Gradual takeover of competing firms, then international expansion, and finally diversification into luxury goods and communications. From his office at the top of the Tour Montparnasse, Zerka now controlled around twenty companies with a combined turnover of several billion euros. The little pied noir who'd started out with nothing had reached the top. The eagle's nest from which he reigned over this empire was a crude metaphor for his social rise. Maxime Zerka rarely went in for subtlety.

His success owed much to his uncompromising nature. Indeed, Zerka was renowned for the brutal way he conducted business. When a company interested him, he never tried to negotiate with the management and shareholders. He knew one tactic, and one only: force. He went on the attack, lowering his weapons only when victory was assured. Anyone who tried to stand up to him was mercilessly crushed. The best anyone else could hope for was not returning home with completely empty hands.

It was not, however, because of Zerka's methods that Sorel's superiors had decided to neutralise him. The world of business did not fall within their remit. Zerka could run his companies as he wished – it wasn't their problem.

But rumours had been circulating for some years about the manner in which Zerka had built up his art collection. According to these whispers, he bought everything within reach, without concern for it origins. He'd never been afraid to purchase a stolen painting. On the contrary, in addition to the savings he made upon purchase, he'd built up an underground network of wealthy collectors prepared to buy the pieces he tired of and ask no questions. In the long run, his manoeuvring would end up destabilising the market, and this was something Sorel's superiors could not tolerate.

A few years earlier, the French police had come very close to catching him. The Foundation didn't exist at the time. Sorel had been informed by a source close to Zerka that he was behind the theft of a Botticelli drawing from a Parisian collector. Unable to intervene in person on French territory, Sorel had provided the local police with a complete file on the operation. It was all there: a photograph of the drawing, the address of the large house in the sixteenth arrondissement where it was kept, and even the name of the man charged with running the operation. All that remained was to watch from a distance, wait for Zerka to take delivery of the stolen drawing and catch him red-handed.

But the new plan hadn't allowed for the incompetence of the policeman running the investigation. Obsessed by hatred of the man Zerka was using to steal the drawing, he'd stepped in too early, ruining everything. Zerka had waited three months, long enough for things to settle down, then made contact with a different network. The Botticelli had disappeared, and Sorel had found his informant with two bullets in his head. He was back to square one. The moronic police had wrecked a golden opportunity.

Sorel had made it a personal matter. He'd demanded – and got – the head of the chief investigator. Despite this meagre satisfaction, he'd been left with a bad taste in his mouth. He went back to the beginning. There was one simple question at the root of everything: why had Zerka taken such a big risk to get hold of the sketch? With his money, he could afford far more important pieces.

Sorel focused on the drawing that Zerka was so interested in. He spent months examining every square centimetre of the reproduction his source had provided. He'd consulted art historians specialising in Florentine art, and read *The Divine Comedy* from beginning to end without finding anything.

Everything became clear when he realised that the key factor wasn't the artist who'd made the sketch, or even its subject, but the name that Botticelli had written on his depiction of Hell. Zerka didn't want the piece for its artistic merit, or for its market value. The fact that it was by Botticelli was of secondary importance to him.

Zerka wanted Vasalis. Or, more exactly, he wanted Vasalis all to himself.

Sorel had identified an essential trait of Maxime Zerka's personality. Many collectors owned more masterpieces than they knew what to do with. Putting together a row of Picassos and Kandinskys wasn't difficult. You just needed good advice, a considerable fortune and, perhaps, a little taste. But Zerka had gone beyond that. He'd reached a point where what interested him was owning what others could not have: the most beautiful version of the *Irises*, for instance, or the only copy of a legendary text. Unique, exceptional things, which didn't come up for sale through the usual channels. In order to acquire them, Zerka was prepared to take extreme risks.

Sorel had pondered at length how to exploit this weakness. The hardest part was finding bait exciting enough to arouse Zerka's desire, and drive him to reveal himself. The trail of Vasalis was the answer. Not without difficulty, Sorel had eventually tracked down the palimpsest of the *De forma mundi* and, in return for a substantial payment, managed to convince the owner to go along with the game.

Once he'd put the plan together, he took it to his superiors. Unfortunately he'd picked a bad time: they were negotiating with Elias Stern to set up an organisation with him to use as a bridgehead in Europe. These brilliant strategists considered this a perfect opportunity to test how the Foundation would work under real-life conditions.

Sorel did all he could to persuade them not to involve Stern in his project, but Zerka's hatred for the art dealer since the *Irises* affair added to his superiors' excitement. If Zerka found out that Stern was his main rival for the purchase of the *De forma mundi*, they thought, it would drive him straight into the trap. Sorel obeyed orders. As principal coordinator, he gave two years of his life to the project.

The first phase of the plan went smoothly. Marie Gervex made public her wish to sell the codex. When Zerka stated his interest in buying it, she pretended to waver between the two offers before finally selling the manuscript to the Stern Foundation.

As Sorel had predicted, Zerka was furious. He even sent one of his men to the Foundation's headquarters to steal the codex as soon as word of its whereabouts got out. Sorel hadn't expected such audacity. He didn't react quickly enough.

A second opportunity arose when Zerka had Marie Gervex killed. By chance, Sorel found himself at the murder scene. He had decided to take a closer interest in Valentine Savi, and had been tailing her since early morning. He'd followed her to the Bibliothèque Nationale, then to Marie Gervex's flat. Despite Stern's faith in the girl, Sorel didn't trust her. And he was right: she was poking her nose into things that didn't concern her. She was a potentially destabilising element. The best thing was to take her out of the game as soon as possible.

When he had realised what the van driver intended to do, Sorel had seen it as a unique opportunity to get rid of her without compromising himself. That damned scooter had ruined everything. After that, Sorel had had to shoot Zerka's hit man, in order to avoid the questions Stern would undoubtedly ask when he found out that Sorel hadn't tried to prevent Marie Gervex's murder.

It had been another lost opportunity, and now Sorel was growing impatient. He felt that if he didn't get results soon, his superiors would sideline him. Stern enjoyed making life difficult for him, and would eventually have his hide. Sorel didn't want to end up in a consulate in some far-flung former Soviet republic. He had no choice now: he had to get Zerka to make a mistake.

With that in mind, he had come to the fifty-fifth floor of the Tour Montparnasse to look for clues, something that would help him anticipate Zerka's next move, and thus force his hand. And for that, there was nothing better than observation in the field.

Something had been bothering Sorel since he got into the office, but he couldn't pinpoint the source of his unease. He switched on his PDA again and opened the file containing the plans of the floor. He saw what was wrong straight away. On the plans, the window occupied only two-thirds of the wall. But now in front of him it took up the entire wall. The dimensions on the plans confirmed his suspicions: Zerka's office had been reduced by about a quarter of its size. From the outside, however, everything seemed to be in accordance with the plans.

Sorel had no trouble solving the problem. He picked up the remote control on the glass table, pointed it where the missing section of the room should be and started pressing buttons on the remote, one after another. Eventually a partition slid aside. Beside the television screen there was a door with a biometric lock with both voice and fingerprint recognition. Sorel knew he didn't have a hope of cracking it, even with the hacking software on his PDA. On the off chance, he tried the handle. It offered no resistance.

The door swung open. A row of spotlights came on automatically, filling the room with a bright, almost blinding light.

Prudently Sorel stayed outside. The room measured about ten metres square. The floor and walls were tiled in white. In the middle stood a stainless-steel table, and above it a halogen dome on a jointed arm like the lights in an operating theatre. Beneath it he could see a large plughole. A sink was fixed to the wall on one side. A stainless-steel worktop ran along the whole length of the wall facing the door. Three wide-rimmed metal trays sat in a row on its surface. From where he was standing, Sorel couldn't see their contents. Curious, he walked forward into the room.

Suddenly there was a brief flash on either side of the door-way through which he'd just stepped. He recognised intruder detectors, invisible from the outside.

With a nervous jump, he turned round and moved towards the door, but he wasn't quick enough. The door closed tightly with the sound of suction.

40

Valentine stared at the note Grimberg had left on the fridge door before leaving. He'd written: *Great evening. Thanks.*

'Prat,' she muttered with a smile, tearing off the Post-it note.

She crumpled it into a ball and threw it across the room. Opening the fridge, she took out a beer.

Valentine yawned. She was exhausted. A coffee would have been more appropriate, but she needed to get some sleep before going back to work at Stern's house. A beer – that was what she wanted so as not to break the rhythm of the evening.

After their talk with Superintendent Lopez, Vermeer had persuaded her to go with him to a trendy bar near the Place de la Bastille. One last drink had turned into a bar crawl around Paris that had lasted the best part of the night. She had drunk and smoked too much, and now she was dead tired. On the plus side, she hadn't had so much fun in ages. For a few hours she'd forgotten all about Vasalis, Stern and the Foundation. Vermeer's therapeutic methods were unorthodox but effective.

She drank half the beer, poured the rest away in the sink and then went to the room that served as bedroom, sitting room, study and storage room. Albert Cadas's file on the Brotherhood of the Sorbonne lay beside the computer. Valentine considered taking a look at it straight away.

But she decided not to, despite her curiosity. There was every chance that David was right, and that Albert Cadas's theory was a web of nonsense. Besides, a full day's hard work on the manuscript awaited her at the Foundation. She couldn't turn up there in this state. She had to get at least a couple of hours' sleep. She was past the age where she could stay up all night. Too bad about the Brotherhood.

She took off her leather jacket and dropped it at her feet. Then she removed her t-shirt, and was about to do likewise with her bra.

Slow applause rang out behind her.

Valentine turned round with a start to see David Scotto sitting on the sofa in the dark. He seemed to be enjoying the show.

She quickly put her t-shirt back on.

'Shame,' said David. 'Those lacy bits at the side are really pretty.'

Valentine was both stunned and furious. 'What the hell are you doing here?'

'I needed to talk to you, and the front door was ajar. I took it as an invitation to come in.'

Valentine cursed Grimberg inwardly. The idiot couldn't even close the door properly when he left.

'How did you find me?'

'I took traces of your DNA from my scooter. I had them tested, made a few calls to influential friends and here I am.'

'After midnight, I'm impervious to all forms of humour.'

Becoming serious, David said, 'You're in the directory, under "Art Restorers".'

Valentine almost threw him out there and then. But she realised she wasn't as angry as she should have been. She was actually quite pleased to see him. She put it down to the combined effects of alcohol and cannabis.

She slumped beside David on the sofa.

'Well, now that you're here, I suppose I can't chuck you out without at least asking *why* you're here.'

'I have a bit of a problem, and I wasn't sure who to turn to. I thought of telling my mother, but she'd have disinherited me if I'd woken her up in the middle of the night. That only left you. Bad luck.'

'I'm not sure I'm the best confidante right now, but go ahead.'

'The guy who beat me up the other night came back this evening. He wants the illumination straight away. If I don't give it to him, he's going to attack a girl I know. You saw what the bastards did to Marie Gervex. I don't want the same to happen to her.'

'Is she your girlfriend?' asked Valentine, still rather drunk.

'She's a close friend.'

'Close enough that you're so worried you can't sleep, and have driven across Paris to talk to me about it?'

David dodged the question. 'I have to get that illumination. The problem is, I don't have the faintest idea where it is. Apart from his office, I can't see where Cadas could have hidden it. I'll never find it without some help.'

'So what do you want me to do?'

'Your man Stern – do you think he'd help?'

Valentine leaned her head on the back of the sofa. She couldn't help closing her eyes.

'I have a horrible feeling he would,' she breathed, just before dozing off.

41

Sorel didn't panic. He was trained to deal with situations like this. He felt a rush of excitement as the adrenalin surged in his veins. The good news was that he'd activated the locking system himself on entering. Unless he'd set off a silent alarm, he reckoned his presence wouldn't be detected until morning, when the staff arrived. Sorel looked at his watch. He had a little over five hours to break out. He had a reasonable chance of escaping, as long as he made his brain function at optimum capacity.

As for the door itself, there was nothing doing. Even with the tools he had with him, he'd never get it open.

Sorel moved across the room. He recognised the items laid out on the trays. They made up a complete set of surgical instruments. This was the second piece of good news: a scalpel was a deadly weapon in expert hands like his. He took one from its sterile holder and slipped it into the pocket of his overalls.

One thing puzzled him, though: why had Zerka installed an operating theatre in his office? Sorel had seen his medical file. Zerka was in perfect health. He had no chronic condition to justify the existence of this room.

He didn't have time to dwell on the question. A barely audible whistling started up. Sorel identified the source immediately. The sound was coming from a vent in the ceiling, above the door. He could see nothing emanating from it, but he knew that gas was filling the room. The security system was more sophisticated than he'd thought. First, the intruder was trapped, and then nerve gas was pumped in to overpower him until security personnel arrived. The files he'd pirated had failed to mention this little detail.

Sorel had faced this situation before. He'd encountered it in training. He knew exactly what to do. He sat on the floor in a relaxation position, back against the wall and legs tucked up, and then placed the scalpel, his Baby Eagle and his watch in front of him. He took a few short breaths, filling his lungs with air. The gas hadn't yet permeated the entire room, but it would only be a matter of seconds.

An untrained individual could hold his breath for less than three minutes. In theory, security systems of this kind were calibrated to pump out gas for slightly longer than the average person could hold their breath. Sorel was banking on its being set to four minutes – this, at least, was what the manufacturers of such systems usually recommended. Sorel practised holding his breath every day, and his personal best was four minutes forty. That left him a good safety margin.

He tried to empty his mind and focus on the regular movement of the second hand on his watch.

After two minutes and fifteen seconds he started to recognise the effects of a lack of air. It was a feeling of general drowsiness. After three minutes, his vision began to blur and the vein at his temple pulsed harder.

Then he heard the sound he'd been waiting for. The whistling stopped and was replaced by a sucking noise. The ventilation system was removing the gas.

Just in time. Sorel was coming dangerously close to his limit, his head was spinning, his vision was dimming. He'd have to take a breath soon if he wasn't going to faint. But he didn't know how long the system would take to vent all the gas. He decided to wait a little longer. He calculated he could hold out for another twenty seconds. In theory, that was enough.

Involuntarily, he shifted his gaze from his watch to the scalpel. Sorel now knew what the room was for. It wasn't a hospital, it was an abattoir.

Suddenly he lost all focus. His body was no longer under control, and he opened his mouth despite himself. In a last flash of clarity, Sorel felt gas combined with oxygen fill his lungs.

42

'The illumination you're looking for is for sale.'

Elias Stern's voice, distorted by the phone's speaker, contained no trace of hesitation.

'How do you know?' asked Valentine, surprised.

'Last week, we got a call from one of my colleagues, an English book dealer. A client of his has put an illuminated leaf on the market. He thought I might be interested.'

'Why did he come to you?'

'He had read on your friend Vermeer's website that I had recently acquired the Vasalis manuscript. According to the book dealer, the page was the one missing from the codex. The one Tischendorf sent to the tsar.'

'Are you sure it's the illumination I've been told to find?' asked David.

'Absolutely. My colleague wouldn't give me his client's name, but, during our conversation, he slipped in that the man worked at the Sorbonne. We did some research, and identified two people who might have the leaf.'

'I suppose Albert Cadas was top of the list,' said David.

'Yes, but he killed himself before we had a chance to speak to him.'

'Who was your second suspect?'

'Well, you, David.'

After a moment of stunned silence, David said, grimacing, 'If your colleague promised you first refusal on the illumination, he was lying.'

He told Stern briefly about his encounter with the Neanderthal and his associate.

'I don't have the illumination,' he concluded, 'and Cadas is dead. If he really was the client, your colleague can wave good-bye to his commission.'

'It wasn't Cadas who put the illumination up for sale. My colleague contacted me again yesterday. He was here in Paris, with his client. Nora traced the call. They were phoning from an office at the Sorbonne.'

'Wait a minute,' said Valentine. 'If I'm understanding correctly, you were offered the illumination before Cadas's death. Is that right?'

'Exactly.'

Valentine pursued her train of thought out loud. 'The seller didn't yet have it in his possession, but he knew it existed and where to find it. He even knew how to get hold of it. I suppose your colleague told you nothing more about his client?'

'No, but now they want to conclude the sale quickly.'

David spluttered with indignation. 'The bastard stole the leaf from Cadas's office! I can see why he wants to get rid of it as quickly as possible.'

'What are you going to do?' asked Valentine. 'Surely you're not going to buy it?'

'It's a difficult decision. The people hunting down the illumination won't let go of David and his friend until they've got hold of it. When they find out that the Foundation owns it, they won't have a reason to threaten them any more.'

'But it was stolen!' cried Valentine. 'You can't just pretend you don't know!'

'If the Foundation doesn't buy the illumination, someone else will and it will disappear. We'll never see it again. Believe me, I don't like it, but we have no choice.'

Stern cleared his throat. 'Mr Scotto, would you mind if I have a word with Valentine in private? What I have to say to her concerns only us.'

David had no objection. He took the face cloth Valentine had found for him and headed for the bathroom.

'Go ahead,' said Valentine, after turning off the speakerphone.

'I've managed to get hold of the valuation report for your sketch. From the Louvre. It wasn't easy.'

'I can tell from your tone that I'm not going to like what you have to say.'

'Indeed. There's something strange.'

'What is it?'

'The insurers had your cleaning solution analysed. There was a problem with it: the acidity level was too high. That's why the ink was erased. Your mixture acted like a bleaching solution.'

Valentine took a few seconds to realise the full implications of these results.

'I don't understand. It was the same solution I'd used in previous restorations. If I'd got the proportions wrong, I'd have noticed. Other works would have been damaged.'

'In that case, we have to conclude that someone tampered with your solution. We have to find out who it was, and why that person changed the mixture.'

The revelation left Valentine speechless.

'Valentine . . .' continued Stern in a voice that was almost affectionate.

'Yes?'

'I'm so pleased you're not to blame. I'd like you to know that I never doubted it.'

43

A perfect cloudless blue, the sky was reflected in the glass walls of the Tour Montparnasse. At a bar table across the square, Hugo Vermeer pointed his camera at the top floor of the building, where a figure had appeared. He just had time to press the shutter release before it disappeared.

He viewed the picture on the camera's display. Despite the distance, you could clearly make out the features of the man caught in profile. Vermeer had never seen him in person, but there was no doubt as to who it was.

'You're about as convincing a tourist as you are a respectable citizen, Mr Vermeer.'

The Dutchman turned towards the young woman in a suit who had just sat down beside him.

'And you're just as pretty disguised as a secretary as you are in your killer's uniform, Nora. You're not going to torture me again, are you? Surely not in public?'

Stern's assistant removed her sunglasses and slid them into her bag. Her expression was perfectly blank, as if Vermeer inspired no particular feeling in her, which was probably the case.

'Can you see anything interesting from here? It isn't the most picturesque part of Paris.'

Vermeer handed Nora the camera. She looked at the picture on the display. She remained impassive as she recognised the man Vermeer had photographed.

'Maxime Zerka . . . He's kept his figure all these years.'

'Do you know him?'

'Yes, unfortunately. He bought quite a few pieces from Elias before falling out with him over some stupid business.'

'The *Irises*,' said Vermeer.

'You're well informed, as always.'

'I don't deserve any credit. Everyone knew about it. Stern was hardly discreet over the matter. He held Zerka up to ridicule.'

'Usually Elias never comments publicly on deals in progress. But Zerka was too pushy. He made the mistake of threatening Elias. Making the whole business public was the best way of getting him to back off. He got what he deserved.'

Vermeer took back the camera, turned it off and slipped it into his trouser pocket.

'Why did you call me, Nora? To see the results of the beating you so kindly gave me?'

'I thought it would be good to patch things up after our unfortunate misunderstanding the other day.'

'I find that hard to believe. I'm wary of customers who don't buy anything, and destroy valuable furniture.'

'I can't disagree. That said, your back seems much better.'

Vermeer was usually indulgent towards pretty women, but Nora's attitude was really starting to get on his nerves.

'I've had enough. You're not what you pretend to be, are you?'

'And what do I pretend to be, in your opinion?'

'A well-bred young lady with a love of books. A deathly dull, shy virgin. Take your pick.'

Nora unbuttoned her jacket and slid the holster she wore in the small of her back round to her hip. Sunlight struck the butt of the gun.

'Let's just say I'm versatile, and that's why the Foundation hired me.'

Her attention was drawn to an elderly woman in the middle of the road. She was trying to save time by going straight across the crossroads, but eventually had to give up and use the pedestrian crossings at the edges of the square.

'Why are you taking an interest in Zerka?' she asked, her eyes fixed on the stream of cars and motorcycles roaring past.

'An old friend advised me to.'

'Did he also tell you to keep a safe distance from the bastard?' On her lips, even insults lost their coarseness.

'No, but my friend can be absent-minded,' answered Vermeer. 'He sometimes forgets important details.'

'I'm serious. Zerka is no angel.'

'That's lucky. Neither am I.'

'Zerka is much more dangerous than those Chechens you met. He won't let you go if you get too close to his little secrets.'

Vermeer was astonished to hear Nora mention an episode from his past that he'd thought was secret. He'd always been careful not to boast about it.

'How did you hear about the Chechens? No one knows about that.'

'The Foundation has very reliable sources.'

Visibly nervous, Vermeer rummaged in his pocket, took out a few coins and set them down beside his coffee cup.

'I've had it up to here with all the mystery. I'm beginning to think your Foundation is involved in more than just art.'

Nora seemed unruffled by his hostility. She answered him without raising her voice.

'You're mistaken. Everything we do is related to art. We simply operate on the margins, like you. Our methods differ, that's all.'

'I love the way you phrase things,' said Vermeer. 'Where did you take lessons in hypocritical waffle?'

He stood up. Nora slid the holster to the small of her back and buttoned her jacket.

'It was Lopez who gave you Zerka's name, wasn't it? Do you really think he did so out of the kindness of his heart?'

Vermeer sat down again. He had lost his colour.

'Oh, come on,' said Nora, 'don't look at me like that. As I said, we're well informed. We know you met him last night at the Lutetia.'

'But . . . how?' spluttered the Dutchman.

'Lopez wants to settle some scores before he disappears from circulation, particularly with Sorel and Zerka. You're his best means of striking at them. When you contacted him, you provided him with an unexpected opportunity to have a bit of fun.'

'What have I got to do with Sorel and Zerka? I don't know either of them.'

'But they know you. Zerka is the main cause of your problems with Lopez. It was he who hired you to steal the Botticelli. Sorel wanted to use you to trap Zerka, but Lopez went over his head.'

'Hang on a minute,' interrupted Vermeer. 'First of all, who is Sorel? A policeman? Some kind of secret agent?'

Nora hesitated. 'Something like that,' she said eventually. 'The Foundation has relationships with a number of government agencies that are also involved in combating art smuggling. Sorel works for one of them. We've set up a sort of association with his superiors. They provide the Foundation with information, and the bulk of its infrastructure. In return, we make it possible for them to intervene in countries where they're not always welcome. We're their cover in Europe, so to speak.'

'Why are you telling me all this now?'

'Because you'd have kept on nosing around if I hadn't. And our operation requires a maximum of discretion. We can't let you go on asking questions all over the place. On top of that, you're in this up to your neck. We'd rather you were on our side. You have the power to do quite a lot of damage.'

'So let me see if I've got this right: you're the good guys, and Zerka is the stock evil bastard?'

'Exactly.'

Vermeer didn't know what to say. He was struggling to take in everything Nora had just told him. Even his most elaborate theories had never touched on such a possibility.

'What happened to me,' he stammered, 'the arrest, being held in custody . . . That was you lot?'

Nora shook her head. 'No, we had nothing to do with that. Sorel tried to use Lopez to catch Zerka, and you ended up in the middle. The Foundation didn't exist at the time. It was set up to avoid such fiascos.'

'For good guys, your methods are rather aggressive, aren't they?'

'The stakes are high, Mr Vermeer. Individuals like Zerka must be eliminated, one way or another. We're talking here about murders, millions . . .'

Nora stopped. She was staring at a man in a suit and tie who had emerged from the main entrance of the building opposite, and was now walking briskly towards the taxi rank. Dozens of similar figures had come out of the Tour Montparnasse in the last ten minutes, but only this man had attracted Nora's interest.

Vermeer took a few seconds to realise why she had fallen silent. 'Do you know him?'

'He's a book dealer. His name's Miller. I wasn't expecting to see him here.'

Vermeer could see from her face that she was thinking fast. The taxi the man had climbed into moved off into traffic.

Nora watched until it disappeared in the distance. Then she stood up suddenly as if she'd just understood something important.

'Come on,' she said. 'Let's go back to the Foundation.'

She made her way quickly across the square, zigzagging between cars with an agility Vermeer couldn't match. It was a miracle he reached the other side in one piece.

As she reached the pavement opposite, Nora waved to the Foundation's Mercedes, which was parked down the street. At the wheel, the chauffeur, Franck, was smoking. He took one last drag and threw the cigarette out of the window.

Nora slowed to let Vermeer catch up. 'I'll phone Elias and tell him we're coming,' she said. 'Get in. I'll join you in a second.'

Vermeer headed towards the Mercedes. Nora signalled to Franck to start up the engine.

At that moment, flames burst from the bonnet of the Mercedes with a terrific roar. Splinters of metal filled the air.

The blast flung Vermeer against Nora. He felt metal fragments pierce his chest and legs. He fell backwards on to the pavement. Above his head, the sky reflected in the tower turned black.

44

David made his way along the Rue des Écoles like an automaton. With his eyes fixed on the ground a metre ahead of him, he walked quickly. He wanted to get this over with.

He hadn't even gone back to his flat to get changed. He was wearing yesterday's clothes, which were all crumpled from half a night on the sofa. He'd had a quick shower after the phone conversation with Stern, and then left Valentine's in a hurry without explaining why.

Stern had confirmed what David already believed: the solution to this affair was to be found at the Sorbonne. Cadas had known the person who stole the illumination, and David knew who that was.

He went through the entrance gate, stopped at the edge of the courtyard and peered round.

He was lucky. The man he was looking for was under a colonnade, deep in conversation with a group of students.

David headed straight towards him. He had no idea what he was going to do, but all rationality had left him. He was angry. Angry because of Albert Cadas's death, because of his foundering academic career. Because of all the things that should never have happened, and had left his life in ruins.

He placed a hand on the shoulder of the man who was the cause of it all. 'You bastard!' he muttered.

The Dean tried to free himself, but David tightened his grip. 'What on earth's got into you, Scotto?'

'Bastard!' David said again. 'How could you sink so low?'

The Dean stared at him in astonishment. 'I have no idea what you're talking about.'

His surprise seemed genuine.

'You pushed Cadas out of the window because he wouldn't give you the illumination, didn't you?' insisted David.

'What illumination are you talking about?'

'The one that was in Albert Cadas's cabinet.' A crowd had started to gather round them.

'Why don't we go to my office?' said the Dean. 'We can discuss things more calmly there.'

'No way! We're going to settle this here and now.'

About ten metres away, the Chief of Security was striding towards them, accompanied by one of his guards.

When he saw them, David let go of the Dean's shoulder, but his anger didn't subside.

'Get out of the bloody way!' shouted Moreau to the students standing between him and the two men. 'Is everything all right, sir? What seems to be the problem?'

David prepared himself for the worst, but the Dean, on the contrary, sought to calm the situation.

'Everything's fine, thank you. Would you mind if we used your office for a few minutes? I need to have a word with Scotto, but my office doesn't seem to be the appropriate place.'

Moreau nodded. 'Come with me.'

He led them to the security office, parting the crowd with arms outstretched.

'Out of the way! The show's over. Back to class.'

David and the Dean followed him. Moreau showed them into the office, dismissing the guards who were there with a peremptory wave.

'Will you be needing me?'

'Yes, definitely. Scotto wants to tell us about the spate of deaths that's struck the university this week. So it'll be useful to have you here. Is that it, Scotto? You know something about Albert Cadas's death?'

David was confused. When he'd got there, he'd been certain that it was the Dean who'd stolen the illuminated page from Albert Cadas's office. But now he was having serious doubts. Or else the man was exceptionally cool-headed.

The Dean smoothed the jacket sleeve that David had been gripping a few minutes earlier.

'If you know something we don't, Scotto, now's the time to tell us. I launched an immediate inquiry into the deaths of Cadas and Fargue. I too have difficulty believing that two accidents could occur like that, so close together. So far, Moreau hasn't found anything, but I have a feeling you can help.'

'So you didn't steal the illumination?'

'I've told you, I don't know what you're talking about.'

His obvious sincerity convinced David. 'Just before he died, Cadas got hold of a medieval illumination. It proved that Vasalis existed. He kept it in his office. I went there yesterday and there was an empty space in the cabinet where it should have been.'

The Dean didn't ask how David had got into an office that he himself had locked after his visit there with Fargue.

'If you're implying that Cadas was killed by the person who stole the illumination, I must stop you now. He was alone in his office at the time of his death. It was suicide. There's no doubt about it.'

'Cadas spent his whole life searching for proof of Vasalis's existence. Why would he kill himself just after finding it at last?'

'If the illumination had already disappeared when he went into his office, it might explain his violent reaction.'

'Except there are no witnesses. So we'll never know.'

The Dean turned towards Moreau. 'You took photos when you were in his office, didn't you? Have you got them to hand?'

The Chief of Security indicated the computer on his control console. 'They're on the hard disk.'

'Let's take a look then.'

Moreau opened the folder, which contained some twenty pictures.

'You took them just after Cadas committed suicide, is that right?' said the Dean.

'Yes. I got there a couple of minutes after it happened. I saw that the office was empty. I went to check the doors of the other offices on that floor. They were all locked. Then I came back here for my camera. My men never left Cadas's office, so nobody could have stolen anything in that time, I'm absolutely positive about that. The office is exactly as it was at the time of Cadas's suicide.'

'Was the metal cabinet open when you went in?' asked the Dean.

Moreau nodded.

'Did you take a picture?'

'Yes, but not close up. I don't think you can see the books inside.'

'Please show us anyway.'

Moreau double-clicked on the file in question. The photograph had been taken about a metre away from the cabinet. It was hard to make out much, as the doors were only half open and the inside was in shadow.

'You can't see a thing,' said David.

'The gap you mentioned – where was it?' asked Moreau.

'In the middle of one of the upper shelves.'

'Let me see what I can do.'

Moreau enlarged the central part of the photograph and increased the brightness. The result was adequate, though not perfect. It was still hard to read the titles on the spines, but you could clearly distinguish the shapes of the different books. The gap between books that David had noticed had been there at the time of Albert Cadas's suicide.

He placed a finger on the screen.

'The illumination was there, look. Someone stole it before

Cadas arrived. That's why he killed himself. He couldn't endure having his find taken from him.'

Moreau gave a muffled cry. 'Hang on! What was the illumination in?'

'I don't know,' said David. 'I've never seen it. Judging by the size of the gap in the cabinet, I think Cadas must have put it in a slim cardboard box, or something.'

'Just one moment.'

Moreau closed the photo file and, with a few keystrokes, brought the screenshot he'd taken for Joseph Fargue up on the display. He pointed out the archive box Miller was carrying under his arm.

'The page could be inside that, couldn't it?'

'It's possible,' said David. 'Who is that man?'

'He isn't a member of staff. He has a foreign name. Wait . . . It's written in here.'

Moreau brought out the notebook in which the names of all visitors to the university were recorded.

'Here we are, I've got it. His name's Miller. Simon Miller.'

'Where was this photograph taken?' asked David.

'The camera that took it is on the landing on the same floor as Cadas's office. Miller left an hour before Cadas committed suicide. He arrived empty-handed, and left carrying those books and the box.'

'If he didn't take them from Cadas's office, where are they from?' asked the Dean.

'That's exactly what Fargue wondered when he saw the pictures.'

'Fargue? You showed him this recording?'

Moreau realised he'd made a mistake mentioning Fargue's visit to the Dean. He wasn't supposed to show the security-camera recordings to just anyone.

He tried to justify himself. 'He was very insistent and—'

'When did he see it?' interrupted the Dean curtly.

'The day he died, not long before his fall. When he saw the

man carrying the books, he lost it. He rushed straight out of here.'

'What's special about those books?' asked David.

The Dean collapsed on to a chair. He held his face in his hands, as if already feeling the storm his next words would unleash.

'Those books are proof that Joseph Fargue's fall was no accident. We have a murderer somewhere in the university.'

David could see in the Dean's eyes that, at that moment, he would have given anything to be a million miles from the Sorbonne.

45

Stern looked sombre when Valentine saw him, from afar, sitting on a chair in the entrance hall of the intensive-care unit at Cochin Hospital. Gripping the knob of his cane, he was staring at the wall opposite. He looked very old and frail. Though impeccably dressed as always, he seemed to be floating inside his suit.

Valentine rushed into his arms. 'What happened?'

'There was an explosion.'

'Hugo . . . Is he . . . ?'

Stern shook his head. 'He's badly injured. They're operating on him now.'

'Is he going to be all right?'

'The doctors wouldn't give a prognosis. They don't seem too hopeful.'

Valentine felt tears run down her cheeks. She hugged Stern, but retreated almost immediately, and wiped her cheeks with the sleeve of her sweater.

'What about Nora?'

'She got off more lightly. Vermeer was standing in front of her when the Mercedes blew up. He took most of the debris. She's a bit bruised, but she'll be up and about in a few days. Franck wasn't so lucky. He was killed outright.'

'What happened?'

'The police suspect foul play. According to their investigators, there was a bomb connected to the starter. They're waiting to conclude the preliminary investigations before they formally declare that the explosion wasn't an accident, but they don't really have any doubts. Luckily the bomb wasn't very big. It destroyed the car, but collateral damage was limited. Otherwise Nora and Vermeer wouldn't have survived.'

Valentine suddenly realised that it was odd Vermeer and Stern's assistant had been in the same place.

'What were they doing together? Vermeer didn't mention he'd be seeing Nora.'

'I asked Nora to go and speak to him. I wanted him to know certain things about the Foundation. They were by the Tour Montparnasse when it happened.'

'Why did they meet there? Hugo hates that area.'

'It was he who chose the meeting place. He must have had something important to do there.'

'Zerka,' murmured Valentine.

Stern stiffened. 'What was that name?'

'Hugo took me to see someone last night. A policeman. He mentioned Zerka.'

'Zerka has offices in the Tour Montparnasse,' confirmed Stern. 'Nora will tell us more when she's well enough to speak. I don't think that'll be too long now.'

His mobile phone rang. He took it from the inside pocket of his jacket.

'This is probably Sorel. I've left him several messages. Hello?'

'Superintendent Lopez speaking. We haven't met.'

'I know who you are, Superintendent. Sorel has told me of your exploits. He doesn't seem particularly fond of you.'

'Could you spare me a few minutes of your time, Mr Stern?'

'When?'

'Let's say in the next half-hour.'

'I'm busy now, Superintendent. Could we make it a little later? I've already been interviewed by your colleagues.'

'I have something interesting to show you. I think it's connected with the explosion. I'd like your opinion.'

'One moment,' said Stern. He glanced enquiringly at Valentine.

'Go ahead,' she murmured. 'I'll stay here.'

Stern went back to the superintendent. 'Very well, Superintendent. I'll come and meet you. Where are you?'

'Have you ever been to the Medico-Legal Institute, Mr Stern? It's not on the usual tourist trail, but the place has its charms, you'll see.'

46

The Medico-Legal Institute was along the Seine, opposite the Gare d'Austerlitz. Stern walked through the imposing entrance to the red-brick building and headed towards a man in an old-fashioned suit who, despite the numerous signs, was smoking a cigarette, leaning against the coffee machine. He was holding a cup, which he raised to his lips as Stern came level with him.

'Superintendent Lopez.'

'Mr Stern. I heard about your assistant and Vermeer. I'm so sorry.' His face expressed the exact opposite, at least with regard to the Dutchman.

'Thank you, Superintendent. What can I do for you? You'll understand that, given the circumstances, I can't stay long. I'd like to get back to the hospital as soon as possible.'

'Don't worry. I'll get straight to the point. Do you know Mr Sorel's whereabouts?'

'I haven't heard from him since last night. He's staying at the George V. You can easily get his room number if you want to speak to him. He's a grown-up. I don't keep track of his movements.'

'Well, you should. Come with me, please.'

Lopez dropped his cigarette butt into the cup, which he threw into a bin. Without bothering to check if Stern was following him, he set off down a long corridor. The double doors at the end bore a sign marked 'No entry to unauthorised persons'.

The policeman pushed open one of the doors, letting Stern through first. Then he went up to a metal door and pressed a button on the wall. A bell rang on the other side of the door.

A voice came over the intercom: 'Hello?'

'Lopez.'

The door opened with a click. Lopez entered ahead of Stern. A man in a white gown came to meet them.

Lopez made the introductions: 'Mr Stern, this is Stéphane Barbé, one of our pathologists.'

Stern had never met a forensic pathologist before. Without really knowing why, he'd always thought the job must leave its mark physically. But Stéphane Barbé looked nothing like the stereotype Stern had pictured. He was young, and his hair was artfully tousled and gelled. An earpiece protruded from the collar of his polo shirt. He removed the other from his ear, which sported a silver earring, and held out a hand to the older man.

'Pleased to meet you.'

'Likewise.'

Barbé indicated the far wall of the cold room, which was lined with stainless-steel drawers.

'Shall we take a look?'

'Yes, let's get on with it,' said Lopez.

Barbé looked first at Stern, then at Lopez. 'Have you warned him?' he asked the policeman.

'Warned me about what?' said Stern.

'Hasn't Lopez told you about the state of the corpse?'

'He hasn't even mentioned a corpse.'

Barbé flashed a look of alarm at the superintendent, who merely shrugged.

'The body was fished out of the Seine this morning, not far from here,' he said.

'And how does this concern me?' asked Stern.

Lopez signalled to the pathologist with a jerk of the chin. Stéphane Barbé opened one of the drawers about halfway up. A body covered in a white sheet lay in it. He lifted the top half of the sheet. It was Sorel.

'Do you recognise him?' asked Lopez.

'Is that an official question?'

'Absolutely.'

'It's Julien Sorel, who was Head of Security for the Stern Foundation. How did he die?'

'He was murdered,' said the pathologist.

Stern had been expecting this reply, but he still looked shocked.

'When did it happen?' he asked.

'We'll have to wait for the autopsy to establish the exact time of death, but it was sometime during the night, the early hours of this morning at the latest. At any rate, he wasn't in the water long.'

'Why did you mention his appearance just now? His face is unmarked.'

The pathologist's expression darkened. 'He was tortured. I've counted around fifty cuts to his chest, arms and legs, as well as some thirty fractures and about as many burns, probably made with a blowtorch, judging by the size and depth of the wounds.'

'My God,' said Stern. 'Was he still alive when they did all this?'

Barbé nodded. 'At first sight, the cause of death would seem to be a massive haemorrhage. He has wounds over almost all his body surface. That means the injuries occurred ante-mortem.'

'In other words, he was bled like a pig,' said Lopez. 'He must have squealed like one too.' He stared at Sorel's waxen face. 'Listen, Sorel was a rotten bastard. No one's going to miss him, least of all me. But it's my job to catch whoever did it.'

'Why are you telling me?' asked Stern. 'You don't need my consent.'

'Indeed not. But everything bearing on Sorel is more or less top secret. I've already reached the limits of my authority. Help me out. I'm not asking much; just put me on the right track. After that, I'll sort myself out.'

'I can't, Superintendent.'

'Why not?

'Because Sorel's superiors would be very unhappy if I revealed the nature of his association with the Foundation. The French authorities are aware of their activities. That's all you need to know.'

Lopez looked pensive. 'If you say so . . .'

Abruptly he pulled off the sheet covering the body, revealing Sorel's naked form. Stern looked horrified when he saw the cruelty that had been inflicted on him.

Lopez seemed pleased with the effect. 'As you can see,' he said, 'only the face and fingers were spared.'

Barbé moved between the policeman and the corpse. Without a word, he drew the sheet back over it and closed the drawer.

Stern took a moment to recover his composure. 'Strange . . .' he said at last. 'Why didn't the killers touch them?'

'They obviously wanted Sorel to be identified quickly,' answered Lopez.

'What's the point of that?'

'It's a message, Mr Stern, and I think it's addressed to you. I'd say someone's decided to give your Foundation a thorough purging.'

47

By the time David and the Dean had finished watching the security video, they knew who'd stolen the illumination from Albert Cadas's metal cabinet. They had also solved the mystery of the books missing from the Research Centre. Regarding the death of Joseph Fargue, they could only make a guess, but deep down they were in no doubt that his fall had been no accident.

One person was to blame for all of it. Even Albert Cadas's suicide could be seen as a consequence of his scheming, as nothing indicated that he would have killed himself had the illumination not been stolen.

Suddenly the Dean paused the video. He turned to the Chief of Security, who was waiting in the doorway that gave on to the courtyard, smoking a cigarette.

'Call the police. And go and check Agostini's office, just in case. If he's there, hold him until the police arrive. Otherwise lock everything and come back here.'

'On my way.' Moreau grabbed his phone from the desk and hurried out. The Dean stared once more at the paused figure of Raymond Agostini on the video. Then he switched off the display in annoyance.

Fargue had stopped too soon when he'd watched the video. Agostini had entered the camera's field of vision first thing in the morning, just after the university opened. At that hour, he could be sure he wouldn't be disturbed.

Getting into Albert Cadas's office wasn't much of a problem. If David knew about giving the door a shove with his shoulder to open it without the key, Agostini probably did too. It explained why there were no signs of forced entry. As for the padlock on the cabinet, the odds were that Albert Cadas trusted his friend enough to give him the combination. Agostini had taken the illumination and handed it to Miller with the books stolen from the Research Centre. Then he must have locked himself in his own office. Contrary to what Moreau thought, the floor hadn't been deserted at the time of Cadas's suicide. The professor of Ancient Greek had still been there when the Chief of Security and his men arrived. He'd simply had to wait a few hours before coming out of his hiding place without being spotted.

Regarding Miller's role, a quick Internet search led David and the Dean to the same conclusion as Joseph Fargue. They could only hope that the book dealer hadn't yet left France with the stolen books, otherwise it was unlikely they'd ever be recovered.

'Why do you think Agostini did it?' David asked the Dean.

'Money, I suppose.'

'But to betray his closest friend like that . . .'

'Amateur psychology isn't my speciality, but I can imagine what went through his mind. He's still got a mortgage to pay off on his house on the Côte d'Azur, hasn't he? Debts, an inadequate salary and an unexpected opportunity: it might be as banal as that.'

David looked sceptical. He realised from the Dean's tone that he didn't intend to delve any further.

'What are you going to do now?'

The Dean shrugged. 'Waiting for the police and letting them do their job would seem to be a wise option.'

'Agostini lives nearby.'

'Is that a statement or a suggestion?'

'More an encouragement not just to sit back when murder and theft have been committed in your institution. You can't evade your responsibilities. You've been more combative with lesser concerns. True, you were in a more comfortable position . . .'

David saw from the Dean's face that the unspoken truce between them had just been broken.

'This is a matter for the police,' the Dean replied curtly. 'I'm not going to go after Agostini with my Swiss Army knife and pocket torch. And even if we did find him at home, what could we do? Jump on him and tie him up, while waiting for reinforcements? Come now, let's be sensible. That would be ridiculous.'

Moreau returned, out of breath. 'Agostini isn't in his office. I left one of my men there, in case he comes back. I've also told the security guards at the various entrances to inform me if he comes past. I thought it advisable not to explain why.'

'You did the right thing. For the time being, it's best that we're the only ones who know. What about the police?'

'They'll be here in ten minutes.'

'Excellent.'

'What now?' asked Moreau.

'Don't you start,' muttered the Dean. 'As far as you're concerned, stay here and wait for the police. Call me as soon as they arrive.'

'All right.'

'What about me?' said David.

'You can get out of here. I'll give your name to the police. And not a word to anyone about this bloody mess.' He pointed a finger at David. 'Do you understand, Scotto? Stay at home and don't speak to a soul. Don't even answer the phone. Let me remind you that a decision regarding your future at the Sorbonne is still pending. If you play the fool, the committee members will be sure to know when they review your case. I can guarantee it.'

The Dean seemed confident of his powers of persuasion, but his threats paled into insignificance compared to those of the Neanderthal. Before the Dean had even finished his sentence, David had made up his mind.

48

Nora winced with pain as she opened her eyes. She looked around the hospital room, bewildered.

Valentine came to sit on the edge of the bed. 'How are you feeling?' she asked softly.

'I ache all over. How do I look?'

'Pretty good for someone who's just miraculously escaped death. Do you remember what happened? The explosion?'

Nora nodded slowly. 'Vermeer?' she asked, her features contorted with pain.

'He's just come out of the operating theatre. The doctors aren't sure if he'll pull through.'

'I'm so sorry. He was in front of me when the car blew up and . . .' She groaned and fell back against the bed, exhausted. Valentine helped adjust the pillow under her head.

'Don't try to sit up,' she said. 'You've had a big shock. The doctors are going to keep you under observation for a day or two before they let you go home.'

A gleam came into Nora's eyes. 'Where's Elias? I have to speak to him.'

'He had to go somewhere. He'll be back soon.'

Nora closed her eyes. For a moment Valentine thought she'd fallen asleep, but then her lips moved.

'Yes, Nora?'

'The drawing . . .'

'Which drawing do you mean?'

'The one from the Louvre.'

'Elias has already told me about the valuation results. I know about the problem with the cleaning solution. You must rest.'

Nora suddenly became agitated. 'My . . . bag . . .' she said weakly.

Valentine got up and looked around the room. Eventually she found the bag hanging on a hook by the door. She unhooked it and brought it to Nora.

'Here it is.'

Nora opened her eyes with difficulty. She pointed at a pocket on the front of the bag.

'There . . .' was all she had the strength to say.

Valentine opened the zip pocket. 'What am I looking for?'

'The letter . . .'

Valentine took out a small envelope addressed to Nora at the Stern Foundation.

'Open it,' whispered Nora.

Inside the envelope there were two typed pages, folded in three. The first page bore the Louvre letterhead and the previous day's date.

Valentine quickly read the beginning.

Dear Madam,

In view of our long-standing relationship with Mr Stern, please find enclosed in this exceptional case the log of Restoration Department entry passes for 11 March 2007. We would be very grateful if you would respect the confidential nature of the information.

This was followed by the standard polite formulas and the signature of the museum's Chief Administrator.

Valentine's hands were shaking. The eleventh of March 2007 was the last day of her former life. The following day she had turned the sketch of St John the Baptist into a sheet of scrap paper.

She looked at the second page. It was a printout headed *Entry Log: Restoration Department*. One column showed a series of identification codes, in numerical order. The entry and exit times of pass-holders were recorded beside each code. Indeed, in order to get in or out of the restoration workshops you had to swipe your ID card through a reader at the door. Valentine had always thought it a simple precaution to deter intruders. She'd never imagined that a record of all comings and goings was stored.

At the bottom of the page, an unknown hand – probably Nora's – had circled one of the identification codes in red pen and written a capital V beside it. Valentine recognised the number she'd been given when she worked at the Louvre.

According to the printout, that day she'd arrived at the workshop at 9.12 a.m., gone out for lunch at 12.33 p.m., returned at 2.07 p.m., and hadn't left until 9.23 p.m.

Strangely, the day of 11 March remained engraved on her memory with absolute clarity, while the following two years were a blur.

Valentine could remember exactly what she'd done that day. She'd left the restoration workshops last, long after all her colleagues. She'd wanted to finish the red chalk drawing by Boucher so that she could start work on the Leonardo sketch the next morning. It wasn't what had been planned, but she was in the habit of completing her work ahead of schedule. She recalled her elation as she closed the door behind her, and how the feeling had stayed with her until the following day.

Excited at the prospect of tackling the Leonardo, Valentine had been unable to sleep and she'd got to the Louvre at dawn, long before anyone else. She'd reproached herself for that sleepless night for a long time. Had she slept, she'd thought for so long, she would have had a clear head when she arrived and wouldn't have made a mistake. Now that she knew how the sketch had been destroyed, she saw things differently.

Nora's annotations didn't only track Valentine's movements. Stern's assistant had ringed one of the other identification codes and put a question mark beside it. According to the printout, the holder of that particular magnetic pass hadn't been in to work that day, but had entered the workshops at 11.40 p.m., leaving just before midnight.

Valentine gave a muffled cry. She knew only one identification code by heart apart from her own, and it was the one Nora had circled. White-faced, she sat down on the bed, eyes fixed on the page.

Nora was fast asleep. Valentine didn't want to wake her. She collected her things and went to find somewhere to make a phone call where she wouldn't be disturbed.

She left the hospital and headed towards a tiny park on the Boulevard Arago, a few hundred metres away, that she'd passed several times. Apart from a group having a picnic on the grass at the other end of the park, the place was deserted. Exactly what Valentine was looking for.

She sat on a bench and dialled a number on her mobile.

'Hi, sweetie,' said Marc Grimberg. He put on a jokily sexy voice, but Valentine wasn't in the mood to laugh.

'Thanks for the note on the fridge. Really nice of you. And thanks for leaving the front door open.'

'You're not calling just to tell me off, are you?' said Marc wryly.

'No, you're right, I'm not calling about that.'

'Go on, I'm listening.'

'I need some information. I need you to cast your mind back. The day before I had my little mishap with the sketch of St John the Baptist, do you know what the other restorers were working on?'

'Well, let me see. As I recall, I wasn't even there at the time. I was away on holiday, remember?'

'Ah, yes . . . Rome, wasn't it?'

'That's right.'

'When did you get back?'

293

Without missing a beat, her former colleague replied: 'The day you had the problem with the sketch. They made an emergency call to see if I could salvage things. I had to catch the first plane back. Thanks a bundle.'

'So how come you used your pass to get into the workshop the night before?'

Grimberg was silent for a long while.

Although the park was almost empty, a man sat down on the bench beside Valentine. He unfolded a newspaper and started reading. Irritated, Valentine shifted to the other end of the bench.

At last Grimberg spoke. 'Why are you asking me all this? It's mad. I was in Rome.'

'I've got a record of all the entry and exit times in front of me, Marc. Your ID number is on it.'

For a moment, Valentine thought Grimberg had hung up. Then she heard the sound of his breathing.

'At eleven-forty p.m.'

'Sorry?' said Grimberg.

'That's the time you went in. It took you a quarter of an hour to alter my cleaning solution, and then you went home to bed. You weren't in Rome, Marc.'

Grimberg didn't try to deny it. His tone became aggressive.

'What do you want me to do, Valentine? Turn myself in? Is that what you want? For me to lose my job as well?'

'I just want to know why you did it.'

'I did all I could. I supported you when you were in a bad way. When you were on the verge of suicide. Remember? I was always there.'

'Bit late, wasn't it? It didn't make up for anything. Why did you do it? I'm not asking so I can use it against you. I just need to know. For myself.'

Valentine's words hit Grimberg powerfully. He started shouting.

'It was a bloody accident! An accident! I didn't think you'd finish the Boucher so quickly. We didn't give a damn about that red chalk drawing. It was a workshop piece, it wasn't worth much. You'd have got off with nothing but a reprimand.'

Valentine tried to dismiss a thought that had just sprung up in her mind. It wasn't possible. She couldn't believe such a stupid explanation.

'You wanted me to ruin the Boucher so they'd take me off the St John the Baptist? You're mad!'

'It was my due, Valentine. I should have been the one to restore it. If they hadn't given it to you, everything would have been fine. It was always me who'd done the important pieces, but after you arrived, I just got the scraps, the unimportant stuff. It wasn't fair. The Leonardo should have been mine.'

His voice cracked. 'It was an accident,' he repeated.

Valentine couldn't listen to any more. She hung up.

The man beside her on the bench folded his newspaper. 'Sounds like you're having a bad day, young lady.'

Valentine really wasn't in the mood to be chatted up by a stranger. She ignored him.

'When things are going badly,' the man went on, 'there's nothing like an evening with friends to relax you, you know.'

Valentine glanced at the man out of the corner of her eye. He looked about fifty, but there was something about him that made her suspect he was older. His smile, his manner, even his clothes, all had something contrived about them, as if he were trying to soften the disturbing hardness of his features.

Valentine turned away with a bored expression. Across the park, the picnickers had gathered up their things and were heading towards the exit, laughing and chatting.

The man waited for them to pass through the gate. He didn't seem prepared to give up.

'Well?' he said. 'What do you think of my suggestion?'

Valentine tried to sound weary and exasperated enough to make him leave her alone. 'You need to have friends you can trust . . .'

The man gave a half-smile. He put the newspaper down on

the bench and moved closer to her, until they were almost touching.

'I don't like to see you miserable like this, young lady. I've got an idea: how about we go and pay our friend Elias a visit? That'll chase away your gloomy thoughts. We can have a glass of champagne in front of those wonderful *Irises*, and chat about the Vasalis manuscript. What do you say?'

Valentine opened her mouth to protest, but she couldn't make a sound.

The man was pressing the barrel of a tiny gun to her hip.

'It's anything but a friendly suggestion, Valentine. I'm afraid you don't have a choice. You had nothing planned for this afternoon, I hope?'

49

Raymond Agostini lived in an apartment on the second floor of a Haussmann block at one end of the Rue Monge. David had been there a few months earlier for a dinner the professor had held to celebrate the publication of his textbook on Ancient Greek literature. As well as David and Albert Cadas, Agostini had invited a few other colleagues and some of his PhD students, including a stunning girl who'd bored David at length about the confusion between unity and homogeneity in Melissos of Samos.

Having searched vainly for another topic that might interest her, David had eventually left her to it. He had spent the rest of the evening chatting to Agostini's wife, a delightful woman who enjoyed Scrabble, healthy walks by the sea and romantic novels. Melissos of Samos couldn't compete.

David had no real idea what he was going to say to Raymond Agostini if he found him at home. He'd try to reason with him but, failing that, he hoped he could at least explain the situation to his wife. If Raymond Agostini had lost his mind, as David believed, she alone would be able to persuade him to tell David where the illumination was. If this didn't work, David had no Plan B. By then he would no doubt be bitterly regretting disobeying the Dean.

He was buzzed into the building along with a delivery man,

passed the concierge's lodge without attracting attention and went up to the Agostinis' apartment. He rang the bell, but there was no answer.

'Mr Agostini,' he shouted through the door, 'it's David Scotto. Can we speak?'

After about thirty seconds, he felt sure there was no one in the apartment. Either that, or the occupants had no intention of opening the door, which amounted to the same thing. Preparing to leave, David took a step back.

It was then that he noticed a dark stain oozing out from under the door and soaking into the mat. Without thinking, he tried the handle. The door was unlocked.

David pushed it open. The pool of blood had spread over half the hall.

The bodies of Raymond Agostini and his wife lay in the hallway, huddled together. The lecturer's head was resting on his wife's leg. His arms were clasped around her waist in a final embrace. Both their throats were slit from ear to ear.

There was another body across the hallway, by the sitting-room door. It lay on its front, head facing the wall. Taking care not to step in the blood, David walked around the Agostinis and went to the third victim.

He recognised the man he'd seen in the security video. Miller had been murdered by a single bullet to the head. A look of deep astonishment was etched on his face. The fingers of his left hand were still clasped around the handle of a brown leather attaché case. It had sprung open as the book dealer fell to the floor, and several books had fallen out. On one of the spines were the words THEATRUM ORBIS TERRARUM.

The cardboard box in which Albert Cadas had kept the illuminated leaf torn from the codex by Tischendorf was beside the body. David knelt down and opened it. As he expected, the box was empty. The illumination had disappeared. This time, David really had lost the trail.

He didn't have time to think about how he'd explain things to the Neanderthal. Behind him, the front door burst open and a voice shouted: 'Police! Don't move!'

David didn't fight as strong hands pinned him to the floor beside Miller's body. Still without resisting, he allowed himself to be handcuffed.

One thought blocked out all others: Anna was going to die, and it was all his fault.

50

Maxime Zerka's Audi A8 Security drove through the open gates into the empty courtyard, the bodyguard with the ravaged face at the wheel, and drew up at the foot of the imposing front steps. No one came out to meet the car. The large house seemed deserted.

Drawing his gun from its holster under his arm, the Neanderthal stationed himself beside the car – a four hundred and fifty-horsepower, bullet- and bombproof monster – and quickly scanned the area. With a nod he signalled to his boss that it was safe to get out, then opened the other door and dragged Valentine out. She tried to break free, but the colossus twisted her arm. She whimpered, and gave up any thought of struggling.

Zerka was last out of the car. He fastened the top two buttons of his jacket and headed towards the steps, followed by Valentine, in the Neanderthal's firm grasp.

Stern appeared at the top just as Zerka was about to start up the dozen or so rough-surfaced steps. The elderly man stood leaning on his cane with both hands.

'Elias!' called out Zerka. 'You look as if you've aged. What's up? Having problems?'

Stern remained stony-faced.

'Are you alone, as I asked?' said Zerka as he bounded up the last few steps.

'You gave me no choice. You've put most of the Foundation's employees in hospital, or the morgue. Only one of my security staff is still standing. He's inside. He has orders not to intervene.'

'All that hard work to end up alone in your palace, like a forsaken old king. How sad!'

'I'm not interested in discussing metaphysics with you, Zerka. Could we settle this matter quickly, please?'

His opponent's polite façade disappeared. 'You piss me off with your superiority complex, Elias. As if you're the only one who's cultured. You'll still die like a dog if I choose to kill you now.'

'But that would be too simple. Your sense of spectacle wouldn't be satisfied. I know you, Zerka: you love spilling blood, but you're just as fond of putting on a show. A car blowing up in a public place, a battered body dumped in the Seine – that's the kind of thing you enjoy. You need your handiwork to be witnessed in order to take pleasure in it. I'm just a lonely old man, as you say. My death will interest no one, unless you blow up the whole district.'

Zerka flashed him a look of impatience. 'Have you got it, as I asked?'

Stern took a red velvet pouch from his jacket pocket and held it out.

Zerka snatched it and pulled off the pouch, dropping it to the ground. A satisfied smile spread across his features as he felt the weight of the Vasalis codex.

'At last. I've been searching for this for so long . . . And do you know the best bit, Stern? I've just acquired the missing illumination. With the Botticelli drawing, I have all the pieces of the puzzle. Vasalis is mine.'

'Just one question. Out of curiosity, did Miller contact you before or after me?'

'Miller isn't exactly a model of professional integrity. He must have told himself that some healthy competition would mean a higher commission.'

'You coveted the illumination, but you didn't want to pay the full price for it. When Miller told you about the Sorbonne, you thought you could get hold of the leaf yourself, but you didn't know where to look, so you tried to get Scotto to find it for you.'

'The idiot failed. I was forced to negotiate with Miller. We concluded the deal at my office this morning, and he handed over the illumination a little while ago, at his client's home.'

'I doubt it was as simple as that. I know you. You're not the type to leave any witnesses.'

Zerka's smile broadened. 'Miller tried to renegotiate the price at the last minute. I lose patience quickly in such circumstances.'

'Why did you blow up the Mercedes? You were about to win, anyway. There was no need for it.'

'The bomb was intended for you. My men spotted your car when they followed Miller to my offices, and suspected you might be in it. Anyway, we knew the game might be up, and I couldn't run the risk. It's a shame you weren't in the car at the time, but you can't have everything you wish for in life.'

Anger flashed in Stern's eyes. 'All those deaths for a palimpsest that you're not even going to try to decipher! You only care that no one else should own it. You're like a spoiled child, Zerka.'

Zerka pointed his index finger at the elderly man. 'Don't give me that crap about the democratisation of culture! You've sold masterpieces to every collector on the planet. How many let the masses enjoy them? I'm sick of you lecturing me on morality. You can go to hell.'

Stern didn't reply. He raised his cane and pointed it at the bodyguard who was holding Valentine.

'You've got what you want. Let her go. She has nothing to do with any of this. It was me who set it all up with Sorel. She shouldn't have to suffer the consequences.'

Zerka gestured to the Neanderthal, who had stopped a few steps down. He gave a grunt of annoyance, and then pushed Valentine violently towards Stern. She stumbled as she reached the top of the steps. One of her knees struck the ground, tearing her trousers.

Stern helped her up. 'Are you all right?' he asked.

'I'll feel better when these bastards have gone.'

'Don't worry. They'll leave now that they've got what they want. Isn't that right, gentlemen?'

Zerka stroked his chin. 'Patience . . . Before I leave, I have one more question for you, Stern: why me? Why did you target me? I'm not the only one.'

'We had to start with someone, and you're the worst.'

'Did Sorel really believe he'd catch me so easily? Did he think I'd simply fall into his trap like a moron? Stupid bastard!'

'He was hoping to find proof of your fraud. You evaded him once before, and he couldn't let it go. He almost succeeded this time.'

'It didn't happen, and it never will. I'm cleverer than you. The law doesn't have the weapons to stop me.'

'We'll adapt. We'll find other ways.'

Zerka started down the steps. 'Dream on,' he said as he reached the bottom.

Valentine called out to him as he was getting into the car. 'What about David? Will you leave him alone now that you've got the illumination?'

Zerka stopped and turned round. 'Scotto proved deplorably inept at his task. The leaf was right under his nose and he still couldn't find it.'

'Please, leave him alone,' said Valentine.

'His life is no longer in my hands. It's already forfeit and I'm a man of my word, at least in this sort of thing.'

The Neanderthal roared with pleasure.

Without a backward glance at Valentine's distraught face, Zerka climbed into the back of the armoured limousine. The bodyguard returned his gun to its holster, then sat behind the wheel and started the engine.

Lowering his window, Zerka called to Stern: 'You're taking

your defeat with great dignity. I'm glad I didn't kill you. I'd have missed this.'

He held the codex at arm's length out of the window.

'One last thing . . . You can keep your fucking *Irises* now. I don't want them any more. I've got something much better.'

The codex and Zerka's face disappeared behind the tinted window. The armoured limousine set off. It drove out through the gates and turned into the Rue des Saints-Pères.

Valentine and Stern stood motionless, side by side, for some time.

Valentine spoke first. 'Is that it? Is that how the story ends? We watch the bad guy leave, and do nothing?'

'For now, Zerka's stronger than us. He's done enough harm. Franck and Sorel are dead, Nora's injured, Vermeer's in a coma . . . Things have got out of hand. We have to stop.'

Valentine opened her mouth to object, but Stern silenced her with a gesture.

'You have to pick your fights, Valentine, I'm telling you this from experience. Zerka won't disappear from the scene overnight. We'll have other opportunities. One of these days he'll make a mistake, and we'll take advantage of it. The Foundation is only just starting its work. As Zerka just said, there are lots of others like him. Today we've failed, but tomorrow we'll succeed.'

Valentine shook her head. 'It's too easy. The bastard can't just get away with it like that. Hugo is in a coma because of him. He might not . . .'

Her voice was choked by a sob. She started to back towards the steps.

Stern tried to hold her by the arm. 'Wait, Valentine. Don't go . . .'

The restorer freed herself with a shrug of the shoulder. She ran down the steps and across the courtyard.

As she reached the gate Stern made a last attempt to stop her. 'Valentine, your future's here, at the Foundation. By my side.'

His voice died away in the silence of the deserted house.

51

Vermeer's chest rose and fell regularly, the rhythm dictated by an artificial respirator. Valentine stared at his clean-shaven face for some time. The nurses had shaved him when he'd arrived in intensive care. Without the stubble, Vermeer looked like a well-fed baby. Usually incapable of staying still, he looked calm, almost peaceful. If it hadn't been for the tube in his throat, he'd have looked as if he were sleeping.

Valentine stroked her friend's cheek with the back of her hand. Vermeer did not react.

'Please don't play Sleeping Beauty for too long,' she whispered into his ear. 'I need you.'

She kissed his forehead, listened for a few moments to the rhythmic hum of the respirator, then straightened up. She mouthed the words 'See you tomorrow' and closed the door behind her.

A black Mercedes, like the one that had exploded three weeks earlier at the foot of the Tour Montparnasse, was parked at the kerb, by the entrance to Cochin Hospital. A man with a blank face and bulging muscles, dressed in a dark suit identical to Franck the dead chauffeur's, opened the car door.

He addressed Valentine politely but firmly. 'He's waiting for you, Miss Savi. If you'd like to get in . . .'

Valentine climbed into the back of the Mercedes and sat down beside Elias Stern.

'You like continuity, I see,' she said. 'What's this one called?'

'I'm an old man, Valentine. I have my little habits. His name is Jacques. How is your friend Vermeer?'

'Hugo's still in a coma. The doctors are optimistic, but they're not sure when he's going to wake up. Have you heard from David?'

'His Foundation research trip is going well. He's somewhere quiet, recovering from all the emotion of recent events. He'll call you soon, don't worry. Did you listen to the news this morning?'

'You mean Zerka? His plane crashed, didn't it?'

Stern nodded. 'Sorel's superiors won't tolerate an attack on one of their agents. In such situations, they have to demonstrate their power to ensure it doesn't happen again. Zerka thought he could escape their retaliation, but those men can reach you wherever you are and, above all, whoever you are. Zerka was wrong to believe he was untouchable.'

'You knew that when he came to get the codex, didn't you?'

The elderly art dealer smiled joylessly. 'I suspected his life expectancy was limited. I know how they work. They maintain appearances up to a certain point. After that, they move to less consensual forms of action. They like to have the last word.'

'Who was Sorel working for? Who are these men, Elias?'

'I'm not sure you're ready to hear it.'

Valentine said nothing, but her tense expression betrayed her impatience.

'Go ahead,' said Stern. 'Tell me what's bothering you.'

'How can you stand it? I mean . . . They've behaved just like him, haven't they? They've murdered him.'

'With men like Zerka, you can't go in for half-measures. I'd have preferred that he was arrested, but the main thing is that he can no longer harm anyone. My personal opinion of the methods used is of no importance.'

'And the manuscript?'

'Unfortunately we've lost track of it. Zerka's offices and all his properties were searched before his death was officially registered. We found the Botticelli drawing, as well as several other stolen pieces, which will be returned discreetly to their owners, but not the codex or the leaf torn out by Tischendorf. We believe Zerka had them with him when his plane was destroyed.'

'So now Vasalis really is dead.'

Instead of replying, Stern handed her a large envelope.

'What's this?'

'It's a permanent employment contract under the same financial terms as the previous one, but this one is open-ended. The Foundation needs people like you. We're not going to cease operations just because we've had one failure. As Zerka said himself, there are many more like him. There'll be plenty of work for us in the next few years.'

Valentine felt the weight of the envelope. It was too heavy to contain documents alone. She looked enquiringly at Stern.

'I've included a small gift, which has nothing to do with the contract. You're to keep it, whatever you decide.'

Valentine opened the envelope. She took out the contract and placed it on the seat beside her, then slid her hand farther inside the envelope. She withdrew the rosewood box that had contained the codex the day Stern came to her workshop.

'The real gift is inside,' added Stern.

Valentine undid the velvet ribbon and removed the lid. The box contained a small book. The binding, with a patina acquired over the centuries, was devoid of lettering. She opened it with an unsteady hand.

The first few pages were covered in tiny handwriting, in dark ink, which was slightly faded in places but still perfectly legible. Written in Latin in primitive Gothic script, the text covered the entire surface of the pages, without margins or paragraph breaks.

'I suggest you go straight to the colophon,' said Stern.

Valentine turned the pages until she came to the inscription at the end of the manuscript. She deciphered it easily.

'Clemens,' she read out. The Pope's signature was followed by a date: 5 March 1267.

Valentine felt her mouth go dry. 'Does this book have a connection with Vasalis?'

Stern's expression was mischievous. 'Despite your friendship with Vermeer, you're singularly lacking in imagination, my dear. This book *is* Vasalis.'

Valentine looked at him, confused.

'What do you mean?'

'Do you know who William of Moerbeke is?'

Valentine knew the name, as she'd seen it in the Vasalis documents that Vermeer had sent her. 'Moerbeke was a scholar. He was one of the first translators of Aristotle.'

'He was above all a trusted adviser to Clement IV, the person to whom the Pope confided his secrets and, when the need arose, entrusted delicate missions.'

He stopped, as if expecting a response from Valentine, which did not come. The restorer simply stared at the Pope's signature.

'Nora has told you about my love of ancient books, hasn't she?'

Disconcerted by this sudden change of subject, Valentine put down the book and stared at Stern.

'I inherited the passion from my grandfather,' Stern went on. 'It was he who began the collection you saw in the library. In 1912, he bought an autograph of Moerbeke's Latin translation of Proclus's *Elements of Theology*. When he had it restored, this little book was found inside the binding. It contains the secret instructions that Clement IV gave Moerbeke regarding Vasalis. This was not long after Heiberg published his article. Vasalis hadn't yet become fashionable.'

'So Hugo's theory was correct . . . Clement IV got rid of Vasalis and ordered Moerbeke to collect all the copies of the *De forma mundi*. Is that it?'

Stern shook his head. 'Clement IV didn't ask Moerbeke to make Vasalis disappear but, on the contrary, to make him emerge from nothing. Clement IV and Moerbeke entirely invented the character.'

'I don't understand.' Valentine was growing still more disconcerted by Stern's explanation. 'According to Hugo, Clement IV did everything he could to ensure that Vasalis was forgotten by everyone. It doesn't make sense.'

'Unless you consider carefully the personality of the Pope. Clement IV was elected to the throne of St Peter thanks to a happy combination of circumstances. He proved to be a competent, honest pontiff, but he soon encountered hostility from a section of the Curia. It has to be said that he didn't really fit the criteria for the post: not only was he French and a widower, he'd also studied law at the Sorbonne, and had no intention of having his conduct dictated by the theologians around him.'

In the file Vermeer had sent her, Valentine had read that after his election Clement IV had had to make the journey to Viterbo, where the papal court then resided, disguised as a monk. Had he not taken this precaution, he would probably not have got there alive.

'To make matters worse,' continued Stern, 'Clement IV included in his close circle the principal proponents of Aristotelian thought. Indeed, Moerbeke had translated the *Politics* several years earlier at the request of Thomas Aquinas, with whom Clement IV had become friends at the Sorbonne. And Aquinas was the main target of conservative theologians who vehemently opposed Aristotle. In their view, in disseminating his theories, Aquinas was guilty of heresy. Once elected, Clement IV tried to protect him. He summoned him to his side at Viterbo, but this was not enough to extinguish his enemies' anger.'

For the first time, Valentine was starting to glimpse a logic to all this.

'Clement IV was caught between two stools,' she said. 'He didn't want to sacrifice Aquinas, but he couldn't alienate the members of the Curia.'

Stern nodded. 'In order to divert the theologians' attention from Aquinas, the Pope asked Moerbeke to give them a bigger bone to chew on. This was how Vasalis came into being. Moerbeke made him the author of a supposedly scandalous treatise, the *De forma mundi*. It didn't matter that no one had ever read it or heard of its author. On the pretext of making all trace of Vasalis disappear, the Pope sent representatives all over Europe charged with dispersing copies of the *De forma mundi*. It was, of course, Moerbeke's fabrication.'

'Was the Metochion codex one of these copies?'

'Absolutely. All that was missing was the finishing touch: Vasalis's spectacular execution. Or rather, if one is to believe the instructions contained in this book, the execution of an anonymous prisoner who'd been rotting in the papal dungeons for years. Clement IV's threats against those who dared refer to Vasalis eventually gave substance to the character. If the Pope gave the impression of fearing him to such an extent, it was inconceivable that he didn't exist.'

'What became of Thomas Aquinas?'

'At first, the pressure on him eased and he resumed his chair at the Sorbonne in 1268. Unfortunately, Clement IV died a few months later, and from 1270 the faculty of arts was subjected to terrible repression, at the insistence of Étienne Tempier, the bishop of Paris. Thomas Aquinas then attempted one final manoeuvre. He used his remaining strength to turn Vasalis into a symbol of the intellectual freedom he sought. After his death, his disciples united behind this ideal and perpetuated it.'

'The Brotherhood of the Sorbonne!' cried Valentine. 'So it really did exist!'

'Probably not with that name, or in the form of an organised group, but yes, the legend of Vasalis was handed down from generation to generation for centuries within the university.'

Valentine suddenly realised the full implication of the art dealer's explanation.

'You didn't really want me to decipher the palimpsest, did you?'

'Even a restorer as talented as you can't work miracles, Valentine. You said so yourself when I first showed you the codex. It was in too poor a condition for you to be able to do anything with it, and I knew that when I went to your workshop.'

'So you've used me. Right from the start.'

'Please don't be angry, Valentine. I wanted to persuade you to work for the Foundation. The codex was the most tempting bait I had.'

The image of Elias Stern entering her workshop for the first time, with his cane and old-fashioned suit, came back to her. That day, she reflected bitterly, she'd thought him an inoffensive old man. She now realised how deceptive his apparent fragility had been. Elias Stern's 'withered rose' exterior hid razor-sharp thorns.

'If you knew the *De forma mundi* was a fake, why have you never said anything? Cadas wasted his life searching for it. You could have prevented that.'

Stern sank back into the seat. Through the tinted car window he stared at the entrance of the A&E Department. An ambulance drove in at high speed, sirens blaring.

'To men like Cadas, the quest is more important than the goal. If he'd discovered the truth about the *De forma mundi*, he'd have set off in pursuit of some other fantasy. It would have made no difference.'

Valentine looked puzzled. 'I still don't understand why you spent a fortune on the palimpsest if you knew it was of no interest.'

'Sorel didn't know that I owned this book when he came to me with his plan. He really believed that the treatise was contained in Marie Gervex's codex. But he didn't care much either way. To him the manuscript was simply a means of getting to Zerka. At the time, I found the irony of the situation rather delightful. Though believe me I regret allowing myself to indulge in this little joke. Sorel lost control of the situation and he paid dearly for it, and many others with him. I would never have undertaken this venture had I foreseen the consequences.'

311

For the first time since the start of the conversation, Valentine saw genuine sadness in the elderly man's eyes.

She placed the book back in the box and held it out to Stern. 'I don't want your gift.'

Stern made no move to take the box.

'Vasalis is a symbol, Valentine. A wonderful symbol of intellectual freedom. No one is more entitled than you to look after it.'

The Mercedes drew up outside the restorer's workshop.

'Incidentally,' said Stern as the chauffeur parked the car, 'your former colleague resigned from the Louvre yesterday. I wanted you to be the first to know. I tried to get them to take you back, but it wasn't possible. The management didn't want to revive the scandal. I'm so sorry.'

'Thank you. There was no need for you to do that.'

'It was nothing. About my proposal, what have you decided?'

'I don't know. I'll have to think about it.'

He placed a hand on the chauffeur's shoulder. 'Jacques, would you mind . . .'

The chauffeur got out and came to open Valentine's door.

'Art Crime Team,' said Stern, as she was getting out.

She stopped dead, one foot on the pavement, the other still inside the car.

'Sorry?'

'That's the branch of the FBI in charge of fighting art smuggling. Sorel was their representative in Europe. I'm not supposed to reveal that. As you see, I have absolute faith in you. I hope it will influence your decision.'

Valentine nodded, got out of the car and closed the door. The chauffeur drove off immediately.

The rosewood box clutched to her chest, Valentine watched the Mercedes disappear. She didn't know yet what she would decide, but she was filled with happiness at the thought that at last she had a choice.

My thanks go to Céline Thoulouze, the enthusiastic, demanding and passionate editor of whom every writer dreams, and to Agathe whose advice has been, as ever, invaluable.

Thanks to Michela and Houssain, for letting me borrow their son's beautiful name.

Thanks to Jean-Luc Bizien, for being as generous as ever.

Thanks to Sophie Thomas, who did such a brilliant job pitching this novel.

And thanks to Deborah Druba, Alain Jessua, Martine Mairal, Nathalie Bériou, Olfa Jouini, Valéry Danty and Gaëtan Esposito for their support.